Casimir Beginnings

J.W. Walker

***

To my amazing wife: I can't wait to make this journey with you. I love you.

***

PART ONE

CHAPTER ONE

As far as she was concerned Claire Keen had been introduced to the Casimir Institute by accident. She was studying Computer Engineering at the University of Washington and working the job fair circuit. She had her eyes on the same things everyone else did; Amazon, Facebook, Microsoft, Apple. There was a lot left to be desired from Claire's interviews with the big tech giants. She saw the potential for a job, but not a lot more. She found herself wandering Seattle job fairs in search of something off the beaten path. Something that would require more than an eye for network design. Even if it wasn't something for the long term; she wasn't ready for the American dream yet.

And Steven Pulling found her. She was shuffling through the University auditorium at her second career fair of the month. She didn't have a good reason to be there. She honestly wasn't interested and had, for the most part, given in to the fact that she'd have to accept the American routine to pay the bills. She'd wait six more months until she finished her Masters program, take some time to enjoy the Summer, then resign herself to the fate authored by whichever tech company was willing to trade her Monday through Friday nine to five. All she really needed was enough money to comfortably keep food in the fridge, the lights on and the water running. Unless she got lucky and something more interesting came up.

Pulling had a small booth near the back corner of the auditorium. And he wasn't exactly forthcoming in who he worked for or who he was looking to hire. He had a couple large poster boards that led passersby to believe his firm worked on clean water projects in war torn countries. But his photos weren't the product of any Bill and Melinda Gates Foundation projects. Just a Google image search and a trip to the university's print center. He wasn't looking for foot traffic at his booth. Steven had picked this spot to observe. Over the years he'd developed an uncanny eye for the specific talents that his organization required.

Pulling spotted Claire the same way he'd spotted many recruits before her. He saw poise and confidence. He saw her moving with purpose, even though she didn't really have one. Besides an eye for talent, Pulling had another advantage. He already knew who he was looking for. He came to Seattle with very few potential candidates in mind. When you possessed the type of technology available to Casimir you had the luxury of advantage when it came to identifying candidates with the right technical skills and future potential for success in a range of interesting and unique assignments. There was very little time wasted in the hiring search. Claire's confident gait through the auditorium only confirmed what he already knew.

Once Steven saw his objective he was ready to deploy the bait. Twenty-three-year olds, especially young attractive twenty-three-year-old women, were unpredictable. But there was one time-tested way to grab their attention, at least briefly. He had pre-staged Jon Haynes on the opposite end of the auditorium. A quick text put Jon in motion.

Jon Haynes' sandy brown hair, boyish face and physical build from his time spent in Special Operations all summed to make it easy for him to meet women. As a guy who learned to blend into his often hostile surroundings during his time in the SEALs, he found that task surprisingly difficult amidst the many wandering eyes on a college campus. But Mr. Pulling had given him a job to do: Blend in, keep a line of sight to the booth, and be ready to carry out follow on instructions. Jon was leafing through some recruiting materials for a structural engineering firm in Oregon, doing his best impression of an unassuming and uninteresting dude, when his phone vibrated in his front pocket:

'I need you to get the attention of the 5'3" brunette in the black blouse and khaki pants about 50 yards behind you. You may choose the method, as long as it gets her to the booth.'

Jon moved quickly at first down the convention aisle. He needed to get in front of her and find a way to get this woman's attention before she complicated his task by wandering down another lane in the endless rows of booths. As he strode to within a few feet of Claire he slowed his gait to only slightly faster than hers. He passed intentionally close to her left shoulder, not trying to draw her attention, but also not trying to avoid it.

***

Daydreaming was a bit of a past time for Claire. She possessed what most would describe as a very vivid--and sometimes imaginative--memory. As she wove along the back aisle of the job fair and glanced absent-mindedly at corporate booths that ranged from medical device manufacturers to small tech startups, she was lost in a daydream of Seattle Sea Fair. The low thrum of career-seekers in the auditorium provided a white noise that transported her to visions of the long days of summer on the Puget Sound. The daydream was so detailed she could have told a story of her time on the Sound like she was just there, a few days ago. But then she was snapped out of it. At first her conscious mind didn't grasp what had brought her back. Some combination of her peripheral vision and a deeply appealing scent grabbed her attention in the here-and-now.

Then she saw him. As he brushed past, Claire caught a fleeting glimpse of an easy-on-the-eyes boyish face. As he continued past she caught herself admiring the view of the backside of the passing stranger. Half embarrassed and half intrigued she followed him with her eyes, now uniquely interested in where he was going.

***

Jon decided it was time to see if he'd caught the lady's attention. He feigned interest in a technology consulting firm and veered over to their booth. He made small talk with a middle-aged balding man who offered a quick video via iPad with a brief history and about life at Barnes & Bowens consulting. Jon graciously agreed to watch the video since it offered him the perfect plain sight disguise as he continued to track his assignment in his peripheral vision. She was getting closer but he couldn't tell if he had her attention yet. Then she conveniently stopped at the adjacent booth. And for just a second he felt her eyes on him. He continued watching the video, now intent on using the time tested, high school crush method of eye contact and a smile to try and reel her in. He sensed her glancing in his direction again and quickly but casually looked right back at her. Noticing a little bit of surprise and maybe a hint of panic on her face, he gave her a barely perceptible smile, maybe closer to a smirk, right as she shot her eyes back down to the pamphlets and blank applications on the table in front of her. That was probably the best he was going to do under the circumstances. He finished watching the video, still unsure if he had the hook in. Then he sat the iPad down on the table, thanked the Brown & Bowens recruiter and made a straight line for the disguised Casimir Institute booth.

***

Did he smile at me? A few minutes ago, Claire was admiring the local scenery and planning to burn the rest of the day running errands after pretending to job hunt. Now this boy, guy, man…whatever he is, was throwing her smiles? She'd always prided herself on her pride and her 'fortune favors the bold' approach to getting what she wanted. It almost seemed like this guy was testing her. Was she steely enough to make the approach? Why not? He could be a fun distraction while she waited for her real life to start. And in her mind there was no doubt she could have him if she wanted.

***

Now standing at the Casimir booth, Jon chanced a glance back up the aisle. There was the brunette, confidence, maybe even arrogance, across her face, looking him straight in the eye and walking toward him with purpose and a slight grin. He almost felt the urge to look away but found himself trapped in something like an adolescent tractor beam. He'd only caught brief glimpses up to now. The girl he was looking at made him forget his assignment. Her shoulder-back confidence immediately inspired his curiosity. And her olive skin, doe-ish green eyes and perfectly proportioned figure inspired something else borne out of male instinct. The short, curvy, bright brunette walked right up to him, took a glance quickly over his shoulder at Steven Pulling and then introduced herself. Not the way he'd expected this to play out.

"Hi, I'm Claire," she said.

***

Claire was infinitely confident in what she was doing. It wasn't until she introduced herself that she realized she hadn't thought through what was going to happen next. Luckily the boy in front of her - yes definitely just a boy - was no slouch with the ladies. He reached a hand out to shake hers.

"I'm Jon. Nice to meet you. Is there something I can help you with? If not, I'd be glad to buy you coffee or a drink later."

Thank God! This guy was quick. He seemed a little uncomfortable, like she'd caught him on his heels. But if he hadn't put his hand out the magnetism she felt might have led her to put a fake-bashful hand on his chest. *What was happening to her?* She felt like she was going to start giggling uncontrollably if she didn't get it together. And now he was asking her out, just like that. Not exactly the way she'd expected this to play out.

***

Pulling watched with smug pleasure. This wasn't exactly what he'd expected, but he knew Claire would not be denied if she wanted something. He didn't know if he could get her interested in young Jon Haynes, but this wasn't his first rodeo either. But while these two were talking like they just met, they were looking at each other like they'd just shared breakfast. He needed to intervene before their focus on each other overran his objective.

"Ehem…My name is Steven Pulling. I see you've met my associate Jon Haynes. Jon and I are employed by a small outfit working on some outside the box projects in southern California."

***

Pulling proceeded to walk Claire through what would turn out to be a series of half truths about the Institute he worked for, particularly how they needed some fresh blood working on their network architecture and data management. Claire feigned interest throughout their fifteen-minute conversation. She really was interested, but also still felt the heat of a blush just under the surface. She learned that the Pulling guy wanted to have her out to his facility to interview and show her the systems for which her network architecture skills were needed. But she was having trouble focusing on the details. She mostly wanted to make sure she left this particular job fair with contact information for Jon. She was not letting this date get away.

Apparently Jon was thinking the same thing. While they both watched Mr. Pulling go on about Casimir and cutting edge theoretical physics and relativity, their primary focus was on their periphals and each other. Claire felt Jon press into her palm. At first she thought he was being weird and trying to hold her hand like they were in seventh grade. As he pulled away she realized he'd stuffed a slip of paper into her hand. Not quite registering how he did that or why, she faked an itch on the side of her face. As she brought her hand away from her face she glanced quickly into her palm at the note:

'Your number here __________'

She flushed a little. They were high-school-flirting with each other right in the middle of a professional meeting; in the middle of a job pitch from a middle aged overly serious professional guy. Jon worked for him and he didn't seem worried in the least about being noticed. But Claire had the tougher job. She definitely wanted Jon to leave the auditorium with her phone number. But she didn't want to appear to

Mr. Pulling to be more interested in the boy than the offer of an interview for a lucrative job at his 'prestigious' Institute. She was also proud enough that she didn't want to appear overly eager with Jon. So she stuck the slip of paper in the front pocket of her khakis. Jon could wait in suspense.

Claire struggled to force her attention back to Mr. Pulling. As she swam her focus back into the details of his impromptu briefing, she caught the tail end of the question.

"So Ms. Keen, would you be willing to come down to Casimir so you can tour the facility and interview for the position?"

In Claire's distracted state she still wasn't quite sure what the job was. But she wasn't really in a good position to refuse. She'd stood in front of Pulling and nodded along, feigning interest, for the last fifteen minutes. It would just seem rude if she backed away now. And what did she have to lose?

"I'd be glad to come down for an interview sir," she said.

"Good. Fill out this contact form and the administrative department will get in touch with you in the next day or two to make travel arrangements."

Pulling handed the form to Claire and she stepped toward the table to fill in her information. As she was writing she pondered her opportunity. Should she put her hope in Jon taking the initiative to get her contact information off the forms? Or should she ensure he had her contact information via the more direct route? As she scrawled her email address onto the Casimir forms she decided she wasn't leaving further interaction with the pretty boy Jon Haynes to chance. And she definitely wasn't leaving her wants up to his interpretation of the situation. She slipped his note out of her pocket and scribbled her number down in the blank provided.

"Thank you again for the opportunity Mr. Pulling. I look forward to seeing you in California," Claire said as she finished up the paper work and handed it over. She ended the meeting with a handshake, then turned to Jon.

"It was nice to meet you as well Mr. Haynes," Claire said as she reached out to shake his hand with the slip of paper containing her phone number concealed in her palm. Handshake complete, Claire saw Jon cut a quick glance down at his palm, then back at her. She gave him the slightest hint of a flirtatious smile as she turned to leave the auditorium.

It wasn't until she was walking down the front steps of the

auditorium, feeling the chill of the January drizzle, when she was struck by a strange realization. She'd just received a job interview offer in her field without ever telling Mr. Pulling a single thing about her, including what field she was in. She'd been way too focused on good-looking Jon Haynes.

CHAPTER TWO

Nine Months Earlier

Lieutenant Jon Haynes was tired. He'd had his SEAL unit in the field for the last 3 days in the mountains of Western Pakistan. As far as special operations wanderings in the Afghanistan-Pakistan border region go, this was a routine op. Fly in to the drop in the hinterlands in the middle of the night, ingress to the target location through the night and early morning. Then get tucked into the hills above the objective and keep an eye out while the sun comes up. His unit was tasked to conduct reconnaissance on a training hidey-hole. If the opportunity presented, they were to grab the top bad guys, dead or alive, then get the hell out. But it all turned to shit about eighteen hours ago.

They didn't see much on the first full day of observation. Some minor movement around the camp. A few minions 'patrolling' with AK-47s, no persons of real interest, and lots of fucking goats. It was starting to look like this was a dry hole. He assumed they'd sit tight for another day, wait for the sun to drop behind the mountains, and then egress to the pickup point. Another location of interest cleared off the map. Easy.

Darkness, and cold, settled in at the end of the first day. Most of the six-man team was dozing near the cluster of packs behind a rock outcropping. A hundred yards down the mountain Jon's night lookout was set. Petty Officer Ramirez, one of his most experienced operators, had the first watch closest to the suspected terrorist camp. Ramirez's primary job was to make sure things stayed as quiet through the night as they had been all day. Behind Jon, about 150 yards upslope, was Senior Chief Petty Officer Jason Jones. The team's senior enlisted man.

He had first over watch. His job was to keep the high perch. One eye on the camp below and the other on the crest of the hill they were stashed on.

Shortly after sunset, the mountains took the remaining light. So Ramirez and Jones dropped their night vision into place and kept the watch as they had countless times before. It wasn't long until it was clear to both that the goats would be their main challenge tonight. A cluster of a half dozen mangy, underfed mountain goats that were loitering north of the compound all day started blindly making their way across the outer parts of the camp. You don't have to watch too many Afghani mountain goat videos to know they're comfortable in the mountains and skittering rocks. As the goats noisily, and blindly, made their way south, Ramirez realized their wide arc for home was going to bring them too close to his position. He was going to have to reposition further south to around the ridge overlooking the terrorist camp, or he'd have to move further uphill and hope to get clear of the wandering six-goat track.

Ramirez chose the latter, favoring the line of sight he knew over watch would have if Ramirez kept him directly upslope. He leaned into his whisper comm and told Jones "Senior-Ram, moving twenty yards your way." Jones confirmed and Ramirez slipped like a ghost up the side of the hill. He was clear of their path and about five yards from a small ridge that he planned to settle behind when the herd was directly below him continuing their trek to the south.

And that's about the time everything went to hell. One of the sure-footed goats must have lost a step because the next thing Jon Haynes heard was a series of thuds and shrill bleats. Ramirez used the ruckus to quickly rise to a crouch intending to scramble into his new foxhole while the noise subsided. But the noise of the tumbling goats brought a new bigger problem. The distinct ca-chunk of a large electrical breaker shutting was the last thing Ramirez heard before he was drowned in light emanating from the camp below. He had no choice now. He broke for the foxhole as a flurry of activity kicked up below.

Realizing they'd been spotted, Jones blew up the whisper comm, "Position compromised!" Haynes was immediately wired. From asleep to fully alert almost immediately, Jon quickly took in his surroundings. Just as he realized Ramirez was likely going to be pinned down by the three terrorists silhouetted in front of the floodlight, the distinct crack of AK-47 fire started up in the camp. At almost the same moment, Jones turned out the floodlight with three rounds from his over watch position.

Recognizing they had a limited window where they'd remain unseen, Jon directed his team, "Wait for the reload then move upslope. Leapfrog and keep them pinned down." His SEALs were immediately in full motion carrying out his orders. With it dark again in the camp, the only targets they had were the flashlights dancing around in the terrorist anthill.

As he stopped to lay down his turn at covering fire, Jon saw that two flashlights were innocently rolling away in the dirt. Two hostiles down. But the cracks and flashes continued and he couldn't see Ramirez in his night vision yet.

"Ram, what's your status? It's time to go. I don't know how long those lights are going to stay out!"

It seemed like forever, but a few seconds later Ramirez crackled over the whisper, "I'm moving L-T. I'm about to be in your line of sight. Aim high!"

Ram popped into view as the rest of the team continued their well-rehearsed defended retreat to the peak of the small mountain. Jon stayed put until Ramirez, almost at a dead sprint, was in his grasp. "Are you hit?" Jon asked. Panting from his uphill forty-yard dash, Ramirez pointed to his right shoulder. He'd been grazed pretty good, but nothing that had to be dealt with right now.

The gunfire continued ahead and behind Jon and Ram but the friendly muffled pops were getting further away as his team climbed the hill. From the foxhole, Jon could also hear the Kalashnikov fire advancing slowly, and honing in on his location. Jon radioed Jones "We may need help from the air to get out of here Senior. How does it look up there?."

"It's clear so far, but can't say for sure until we get topside," Jones responded quickly. About ninety seconds later, as Jones reached the top of the mountain, he realized it was worse than they thought. Near the peak of the taller adjacent mountain to the north he saw three sets of headlights bouncing around and clearly headed in their direction. He also thought he could faintly hear the rumble of a diesel engine. There weren't many vehicles in these hinterlands, not to mention rapid responders armed and ready in the middle of the night. Something was very wrong. Jones radioed back, "L-T, there's reinforcements coming. At least three trucks and one of em's big."

It didn't make sense, but that didn't change anything. They needed air support and an evac quick. This was a hotspot and the intel had missed it. Jon whisper-comm'd back "Senior, whatever you have to do, get in comms, get us some fire support and get us a ride home!"

After that Jon was in overdrive. He drug Ramirez up the hill with disregard for the fire coming at them from below. He needed to get to his team and figure out how to get them out of here before they were pinned down on all sides. He only had a few more yards to go and could see the shadow of the rest of his team dropping down the other side of the ridge into cover. He closed the last few paces quickly, then lost his grip as Ram slipped on the loose gravely rock near the peak. As he reached back scrabbling for purchase on Ram's uniform to haul him the rest of the way, two rounds ripped through Jon's right leg. One took him in the meat of the calf, probably through and through, but the second slammed into bone right below the knee. When the second round landed he was at full strain leaning back, pulling Ram up. The searing shock loosened his grip on Ramirez and he stumbled backward over the top of the ridge. Before Jon knew it, he had somersaulted backward twice and was picking up speed down the backside of the mountain. He was starting to lose equilibrium from the fall. And the shock of what was probably a broken leg, maybe even a shattered right knee, was causing his vision to go gray around the edges. The last thing he remembered was a crackle over the radio, "Jason's down, 100 yards north on the ridge!"

What came next was a blur. Jon didn't remember finding the bottom of the backside of the mountain. He blacked out at some point on the way down. Just beneath the surface of consciousness that he couldn't quite swim up to, he felt a heavy weight of dread. His bleary nightmares were full of helicopter engine noise, yelling and swearing. He almost fought his way to a breath of reality but as he got close, the pain in his leg was blinding, all-consuming. A morphine needle slammed into the opposite leg and he swam right back down into his feverish dreamland.

Jon remembered a fast push across a tarmac. He wasn't the only one on a gurney. Next was what felt like forever in and out of sweaty sleep on a plane; probably a C-5. Then he was in a hospital. He remembered seeing Ramirez next to his bed, head in hands. What the fuck happened? He remembered needing to piss and finding a portly nurse hustling into the room to help him across to the bathroom.

Time slipped through his fingers. He felt feverish. In one of his half-conscious dreams he saw a man he'd never met sitting by his bed telling him that he'd let Jon's parents know he was fine and would make a full recovery. Where the hell was he? Why did his right leg feel like it was sealed in a coffin full of ants? For the next few days (or weeks, or months?) Jon was in a semi-conscious morphine induced stupor. When he was awake the world around him didn't feel real. He ate, drug his heavy brick leg to the bathroom, usually with assistance, and tried to dig around in his own mind to figure out why he felt like there was an enormous black cloud hanging just out of his mental reach. He had to figure out what this self-made secret was. On some level he didn't really want to know, and every time his medicated sleep stupor took him back down he felt like he wasn't quite strong enough to force himself to go get answers. That feeling of weakness was most palpable when he'd groggily crack his eyes open and see Ramirez there again and again, each time with the same look of sickness and dread seeping between the fingers of the hands against his face.

Then Jon woke up. Like really woke up. One morning he opened his eyes and saw sunlight pouring in the window to his right. He was definitely waking up somewhere unfamiliar with a touch of Deja vu. Like waking up from a dream but feeling like there's one foot still in the dream world. He knew this was 'real life' but still had a detached feeling; like a hangover without the headache. He sat up in bed and got ready to make his way to the bathroom across the room. That was when he realized the brick of a cast on his leg wasn't part of the dream.

As he stared at his atrophied right leg his stomach tightened. And then a familiar train of dread and despair hit him. The mountain in Afghanistan…he remembered taking a hell of a fall, he remembered the acute pain of the two bullets in his leg. He also knew neither of those explained the deep feeling of loss that felt like it was sitting on his insides. He pushed it aside for the moment and stumbled across to the bathroom. He took a good long piss and found a toothbrush and razor waiting for him at the sink. After ten minutes spent making himself feel human again, he stepped back out of the bathroom. And there was Ramirez.

"Hey L-T," said Ramirez. He seemed like he was struggling to keep his eyes up. Definitely not normal for one of his most steely eyed operators. Maybe it was all in his cloudy head.

"What's wrong Ram?" He asked casually in case he was wrong.

"How much do you remember about taking those rounds in your leg a few weeks ago?" Ramirez asked him.

"A few weeks ago?! I guess we have more to catch up on than I thought. First off, where are we?"

"We're in Stuttgart boss. You took two rounds. One really nasty near your right knee. But I think what jacked you up most was the tumble you took down the mountain when you lost hold of me. We drug you about a mile while we waited for the evac. Ultimately, we decided to lay low rather than take on the entire anthill we'd kicked over. You were out cold the entire time and honestly, I'm just glad to see you still remember how to speak English."

"So what else is weighing you down?" Haynes asked. Ramirez paused and stared down at the hospital room floor. Haynes braced.

"Jones. He went down at the same time you did. He was K.I.A., L-T."

There it was. Haynes knew he'd lost someone; deep down he knew it. He couldn't place it and the conscious part of his mind refused to acknowledge it. But Ram just made it real. Couldn't run from it now. He was awake, this was real, and Jonesy was gone.

Jon felt a little uneasy on his feet and hobbled back over to sit on the bed. He stared a long way out the window at the adjacent parking lot. Not really looking at anything in particular. His mind had already started racing through the chaos of the night in the mountains. The questions of what he could have done better, different.

"Does his family know?" Haynes managed to choke out.

"They've been notified in the official channels, but no one from the team has talked to them or been to see them. Do you want to call Sheila and talk to her yourself?"

"I don't think so. Not yet at least. I need some time to figure out what I'd say. It'd probably be better if I went to see her in person. How long are they saying I'm going to have to stay here?"

"Not sure boss. They've mostly been worried about getting you conscious again. Now that you're up we can probably talk them into sending you back to the States for the rehab part," Ramirez replied.

Jon and Ram made small talk in memory of Senior Chief Jones for the next few minutes. Both of them using it like good warriors should, to process the loss of a friend. Eventually the small talk dried up and Ramirez found an excuse to leave Haynes alone with his thoughts. Jon was relieved but also terrified to be alone with his swirling, racing mind. He lay in the uncomfortable hospital bed for what might have been hours, or maybe only a few minutes, until there was a soft knock at the door.

Jon managed to let out a soft grunt acknowledging the visitor. A medium height, slightly heavy, regular run-of-the-mill white guy in glasses came through the door. As Jon glanced up at the incredibly average bureaucrat of a man he had another strong sense of Deja vu.

"Mr. Haynes, sorry to disturb you. May I sit down?" said the plain guy.

"I guess so, but what can I help you with?"

"My organization has become familiar with your case over the last few weeks and is interested in offering you an opportunity of sorts. After you make a full recovery of course," replied plain guy.

Jon was annoyed. "Normally people I've never met introduce themselves first. Especially people I meet for the first time while I'm lying in a hospital bed in a cast and gown. Please start from the beginning sir."

"My apologies. I represent an organization called Casimir Institute. We work on a lot of things I won't go into right now, but suffice to say there is a lot of interest in the work we do from those whose interest we do not seek. As such, security is very important to us. We're interested in men with your particular set of skills to stress test and ultimately enhance the security at one of our most prized facilities."

Now Jon was past annoyed. He was only two weeks removed from taking two bullets for his country in the backwoods of Afghanistan and falling God knows how far down a mountain; a fall from which he had just reclaimed full consciousness. Moments earlier he found out that he'd lost the senior man on his team and a close friend. He was still in a morphine haze and as far as he knew he hadn't even left this room since they stitched up his leg. And the assholes that run this place were letting recruiters in to badger him with job offers. He still had a commission and was on active military duty. Either this guy was Houdini or someone was asleep at their post in this hospital.

"Look buddy, I'm not sure who decided it was a good idea to let you in here. I'm also not sure why you think it's a good idea to try and pitch me on some half-explained security job while I'm laid up in the hospital, but I'm not interested. You couldn't even be bothered to offer a name and a handshake? Kindly get the hell out and let me be."

The plain guy seemed to take his verbal lashing in stride. As if he'd expected it. He paused for a moment, pushed his large metal frames up on his face, and then responded as though he hadn't been ordered out of the hospital room by a wounded warrior.

"Lieutenant Haynes, I sincerely apologize if my approach has rubbed you the wrong way. I should have started by offering my sincerest condolences for the loss of your brother in arms. Perhaps I should have followed that up by saying that regardless of whether or not you accept my offer of employment, the Casimir Institute would like to honor the service of Senior Chief Jones by establishing a small foundation in his name as well as ensuring his family is cared for financially. I understand his wife Sheila might even be interested in leading such a foundation if given the opportunity. I plan to offer her that opportunity. The only string attached is that you come tour our facility at a time that's convenient for you and that you hear me out. And my name is Steven Pulling."

Jon was pretty sure this was the next scene in his concussion induced fever dream. Plain guy was making ridiculous promises based on information he couldn't possibly have.

Jon massaged his temples, trying to clear his thoughts. "Look, Mr. uh, Pulling, I appreciate your generous and strangely specific offer, and your persistence. But as you can see, I have a couple bullet wounds I'm dealing with. Not to mention that I'm laid up in Germany and still a commissioned member of the military. While I'm somewhat curious as to how you came to know about me, my location and so much detail about my unit's members and recent operational action, I'm not interested in any once in a lifetime, Publisher's Clearing House offers. Like I said, maybe a bit rudely before, I'd appreciate it if you left me to my rest and recovery."

Once again, Mr. Pulling gave nothing away with his reaction to Jon's rebuttal. He just sat there like an android processing a complicated algorithm. After a few seconds he adjusted his frames on his nose again and replied in the same measured monotone. "I'm sorry to hear that Jon. But as you wish. I'll take my leave of you now. Here is my contact information if you have a change of heart at a later date."

With that, Pulling slid a very simple gray business card onto the bedside table, stood, turned, and departed in the same unassuming and awkward fashion as he had arrived.

Relieved, Jon laid his head back on the flimsy hospital pillow and tried to sleep. He forced his body to relax but his thoughts raced him right back down the rabbit hole of despair, albeit now a rabbit hole with some new questions and a few new concerns.

CHAPTER THREE

Jon eased his way down the steps and into the wading pool. He didn't have to learn how to walk from scratch but he wasn't exactly running five miles a day either. For the last month and a half he'd been grinding out physical therapy sessions for as long as his leg could handle each day. He was no slouch in the gym before he was wounded, so most days he was at work rebuilding himself for six to eight hours; plenty of time alone with his thoughts. The first few hours were spent doing whatever low-grade torture the physical therapist dreamed up for the day. The remainder were spent working the rest of his body back into shape to the extent his leg would allow it.

Jon didn't mind the time with the therapist. She was easy on the eyes. About his height, 5′-8″ or 5′-9″ fair skinned and fit with strawberry blonde hair. Definitively not his type, but he was able to make the daily grind of physical therapy pass by a little quicker toying and flirting with her as a distraction. Jon was infinitely confident that she was into him, as most unmarried women his age were.

While he didn't spend a lot of time thinking about the future, Jon was pretty certain that it still included the SEALs. So most of his physical rebuilding was focused on getting his body back to what was required to get into the field and do his job. He was making progress overall but full mental confidence in his right leg was a long way off. Jon's bigger concern was that he had a hard time visualizing his return to the operational SEAL teams. He loved being in the field. He had a hard time picturing himself in any other role, but he also wasn't completely on the other side of what it meant to lose a man in a firefight. The darker side of his mind kept telling him that until he got back to real work, he wouldn't be able to fully come to terms with Jonesy's death. From the moment Jon had his lights knocked out as he tumbled down the hill in Pakistan, nothing in his life had been routine or normal, which kept the grief and regret at arm's length. He tried to tap into it during his training sessions, but being holed up in a hospital, largely alone, was a lot different than running through the paces of training and operating with a close-knit team of SEALs.

After the initial surgery to repair his right knee and fibula Jon spent a few more weeks in the hospital in Germany. He'd been back in Southern California for a month now. The first few weeks of healing and recuperation of his leg had gone off without much of a hitch and he had been working through the paces of physical rehab ever since. Other than right before he went to see Sheila Jones, he hadn't thought much about Steven Pulling - the unwelcome visitor he had in the hospital in Germany. But that changed quickly when Jon looked up from the end of the wading pool and saw him casually standing and staring less than ten feet away. Jon made eye contact and that appeared to be all the invitation Pulling was waiting for.

"Hello Lieutenant Haynes. Have you had any further thoughts on the offer I made you back in Germany?"

"Haven't thought about it much. Do you have some sort of all access pass to military medical facilities? This is getting ridiculous," Jon said, buying time to process what was happening as he made his way to the edge of the pool.

While Jon remembered feeling irritated, bordering on furious, the first time this awkward middle aged bureaucrat showed up, there was something about seeing him standing here now, knowing the pain Sheila and her kids were going through. It suddenly seemed like it might be real. And it was too serious a situation, detached as he might feel about it right now, to disregard this guy. The shoulder sagged looks he saw at the Jones house last week weighed heavy on him.

Up to now he'd focused the emotional energy built up in that afternoon at the Jones' house into physical energy. A seemingly endless supply of physical energy that he'd harnessed to work his leg and body back into fighting condition. He was going to make his recovery and honor Jason's memory by getting back to work. Sooner rather than later, and better than ever before. He wasn't particularly convicted about it, but that's the sort of thing people did in this situation, right?

As he stared at Pulling standing alongside the physical therapy wading pool, he realized on some level that he was going to hear this guy out; maybe take him up on his offer for Sheila's benefit.

Regardless of how ridiculous it might seem, no one hunts their quarry down in Germany, makes too good to be true promises, and then shows up again in San Diego, without even a hint of interest returned, still persistent in his pursuits. Jon had to respect the tenacity of the guy. He also had a strange respect, or maybe a tinge of fear, for how easily Pulling seemed to be able to track him down. Yep, maybe that was it. Jon was spooked by a plain high school chemistry teacher-looking guy. And on a macho level, that really bothered him. He needed to meet this head on. See what this guy was about and get a better idea of how he knew everything about Jon and his medical treatment…and about Jonesy and his family. Jon was also curious how this civilian frump of a man managed to walk right into two different medical facilities on military bases in two different countries like he had a map and the night janitor's keys.

More importantly, he wanted to do something real for Sheila and her kids. Going back out and fighting more bad guys would be great. And Jonesy would love it. But Jonesy also loved his kids. Taking another couple bullets in some forgotten corner of the world wouldn't do anything for Sheila, Jason, their kids, or Jon. Ever since he stood waiting on the front porch of the Jones' house a couple miles from the San Diego beaches, he knew he owed them something more. Jason may not have died knowing he would save Jon, but Jon owed him nonetheless. Senior Chief Jason Jones had carried out the orders that got him killed, saving Jon and the rest of the team in the process.

Jon climbed out of the pool and started to towel off.

"Lieutenant Haynes, I assure you there is nothing nefarious about my proposal. My organization is interested in acquiring your services. We're also interested in honoring a hero by helping his family. What will it take to convince you of my sincerity?" asked Pulling.

As he softened to the whole idea Jon lowered his guard slightly, willing to entertain the details. "If I go along with this, what does it look like? Where, when, how long?"

"You could specify the timing Mr. Haynes. Depending on your recovery and rehabilitation we'd be glad to host you for a tour and overview whenever it's convenient for you. As far as the location, extensive travel will not be required. The facility of interest is a short drive from here."

"And what exactly would I be doing for Casimir. Anything more specific than facility security?"

"Unfortunately Mr. Haynes, those details will have to wait. We will be able to discuss more thoroughly when you visit, but even then I suspect you will be unsatisfied with the level of detail I can provide. Certain aspects of our operations are only divulged to those in our employ with a need to know. I'm sure you understand."

"Ok...I guess. Please forgive my skepticism, but were you serious back in Germany when you said that you'd take care of the Jones family and the foundation as long as I came out for a visit?"

"Absolutely, Mr. Haynes. We'd be honored to do so. Frankly I'd be supportive of those actions independent of your entertaining my offer of employment. But the gentlemen I work for drive a harder bargain."

"Fair enough. You've convinced me sir. How soon can I come out and how do we set this up?"

Jon saw the slightest hint of a satisfied smile creep across Pulling's face.

CHAPTER FOUR

After spending the early morning driving ninety minutes into the desert east of San Diego, Jon pulled his F-150 up to the gate and handed his Navy ID over to the security contractor manning the shack.

"I have an appointment with Mr. Pulling," Jon said as the guard handed his ID back to him.

The guard started flipping through a clipboard list without comment. The facility Jon saw through his windshield was nothing but underwhelming. It looked like countless other side-of-the-interstate warehouses where the average passerby wouldn't have the slightest clue what happened inside and probably wouldn't think twice about it. To Jon's trained eye the only thing remotely notable about this particular facility was the razor wire fence creating a half-mile standoff from the building. The guard seemed to find what he was looking for.

"Ok Mr. Haynes. You can park your vehicle in the lot to your right and someone will be out to meet you shortly," said the guard.

The lot wasn't inside the main facility fence. Jon pulled into the lot and eased into the first spot, only about 30 yards from the guard shack. He shut the truck off and sat looking at the facility while he waited for whoever was coming to retrieve him.

While he waited Jon reached into the center console of his truck and fished out a prescription bottle of pain medication. He wasn't supposed to drive when he was on the pills, but he was starting to feel the dull ache returning in his right leg. He also figured since he was getting a chauffeur for this outing he could afford to take the edge off. It certainly wouldn't hurt his focus. The meds didn't dull his mind, just his reflexes.

The duty of warding off the mental distraction of pain all morning wouldn't help him figure out how Mr. Pulling and this company seemed to know so much about him. He still wasn't particularly interested in leaving the military for this job, but he wasn't going to drive all the way out here without trying to figure out how the Casimir Institute knew so much about him and his unit, or why they were so acutely interested in him.

Jon swallowed the pills as he let his mind chew on these questions. As he took a pull from his water bottle to wash it down, he saw the familiar but unmemorable figure of Steven Pulling approaching in an electric golf cart. Pulling pulled past the gate and into the parking lot. Jon took his cue and got out of the truck to rendezvous with his escort.

"Hello Jon, I hope your drive out was uneventful," Steven Pulling called from the driver seat of the cart.

"Good morning. The drive out was fine," said Jon.

"Please get in and we'll get started."

Jon swung down into the passenger seat of the cart and Pulling quickly pulled away to head back toward the guard shack. The guard waved them through and they headed along the straight road toward the non-descript warehouse. They were halfway between the gate and the building before Jon realized Steven hadn't said a word.

"So Mr. Pulling, I'm here now. Can you tell me anymore about your organization's interest in me? I'd also really appreciate any insight you can give me into what you guys do out here."

"I'll take your questions in order Mr. Haynes. Casimir Institute has some unique methods for identifying talent. Your name was high on our list. While I regret the circumstances under which I made my initial offer, we had our eye on you before your last outing in Pakistan."

"Who said I was in Pakistan? And you still haven't answered my question."

Pulling moved right along, unfazed. "To answer your second question, Casimir Institute is focused on theoretical physics turned practical. Specifically, our focus is in application of cutting edge applied physics research in areas of nanotechnology and computing. Suffice to say, Mr. Haynes, we have some potentially valuable trade secrets and research we want to ensure is protected from the prying eyes of other commercial interests. The name Casimir actually originates from our founders work in the application of the Casimir Effect to developing advanced silicon-based microprocessors. I'm sure you can imagine why we'd want to protect this work."

"Sure" Jon replied. He couldn't actually. He had no idea what Pulling was talking about. He was lost at 'theoretical physics.'

As they approached the east side of the warehouse Jon noted only one access point to the main building, at least on this side. It was a normal-sized door with an adjacent window and call box. There was also some sort of electronic pad, perhaps biometric, on the opposite side of the door. Jon assumed they were headed there to park but then Steven veered the cart to the left, paralleling the east side of the warehouse structure.

As Pulling steered the cart alongside the building he started up again in his tour guide voice. "Around the corner ahead on the south side of the building is our security outpost. Before we get there, you should know that I've advertised you as a security consultant that we're bringing in to evaluate our systems and security practices. It's been billed as a routine check. An independent assessment of our day to day practices."

"When you say advertised...?"

"Your presumption is correct. You are not really here to perform a routine assessment of security. But you should take good mental notes on what you see, and get to know the security team."

"I don't understand."

"You will. Please Mr. Haynes, be patient. And while we're in the security outpost I'm going to refer to you as Mark Johnston, Head Security Consultant at Gateguard Security. Try to play along."

As he was talking Pulling edged the cart around the corner and Jon saw the security outpost come into view beyond the warehouse. It was concrete block construction and not much larger than a typical construction trailer. There were a few antennas and satellite dishes on the roof, which indicated to Jon at least some advanced communications capability.

They drove in silence across the concrete valley between the warehouse and the security building. Jon looked over his shoulder at the south end of the building and noticed a large loading dock and adjacent sliding barn door on this side of the building. He also felt a faint humming that seemed like it resonated in the base of his skull. Maybe the pain meds were playing tricks on him. But he was curious about the facility and Pulling seemed to be in a more forthcoming mood.

"Where's that noise coming from?" Jon asked.

"I'm not sure what you mean Mr. Haynes."

Jon backed off. "Never mind, its probably in my head."

As the cart got further from the building the humming seemed to fade. Jon turned his attention to the security shack in front of him as Pulling stopped the cart near the main double doors that faced the warehouse. Pulling climbed out of the cart and headed for the doors. Jon followed.

Pulling swiped a badge at the card reader next to the door and waited for the clunk of the releasing locks. Then he swung the door open and Jon followed him into the small lobby. Ready to greet them behind the desk was a young, fit guard sporting a typical rent-a-cop uniform; the same make and model the ID checker at the front gate had been wearing. He seemed to straighten as Pulling walked up to the desk.

"Hello Mr. Pulling. I assume this is Mr. Johnston from Gateguard?"

"Indeed it is."

"I'll call Mr. Whitlock and let him know you're here," said rent-a-cop.

A few minutes later a tall lanky, just past middle-aged man came around to the lobby. Jon noted a Clint Eastwood quality to him.

"Hello Mr. Pulling," said Whitlock, acknowledging Steven Pulling with a slight nod. He then turned to Jon and extended a hand. "And you must be Mark Johnston. I'm Craig Whitlock, Head of Security for Casimir Institute. I trust you'll find your evaluation of our operations to be uneventful. Should be the easiest money you've made in a while." Whitlock shot a thin, smug grin at Pulling as he said this.

"Now Craig, as you know, we're not bringing in Gateguard because we think you're missing the mark on the security of this facility. Mr. Johnston is here to give us an independent assessment and a clean bill of health on your operation."

Jon was starting to think he might be getting in over his head. He came out for an interview. Mostly to help Sheila, but also to satisfy his own curiosity. Now he was being made complicit in deceiving an entire security team while still on active duty. He'd been on site for half an hour and still didn't know why he was actually here.

Pulling continued. "Craig, Mr. Johnston is only out for his initial site visit today. If you'd be so kind, I'd like you to give him the overview of your operation. I'll come back shortly to collect him for a brief tour of the warehouse."

"Understood," grumbled Whitlock. "Mr. Johnston, if you'd follow me around to the back I'll give you the run down."

Jon stepped around the front desk to follow Whitlock through the door that presumably led back to the rest of the security outpost. As he did, Pulling headed for the door with a promise to return to collect Jon soon.

As Haynes headed back he pondered the current situation. Rather than following his instinct and keeping his distance from Steven Pulling, he had taken the bait and followed his curiosity to this 'interview.' Now he couldn't help thinking he was unwittingly being forced into involvement in some strange form of internal corporate covert action. As he stepped through the door into the main room of the security building, he reminded himself that he was about to deceive the security director for an unknown reason. And by the way, he was still an active duty commissioned member of the military. He needed to tread very carefully. Jon decided he would say as little as possible and let Mr. Whitlock do the talking.

Lucky for Jon, Whitlock appeared just as anxious as he was to get the tour over with. "Welcome to the back room Mr. Johnston. From here we monitor the full suite of sensors that give us situational awareness of the facility exterior. We have remote video feeds that watch the perimeter as well as remote sensors that trigger on activity between the perimeter fence and warehouse. You'd be amazed at how many desert critters manage to set them off on an average night."

Whitlock walked Jon over to a large bank of video monitors with an adjacent computer workstation containing dual monitors and an open application that appeared to control the cameras and sensors.

As Whitlock continued the basic overview Jon nodded along and continued to take in the layout of the room. He stuck to his guns and didn't ask questions. But he was also nagged by Pulling's earlier advice that he take note of the security setup.

"There's no fancy high speed Internet out here in the desert so we also have a full satellite communications suite that provides both data and voice links to the outside world. So we can call for police or other emergency support if needed," Whitlock continued.

"That's pretty much it. Cameras and sensors on one side and communications on the other. Through the back door is our equipment storage area and the rear exit of the building. We've got a couple carts and trucks out there that we use to get around and respond to anything that pops up."

Jon was fighting back the urge to ask questions. As his pain medication set in he felt his caution receding. Why did security not monitor the inside of the warehouse building? And they were only about sixty miles outside San Diego. Why was there no connectivity with the outside world? But Jon swallowed the urge to ask. He still wasn't clear on why he was here so he wasn't sure what doors he might accidentally open with a line of questions. In addition to connectivity and monitoring of the warehouse, Jon was growing curious about weapons. None of the security personnel in this outpost were armed and he couldn't remember if the guy at the gate was carrying. But Jon could tell there wasn't much else he was going to learn about security from Whitlock. He didn't want to ask questions and the security director didn't seem all that interested in volunteering information.

As all this was swirling in his head, Jon followed Whitlock back out to the front of the building and saw Pulling's golf cart rolling up near the double glass doors out front. Whitlock held the door open for Jon and they exchanged forced pleasantries as Jon departed the security outpost and walked back to the cart.

"I trust your visit went well?" asked Pulling.

"I'm not sure," Jon replied. "Why am I here again? I have plenty of questions about the setup in there but your security director didn't seem real happy to have me around. So I decided it was best to play the quiet game rather than risk giving up any clues as to the secret mission you haven't told me about yet. Are you ready to tell me what I'm really doing here? I just spent the last few minutes as Mark Johnston, which I'll remind you is not my real name, and when I drove out here I thought I was interviewing for a job at your Institute. Can we kill the suspense and skip to the punch line?" As Jon went on he struggled to contain his frustration and sarcasm.

"We're almost there Mr. Haynes. Let me take you through the warehouse first. Then we can talk about the real terms of the employment I'm offering."

Jon rolled his neck to try and ease the irritation he was feeling. As he settled back into the golf cart that was now rolling toward the warehouse, he felt the return of the deep hum that he'd felt before. It was definitely emanating from the warehouse up ahead and seemed to build as they got closer. Jon did his best to put it out of mind as Pulling whirred the cart around the southeast corner of the building and parked near the single door.

"Alright Mr. Haynes, we're going to have to go through visitor control when we get inside the building. As far as the security personnel are concerned, you're still Mark Johnston from Gateguard Security. I have already provided all your identification information to them so it should be as simple as turning over your cellphone and picking up your temporary identification badge. If you have any questions, please get them out of your system now. Once we get inside I'd prefer if you let me do most of the talking. Please focus your considerable skill on observing your surroundings and saving any inquiries until we're back outside."

Jon sighed. "My list of questions is far too long to get out of my system right now. And what the hell. I've managed ok so far. Let's just go for it."

Again Pulling swiped his credentials across the security panel near the door. But this time he followed with a press of his thumb that caused the entire panel to illuminate green. Then the door locks clunked open. Pulling and Haynes stepped into a very small lobby area with two chairs, a small magazine table and a one-way mirror with an inlaid speaker. Next to the two-way mirror was another door.

"Good morning Mr. Pulling," came the voice from the speaker. "This must be Mr. Johnston."

"Indeed it is," said Pulling as he reached into the slot below the mirrored glass. He withdrew a green-yellow Casimir badge with Jon's photo on the front and Mark Johnston, VISITOR, ESCORT REQUIRED, printed on the bottom. He handed the badge over to Jon and instructed him where to clip it on his shirt collar.

"I'll need you to leave your cell phone here with me Mr. Johnston," came the voice from the speaker. "Please power it off if you don't mind. As you can probably imagine, it's a little annoying when I'm holding phones with alarms, alerts and ringtones that I can't turn off going non-stop back here in my little booth."

"No problem," said Jon as he thumbed the power off on his phone and passed it through the slot. Then the guard released the lock on the interior door and Pulling led Jon through into the large open portion of the warehouse.

Jon wasn't sure what he'd expected to see inside the massive structure, but this wasn't it. Interconnected catwalks suspended from the ceiling, supported along their length by steel columns cut the sightlines of the structure into a grid pattern. The ground floor was largely obscured by row upon row of servers. And between the servers on the ground and catwalks overhead there was an intricate network of steel fluid piping and electrical conduit that Jon assumed was cooling, power, and data connections for what had to be the biggest conglomeration of computing power he'd ever seen. He hadn't ever seen data centers of tech giants like Facebook and Google, but this is what he imagined they might look like.

Rising above the server racks near the center of the warehouse was a large flat-topped concrete rectangular structure. The catwalk grid was tied into and using it for support at the center of the space, but the structure was much too large for that to be its only purpose. Sitting atop the structure was a large winch and a small metal closet-sized building. Jon could only see the top portion of the huge concrete monument that rose above the sight line of the server farm.

The outer perimeter of the warehouse floor was polished concrete but ten yards from the outer wall where the rows of servers began, the flooring was elevated about two feet. Jon presumed the void between deck and concrete housed even more interconnecting wiring and cooling piping. Jon looked down the polished concrete walkway to his left and right. He had a clear line of sight all the way down to the warehouse exterior on either side, indicating that this side of the warehouse at least, was laid out in a symmetrical grid pattern.

Pulling glanced at Jon as he finished surveying the scene just inside the warehouse door. "Are you ready to walk about Mr. Haynes?" asked Pulling as he started down the side of the warehouse.

"Sure," said Jon as he followed Pulling along. "What exactly am I looking at?"

"Servers Mr. Haynes. This warehouse houses significant processing power and data storage. Everything the Casimir Institute is working on is run on these machines. Our network engineers are able to reconfigure the system as required to provide computing power for any project or calculations our researcher scientists require. And we use a proprietary artificial intelligence system to optimize the usage of the data and processing."

"If this is really just a big data center, I don't understand the need for all the security, or me for that matter," replied Jon.

Pulling rolled his eyes at the statement. "Mr. Haynes, all together this warehouse constitutes one of the most advanced supercomputers in the world." The tone of his voice indicated this should have somehow been obvious.

They arrived at the corner of the building and rounded the final row of servers. Jon noted the large garage door he'd seen from the outside and a gap in the server grid. As they continued the stroll around the building's perimeter Jon felt the final bit of tension he'd been holding onto ease out of him. His pain meds were operating at full effect now. He'd have to be careful to keep his curiosity in check while his impulse control was inhibited. To distract himself he continued his scan of the security setup.

Interesting. You couldn't swing a cat outside the building or anywhere on the perimeter grounds without hitting a remote camera. But there were none visible so far inside the warehouse turned data center. There were also no people. He'd seen one twenty-something woman walking the catwalks on the far end of the building, maybe reviewing logs on some of the instruments monitoring the behemoth computers. But no one else besides him and Pulling. Jon filed the lack of personnel and monitoring into his growing list of questions, saved for whenever Pulling allowed for them.

As they continued along the southern perimeter of the warehouse, approaching the garage door Jon gained a clear line of sight to the concrete structure at the center. A few things came into immediate focus.

The hum he'd previously attributed to the row upon row of servers was emanating from the structure. It had to be. The focus and intensity of the sound – or feeling – increased almost as soon as he could see the structure's base. He also saw the first signs of interior security. A guard, much more mercenary-professional than Craig Whitlock and gang, was standing sentry at a vertical lift door at the base of the center structure. He also saw the familiar dark orb of a remote camera positioned over the same door. A door that mirrored the size of the exterior garage door it was aligned with. Its purpose was now obvious to Jon, as was the purpose of the structure that housed it. The concrete tower contained a very large subterranean elevator.

This was far and away the largest elevator Jon had ever seen. Easily big enough to fit a large tractor-trailer or construction machinery. And he instinctively knew that Pulling was primarily concerned in protecting whatever was at the bottom. Given the size of the elevator, Jon also felt strangely certain that the warehouse he was standing in was only the primer, the entry foyer, or the front for the far grander facility housed below ground.

"Mr. Pulling, what's down there?" asked Jon, forgetting his charge to hold all questions until the end.

"Very good observation Mr. Haynes, but that is beyond the scope of today's tour. Please save any other insightful questions for the completion of our walkabout when we're back outside," replied Pulling, flashing the slightest hint of a satisfied grin.

Steven Pulling and Jon Haynes continued what would prove to be an uneventful circumnavigation of the warehouse over the next twenty minutes. As they returned to the side door they'd entered through, Jon confirmed that this and the garage door were the only entry points. He'd also confirmed that the only personnel in the warehouse beyond he and Mr. Pulling were the black clad security guard at the lift and the lone log-taker up on the catwalk. There was certainly more than meets the eye to this facility, and it was most certainly all below ground.

Pulling gestured toward the door, indicating to Jon that the tour of the interior was done and they were headed back outside through the security vestibule. Jon stepped through the door and up to the security window.

"I hope you enjoyed your tour Mr. Johnston," said the invisible guard on the other side of the one-way glass as he slid Jon's phone into the slot. Jon palmed his phone and dropped it into his front pocket as he followed Pulling out the door into the bright desert sun.

Jon followed Steven back to the cart and slid into the passenger seat. As he did Pulling cleared his throat, "Ok, Mr. Haynes. I know you have questions. Fire away."

Jon hesitated, trying to clear the slight fog caused by his pain medications. Based on all previous interactions with Steven Pulling he needed to craft his questions carefully and fire for maximum effect. He couldn't be sure how long the answers would be available.

"Why is the access to the underground lift inside the warehouse secured by someone that isn't part of Whitlock's security team?"

"Very good Mr. Haynes. The warehouse does in fact house an access point to a secure subterranean facility. Please go on. What other questions do you have?"

Jon bit back the frustration of receiving another half answer from Pulling. "Why is the complex almost completely cutoff from the outside world?" he asked next.

"Another fantastic observation Jon. As I'm sure you noticed we maintain the ability to connect to the outside world via the security outpost. Any communications or connectivity beyond the essentials required for summoning emergency services were evaluated as a potential security concern."

Jon was about ready to give up. Other than confirming his

observations Pulling wasn't giving up anything. But Jon pressed forward. "Why isn't there any security monitoring inside the warehouse? Other than the access control at the door we came through, there was no one from Whitlock's team inside and no monitoring equipment keeping an eye out from the outpost."

"Well done LT Haynes. When I saw the glassy look in your eyes I was slightly concerned that the medication you took to ease the pain in your leg would also dull your knack for surveillance. Mr. Whitlock's security group is solely tasked with protecting access to the campus and its exterior. They do not possess a need to know regarding the operations within the facility. And should we find ourselves in need of outside assistance, it provides Mr. Whitlock, who would coordinate any such assistance, with a degree of separation from our operations."

Jon sighed as he realized the rabbit hole only went deeper. The cart was halfway back to the front gate to return Jon to his truck and, while he had a trove of new questions, he didn't have any new clarity on his original purpose in making this visit to Casimir.

Pulling continued, "The intuition demonstrated by your questions, after such a short time at our facility indicates you're exactly what we're looking for at Casimir. Consider your interview a success. Are you interested in hearing the terms of my offer Mr. Haynes?"

"I am...I think. But first, what about your promises regarding Senior Chief Jones' family? I'll admit you've got my attention with this secret underground desert facility, but I came here because I wanted to see my friend honored and his family cared for."

"That will all be handled within the month. You don't have to concern yourselves with the details unless you want to. I will ensure the logistics and financials of establishing the foundation are handled. The remainder of the foundation's operations will be as determined by the Director, Mrs. Sheila Jones."

Jon was slightly taken aback. Maybe this was real after all. "Almost seems to good to be true Mr. Pulling. If it's all right with you I'd like to tell Sheila myself. Lend some credibility to the whole thing and try to keep her from fretting with the same doubts about you that I still have."

"Very good Jon. We'll arrange for that to happen in the coming weeks. Regarding my offer of employment; you would have to leave the Navy. I have some influences that can help that happen quickly but it will have to start with you submitting your intent to resign your commission. Is that going to be a problem?"

Jon let out a resigned chuckle. "I'll admit I'm very interested sir. At the very least I'm extremely curious. But you really haven't told me anything yet. So I don't think I can answer your question. How about a little more on what you're offering?"

"Understandable. You would be working for the Casimir Institute in an unconventional capacity. You will be employed as a special assistant working directly for me with minimal contact, at least initially, with the rest of the Institute's personnel. Your compensation will exceed your military pay and benefits by a large margin so you needn't be concerned with the personal finance aspects of my offer."

Pulling let this offer hang incomplete as their cart passed through the main gate. He veered toward the parking lot where Jon's truck was parked and shot Jon a slight eyebrow raise, waiting for his response. As Pulling eased the cart to a stop along the driver's side of Jon's truck, Pulling asked, "So Mr. Haynes, do you want to be a part of Casimir Institute? I won't say you have to take it or leave it now, but a series of significant events is on the near horizon and I need to fill this position sooner rather than later. You are far and away my preferred candidate."

That wasn't entirely true. Pulling didn't tell Jon that he was the only candidate.

"I don't know why, but I want to seriously consider your offer. But you've got to give me something I can work with. This is a major decision that you're asking me to make without all the cards on the table."

As Jon stepped out of the cart and reached for his keys, Pulling stared straight ahead at the distant warehouse they'd just left. He seemed to ponder how much he was willing to say as part of this negotiation.

"Mr. Haynes, I appreciate your interest, your diligence, and especially your persistence. I hope you'll understand that the specific details about the position I'm offering you are extremely sensitive and will be revealed in due time." Pulling paused, considering how to proceed. "There are certain things I simply cannot reveal until the time is right and you are... eh, part of, shall we say, the inner circle."

Pulling seemed to relax a little and grabbed the steering wheel of the cart, readying to drive away. As he prepared to nudge the accelerator he looked at Jon again. "But to help in what I'm sure is a difficult decision, I can offer some insight into your first assignment." Pulling pointed at the warehouse. "I'll need you to covertly gain access to the underground facility beneath that warehouse."

"I look forward to hearing from you Mr. Haynes. Please don't hesitate too long in your decision."

Pulling smiled like he already knew how Jon would decide, then drove back toward the gate, leaving Jon alone in the parking lot.

On auto-pilot, Jon thumbed the key fob and climbed into the driver's seat of his truck. As he started the truck to make the drive back to San Diego, he already knew he was going to leave the Navy and go work for the mysterious Steven Pulling and his shadowy Casimir Institute. He just wasn't sure why.

CHAPTER FIVE

Present Day

Jon didn't wait long to get in touch with Claire. He was scheduled to fly back to San Diego two days after the job fair. It might be a long shot, striking up a long-distance relationship – or fling – on short notice. When Pulling drug him up to Seattle to play lady catcher at the job fair he definitely hadn't planned on actually trying to catch one for himself. But Claire had something magnetic about her.

Sitting in his hotel room in downtown Seattle Jon held Claire's quickly scrawled phone number in one hand and his cell phone in the other. He'd looked at both a few times in the last hour. Each time brought a bout of nervous energy and unfamiliar butterflies.

Jon was not anxious or uncomfortable around women. In his experience, conversation and flirtation with the opposite sex came naturally, almost effortlessly. He wasn't a pursuer of long relationships, nor was he after casual sex. He typically found little resistance in drawing the interest of the women he found interesting. For Lieutenant Jon Haynes, dating and the like was something that just sort of happened on its own, without much effort or foresight. And, not surprisingly, he had never had anything that the majority of the adult dating world would describe as a serious relationship. He was the heartbreaker, not the heartbroken.

So...why was he nervous and hesitating? It wasn't from fear of rejection or lack of confidence. But there were plenty of things in Jon's life that had required him to step across the threshold of fear. He knew how to summon courage, look fear in the face, sack up, etcetera. He also never thought he'd need to exercise that skill set to call a girl. But after an hour of indecision, he was there. He forced the butterflies down as best he could and dialed Claire Keen's cell phone.

While it rang he realized in working up the nerve to call he'd forgotten to think about what he'd say when she answered. He suddenly hoped for voicemail. Nobody answered cell phone calls from unknown numbers anyway. He'd ride this out and think of something.

"Hello?"

Crap

"Hi…uh Claire?"

"Who is this?" came the reply. Not entirely impatient, but close.

"Sorry, It's Jon. Um, from the job fair?"

The voice on the other end brightened. "Oh, Jon! So nice to hear from you," she said with a hint of playful sarcasm.

Jon knew the right moves here. Make cool and casual small talk about his visit to Seattle or whatever else came to mind. Then call the play and ask to take her to dinner before he was scheduled to leave town. But he was holding onto his composure by a thread. He needed to be off this phone call before he made an ass of himself.

"I was wondering if you're free tomorrow for dinner," Jon blurted out.

"Sure. Did you have somewhere in mind? If you don't know the town I can probably make a suggestion or two."

Jon felt his nerves ease as he registered the eagerness in her reply. "I'll definitely take the recommendations of a native. I don't know much other than what's within a few blocks of my hotel."

"Ok, I'll think of something and let you know," she said.

"Perfect. How does seven o'clock tomorrow night sound? I'll pick you up at your place and we can head over to wherever you pick. Just text me the address."

"That's pretty presumptive of you Mr. Haynes," Claire said with a hint of teasing in her voice.

Jon hesitated a beat, not entirely sure if she was kidding. "I…uh, sorry-"

"I'm kidding Jon. I'll text it to you and see you tomorrow night. Goodbye Jon Haynes."

"Bye." Jon was about to thumb over to end the call when he realized she'd already hung up. He set his phone on the end table by the sofa and took a deep breath. He had nerves and adrenaline thrumming through his veins like he'd just finished a live fire training session and needed a few minutes before he'd stop seeing the world through a straw. As the minutes passed his phone vibrated on the end table with a text message alert. It was Claire. He snatched the phone and looked at the message. There was an address for an apartment about ten blocks from his hotel and a couple suggestions for restaurants. Jon relaxed further and eased himself back on the hotel sofa. He had about twenty-four hours to figure out how he was going to take this girl on a date without acting like a seventeen-year-old teenage nervous wreck.

***

Pulling didn't have any appointments or assignments for Jon the next morning. The only direction he'd given was for Jon to enjoy Seattle and stay out of trouble while Steven called on a few associates in the local area. When Jon first saw the schedule for this trip he was moderately excited to spend some time exploring Seattle. But now he had a date on the books with a girl that made him inexplicably nervous, and he had no way to distract himself until it was time to go pick her up.

He began the day researching the couple restaurants Claire had proposed. He was leaning toward the Asian Fusion restaurant near her apartment but he had plenty of time to walk by and check it out during the day. He also took a look at the forecast. It was typical Pacific Northwest January weather. Mid to low forties throughout the day and evening, cloudy, with a persistent drizzling cold rain. He'd need to go spend a few dollars on a better coat. Obviously he wanted to look good, but equally important he needed to stay warm. Even though his physical therapy was done and his wounded leg back at full capacity, cold damp conditions still brought a distracting, throbbing pain if he let the cold seep in.

Next, he scoured the Internet on his phone looking for bars and lounges near the restaurant. Jon had learned in the dating game that you had to have a plan to prolong the night if things were going well. Real life wasn't the movies. Real people don't just go home together and try on their birthday suits because they had a nice conversation over dinner. Jon preferred to have a plan to follow up dinner with drinks somewhere quiet and casual if the evening was on the right track. It was an unassuming move, allowed for continued conversation with added social lubricant, and if he didn't tell the date that it was part of the plan, he wasn't obligated to do it if things weren't going well and he preferred to end the night early. After a few minutes of looking he found the perfect spot. A speak easy style bar a few blocks from the Asian Fusion place. He also noticed in his search that Seattle loves Asian Fusion.

Ok, now he had the plan. He knew he needed a jacket. But it was eight in the morning. How to kill the remaining eleven hours without getting inside his own head thinking about how to handle the 5′3″ brunette that made him as nervous as a scrawny seventh grader at a school dance.

Over the next few hours Jon made his way to the mall, picked up a North Face jacket at a significant hit to his wallet, and took a walk past the restaurant and the speak easy to make sure he could find them. He thought about walking past Claire's address to make sure he could find it, but he was quickly learning about the chill that came with Seattle in January. He also didn't want to accidentally bump into Claire or someone she knew and come off as a creepy stalker type. So he went back to the hotel and grabbed lunch in the lobby restaurant.

After lunch he tried to distract himself in his hotel room but it wasn't working. He turned on the TV, found a cable news network, and tried to take his mind off the girl he was all too excited to spend the evening with. Before he realized it, Jon was playing greetings, flirtatious lines and jokes on repeat in his mind, trying to pin down how he would keep conversation going with Claire and impress her with his charm and wit. He was right back in his own head. Nothing good could come from this. His only real distraction was the dull throb in his right leg, probably brought on by the cold, damp Seattle weather. He decided to take a couple pain pills and see if he could catch a short nap to pass the time.

When Jon awoke it was past sunset and twilight had settled across his room. The change in lighting registered and caused him to jerk fully alert. He was late and was going to ruin his shot with Claire. Then he glanced at his watch and remembered that the winter days in the Pacific Northwest were obscenely short. It was just before five o'clock and he still had two hours until he was supposed to meet Claire at her apartment.

He took his time readying himself and set out to walk the ten blocks to Claire's apartment an hour before he was supposed to arrive. He made his way through the cold rainy Seattle streets absentmindedly. He had committed his walking route to memory before he left the hotel so he had plenty of mental bandwidth to distract himself with the city landscape – as well as a healthy dose of self-doubt and the nagging question of what he was really after on a business trip date. On the one hand his infatuation, and probably his lust, for Claire were pegged high. And she'd agreed to go out with a guy from out of town. The physical attraction and no strings elements of this situation were hard to miss. With a few things breaking his way, Jon could see tonight ending in Claire's apartment or his hotel room. But Jon kept getting hung up on whether or not that's what he wanted. He didn't really know Claire at all, but he felt like he did. There was an attraction between them. But more like something that exists between charged magnets than between young attractive people. It might mean he was out of his depth with Claire and would need to fight his more instinctive urges until he had a better handle on the grown-up emotions involved.

***

Claire stood in front of her bathroom mirror evaluating her outfit. Like any woman, Claire spent plenty of time in front of the mirror readying herself for a night out. But unlike most women, Claire hardly applied makeup at all. Lipstick if the occasion was right for it, eye shadow and liner for really fancy outings. But beyond that she steered clear of the makeup counter. She was genetically gifted with nearly flawless olive skin and a Polynesian mother that ingrained in her, from an early age, an appreciation for the need to take good care of it. A layer of makeup on her face made her feel fake and half suffocated. So instead she spent her prep time over analyzing her clothes.

Tonight she was planning to wear a deep green top with a semi-plunging neck line – plunging enough to be interesting but not overly inviting – and designer jeans with knee high boots. It didn't take her long to get dressed. She was already well into the psychoanalysis of the clothes she'd donned. She'd made her way through the full gamut of viewing angles. Then her roommate Amy had been invited in to the fray to judge whether or not her top and boots made her look 'slutty' and whether or not the jeans made her butt look good.

Over the year they'd lived together and the five years they'd known each other Amy had grown to virtually worship Claire's natural beauty and sense of style. So naturally, Amy approved and had suggested a three-quarter length black pea coat and black clutch to finish out the outfit.

Claire was ready to go but Jon wasn't supposed to arrive for another fifteen minutes. Now she was avoiding overeager waiting by the door of the apartment. She loitered in front of the mirror under the guise of checking herself out. In reality, she was trying to see into the near future wondering how and where this date would lead and asking herself what she wanted from it. The average guy that picked up a date while out of town on business usually had pretty clear goals. Long term commitments were not something you left town searching for. And given how eagerly she'd agreed to the date it wouldn't be unreasonable for him to have certain expectations of how tonight was going to end if he played it right. And he would be right. Claire knew based on the few minutes she'd spent with him that if he was a non-creepy gentlemen type, maybe a little shy but funny, she'd have a hard time keeping her cute outfit on at the end of the night.

Then came the knock at the apartment door. Time to play it just a little bit coy. "Amy can you grab that? I'm almost ready," Claire called out the bathroom door.

Claire heard Amy answer the door followed by a muffled exchange between Jon Haynes and her roommate. A few seconds later Amy tapped on the door to Claire's room and emerged with an excited smirk on her face.

"OH MY GOD," mouthed Amy in a near silent whisper. She elbowed Claire playfully just below the ribs. "He's not cute. He's hot...You're so screwed. Pun intended," Amy whispered between bouts of the giggles.

Claire rolled her eyes as she threw a few odds and ends in her clutch. Then she headed out of her room into the living room. Jon was standing in the dining area between the kitchen and living room looking slightly uncomfortable.

"Hello Jon Haynes," said Claire, trying to exude the confidence she suddenly found lacking. She wasn't nervous sixty seconds ago, but as soon as she saw him she felt butterflies and a touch lightheaded at the quick rush of adrenaline.

"Hi. Are you ready to go?" he asked. As Claire took in Jon's schoolboy outfit she relaxed a little. The boyish face and the oversized raincoat made her think, strangely, of Paddington Bear. The childish image helped her suppress the nerves enough to maintain her confidence as she slung on her coat and made a show of hooking her arm in his before heading out the front door.

As they walked out of her apartment building, Jon told her he'd chosen the restaurant closest to her apartment to keep them out of the rain. Claire noticed one of the tags still on the sleeve of his new jacket and was quickly aware how uncomfortable he was in the rainy northwest winter weather. She would go along without teasing him for now.

They didn't talk too much on the short walk over, only casual pleasantries. She also lost the Paddington Bear image. His stride was confident and his strength obvious. Even through his jacket she could feel it in the hook of his arm. As he opened the door to the restaurant and led her in by the small of her back she was very aware of the subtle firmness of his touch. She sighed imperceptibly. They hadn't even sat down for dinner yet but she felt the familiar warm chemical tug of adolescent lust.

***

As they entered the restaurant Jon let out an internal sigh of relief. Despite his nerves he'd managed to make the pickup and short walk to the restaurant without making a fool of himself. The distraction of the rainy walk and the confidence that comes with having a beautiful girl on your arm had caused the flood of nerves to recede. But as he stepped behind Claire into the warmth of the restaurant, the butterflies battled their way back into the fray. Small talk was over. They'd now sit across from each other at a table in a trendy restaurant. He'd have to look her in the eyes – not hard to do - and make real adult conversation.

The restaurant was about right. Not too upscale to make things feel stuffy but nice enough that it didn't feel like he'd taken her out to slum at a burger joint. The décor was a little loud and very trendy but the music was more subdued – mostly white noise that was just loud enough to carry on a conversation without letting it filter out to the surrounding tables.

The place wasn't particularly crowded so they were taken to a table almost right away. As the hostess led them to an intimate table made for two and set down the menus, Jon was on auto pilot. He eased Claire's chair away from the table and offered it to her naturally. Then he sat down across from her and felt an unfamiliar lump in his throat. He was suddenly very self-conscious.

"So Mr. Jon Haynes…" Claire drew out his name with a hint of flirtation, or coaxing. "What do you do for Casimir Institute?"

Jon felt he'd been given another reprieve by his attractive companion. She was going to make the conversation go. But damn. In all his nerves and distraction he'd failed to consider that she'd be curious about his role at Casimir.

"I guess you could say I'm a security specialist. But I've only been there a few months and am still learning the ropes as a sort of executive assistant to Mr. Pulling." Jon hoped she'd take his vague explanation at face value. He would also spin it back on her to move the discussion in another direction.

"What about you? Are you planning to come down to San Diego for the interview Mr. Pulling offered?"

"I think so. I hadn't ever really considered the idea of living in Southern California. Most people in my field end up in Northern California or staying here in the Seattle area. But I'm also a little bored with the idea of finishing school and just plopping in to a regular job at some big company. The routine and structure of something like that sounds boring, and maybe even a little scary, you know?"

"I do actually. Before I went to work for Casimir I was in the military. I ended up there mostly because I was afraid of the idea of pushing a desk right out of college. I wanted excitement and adventure…I liked the structure but didn't want the routine, so the military seemed like a good fit." Jon trailed off, realizing he didn't want this conversation to become about him. Too many off limit topics he'd have to side step.

"So what field are you in exactly?" Jon asked.

"I think the most accurate thing you could call it is network engineering. Unless you're a computer geek you'd probably find it pretty boring. Basically I'm studying to design, build and maintain large scale computer networks."

"Does that make you some sort of cyber security whiz kid?" Jon asked with a slight wink, legitimately curious. Most of his interest in Claire was driven by his carnal curiosity about the curve of her figure but there was some professional mystique too. Pulling hadn't bothered to brief him up on why they needed to come up to Seattle and coax this particular coed into an interview at Casimir. IT professionals were a commodity in most major cities nowadays, so Steven's specific interest in Claire still didn't quite make sense, making her all the more interesting.

"No, I don't do the security stuff. I try to make the network perform at its best. The security guys end up piling on a bunch of extra code to keep bad guys out and play big brother to the good guys. It ends up taking a huge bite out of the capability of most networks." Claire paused, a hint of frustration visible in the crease of her brow. "Uggghhh. Don't get me going on my geek squad political topics." A sly smile replaced the furrowed brow. "Why don't you just think of me as the cute-sexy hacker from one of those crime scene investigation shows. I even have some trendy librarian glasses I can throw on if that helps the image."

"I can manage that," Jon replied with another weak attempt at a suave wink. Unable to tell how his cheap attempt at returning Claire's flirtation was received, Jon continued to follow his playbook – keep the girl talking.

"So are you from Seattle originally?" Jon asked.

"Sort of. I'm from across the Sound. It's a short ferry ride over here, but much more of a small-town lifestyle," replied Claire.

From there the conversation between them moved on its own momentum. Jon felt like he'd applied the necessary energy – and nerves – to get the train started, but now the weight of their interest in each other kept it moving. Drinks arrived, appetizers were ordered, entrees were served. None presented more than a slight bend in the tracks of their conversation.

They discussed family. Claire grew up in a Brady Bunch house, her mother and step father marrying already with kids from their previous marriages. Jon came from a more traditional, and rare, household where his parents were still married and seemed happy together. They discussed growing up, high school, college, work. Everything seemed to move on its own. Neither of them glanced at a watch. There were no awkward pauses or discussions of the weather. Before Jon realized it, the check was sitting on the table. He collected it and paid the tab mindlessly, lost in Claire's childhood story of a family road trip through Arizona with no air-conditioning.

Jon's credit card returned, the table was bussed, and their waitress made two different stops at the table to see if they needed anything else. This all went unnoticed by Jon and Claire. On the waitress' third stop at their table Jon snapped out of the trance long enough to get the hint.

"Claire, I think the waitress is ready to get new paying customers at this table. You want to walk over to Bathtub Gin? I've never been but it comes highly recommended."

Claire feigned irritation at the recently departed waitress. "Sure. It's a cool spot. Pretty intimate setting though. Are you thinking about trying to get me drunk?"

Jon felt a little warmth creep up around his collar. He still wasn't sure what his end game was with Claire, but she had cut right to the quick on his normal formula for a date. He felt exposed…but still very confident.

Glancing at his watch Jon realized they'd been at dinner for coming up on two hours. As he pushed back from the table Jon had a helpless feeling. He'd completely lost track of time. He'd been so drawn in to every word Claire had said. He could describe every detail of her face. He could repeat verbatim everything she'd said about how her younger brother used to get in neighborhood fights growing up. He knew her grandmother's maiden name. But he wasn't sure how much he'd eaten or even what he ordered. It was as though he and Claire sat down to dinner and started moving at a different speed than everything else around them. It reminded him of something out of a science fiction novel where time moves at a different speed and people age differently on spaceships flying at hyper speed. Two hours had just elapsed for the rest of the world. For him only a few minutes. And he wanted more time.

***

As they got up to leave the restaurant, Claire knew she liked where this was headed. Jon was a great listener and was at least interested enough to want to keep the night going.

Nature dictated that every man was drawn to the female form. Claire knew this and intended to make use of it to continue to signal her interest. As he opened the front door of the restaurant to lead her back out into the rainy Seattle streets she again felt the strong but subtle presence of his hand at the small of her back. As they came through the door she decided to take his touch as an invitation. She slid her left arm under his right and rested it on his waist. Then she gently leaned her body into his as they walked, letting the curve of her breast press against the right side of his body. Jon took the invitation in stride and brought his arm up to rest around her shoulder. Neither of them missed a step and Claire felt a thrum of excitement in the pit of her stomach. They fit together perfectly.

They walked like this for the three-block trip to the bar-lounge where they'd continue their date. On the way there Jon seemed content to just walk, the magnetism of their first real physical touch stealing away the conversation that had flowed so freely at dinner a few minutes ago. So Claire decided to try and learn a little more about him.

"So what did you do in the military?" she asked. Claire thought she noticed a slight tension build up in Jon's midsection as soon as she asked the question.

"I was in special operations with the Navy." Jon's reply was abrupt. Maybe this was a sore subject. But Claire was humming on the adrenaline of their touch and his so far uncharacteristic response to her question made her intent on pressing forward.

"So you were a SEAL or something? How long were you in the Navy?" she pressed casually. With the second, clearly unwelcome question, she thought she felt him pulling away from her just a little bit.

"Yeah, I was a SEAL. I spent just over four years in. I separated about 4 months ago to start working for Casimir."

Claire was getting the signal that he didn't want to talk much about his military work. Not that she should care. This was a casual first date between a couple people that didn't even live in the same city. Why was his unresponsiveness nipping at her pride? She fought back the urge to continue pressing the topic, instead favoring the light conversation and chemistry they'd had at dinner.

She moved past the unwanted line of questioning by pressing in closer to him, feigning a need for shelter from the cold drizzle. They turned down the alley to the speak-easy and she shifted the conversation to a lighter topic.

"What do you do to stay in such good shape?" she asked, sliding her hand up and down his back.

***

Jon was a bit flustered at the warm feminine curves pressing into him and the hand moving suggestively along his back. As the doorman waved them into Bathtub Gin, Jon was slightly relieved at the casual excuse to break free of the pseudo embrace they'd been in since leaving the restaurant.

As they stepped into the bar a hostess led them to an isolated two-person table down a half set of stairs near the back of the dimly lit establishment. Once they sat down and started to peruse the drink menu Jon found himself looking for an excuse to get close to Claire and re-establish contact. He was surprised at how well she fit under his arm; less surprised at the urge he had to touch her skin. It didn't need any help, but the soft light of the speakeasy gave Claire's skin an even more inviting glow.

After ordering Bourbon on the rocks for Jon and a Nantucket Mongoose for Claire, they chatted aimlessly. Throughout their conversation Claire seemed to find excuses to run her hand along Jon's arm or gently touch his chest. Jon didn't fail to notice and took the signal, eventually putting his arm over her shoulder to pull her into the prototypical couples embrace they'd shared on the walk over.

With her body nestled into his again, he regretted being curt toward her earlier questions about his time in the military.

"Sorry if I was short earlier when you were asking about the Navy. There's still some pretty fresh scars there," Jon offered.

"Thanks, but it's okay. You don't have to talk about it if you don't want to. I understand."

Jon didn't want to talk about it – normally. But either from the warmth of the Bourbon or the warmth of the girl, he felt at ease about it in the moment. With all the specific (and classified) details left out, he recounted the story of his last SEAL deployment, the loss of Jason Jones and his long road to recovery from the two bullets in his right leg.

As Jon retold the events he was entranced by the way Claire seemed to follow each word. He couldn't say for sure that she was genuinely interested, but if she wasn't she was a hell of an actress. Her eyes were engaging, looking up into his every word. The emotion he felt at various parts of the story seemed to be reflected back in her facial expressions. For the second time tonight, time seemed to take on a plastic quality. Bending around them to form a cocoon, events within moving at their own pace compared to the rest of the room. As he went on more drinks came. Their embrace at the table seemed to become more intimate.

As his inhibition receded further, Jon described his initial introduction to Steven Pulling in the hospital in Germany. He started to talk about how part of the reason he ended up working for Pulling was the generous way he'd offered to take care of Sheila and the kids, but he caught himself straying into dangerous territory and trailed off. As much as he was enjoying Claire's company, the curve of her body under his arm and the gentle but electric feel of her skin, he swam back up to reality, reminding himself that she was only a few hours removed from being a complete stranger.

As he snapped back to now, albeit somewhat dulled by the booze and hormones, Jon needed to change the subject. He went with what came naturally given the circumstances.

"Do you want to get out of here?"

***

"Sure," Claire said, ducking out from under Jon's arm and gathering her coat. As she did, she got a little self-conscious at how quickly she'd taken the offer. But Claire assured herself that just because she'd agreed to leave the bar didn't mean she'd already decided to sleep with him. But if he pressed his advantage she was pretty sure she wasn't saying no.

As they got up from the table and headed up to the door Claire felt a flush rise in her cheeks. She was a little drunk, but even more excited. She silently reminded herself that she left on this date acknowledging the possibility of a one-night stand with a good-looking guy from out of town. But in the last hour he'd poured out something more than witty banter and pickup lines. Jon Haynes was a looker for sure. He was also a good storyteller, and funny in a dry sarcastic sort of way. But there was something more to him than he wanted to let on. The dark intimacy of the bar they were in, combined with the booze, seemed to ease him out of his protective shell for a few minutes at least. She wanted to learn more. However, Claire knew the flush in her cheeks and the butterflies in her stomach were more founded in the physical attributes of Jon Haynes than their brief emotional connection.

Once they were outside Claire slipped back under Jon's arm; a position she found she fit into quite well, and one that seemed to give her subliminal power over him. At the same time, he flagged a cab at the end of the alley. Once they'd climbed into the back-seat Jon gave the cabbie the address of his hotel.

As the cabbie weaved through the light midnight Seattle traffic Claire decided she was going to accept Jon's upcoming invitation. Physically, the answer was obvious. She would have a good time with him; no doubt in her mind. And he was no sleaze. She got the impression he didn't have a hard time picking up women, but that it also wasn't a regular occurrence. Normally in a situation like this Claire would play coy, building the anticipation and excitement for a second date. But she really liked Jon and, because of geography, there was no guarantee in a second date. She could at least have fun tonight.

A few short minutes later the cab pulled up in front of Jon's hotel and they made their way quickly inside, free from the rainy cold. Jon grabbed Claire's hand and started to lead her over to the lobby bar.

"Nightcap?" Jon asked with a flirtatious smile.

The anticipation was going to drive her wild. She saw the elevator bank off to the right and pulled him that way instead.

"Sure. Which room is yours?" she asked, more than suggestively as she spun around to face him while continuing to walk backwards toward the elevator.

"Oh. It's 523. But you have to have one of these room keys to get the elevator to work," said Jon, teasing her with the keycard he'd just drawn from his jacket pocket.

Claire flashed a playful but seductive look at Jon as she took the key from his hand. She spun back to face the elevators as she slid the key into the back pocket of her jeans. Her mind made up, she was leaving no room for mixed or missed signals.

***

As the lobby elevator door dinged open, Jon followed Claire in. He was nervous. He knew first time sex with a very attractive woman was in his immediate future. Despite his confidence in this sort of situation, it was impossible not to be nervous. His heart was hammering. He knew his face was flush. The first signs of sweat were on his palms and he could hear his pulse in his ears.

Claire leaned against the side of the elevator nearest the button panel. Jon gawked at her nervously as she reached over and pressed the button to send them up to the fifth floor. As the elevator doors slid shut they stared at each other, Claire donning a slight smile – maybe a smirk – and leaning against the elevator car's railing. Jon stood just inside the door trying his best to be casual, cool.

There was no one else on the elevator as it started its ascent. Claire was putting out every signal of invitation in the book and, by Jon's estimation she was fully in charge of the situation. He wanted to change that, if for no other reason than to stop standing in the elevator helplessly, anxiously staring at her. He summoned the best imitation of fearlessness that he could and stepped to her side of the elevator. Without a word he slid his hand onto the nape of her neck and pulled her toward him. He kissed her. She returned the gesture with eagerness, parting her lips and leaning into him.

As the elevator continued so did they. Jon's hands in her hair, Claire's around his waist. Jon would have been content to stay in this elevator all night. The way they fit together in this embrace felt right. Satisfaction and contentment, like when you find two pieces of a particularly difficult puzzle that fit together perfectly. But the kiss ended and they reluctantly pulled apart as the elevator decelerated and the doors chimed and slid open at his floor.

They both laughed to relieve the tension as they walked impatiently to Jon's room. As they approached the door Jon reached into Claire's back pocket to retrieve his room key, not missing the opportunity to appreciate the curve of her backside. He quickly unlocked the door and they were kissing again before it swung shut behind them.

They stumbled from there to the couch in the small living room area without ever breaking their embrace. Jon backed his way onto the two-person sofa and Claire quickly followed on top of him. They explored each other hungrily for the next few minutes until Jon broke the kiss just long enough to get in a word.

"Can I make you a drink?"

"Sure," Claire replied, flushed and brushing her hair back in place with her fingers.

Conscious of his excitement, Jon took a second to adjust his jeans before getting up from the sofa to head over to the mini bar. Jon was flustered. He fumbled for a few miniature liquor bottles, ginger ale and a Coca-Cola and started to mix haphazard cocktails. As his heart rate slowed his head cleared long enough to let other-than-carnal thoughts in.

He'd had a great night with Claire. They talked and enjoyed each other effortlessly. Their hungry teenage make out session had also been very enjoyable. Any remaining thoughts he'd been having of an out of town one-night stand were evaporating while she waited patiently on the couch in his hotel room to share a nightcap. Jon started to negotiate with himself. He would really like to sleep with her tonight. They had chemistry, both personal and physical. There was no chance the sex wouldn't be good – probably great. But, sex or not, he knew he wanted to see her again. It didn't matter if he needed frequent flyer miles or a bus pass to get back and forth from California, he wanted to keep seeing Claire Keen. Thus the nagging, mature question made its way to the front of his mind. Could he take her across the room to his hotel bed, make sweaty hungry love to her, and not have this date become just a one-time thing on a business trip? He carried the drinks back over to sit next to Claire on the couch.

"I had a good time tonight," Jon said, cringing at the cliché awkwardness of his delivery.

"Me too." Claire smiled back at him.

Jon decided to put all his mini bar thoughts out in the open and see where things landed. "I definitely want to see you again, if you're interested…"

Claire didn't respond immediately. Still smiling, she raised her eyebrows slightly, urging him to continue.

"Ok. I also would really like to take you over to that bed and finish that kiss. I think we could make this a really memorable one-nighter; maybe an all-nighter. I guess what I'm trying to say is…"

"I know what you're trying to say," Claire interrupted. "I was thinking the same thing. We don't have to sleep together tonight. I'm going to take the interview with Casimir. If nothing else, it gets me a free plane ticket to take you up on your offer of a second date. I'm sure you know how to show a girl a good time in San Diego," Claire teased.

"So, yeah. I'll admit I was ready to show you my less modest side, but we can save that fun for later. Build the anticipation. I'll let you see me home to my apartment and we can both cool off for the night."

Jon let out a sigh of mock relief. "Ok Ms. Keen, how about I call you a car home and walk you out. I don't trust myself to take you all the way back to your apartment. After you leave I'll probably just stand out in the cold rain for a while. Then maybe I'll be able to get to sleep tonight," Jon said with a suppressed chuckle.

"Deal," said Claire as Jon thumbed through the screens on his phone to direct an Uber to his hotel.

Claire and Jon chatted a little awkwardly for the next few minutes finishing their drinks and waiting for Claire's car to arrive. Jon took Claire's empty glass over to the mini bar then grabbed her coat from the floor by the door where she'd dropped it during the more intense activity earlier.

At the door Jon held Claire's coat for her as she shrugged into it. As he let the coat fall onto her shoulders he couldn't help himself. He slid a hand around her midsection and turned her slightly toward him to kiss her again before they went out the door.

"Screw it," Claire mumbled as she turned to fully face him and press into him again. As she said this Jon felt her with one hand pulling open the buttons on his shirt and with the other dragging him toward the bed by the waistband of his jeans.

The Uber driver called three times before giving up and charging Jon the no-show fee. Jon and Claire were lost in each other for the next few hours and never noticed.

CHAPTER SIX

Claire stood on the sidewalk outside of a rented office in downtown San Diego wondering what she'd gotten herself into. Up to this point she'd thought she was coming to California to interview with a prestigious, albeit mysterious, privately funded institute that was doing cutting edge nanotechnology research. But when she'd arrived at the address she found a street level office space in an unassuming downtown building. Looking through the dirty front windows she didn't see anyone inside. It was nine-thirty in the morning; there should be somebody at work by now. She also had the distinct impression that the space she in front of her was a furnished rental space. The kind usually rented by self-employed accountants that needed a space other than their living room or garage to get some work done.

Well if this was a bust, at least the weather in San Diego was amazing so far. Mid-sixties with warm sun shining – in February! Worst case she'd get in an expense paid trip to visit a few Southern California beaches and break up the dreary Pacific Northwest winter. And she would get to cash in on the promise of a second date with Jon Haynes.

He was the main reason she'd agreed to come down for the interview in the first place. She'd gone out with him on a gut feeling, and an unsophisticated crush. Then they'd ended up spending the night together, despite their combined best efforts at patience and maturity. Now she couldn't stop thinking about him. Before she succumbed to her more primitive urges and dragged him into his hotel bed, she had a really great time with him. She had an even better time after she seduced him. The entirety of her evening with Jon Haynes had been playing on repeat in her mind's eye for the last two weeks and she couldn't wait to see him again.

She'd flown in from Seattle the previous night, courtesy of the Casimir Institute. She was scheduled to meet with Pamela Lindy, Assistant Director of HR at Casimir, at nine forty five at the address in downtown San Diego where she now stood. She'd misjudged the walk from her hotel and was a few minutes early. Claire no longer had an image of prestige and mystique about the Casimir Institute, but at least she had fifteen minutes to figure out how she'd tell Ms. Lindy that she'd made a mistake and wasn't the right person to come on as their network engineer. What kind of sophisticated network could they even have at a rented storefront office where no one showed up to work until after nine in the morning?

As Claire stood out front and deliberated the best way out of her impending interview, she noticed someone bustling around inside, near the back of the office. Without thinking Claire waved and smiled at the plump blonde woman as they made eye contact. The woman waved back and held up her index finger to indicate she needed another minute with the files she was busy arranging on the back desk.

A few minutes later the plump woman looked up, flashed Claire a big smile, and straightened her blouse and knee length skirt as she started toward the front door. After fumbling with the lock for a few seconds she swung the door open, donning the same exaggerated smile.

"Good morning. I'm Pam, can I help you?" asked the plump woman, extending her right hand as her left held the door open.

"Hello," said Claire, returning the gesture and shaking her hand. "I'm Claire Keen. Sorry if I'm a few minutes early for my appointment."

"Oh, no problem. Come on in. I was getting the office opened up and set up for your interview," said Pam, motioning Claire to the desk at the back where she'd been shuffling papers a few minutes earlier. "Please take a seat. I just need a minute to finish up."

Claire settled into a chair opposite the desk as Pam hurried through the office turning on fluorescent lights and starting a coffee pot. As she looked around the office Claire saw no evidence that the Casimir Institute even had a computer network that required engineering. There was a laptop facing away from her on the desk and there was a LaserJet printer on top of a stout file cabinet along the opposite wall. Otherwise the place was filled with abandoned desks, tables and chairs. In the moment, Claire wondered if part of Steven Pulling's spiel back at the job fair had contained some important details she'd failed to pay attention to while she was distracted by her schoolyard flirtation with Jon.

Pamela Lindy made her way around the desk, her cheeks slightly flushed after bustling throughout the office. She pulled the chair back on her side of the desk and sat across from Claire, interlocking her fingers and resting them on the desktop.

"Thank you for making the trip down to San Diego Ms. Keen. I hope your flight went smoothly and the hotel accommodations are ok."

"Everything's great. Thank you," Claire responded. "But I have to admit, this isn't what I was expecting. Mr. Pulling gave me the impression of a much larger operation. I'm not sure my skill set is suited to the scale of things here, Ms. Lindy."

Pam chuckled. "Oh, I'm sorry Ms. Keen. Mr. Pulling must have left a few things out when he invited you down for an interview. Just hear me out before you give up on us."

Claire was embarrassed. She'd revealed too much about her first impression of Casimir. And clearly she'd gotten something wrong. Probably should have kept her mouth shut until she was more certain of the situation. She also noted a hint of irritation, or anger, flash across Pam's formerly bubbly countenance.

"I'm sorry Ms. Lindy. I didn't mean to jump to conclusions," Claire backtracked, feeling flushed.

Pam sighed. "Water under the bridge Ms. Keen. As you may have begun to realize, this is not Casimir's primary facility. We keep this modest off-site office so that we have a comfortable place to cover some administration and ground rules before we make our way over to the Institute. I assure you our actual campus is much more interesting and substantial."

Pam paged through one of the folders on the desk and withdrew a form printed on legal paper. She glanced over it before flipping it onto the desk in front of Claire.

Pam resumed her formerly bright and bubbly manner. "Ok Ms. Keen, this is a pretty standard non-disclosure agreement. I'll need you to read over it and sign then print your name and the date at the bottom. This form legally obligates you to not discuss anything you see at our campus today without express permission from Casimir Institute Security."

Claire was floored. After getting a look at the office and assuming away the interview, she'd let her focus drift to her real reason for being in San Diego - Jon Haynes. Then she'd been caught off guard after running her mouth and dismissing the interview too quickly. Now she was sitting across from an outwardly pleasant middle-aged woman – who'd shown evidence of hidden claws – and a legally binding non-disclosure agreement. What had she gotten herself into?

I really should have paid better attention at the job fair…

As Claire read through the legalese she didn't find anything too concerning. No implied permission to use her body for scientific research or sell her organs on the black market. Seemed low risk. And an interview that required a non-disclosure agreement? The mystique and intrigue alone were enough to get her to sign the form so she could see what happened next. Claire scrawled her signature on the form and spun it back across to Ms. Lindy without asking a single question. Pam took the form with a smile, folded it back into the file folder and started to push back from the desk.

"Alright Ms. Keen, now that the paperwork is out of the way we can head over to the campus. We have much to discuss on the way, but we have plenty of time. We're headed about an hour and a half into the desert so if you need to use the bathroom now would be a good time."

***

After driving through nothing but desert for the last half hour, Claire was relieved to finally see the warehouse up ahead. She had spent the first forty-five minutes of the drive listening to Ms. Lindy give an overview of how her interview would be conducted and the specific ground rules of her non-disclosure agreement. When that conversation had run dry they tried to make small talk for about fifteen minutes before giving in to silence. Pam eventually tired of the silence and turned up the radio. Luckily, Claire didn't mind the Oldies.

They approached the warehouse by way of a small two-lane road. There was nothing else around other than desert terrain, the warehouse, and the serious barbwire and chain link fence that stood off from the warehouse by a half mile.

As they pulled up to a small guard shack, Pam rustled in her purse, withdrawing a badge with her photo on it, and asked Claire for her driver's license. Pam presented both to the guard with a smile. The guard quickly handed Ms. Lindy's badge back through the window and took Claire's ID into his shack. After he spent a few minutes comparing Claire's ID with names on a clipboard list, the guard returned.

"You're all set. Have a nice day ladies," said the guard as he palmed a button inside the shack, opening the gate in front of Pam's car.

As Ms. Lindy pulled the car through the gate and continued toward the warehouse she struck up the conversation again. "Everything you've seen thus far, including the location of this warehouse and its association with the Casimir Institute is not covered under your NDA. We're going to head around the building and park, then we'll get some more appropriate transportation for the rest of the trip."

"The rest of the trip?" asked Claire, her disappointment obvious.

Pam smiled and let out a short laugh. "Don't worry Ms. Keen. The rest of the trip will be much more exciting. And everything you see once we enter the subterranean lift is covered by the agreement you signed earlier. So get all your questions in while we're here on the tour. Once you finish up today's interview there won't be any further opportunity to satisfy your curiosity unless you're offered and accept a position here."

Claire had no response. She waited quietly, nervously, for Pam to put the car in park. As they climbed out of the town car that had brought them this far, Pam led Claire to a row of electric golf carts parked adjacent to a large garage door on the side of the warehouse. Before she sat down in the first cart in the row, Pam turned around and waved her arms in the direction of a small concrete building about a hundred yards away. As she turned back and sat down in the cart, a loud siren sounded three times and the garage door to their left came to life and began sliding open.

Pam backed the cart away from the building and sent the cart whirring toward the opening garage door. As the cart rounded the turn into the warehouse Claire's breath caught in her throat. The space inside the door was filled with row upon row of top of the line servers all networked together through a series of cabling that ran up to interlaced catwalks suspended from the superstructure. Those catwalks all converged on a massive concrete structure in the middle of the warehouse.

As Ms. Lindy steered the cart through the exterior door, Claire quickly realized the concrete building was their intended destination. Now inside the warehouse, another flurry of activity began. The siren blasted three times, and this time the garage door behind them slid closed while another one of similar size on the front of the concrete building ahead of them began opening.

Pam brought the car to a stop outside the open door. "Are you more interested in our operation yet Ms. Keen?" asked Pam. As Claire tried to form a response, another guard - this one clad in black and much more serious looking than the guard at the front gate – stepped over to Pam's side of the cart and looked at her expectantly. She produced her badge again and handed it over. The guard took it and walked briskly over to his post adjacent to the door. He came back shortly thereafter, approached Claire's side of the cart and handed her a bright red badge. Before she clipped it on her blouse she flipped it around and saw in large font:

VISITOR - ESCORT REQUIRED AT ALL TIMES

The guard then walked around the front of the cart and returned Pam's credentials. As he prepared to step back to his post he looked sternly at Pam. "Ms. Keen has been logged entering the facility with you as her escort. You are responsible for her whereabouts at all times while she is on the campus. Do you have any questions about your responsibilities as escort of an uncleared visitor, Ms. Lindy?" asked the guard.

"I do not, thank you." Pam smiled, her cheery persona very much on display for the guard.

"Very good. Then unless you have any remaining questions you are cleared for entry. Please pull your cart onto the lift and remain seated until the bell sounds after the lift is moving."

"No questions. Thank you again," Pam replied as she eased the cart forward through the door and onto the center of the platform.

As they pulled forward, Claire caught herself gawking at her surroundings. The lift platform was massive. Easily big enough to fit a tractor-trailer with room to spare for the driver to get out and walk around. She followed Pam's lead and stayed seated in the golf cart that was now parked in the center of the massive elevator. The door behind them whined shut and was immediately followed by a long low tone and the sound of heavy machinery coming to life. The lift shuddered momentarily and Claire had the familiar elevator sensation of moving down. Claire glanced at Pam to see if it was ok to get up from the cart. Pam remained seated and returned Claire's look, the same cheery smile still plastered on her face.

Anticipating Claire's question, Pam jumped in "Sit tight for a minute Ms. Keen. It's a long way down and this big thing takes a little while to get up to speed."

As if on cue, Claire felt her stomach lurch with the kick of downward acceleration as the elevator increased its descent rate. There were no windows in the oversized compartment, so she couldn't be sure, but Claire felt confident they were moving at the speed of a skyscraper express elevator. Moments later a series of two low tones sounded.

"If you want to get up and walk around now you can Ms. Keen. It's a short ride so don't go too far, and make sure you come back to the cart when the bell goes off again. This thing stops pretty fast so you want to be sitting." said Pam.

Claire hesitated at first but her curiosity got the best of her. She stood, one hand still on the outside of the cart, and surveyed the giant elevator. The lift was a large rectangle, easily thirty feet wide and twice as long. The floor was smooth concrete but the walls and ceiling looked like nothing more than corrugated sheet metal with a few significant supporting steel beams interspersed along with some fluorescent lighting ballasts that bathed the lift in artificial light like a hospital hallway. There couldn't be much insulation in the surrounding walls either. The sound of the machinery running the lift was loud and inescapable. Overall there was nothing too fantastic about the lift, other than its size and the speed something of this size was able to move. It was definitely function over form.

Satisfied she'd given herself the grand tour of the elevator, Claire sat back down in the cart and waited for the next surprise.

After a few minutes, stretched further by her anticipation, Claire heard the low tone sound from the overhead again. A couple seconds later Claire felt twice her weight as she was pressed into the seat of the golf cart by the elevator's rapid deceleration. As the feeling eased Claire could sense that the elevator was now crawling to the end of its travel.

"How far below ground are we? How fast were we moving?" Claire asked, failing to hide her child-like excitement.

Pam giggled. "Everyone asks that. Just sit tight. You're going to have a lot more questions when those doors come open."

Right on cue the lift came to a full stop, the elevator tone sounded a final time and the doors behind them started to slide open. As they did, Pam pulled the cart forward and, with plenty of maneuvering room on the giant lift platform, swung around in an arc back toward the doors.

As the cart pulled clear of the lift door and into the heart of the subterranean facility, Claire's curiosity receded behind a curtain of absolute shock. She was tempted to pinch herself to swim up from a dream. There was no way this was real. She was entering the science geek version of Willy Wonka's factory. What stretched in front and above her was a dome bigger than any baseball or football stadium she'd ever seen. The supersized elevator shaft they'd come out of appeared to mark the center of the dome. As Claire gawked up at the ceiling above her she saw massive trusses running from the concrete elevator shaft down towards the ground at the perimeter. A perimeter that was so far away Claire thought she could see a slight curvature in the floor.

Paying no attention to where Pam was taking her in the cart, Claire noticed she was no longer bathed in fluorescent light, but rather, it felt like daylight had penetrated the earth above her. She felt heat radiated in the light. And to the right of the cart she saw they were being followed by a shadow of mid-morning height.

The awe and overload continued. As Claire tried to reconcile their depth below ground with the sunlight overhead, she started to register the other structures around her. As the cart sped directly away from the elevator Claire had the feeling that she was on a windshield tour of a large suburban business park, or a small college campus. The buildings were...normal. And numerous. Claire had the impression they were driving down Main Street. A thoroughfare that dominated the middle of the underground campus.

To the right of the main drag were a half dozen three to five story buildings that had all the trappings of administrative office buildings that could be found in any suburban business park. As Claire twisted in her seat to look back past the concrete tower she fit another piece into place. A large conduit emerged from the side of the concrete tower and into a single-story structure immediately adjacent. From that smaller structure emerged lesser conduits that ran to each of the six nearby buildings and one that went into the ground in the direction of the road.

The left side of the road was much more industrial. At a glance it looked like everything that would be needed to run the utilities of a miniature town. Claire saw sewage processing, pump stations that probably sent potable water throughout the small city, and electrical transformers of various sizes and the lines and conduit that carried the power out through the town. The underground facility appeared to have all the trappings of being self-sufficient. As Claire struggled to let her mind accept the massive reality in front of her, Pam pulled the wheel of the golf cart to the right and sent them humming into the business park side of the underground town.

As they made their way between two office buildings Claire started to appreciate the depth of the facility. The buildings she'd seen on the right-hand side of Main Street weren't just facades or small buildings. Each of them had the depth of a full city block. As they made their way toward the perimeter of the dome Claire noticed that the building complex on her right had balconies on all four floors and on all sides of the buildings. Each of the balconies was unique, furnished with typical apartment patio furniture, clothes lines, and even a hammock in a few cases. As she gawked at the building they passed an opening in the side, where Claire could see multi-floor stairwells on either side and an open courtyard in the middle.

"Are those apartments?" Claire asked no one in particular.

"Yes. Depending on their type of work, many of our staff find it necessary to live in the facility full time," Pam replied, resuming her tour guide voice. "We can talk more about the accommodations later, if you're interested. If you look to your left you'll see the main office building. All our administrative staff and the Institute's corporate leadership keep their offices here. It's like any sun drenched office building you'd see anywhere else in Southern California. Except this one happens to be underground."

The mention of sun brought another odd reality to the surface of Claire's awe induced stupor. "Where is that intense sunlight coming from?" Claire mumbled. "I don't think it was this warm and sunny when we came into the warehouse up on the surface."

Pam squealed with excitement at Claire's question. "That is one of our favorite toys to show off down here. The ceiling of this dome cavern is lined with a sophisticated LED membrane. Using some of our most cutting-edge nanotechnology we've been able to miniaturize the LEDs within the membrane and then program a sequence to their operation that can simulate the Southern California sun traveling through the sky over the course of the day. You can actually get a 'sunburn' down here," she giggled. "It also happens to be great for managing the circadian rhythm of our staff that live in the facility."

Pam shifted topics. "Ok, Ok. I get really excited showing new people around down here. But we have to stay focused. The headquarters building I was talking about. That's where we're headed for the sit and talk part of your interview. You're going to be meeting with Ms. Victoria Stein, the Network Lead. We can get more into our corporate structure later if we have time, but for now, think of a Lead as the equivalent of a corporate vice president. If you come to work with the Institute, she would be your boss's boss's boss. So try to make a good impression."

Claire snapped back to reality. She only had a few minutes to put her curiosity on hold and focus on nailing the interview. She concentrated on getting her mind right as Pam drove up to the entrance of the office building and parked the golf cart. As Claire stepped out and followed Pam to the front doors, Claire felt nervous energy building in her stomach. She felt under prepared. Pam opened the door and led her into a lobby with modern décor. Claire's lack of preparation had been motivated by her lack of real interest in Casimir, but after what she'd seen 'outside' on their way to this office, she couldn't imagine working anywhere else. She needed to pull herself together before she met Ms. Stein. She'd stay composed and do her best to recall everything she knew about Casimir. And she'd look for ways to highlight how her skill set could make the Institute better. This was going to be tough. She knew very little about the job she now desperately wanted.

As Claire's mind raced, Pam led her up an elevator and through hallways within the headquarters building. Claire was busy in her own head putting together words that captured why she wanted to be a network engineer in the first place; things that would highlight her ability to solve complex problems. She assumed that any company that operated somewhat secretively in an underground cavern in the desert must have complex problems that needed to be solved. Before she knew it Claire was standing in an anteroom outside an executive office with large cherry wood doors. There was a secretary seated to the left of the main office doors and Pam was chatting with her.

"This is Claire Keen, here for her interview. I'm registered as her escort so give me a ring when the interview is wrapping up and I'll come back and collect her for the rest of the tour," Pam said to the secretary.

"Sure thing", replied the petite auburn-haired secretary. The secretary then acknowledged Claire with very serious eyes. "Have a seat. I'll let you know when Ms. Stein is ready."

Claire sat in the anteroom and tried to distract her hamster-wheeling mind. But every time she tried to slow down her thoughts and relax she felt cold fingers of nervous fear wrapping around her stomach. She decided it was better to stay on edge by running her brain a mile a minute than to let nerves overtake her. Hopefully the interview started soon. Sitting and waiting was going to be exhausting.

After a little less than five minutes, which felt like forever, the heavy cherry door thumped open and swung back from the anteroom into the office. Standing in the opening was a slender woman, probably in her mid to late fifties, with shoulder length jet-black hair. Claire was immediately intimidated by how pretty she was. Ms. Stein must have been a knockout when she was Claire's age. Definitely not a Pepsi and Cheetos computer nerd. To go with her striking appearance, Ms. Stein had age lines surrounding her eyes - eyes that looked like they could detect bullshit and see into a person's sole. Claire had made it this far in life by trusting the gut feel of a first impression. Her gut was screaming at her to be direct, one hundred percent genuine, and honest in all dealings with Ms. Victoria Stein.

Claire stood as the Casimir Institute Network Lead strode over to greet her. "Welcome to the Casimir Institute Ms. Keen," said Stein. "Please come into my office and we'll chat."

As Claire followed Stein into the spacious office she couldn't remember if she'd said a single word in response to Stein's invitation. Even Stein's voice impressed Claire. It was deep but still feminine with the lightest hint of a British accent. Claire had only been in her presence a minute, but she was already envious of, and intimidated by, the secretive business world velociraptor that she now needed to impress during their 'chat.'

"Let's sit shall we?" Stein said as she gestured to a pair of plush chairs set around a coffee table in one corner of the office. As the two ladies sat, Stein did exactly as Claire expected and wasted no time getting down to business.

"Why are you interested in the Casimir Institute Ms. Keen?"

"To be honest ma'am, I'm more curious and intrigued than interested," Claire replied, sticking with the honest and direct approach.

"Go on," said Stein. A slight smile cracked on her face as she leaned back in her chair.

"Well, I can't say with anything approaching honesty that I'm interested in Casimir. I don't have even a sense of what the Institute does. I can't be interested in something I don't know anything about."

Claire paused to assess how her opening volley was received. After a couple seconds with no reaction from Victoria Stein, Claire pressed forward.

"But I am intrigued. And my curiosity about this place is through the roof. If someone let me, I'd take one of those golf carts and drive all over this facility. It's one of the most incredible marvels of engineering that I've ever had the opportunity to see in person. I'm sure I have a lot to learn still, but from the initial ride over to your office, it appears to me that you have built a self-sustaining underground world wonder. There are embattled governments that would pay billions for that capability alone."

Claire paused to breath. Hopefully she wasn't coming on too strong. She prayed there weren't some basic facts about Casimir that she should know and didn't. It would be really embarrassing if a Google search could have told her that they refurbish old PCs and she showed up to the interview without the slightest clue. So Claire withstood the urge to continue and waited for Ms. Stein to respond.

"Well it's nice to have someone appreciate what we've built down here. Those of us that work here every day have a tendency to take this 'marvel' for granted," said Stein. "So tell me Ms. Keen, what value would you bring to Casimir?"

Claire let out a long breath and glanced up at the ceiling, pulling the right words together. "I'm dedicated. Especially when I'm challenged." Claire paused, not sure where to go next. She knew how she felt and where her internal sense of confidence came from, but she wasn't sure how to put the words together in a value proposition that this mystery company would find desirable.

"Go on Ms. Keen," Stein beckoned with the same slight smile from before.

Claire wasn't going to get out of explaining herself. She took a deep breath and continued. "I guess you could say that I don't know how to quit on a challenge. It's really the reason I got into network design. There are an infinite number of complex problems to solve in networking. And there's diversity in it. I feel like I could design networks and solve complex computing problems for the rest of my life without ever settling into the doldrums of a routine. There are always new challenges." Claire paused, confident she'd put it the best she could. If Casimir didn't want her after that explanation then this probably wasn't a good fit anyway. But the momentum of her thought process carried her forward. "I think that's why I was so intrigued by Casimir. I'll be honest; I don't understand what you guys do. But the mystique initially got me interested enough to come down here for the interview. And then, once Pam brought me out to the facility and I saw this complex sprawled out as those lift doors came open, I knew I wanted to be a part of it. If you bring me on, you'll get every bit of my motivation and determination. I can tell Casimir is on the cutting edge of something, so I have no doubt that the challenges will keep me one hundred percent engaged."

"Very well put Ms. Keen," said Stein. "Your passion makes me feel motivated to work harder for Casimir."

Stein stood and motioned for Claire to follow. As she reached for the door to leave her office and head back to the anteroom, Victoria shifted modes. No longer an inquiring interviewer, her demeanor shifted to something slightly more like Pam Lindy; an excited tour guide.

"Let's go find Ms. Lindy and take you on a more thorough tour of the facility. Hopefully I can shed some light on what we do here. Then, if you're still interested, we can discuss the terms of your employment."

Claire let out a silent sigh of relief as she stepped back into the anteroom.

CHAPTER SEVEN

Three Months Earlier

Two months after taking the job as Steven Pulling's 'special assistant' Jon Haynes was frustrated. He'd given up his military career and was starting to doubt his decision. Since accepting Pulling's offer of employment Jon had poured over everything about the Casimir facility that he could get his hands on; which wasn't much. He'd even convinced Pulling to give him a little extra cash so he could pay for commercial satellite imagery of the Casimir complex and the adjacent properties. He had scoured the images in detail, like he would for a reconnaissance mission in his past life. But no vulnerabilities jumped out at him. In fact, nothing jumped out at him. He saw the warehouse complex and an adjacent desert filled with solar panels, probably supplementing the energy requirements of whatever was happening in the below ground facility. Fortunately, the Casimir complex wasn't in remote hostile territory in Afghanistan so Jon decided to take a trip out to explore the outlying areas that he hadn't seen on his original visit.

Jon made the hour and a half trip out to the Casimir facility multiple times over the two months since he'd accepted employment. So far he hadn't learned much. He'd confirmed the satellite imagery as best he could from his vantage point on the ground outside the fence line. There were fences, desert and solar panels.

But today he'd come with additional resources and was intent on probing further into the outskirts of the Casimir property. He planned to launch a small unmanned aerial vehicle ('drone' in popular terminology) and get a slightly better vantage on the outlying parts of Casimir's property than he'd been able to get from the satellite images. Unfortunately, he was working with commercial technology that he'd acquired from an online retailer. Partly because he wanted to maintain deniability in the event that Whitlock's security team had the ability to detect small airborne invaders, but also because he didn't have the resources or connections to acquire anything higher end like he would have used with special forces. Ready for the day's flight, Jon stepped out of his truck on the abandoned desert road and set up shop for flight ops. He'd done his best to look like a drone enthusiast out to satisfy an innocent desire to fly over the desert and capture some cool HD video he could post to YouTube.

From the tailgate of his F-150 Jon launched his drone, ascended to a 100 foot altitude, activated the live video feed on the controller, and sent the vehicle humming across the fence line to begin surveying the Casimir property. In addition to getting some better images of the property, Jon also hoped to elicit a response from Whitlock's security team. He assumed an operation as advanced as Casimir's likely had remote sensors that would pick up a common toy like this. Even if he lost the investment in the drone, he'd at least get to observe Whitlock's security team responding to intruder detection.

Half an hour passed. As Jon pushed the drone further from the fence line over the solar panel field, his confidence increased. There was no VHF radio chatter or other evidence of a security response. He'd found his first solid evidence of a hole in their security. But the question remained whether or not there was anything in the far reaches of the Casimir property that was even worth protecting.

Jon dropped the drone down to a fifty-foot altitude for an even closer look. As he nudged the throttle forward to continue further west into Casimir territory he noted three solar panels that bulged up above the rest, as though they were sitting atop the crest of a sand dune. He slowed the drone into a hover over the three standout panels. Once he had the drone stable he zoomed in the HD camera mounted on the drone to try and get a look between the panels. The panels were too close together to make out anything noteworthy.

He dropped the drone down to a twenty-foot altitude. He couldn't risk getting much lower. Jon was pretty good at flying the drone but the closer he got to the ground the less time he had to adjust the controls if he started to lose altitude. While he had decided that Whitlock's security team had no ability to detect a drone in the air out here, Jon did not want to find out what happened if he bounced the drone off one of the solar panels.

Steady at a twenty-foot altitude Jon took the camera to max zoom while hovering directly over a seam between two of the solar panels on top of the dune. Because of the sun directly overhead all he could see between the panels was dark gray shadow over sand. He was quickly becoming convinced that his one item of interest for the day was going to turn out to be nothing more than a bump with a little more sand than the other areas around it. He maneuvered the drone around to try and change the line of sight, just to be sure. As he eased the drone into a hover over one of the panels adjacent to the elevated ones he finally found something worth getting excited about. It was dark between the panels and hard to be sure, but Jon was pretty confident that he was looking at an area that was more shaded than the rest. Even more exciting, Jon saw something other than sand. As he stared at the image on his controller he saw a lip of concrete, and just beyond that, pitch black. There was something under the elevated solar panels, but Jon was going to have to cross the fence line and go in on foot to get a better look.

Jon snapped a few still images from the HD camera and then pushed the drone back up to a hundred-foot altitude. Still in a hover, he spun the drone around, slowly surveying the surrounding area for any signs of other elevated dunes. After a few minutes of staring at the same endless field of solar panels in three directions, Jon spun the drone back toward him and throttled toward the fence line.

He brought the drone down to land next to his truck on the dirt road, shut off the quad rotors, and considered his options. He could take a little risk and walk the quarter mile into the solar panel covered desert to get a first hand look. Or he could set an appointment with Craig Whitlock for his 'consulting visit' to see if he could learn anything else about how the security team monitored for intruders in the desert. He decided the conservative option was best. He tossed the drone in the backseat of his truck and climbed into the cab to drive away.

But as he turned the truck around on the dirt road, still very aware that his presence over the last hour had drawn no attention, he shifted back in to park. He debated internally with himself the risk of crossing the fence line for a quick look. *What's the worst that could happen?* Even if he triggered an alarm and a rapid response team swarmed him, he was a security consultant that had come out to inspect perimeter security. He could feign satisfaction at Whitlock's team passing the test of his security probe.

Jon grabbed his phone from the center console, and climbed out of the truck. He walked directly to the fence line and ducked between two strands of barbwire. He took a direct route to the three solar panels of interest.

When he was about a quarter mile inside the fence line he was hit by a pang of conscience. He looked back and realized his heavy steps through the deep dry sand were leaving very obvious tracks. He should have grabbed something to cover the tracks on his way out. But at this point he was invested. He'd decide when he got back to the truck if he had time to return to cover his tracks. Jon put the concern out of his mind, trusting that his security consultant cover would win the day if he were discovered.

Fifteen minutes after he ducked under the fence Jon approached the three solar panels on the sand dune. From his new vantage point walking at eye level to the solar panels, with a clear line of sight beneath them, Jon knew he'd found what he was looking for before he got there. From over a hundred yards away the concrete tunnel, headed down into the desert floor at a thirty-degree angle, stood out clearly. Jon closed the remaining distance snapping photos on his cell phone from various angles as he approached.

Jon stopped directly in front of the opening. He smiled as he looked down the four and a half foot diameter concrete tunnel diving under the desert floor. He turned on the flashlight on his phone, silently kicking himself again for being too impulsive to remember to grab the big Mag Light from his toolbox. Unfortunately, Jon could only see ten feet into the tunnel before the pitch black consumed the cell phone's light.

Jon snapped another dozen photos of the tunnel mouth, frustrated at his lack of planning lending to sub optimal execution, but satisfied that he'd finally caught a break in his efforts to access the facility.

As he walked back toward the fence line and his truck, Jon knew the next step was to set his meeting with Whitlock. And now he had something definitive to look for during his second trip to the Casimir security headquarters.

***

Craig Whitlock, head of security at the Casimir Institute, was not excited to hear from Mark Johnston from Gateguard Security. But after a few unreturned phone calls and some persistence, Jon, under his alias, was able to get Whitlock to commit to meet with him for his follow up on the bogus security consultation.

Jon arrived at the Casimir facility mid-morning and, just like the first visit, checked in at the guard shack where he was directed to park outside the gate in the visitor lot. After waiting and sweating in the desert heat for thirty minutes, Jon saw Whitlock headed his way in one of the Casimir electric golf carts. Whitlock pulled into the parking lock behind Jon's truck.

"Good to see you again Mr. Johnston, I'm sorry to have kept you waiting," said Whitlock, failing to hide his sarcasm. Jon suppressed his irritation at the obvious delay and overt cynicism.

"Thanks for agreeing to meet with me," Jon replied with all the professionalism he could muster. "Based on what I saw on my first visit, I hope to make this a quick follow up, then I'll get out of your hair and get you my report and recommendations in a couple weeks."

"Recommendations?" Whitlock asked.

"Well..."

Before Jon could explain Whitlock cut him off. "Just get in the cart. I'll take you over to the outpost and we can get this done with."

Jon forced a smile as he climbed into the passenger seat. Whitlock then accelerated quickly through the gate and toward the outpost building. There was no conversation exchanged, as Jon couldn't come up with a way to make casual or business-related conversation. The hostility was obvious and overt. Jon needed to get whatever information he could about security in the outlying solar panel fields, and any insight into where the concrete tunnel would lead. Then he needed to find a way to end this visit. The longer he exposed himself to Whitlock's hostility, the more likely it became that he would lose his composure and offer Craig Whitlock an attitude adjustment.

As they neared the outpost, Jon decided not to give up on trying to be professional; maybe he'd even get on Whitlock's good side. It never hurt to turn potential adversaries into allies. As long as Jon played his cards close, he really had nothing to lose in establishing a friendlier rapport.

"Listen, Mr. Whitlock, maybe we got off on the wrong foot. I know it probably feels like I'm here to tell you all the ways that you could be running your security shop better. Maybe you're even thinking that I plan to tell your bosses that you're doing an inadequate job of keeping this place secure. That I might report in such a way that places your autonomy, or even your job at risk."

"Hmmph. Most people don't hire independent consultants when they think things are going well," grumbled Whitlock.

"Maybe your perspective is wrong. Everything I know says that

Casimir is working on something important that they really want to protect. Maybe your company asking me to do this review has nothing to do with your performance, but everything to do with an increasing sensitivity to what you have to protect." Jon was laying it on thick and Whitlock's almost imperceptible reduction in hostile body language indicated it might be working.

Jon continued, now aiming to boost Whitlock's confidence. "From what I've seen so far you're running a fine operation here. You seem to have a highly professional staff that knows how to follow protocol, a good concept of operations, and top of the line equipment that's well maintained. Those are three pillars of a strong security posture."

"Thank you," Whitlock replied. It seemed sincere. That was a first.

As the cart pulled up to the outpost and Whitlock got out to head for the front door, Jon stopped him. Time to finish negotiations and turn this guy into an ally. "Listen Craig, for what it's worth, I plan to give you a copy of my draft report before anyone else sees it. I'm going to ask you to review it for accuracy and give you a chance to comment on any of my assessments and recommendations before I finalize it and send it to anyone else at Casimir. So please, give me the benefit of the doubt and work with me on this. I'm not out to get you. You don't survive in a business like mine if you just walk around pissing off every security division director at every major company."

Whitlock cocked his head ever so slightly and looped his thumbs in his front belt loops. "Maybe I had you pegged wrong Mark Johnston. You're not going to convince me to be excited about you being here. But I appreciate you being direct with me. I also appreciate you standing your ground. Most people don't do that these days." Whitlock smiled just a little and extended a hand.

Craig and Jon/Mark shook hands.

"Now that we have that out of the way, let's get you a more detailed look at security HQ. Then we can look around wherever you need to get your inspection done with," said Whitlock as he pulled open the outpost door and gestured for Jon to head inside.

***

After thirty minutes on the HQ watch floor and a detailed briefing from one of Craig Whitlock's deputies, Jon was convinced that there was no monitoring of the concrete tunnel he'd found in the desert. This team was highly focused on keeping the complex around the warehouse free of intruders. They could catch a coyote on remote sensors that had gotten past the guard shack. But you could drive a

Mac truck through the solar panel field and they probably wouldn't notice until the power went out.

Unless they were deliberately hiding something, they didn't have any situational awareness of the outlying solar field. They were so ignorant of that part of the facility that Jon found himself questioning whether or not it was even connected to the underground complex at all.

Jon decided to use his remaining time with the Casimir Institute security team to try and learn the extent of their role here. He was certain that there was something of significant interest in the underground complex, but it didn't seem like this security team had the slightest clue, or any responsibility for protecting it.

"Mr. Whitlock, can I have a couple minutes in private?" Jon asked.

"Sure thing Mark. And please, call me Craig." Craig motioned toward the office in back, just off the watch floor. Jon followed him in and Craig shut the door. It was a little too small for two grown men to stand away from the desk without being awkwardly close. So Craig relieved the intrusion of personal space by taking a seat at his desk. Once seated, he motioned to Jon to go ahead.

"All right Craig, I know you value your time, so I'm going to get right to the point," Jon began. "From my initial visit out here with Mr. Pulling, I know there is an underground portion of this facility that's at least big enough to justify a supersized lift that could hold an Abrams Tank. But as I look at what your men are watching and where they're patrol routes take them, I don't see any security footprint in the underground portion of the facility, or even much of one inside the warehouse to monitor access to the elevator. This seems like a pretty big seam in your coverage. Can you help me understand?"

Craig shifted in his seat and stroked the stubble on his chin. "Pulling didn't talk about this with you at all?" The edge of irritation had returned to Whitlock's voice. "I guess he figured an independent security consultant wouldn't notice a hole you could literally drive a truck through. Or he figured I'd find a way to explain it away." Craig was back to dripping with sarcasm and frustration.

"Sorry Craig, but I don't know how to respond to that." Jon focused on maintaining a neutral expression lest he give away his excitement. He might have found the seam he needed to exploit.

"It's not your fault," said Craig, shaking his head. "I've been frustrated for years with this setup. If your assessment were to mention it as a potential vulnerability that might be really helpful.

And of course it would make Casimir more secure going forward."

Jon noted that last consideration was tacked on for show. Craig Whitlock clearly had an axe to grind with his bosses.

Jon decided to lead the witness to get to the point. "Are you saying that you don't have any security footprint inside the warehouse or in the underground complex?"

"That's what I'm saying. I don't have a footprint there."

"So...."

"Look Mark, I want to explain this to you. I feel like we can help each other out. But before we go further you have to agree that what I'm about to tell you doesn't go into your formal report. I could lose my job. The most you can say officially is that you found a seam, or a gap, in security inside the facility. Nothing more."

Since Jon wasn't planning to write any sort of real report, this decision was easy. "Agreed."

"I'm in charge of external security. That's it. I'm kept intentionally out of the loop on operations and security protocol inside the facility. I also don't control access to the real facility."

"Are you telling me the chief of security doesn't control access to the most sensitive part of the facility he's in charge of?" Jon asked.

Whitlock looked down at the floor between his feet, trying to decide how much he could or should say next. Jon pressed forward, steering the discussion.

"You said you're intentionally kept out of the loop. What do you mean?"

"Mr. Pulling calls it a firewall. As far as I understand it, I'm the face of the organization's security, which makes me a potential target for corporate espionage and things like that. So technically, I could be comprised, kidnapped, what have you, and that wouldn't directly lead to someone being able to access the most sensitive portions of the facility." Whitlock was starting to squirm, getting increasingly uncomfortable as Jon approached direct questions of underground facility access.

Jon went for the jugular. "Who's in charge of access and security of the underground facility?" This info would be key if Jon was going to get inside. The more he probed Whitlock, the more he realized he wasn't ready to attempt to access the facility yet.

"I don't know," Craig replied, frustration evident. He seemed vulnerable, bordering on insecure. "I told you I'm firewalled from knowing what really goes on here."

"But you've had this job for what, five years? Surely you have some idea who's running the security forces below ground. Some idea of their operating patterns."

"Of course I do." Craig was looking at Jon again and almost yelling. "I'm trained to watch people, identify patterns, recognize threats. And I'm not sure, but I think the fact that I know what I know might be enough to get me fired. You've pushed this discussion far enough Mr. Johnston. I'm not comfortable discussing this further and we've gone beyond the scope of your consultation."

The quick relapse to a last name basis indicated to Jon that he was out of rope with Craig Whitlock. One last question…

"I understand Mr. Whitlock. I'll drop the issue and keep your name out of it if you'll just point me in the right direction to continue my inquiry." Jon said this with the clear implication that he had Craig in a corner. "I have no intention of dragging you into the next steps of my consultation, but you have to help me past this dead end, Craig."

Craig slumped back in his chair and rubbed his temples. Then he ran his hand through his salt and pepper hair before making eye contact again. "I thought you might be a standup guy Mr. Johnston. But now I'm not so sure. A few minutes ago I decided to be honest with you. Now, it feels a lot like you're coercing me."

"I'm sorry you feel that way Craig," said Jon, not backing down.

Craig was staring at the floor again. "Talk to Pulling. Tell him you saw a bunch of obviously ex-Special Forces types inside the warehouse and hanging around the lift access. And don't fuck me. Tell him I clammed up when you tried to ask questions about them."

"No problem Craig. Now why don't you give me a lift back to my truck and I'll be on my way."

***

As Jon merged onto the freeway heading back toward the coast, he checked his phone, mounted on the dashboard of his truck. He had cell phone reception again so he dialed Steven Pulling and put the phone on speaker. Pulling picked up on the first ring.

"Hello Jon Haynes. I trust all is going well with your consultation?"

"Actually, that's why I'm calling. I won't bore you with the details, but I did a lot of looking around in pursuing my assignment and I just finished my follow up visit with Craig Whitlock. I noticed that he doesn't seem to have anything to do with access or control of the underground facility." Jon let that hang to see if Pulling would take the bait. He didn't.

Jon continued, trying to get Pulling to talk. "I also confirmed what I suspected on my first visit. There is a completely different outfit running security for the underground facility. And I have no access to them."

Finally Pulling spoke. "It sounds like you've gained a full understanding of the challenge of your assignment Jon. To what do I owe the pleasure of this phone call?"

"I um…" Shit. Jon silently chastised himself. He made the call before he'd flushed out his tactics. "I'm frustrated Mr. Pulling. You tasked me with gaining access to a secure facility. That's something I know how to do. But when I've been given this type of assignment in the past I had intel and an objective once I'm inside. You've given me neither. All I have is a few bucks for commercial imagery and a false identity that gets me access to work with a washed-up Clint Eastwood who's firewalled from the real target." Saying it all out loud brought the last two months of frustration to the surface. Jon finished on a crescendo and pounded the steering wheel.

"Please Jon. Don't allow your emotions to cloud your judgment. As I said, you have identified the challenge of your assignment. I wouldn't have asked you to do it if I didn't think you were capable."

Jon took a deep breath. Pulling was rattling him. Jon had made this call with the intention of shaking some new information from Pulling and it wasn't working. He needed to change course or end the call. He had an idea.

"I appreciate your confidence in me," Jon said, exaggerating his regain of his composure. "And on the bright side, I think I've found my access point to the facility. I still have a lot of planning and some additional research and reconnaissance to do, but I know how I'm going to get down there."

Jon paused to gauge Pulling's reaction. Receiving none, he continued. "Based on what you've told me thus far, if I'm successful in getting into the facility undetected, regardless of what happens once I'm inside, I've succeeded. Mission accomplished."

Jon paused again. This time letting silence prevail until Pulling responded. Jon let a satisfied smile spread across his face as he glanced from the road down to his phone. Had he actually managed to take Pulling by surprise?

***

Steven Pulling leaned back in his chair. None of his projections had Jon Haynes finding his way into the facility this quickly. He needed to stall him; he needed to shake Jon's confidence enough to keep him in the reconnaissance phase. He wouldn't have the right personnel in place for the next phase of his plan for another two or three months.

"Mr. Haynes, I hardly think a haphazard entry into the facility is wise at this point. You were just lamenting your limited intelligence on the site's physical makeup and security." Pulling paused. He needed something more convincing. A stronger deterrent. "And once you're inside how do you plan to get back out Jon?"

Steven waited for Jon to respond. If Jon pressed his plan to breach the facility now he'd have to take more direct action to slow things down.

"Worst case I'll egress via the same route I came in. If the opportunity presents, I'll attempt to leave via the lift in the warehouse, but I'll take what the situation gives me. Worst case, I get in to the facility, get a better idea what's down there and have to make a hasty retreat to avoid detection. I think I know enough right now to run that op in the next few weeks."

Steven sat forward in his chair and propped one elbow on his desk. Frustrated, he ran his hand through his thinning hair. This was unacceptable and totally contrary to his projections. If Jon Haynes accessed the Casimir facility now, whether successful or not, the timing would be all wrong. Steven would be hard pressed to assemble the teams he'd spent the past two years scouting.

"It seems you're closer to your objective than you originally let on Mr. Haynes. Excellent work. However, I'm afraid I'm going to ask you to put this effort on hold for a short period. I have another short duration assignment for you."

"Are you kidding? I call to ask a few questions, let you know I'm nearly ready, and now you're putting the op on hold?"

"I assure you Jon, this assignment is equally as important as your current efforts." Pulling was holding on to the plan by a shoestring. Directly intervening in Jon Hayne's progress toward accessing the facility ran contrary to the natural progression that was supposed to bring the team together. This introduced a new variable; it made the long-term outcome unpredictable. But what other option did he have? If he let Haynes access the facility now everything would go completely off plan.

"If this new assignment is so important, why am I only hearing about it now? Right after I told you I'm making final preparations to access the facility?" Pulling needed to tread carefully. Jon was clearly upset…and suspicious.

"Jon, I realize I haven't given you much reason to trust me, but I need you to do so now. I brought you to Casimir because you are uniquely qualified to assist me in a number of priority projects. Accessing the facility is certainly one of them, but it's not particularly time sensitive. This other project is. I'd planned to call you about it next week. But since we're talking now I figure you can have a few extra days notice. Not to mention that the covert access project clearly has you frustrated. A few weeks away might be good for you. Give you an opportunity to take a step back and return in a few weeks with fresh perspective."

Jon sighed. "Understand all sir. I work for you. What's the assignment?"

"After the holidays you'll be traveling with me to the University of Washington for a series of meetings and a recruitment opportunity. I'll email you the details later this afternoon. Good bye Jon."

Steven Pulling hung up the phone without waiting for a response.

CHAPTER EIGHT

Present Day

Claire swiped the key card at the door to her 10th floor hotel room in downtown San Diego's Gaslamp District. She felt like she was floating. Victoria Stein had toured her around a facility out of a scientist's wet dream. Then offered her the opportunity of a lifetime. She was going to be a network engineer for a disruptive organization with leading edge artificially intelligent networks supporting out of this world research in computing and nanotechnology. And there was Jon Haynes to look forward to.

Claire dropped her bag and room keys on the table and flopped backwards onto the bed. She thought about Jon. Claire normally wasn't one to chase a man she was interested in. Usually she didn't have to. But with Jon she'd put herself in the driver's seat because of her seduction at his Seattle hotel. Did that change things?

Complicating Claire's calculus were the terms of her new employment at the Casimir Institute. She was scheduled to begin her indoctrination in two weeks, and the three-month introductory training period required her to live full time in the underground facility. If she did nothing to initiate contact with Jon Haynes she risked him being unavailable when she emerged from the facility three and a half months from now.

She was at a decision point. Jon knew Claire was in San Diego but she hadn't heard from him yet. Her pride screamed at her not to pick up the phone and call him. But everything else told her she should. She didn't have time to wait for him to make a move.

She had two short weeks to go back to Seattle, get her life sorted out, and ship everything she owned to Southern California to sit in storage until her training was done and she could sort out the next phase of her life. All the excitement and anticipation built up a bow wave of stress. And she knew one sure fire way to relieve stress.

She sat up and stepped over to retrieve her phone from her bag. She opened her contacts, selected Jon Haynes and then sat back on the bed, staring at the phone. Realizing her pride wouldn't let her call him she opened up a new message. Before she could think about it any further she quickly typed and sent her message to Jon: 'Interview went great!'

She sighed and flopped back on the bed. Claire tossed the phone down beside her thinking she'd try and nap for an hour or two. Maybe she'd hear back from Jon, maybe not. Either way she'd book a flight back to Seattle tomorrow morning, then spend tonight exploring San Diego. Her new hometown…sort of.

As the stress started to recede and she felt like sleep might find her, her phone signaled a new message. Instantly fully alert, she grabbed the phone and read the response from Jon: 'That's great. Are you up to dinner and drinks tonight? I'd love to hear more about it.'

Claire was smiling ear to ear. But she'd let Jon wait in suspense for her reply. She tossed the phone back on the bed and let sleep take her.

***

Later that night Jon met Claire in the lobby of her hotel. He was initially annoyed that Claire had waited so long to respond to his invitation for a second date. He figured this might be one of those dating games where you try not to appear too eager. Some strange way to maintain the upper hand, or not scare the other person off by showing that you were too into them. Jon hated those games and it was one of the reasons he'd steered clear of casual dating. That and the frequent classified deployments to all the finest terrorist hideouts the world had to offer.

Ultimately, it wasn't hard to move past the irritation. He wanted to see Claire again. He'd spent plenty of time over the last few weeks thinking about their night together in Seattle. Most of those thoughts were centered on the time they spent in his hotel room. But he was also drawn to the less carnal aspects of their evening. He caught himself daydreaming of the way she felt under his arm when they walked in the Seattle rain. He felt warm and comfortable when he passed someone wearing her perfume. He liked the sound of her laugh, the depth of her eyes and the touch of her skin. Jon had something for Claire that amounted to more than an infatuation. He'd make sure and tell her that directly. Maybe that would get them past the need for any more dating games.

The most irritating part of all this was that Jon knew Claire was confident. Most girls he'd seen play these sorts of games did it from a place of insecurity. From not wanting to appear too excited. It was easier to accept rejection if you could convince yourself you weren't interested in the first place. *Surely Claire knew he wouldn't reject her.* Clichés aside, women really were impossible to understand.

There was another wrinkle to the situation that Jon couldn't seem to set aside. Steven Pulling had put an all stop on Jon's original assignment to get into the underground Casimir facility and diverted him to a recruiting mission. There were other meetings Pulling advertised as part of the trip, but Jon quickly realized he had no role in those discussions. He wasn't invited to half of them and the ones he was present for he served all the purpose of a potted plant. It seemed too convenient that Jon had been pulled for that assignment and so quickly hit it off with his target for recruitment. And in hindsight Jon understood that she was the only target. Was she the only reason he was on that trip? It could all be coincidence, but he couldn't help wondering if there was more to the the story than he was being told. And he had to admit, all the mystique of Steven Pulling, the Casimir Institute, and the coincidences or connections he hadn't yet put together, made Claire all that much more enticing. His instinct told him that he was being manipulated. Under normal circumstances, the suspicion alone would be sufficient cause to abort. But Claire Keen did not represent normal circumstances.

When Jon stepped into the lobby and saw Claire sitting on the sofa waiting for him he was over it. He immediately became unconcerned with any dating etiquette or Steven Pulling cloak and dagger games. He slowed his gait to appear confident and nonchalant as he approached her.

"Hi Jon Haynes," Claire said with a flirtatious smile. "I've had the best day so far. I hope you're up to the task of keeping the trend going." Claire laughed out loud at her own tawdry line.

"Hello Claire. You look great; I'll try my best to live up to your expectations," Jon said as Claire stood. They leaned in to each other for a friendly greeting sort of hug. Jon decided he could do a little better and kissed her gently on the cheek. With no particular plan for their evening they took seats next to each other on the lobby sofa.

***

"Alright Claire, you're in San Diego, interview is done, and you have my undivided attention. Did you have anything particular in mind you wanted to do or see while you're in town?" Claire felt resurgence of the excitement she'd had this morning; before everything changed at her Casimir interview.

"Um, I guess I really hadn't thought about it much. This all came up so fast, then I was mostly focused on the interview." Claire decided a little white lie was ok. She hadn't been distracted in the least by the interview until it was already happening. The real occupier of her thoughts had been Jon. She hadn't quite gotten around to searching Yelp for good restaurants or TripAdvisor for the best sites worth seeing in San Diego.

***

Jon suggested the hotel lobby wasn't the best spot to get their night started so he invited her to get a drink at the hotel's rooftop bar while they planned out the rest of their evening. It was one of Jon's favorite places downtown and he was pretty certain it was early enough that it wouldn't be crowded or loud yet. As they walked to the elevator Jon slipped his arm over Claire's shoulder and pulled her into him. Just like their first night together in Seattle, she responded, wrapping her arm around his waist. As they stood waiting for the elevator Claire let her head rest back against the front of Jon's shoulder. The simple touch snapped them back into the place where time slowed down. Jon couldn't be certain but he was fairly sure Claire felt it too. Their breathing slowed. They savored the moment. Maybe the elevator would never come and the night would never end.

***

Whether it was seconds, minutes or hours later, the elevator arrived and they broke their embrace to make room in the elevator for the other five people that were also headed up to the popular rooftop lounge. As the elevator made its way to the top of the building Claire slipped her arm around Jon's and leaned against his shoulder. This sort of puppy love thing wasn't normally part of her game, but she wanted to touch him. And he didn't seem to mind. The elevator tone marked their arrival and Jon, Claire and the five anonymous strangers they'd shared their ride with piled out and headed towards the lounge's bouncer. Once inside, Jon led Claire by the hand to two seats along the roof's edge. It was a perfect spot. They had a bird's eye view of the city and PETCO Park. They were near the edge of the roof, away from the other patrons. The music was loud enough to add to the atmosphere but not too loud to impede conversation.

Jon pulled a chair back and offered it to Claire. Once they were both seated he placed a hand gently on on the back of her chair, allowing his fingers to brush against the skin between her shoulders. Jon looked at her and Claire felt an excited tingle as she met his eyes. Something was happening, and she could feel a little adrenaline start to surge in her stomach. Claire was certain Jon was headed in for a passionate kiss that would thrust them right back to the level of fervor they'd had last month in Seattle. She tried not to appear too eager as she waited for Jon to make his move.

As if he'd read her thoughts Jon leaned down and in towards Claire. At the same time, he moved his hand up from her shoulder to the back of her neck. With confident strength he pulled her in to kiss her firmly on the mouth. She received it with an all too obvious hunger. After a few seconds Jon slid his hand off her neck and backed slowly out of the kiss.

Jon nervously cleared his throat. "Sorry. I had to do that. Let me get us some drinks. I was thinking a Moscow Mule sounded pretty good. What are you having?" Jon asked. Claire tried not to let the disappointment show on her face. A moment ago she was lost in the middle of a very romantic rooftop kiss and a strong embrace. It had ended too quickly and converted to a very intimate request for her drink order. Not displeasing, but not the grander gesture she'd been expecting, and wanting. She decided the small gesture was ok for now. The night was still young.

"Moscow Mule sounds great," Claire responded, throwing a big flirtatious smile at Jon to hide her regret that they weren't continuing into a hungry make out session in the trendy bar. Jon walked away to get the drinks as Claire fought to steady the freight train of her mind. Be natural. Stop reading into everything.

***

As Jon walked to the bar he sensed something was off, if only slightly. He'd graciously offered to go get them drinks and let her enjoy the sights of the bar and the purple sky that accompanied the half hour right after sunset. It was an atmosphere that was sure to impress. Instead of fawning over his chivalry, Claire seemed irritated, or hurried. She hid it pretty well, but he could see it simmering below the surface. Jon arrived at the bar and absently drummed his fingers on the marble bar top.

"What can I get you?" asked the bartender, tugging Jon back to reality.

"Two Moscow Mules. Top shelf," Jon replied, barely making eye contact with the bartender. As the bartender worked, Jon first admired the twelve-foot tall waterfall behind him. Then Jon hazarded a casual glance back at Claire at the other end of the rooftop. He was hoping that she'd be anxiously following him with her eyes, awaiting his return. Instead she had a thousand-yard stare fixed on the downtown landscape. And the slightest smirk indicating she was lost in thought, scheming maybe?

Jon wasn't sure how he'd done it, but he seemed to have date number two with Claire Keen off to an odd start. Strange, since their touch in the lobby had the same electricity they'd had a few weeks ago in Seattle. Either Jon had done something wrong or she had something else on her mind. Something that she didn't want to discuss but that he was expected to understand and be ready to listen to anyway.

Jon glanced back at the bartender just as he was squeezing limes into the two bronze mugs. Jon slid him a credit card and told him to keep the tab open as he grabbed the two mugs and headed back to Claire. As Jon made his way back to the table, he decided he had no idea what might be bothering Claire and that there was no point in trying to figure it out right now. His best play was to stay confident, portray a slight aloofness, and listen to whatever she had to say. He arrived at their roof edge seats and slid Claire's drink in front of her.

"Let me know what you think," Jon said as he sampled his drink and motioned for Claire to do the same.

"Oh, it's good," Claire responded as she set the mug back on the marble bar top.

Jon let silence reign for a moment, trying to discern the best tactic to get Claire back into the evening. The topic of her recent interview was an obvious choice, but if her experience with Casimir was anything like his, she wouldn't be able to say much.

***

"Tell me about your interview. Are you taking the job?" Jon asked. Claire knew this question was likely but she'd failed to prepare a response. She'd assumed that Jon, a fellow Casimir employee, probably had to sign a bunch of non-disclosure forms just like she did. She'd convinced herself that those forms would be enough to prevent it from being a topic of conversation tonight. Obviously she was wrong. She needed to quickly figure out how to navigate this minefield. She was also well aware that she'd been throwing a bit of an odd vibe since Jon had broken away from their stirring kiss when they'd first arrived on the roof top . Shutting down the first line of conversation that Jon tried to open wasn't going to help things. She decided to proceed cautiously.

"It went really well. They offered me a job, maybe a dream job, and I'm starting the training program in a couple weeks." Claire immediately wished she'd read the non-disclosure agreement more carefully. She was pretty certain she was allowed to tell people where she worked. She was also pretty sure it was ok to say that she was taking part in a three-month indoctrination program. But if she was going to continue dating Jon, she was eventually going to have to tell him that she was going to disappear off the face of the Earth for that three-month program. She needed to decide, quickly, how she was going to explain that without revealing details about the underground facility? Surely Jon Haynes, former Navy SEAL and all around badass, was 'read in' to the secret underground technological marvel.

"That's great. Does that mean you're moving down here for good?"

"Yeah. I'm flying home tomorrow to get stuff in order so I can move down here before the training program starts."

"Wow. That happened fast. Do you need help finding a place?"

Claire hesitated. "Umm…no, not really. Maybe in a few months. For now, I'm going to move my stuff into a storage unit. Not much need for a place right at first." She decided to stop there, hoping Jon would understand the implication. He'd probably been through a similar indoctrination program when he started at Casimir. In fact, she really wanted to ask him about it to see if he had any advice or pointers to help everything go smoothly. Again, she wished she'd read the fine print in the non-disclosure agreement.

Claire continued with the non-specific, cautious approach to the topic. "Any helpful tips for someone just starting the training program?" She'd follow Jon's lead. If he thought it was ok to discuss then it probably was.

***

Shit. Things were about to get awkward if Jon didn't think fast. Claire was anxious about starting her new job and wanted her pseudo-boyfriend to give her the inside scoop. But Jon had no scoop to give. Claire probably knew more about Casimir than Jon did. Somehow being a special assistant to the enigma known as Steven Pulling left Jon feeling like a mushroom…kept in the dark and fed nothing but shit. Jon had some great ideas about how to break into Casimir's below ground crown jewel facility, but he didn't know a thing about their trainee summer camp program.

Given all the secrecy surrounding Casimir, Jon saw only one safe option. "It's probably best if we don't discuss it here. Can we put a pin in that topic for now?" If Casimir Institute buried their trainees under the same layers of secrecy and compartmentalization that they did their security personnel, Claire would get the point and move on to other topics…hopefully.

"Of course. Sorry to talk shop. I just have a little case of new job jitters," said Claire.

Jon sensed the slightest relaxation from Claire as they agreed to dismiss the topic for the time being. She seemed a little uneasy asking about Casimir and appeared relieved to let the conversation shift to other topics. Strange.

Suddenly Jon was more curious than cautious. He fought the urge to probe the issue further. All his instincts screamed that Claire was an excellent intelligence asset for his assigned covert entry mission. But if he started harvesting intel from a girl he was legitimately interested in, not to mention one he'd been intimate with, he'd be no better than the pukes at CIA who manipulated people for a living. He decided to abandon the topic altogether.

Jon forced himself to relax and slid his arm over the back of Claire's chair again, letting his hand brush against her opposite shoulder. "This view is amazing isn't' it?" The brilliant post-sunset purple was quickly giving way to deep blue, with the black of night close on its heels.

***

Her first instinct had been right. It obviously wasn't ok to talk Casimir business in public. But she really wanted to know what she'd gotten herself into. While she felt a little guilty using him for inside information, Claire couldn't help but take advantage of the situation. With Jon as her inside man she could get a leg up on her training if she could get a little info out of him. She'd try again later if they found themselves in a more private setting. Claire had been looking forward to this date for the last couple weeks; best to get over her frustration and enjoy the night with Jon.

Claire forced away further thoughts of her impending training and focused on reclaiming the connection she and Jon had back in Seattle. She took the invitation of his arm draped across the back of her chair a step further. She lifted his wrist to pull it around her shoulder and simultaneously nestled her opposite side into his chest. They were quiet for the next few moments, watching the post-sunset light fade behind Point Loma.

"You're right. This is beautiful," Claire said picking up Jon's more casual line of conversation. They spent the next half hour mostly quiet, enjoying the changing color of the western sky while they sipped their drinks.

With the sun set, the night sky gave itself up to full darkness. Jon turned to look down at Claire. "Another drink or do you want to move on to dinner?"

Claire briefly considered just inviting Jon back to her room in the hotel to rekindle their reckless passion and get over the awkwardness brought about by discussions of the Casimir Institute. She decided to let logic prevail over lust. "Dinner sounds good. I've been told I should make sure I eat Mexican Food while I'm in San Diego."

"I could do Mexican. There's a few great places a short walk from here."

***

A few minutes later Jon and Claire were back on street level stepping out into the cool San Diego night for the short walk to the tequila and taco bar Jon had in mind for the next phase of their evening. Jon felt a hint of chemical relaxation from the first drink of the night back at the rooftop bar.

He decided to use his slightly blunted inhibitions to regenerate physical contact with Claire. But instead of the arm over the shoulder embrace that they'd both found so appealing thus far, Jon decided to change things. To keep Claire off balance. As they walked away from the hotel in the direction of the restaurant, Jon grabbed Claire's hand and intertwined her fingers in his. As they walked they discussed the best places to live in the city and how much moving sucked; both steering well clear of any discussion of Casimir while recognizing the obvious link their work now placed between them.

As they approached an intersection and slowed to wait for the WALK sign, Jon decided to take a more assertive approach with Claire. He took the hand he still held and folded it behind to her lower back. In doing so he twisted her to face him and kissed her greedily.

Jon saw the sign change in his peripheral vision and pulled away gently from the kiss. He didn't fail to notice the welcome invitation it received from Claire. "Sorry, I needed to do that," Jon said as they started across the intersection.

"You needed to do that?" Claire responded, with a coy satisfaction in her tone.

Fifteen minutes later Jon and Claire sat at a high-top table sipping top shelf tequila from salted glasses with lime wedges perched on the rim. Aided by the drinks, the conversation between them flowed easily. They hardly noticed the waiter standing next to the table waiting for a break in the conversation to take their dinner order. Eventually they made their order and the waiter broke off to get it started in the kitchen.

While they waited for food to arrive Jon allowed his liquid courage to motivate him to take the conversation back in a serious direction. "Where do you see yourself in five years Claire?" Jon asked, smiling.

Claire seemed to hesitate; surprised by the sudden turn from casual banter to serious 'relationship' talk.

Jon continued, "If we're going to get to really know each other…"

Claire glanced at the ceiling, formulating her response. "It's funny you ask. The whole reason I ended up here, taking this interview with Casimir and this job; it's because I don't know where I want to be in five years. I only seem to know where I don't want to be. I'm not ready to take a 'normal' job like everyone else yet. My gut says there's something more than a normal American nine to five out there for me." Claire paused, looking at Jon again, probably to gauge his reaction.

"Go on," Jon said, pushing a loose strand of hair from her face. "I'm interested in the inner workings of the beautiful mind of Claire Keen," he said, smiling in an inviting way he was certain would keep her talking.

"I don't mean to say I'm somehow different or special. Just, I don't feel like I'm meant to push a desk or have a routine for the next thirty years. At least not yet."

Emboldened by a couple more sips of tequila Jon edged forward. "Is that why you signed on with Casimir?"

"No…At least not at first…Maybe." Jon sensed Claire wasn't entirely sure why she signed on with Casimir.

Claire looked at Jon thoughtfully, her right hand gently touching her chin. "You sort of lured me to Casimir, you know."

Jon felt his pulse quicken and his face flush. Hopefully the dim restaurant would disguise his obvious reaction. Jon said nothing and let Claire continue.

"I mean, I would never have been offered the interview if you hadn't been making eyes at me in the job fair auditorium, baiting me to talk to you. Then you asked me out. Then Mr. Pulling offered to have me down here for the interview. Then we...well you remember."

Claire glanced up at the ceiling, processing her next thought. "It's all linked for me. Although it wasn't this morning. At first the interview was interesting but mostly a means to an end. I wanted to see if what we had together our first night was just fun and fleeting, or real." Claire hesitated and made quick eye contact with Jon.

Jon sensed she was suddenly self-conscious. Maybe worried that she was coming on too strong or revealing too much about her interest in him.

Jon placed a hand across the table on her forearm. "Well I'm really glad you came. It would have been expensive for me to fly to Seattle to see you again."

Claire smiled. Relief danced across her face. Her eyes stopped darting from ceiling to floor and she made eye contact with Jon. "But then I went out to the Casimir facility. It's the most amazing thing I've ever seen. I knew immediately that I wanted to work there, to be a part of it; that amazing things must be happening in a place like that. I knew it definitely wouldn't be the dreary routine I was afraid of falling into. It was something bigger. Something important."

"Do you know what you're going to be doing for Casimir yet?" Jon asked.

Claire ignored his question. "This afternoon I realized it was all linked. There's no way it isn't. You and Steven Pulling show up to the job fair. Then you and I, err, get to know each other. Really hit things off. Then I come down here for an interview to find that I've been invited into a self-sustaining technological marvel underneath the California desert. A facility that, from what I can tell, is housing high end computing research, maybe even an advanced AI. A place so huge they built in their own artificial sun!"

Jon tried not to react. As far as Claire knew, Jon had been down there too. Just then the waiter returned with their dinner and they both ordered another drink.

They started into their food and slipped back into casual conversation. About the food, best beaches and sites to see in San Diego and best neighborhoods for young professionals. They talked about traffic, weather, family.

As they finished their food and had almost polished off drink number two, Jon tried his question again. "Do you know what you're going to be doing for Casimir when you start?"

"Sort of," Claire responded, now following Jon into this topic as if it were no more significant than how many inches of rain Seattle received last year. "It's some sort of network engineer position. But first I have to live down there full time for three months for the indoctrination program."

Claire wiped her hands with her napkin, set the napkin on her finished plate and pushed the plate toward the center of the table. She returned her full attention to Jon.

"I'm pretty excited about getting to know more about the facility. But I am a little nervous about disappearing underground for twelve weeks. Especially since I have no idea what it means to be 'indoctrinated' into the Casimir Institute." Claire paused.

She raised an eyebrow and looked at Jon. "I was actually hoping you'd give me a little insight into what I should expect in the training program."

Jon pushed the last bite of his taco into his mouth; buying time so he could quickly weigh his options before responding. Not only had he never been through the training program. He'd never stepped foot in the secure, subterranean portions of the facility. There was no way to respond to her query honestly without revealing that the nature of his employment with Casimir was very different from hers. He also knew he didn't want to build his foundation with Claire by misleading or lying to her.

"I'm not going to be much help for you there," Jon started.

"Bummer," Claire replied. "Do the ex-military guys get different training than the computer nerds?" She smiled.

"Um, I wouldn't know that either. I didn't go through the training program and have never been below the above ground warehouse."

Claire's eyes widened and her mouth fell open.

***

Claire's stomach was in knots. She'd revealed all sorts of details to Jon, certain he was 'in the know.' Now she'd learned that she had a more extensive knowledge of the Casimir Institute's amazing facility than her former Navy SEAL companion that had been working for the company for months. *Had she violated her vow of secrecy before her first day on the job?*

Claire wasn't sure what to say. She was frozen with something resembling fear. Thankfully Jon kept talking.

"I hope you don't think I was trying to mislead you," Jon said with a hint of remorse on his face. "I'm still trying to figure out what is and isn't off limits for conversation when it comes to Casimir."

Jon ran a hand through his hair, his remorse shifting to frustration. "When I was in the military it was pretty clear what was and wasn't off limits for discussion. At the top of the page it said CONFIDENTIAL, SECRET, TOP SECRET. Always clearly marked and the rules were always clearly understood. Now all I have is an agreement that says I won't reveal 'details about the Casimir Institute and its operations.' I don't think I know any details about the Institute or its operations."

Claire could see Jon's frustration clearly. It was oddly reassuring. She was trying to overcome her fear at the sudden realization that she'd likely violated her non-disclosure agreement and put her job at risk before it started. Claire quickly decided her best bet was mutually assured destruction.

"Well, you know my part of the secret. Now show me yours." Claire forced a confident smile at Jon. "What do you do for the Institute Jon Haynes?"

"I'm a Special Assistant to Steven Pulling," Jon replied quickly before breaking eye contact.

Claire tried to be patient while Jon obviously wrestled in his head with what to say next. A moment later Jon looked up again. All remorse, frustration and confusion had faded from his countenance. He had a determined look that was both deeply attractive, and a little intimidating.

"I'm assigned to break into the underground facility."

For the second time in the last five minutes, Claire's eyes went wide, and her mouth hung open involuntarily.

CHAPTER NINE

One Month Later

Claire awoke in her new apartment to the sound of her screeching alarm clock. Most people would tune their alarm to a radio station or some soothing sounds. Claire was a heavy sleeper and found that if the sound wasn't incessant, horrible noise, she'd sleep right through it. She stood up next to her bed and stretched before silencing the alarm clock, walking to the window and throwing open the curtains to bathe the room in 'natural' light.

Claire was one week into the training program at Casimir Institute and three weeks removed from the night out with Jon Haynes where he'd revealed to her his mission to break into the highly secure facility she currently called home.

The date three weeks ago had ended well. Not as well as she would've liked but the long-term prospects were good. After the revelation about Jon's unconventional role at Casimir, their conversation went dry, as neither was sure what else to say. Jon paid for dinner and the two walked through the cool San Diego night back to Claire's hotel. Like a gentleman, Jon dropped her off there with an affectionate kiss and promised to see her again during the two weeks she had before starting her training.

Claire had spent the following week in Seattle packing her things, shipping them to a San Diego storage unit and settling up a few other affairs before she moved to sunny Southern California for the foreseeable future.

The Pacific Northwest was her home. But instead of sadness at leaving the place where she'd grown up, made most of her memories, and had most of her friends, she was filled with eagerness and anticipation. She was excited to immerse herself in the mystery and intrigue of the Casimir Institute. She had the butterflies of eagerness about spending a little more time with Jon before she began her training.

While she was in Seattle setting her life in order, Jon made sure to contact her daily. They texted, talked and video chatted throughout the week. Halfway through the week, Jon informed her that she was now his girlfriend. Claire accepted his confident proclamation gladly. In the past she would have bristled at the idea of a man claiming her rather than asking, but with Jon she somehow found it endearing.

As she stood in front of her window deep underground in the Casimir facility, she remembered warmly the three days they'd spent driving her car from Seattle to San Diego. It had been Jon's idea. By his logic, she was his girlfriend now, he wanted to see her, and he wanted her to be safe. So, their third date happened over a three-day road trip. Jon convinced her that they should take the Pacific Coast Highway. It added time to the trip, but not much. And it let them see all the best sites along the California coast, even if most of them were seen only through the windshield of her Ford Edge.

Claire hated driving but loved being around Jon. It was the perfect psychological trick to play on herself. Instead of hating every minute on the road, she hoped it would never end. The conversation flowed easily. They also grew more comfortable just being with each other. Letting silence reign while enjoying the presence of the other.

The first night they'd stopped in Crescent City, a small coastal town near the California-Oregon border. When they stopped, Claire took note of the fact that Jon asked for a room with two double beds. Claire wanted to revisit the passion of their first night together but decided to let Jon's etiquette deter her primal instincts.

Near the end of the next day's driving, as they crossed the Golden Gate Bridge, sun starting to set over the Pacific Ocean to their right, Claire realized that she loved Jon Haynes. And while she wasn't certain enough to say it, she thought there was a better than even chance that he loved her too.

They stopped the second night in Monterey. Once they'd checked into the hotel Jon made a bee line for the shower, anxious to rinse off the days' time spent in the car. At first Claire had patiently waited her turn for the same. But her feelings and her hormones got the better of her. With eagerness coursing through her fingers she placed the 'Do Not Disturb' sign on the door of their room, impatiently removed her clothes, and stepped into the hotel bathroom.

Standing at her window in her Casimir Institute apartment, Claire vividly recalled asking Jon if she could join him in the shower. He obliged and they never made it out for dinner that evening. It might have been one hour or seven. But that night Claire slept better than she ever had. Not just because of physical exertion or satisfaction. But because she felt safe and...loved. Jon hadn't said the words; neither had she, even though she felt them in a way that threatened to burst from her mouth. Nevertheless, she knew the way Jon treated her was borne out of more than infatuation, good manners or chivalry.

They'd both awoken mid-morning the next day, intertwined like a human pretzel. They enjoyed the pleasure of each other's company again before checking out and hitting the road for the final leg of their road trip. They made the rest of the drive to San Diego mostly silent, fingers intertwined on the center console of her SUV, enjoying the ever-changing scene of the Pacific Ocean to their right.

Knowing Claire was in the final countdown until her three-month indoctrination at Casimir, they'd spent every day together over the next week. Claire was staying in Jon's apartment and barely had time to get her affairs in order. Everything seemed like a sideshow when compared to the time spent with Jon.

On the last night before she was to report to Casimir to begin her training, Jon cooked her dinner and they planned to spend the evening in his apartment. As they ate Jon nervously revealed to her that he had fallen in love with her. That he would wait as long as necessary for her to emerge from Casimir so that they could continue to see each other. She barely let him finish his declaration before the same revelation burst from her lips. And as soon as they'd agreed that they would continue their relationship after Claire's training (Jon assured her that he could treat this absence like any of the many deployments of his past life), Jon revealed that he was only weeks away from making his attempt at breaking into the underground facility.

Claire was nervous at first; worried that she might get caught up in something that would affect her long-term prospects at Casimir. But by the time Jon dropped her off downtown the next morning to board the van with the three other anxious trainees, Claire decided she wanted to see Jon succeed more than she cared about her own opportunities.

As she kissed him goodbye, she told him to find her once he was inside. She committed to give him a place to hide until he figured out his next move. He smiled and said nothing else.

Claire tried to push Jon out of her mind and focus on preparing for her next day's training. But as Claire stared out the window on the morning of day seven, just as she had on day six and would on day eight, she hoped today would be the day Jon arrived so they might have their reunion.

CHAPTER TEN

A couple hours before dawn, Jon parked his truck two miles from where he planned to cross onto Casimir property. If the security team detected an intruder, it was at least worth trying to throw them off the trail of where he breached the facility. He was confident that he could get inside; less confident that he could remain covert, per his assignment, and evade capture once there.

Jon took solace in Claire's commitment to harbor him once inside. But in his final days of preparation, his confidence in being able to quickly locate Claire in the massive facility wavered often. During their many days and nights spent together before she'd left for indoc training, Jon had put together a decent mental image of the facility. Based on what he thought he knew, his best chances to gain access, avoid detection and find safe haven with Claire was to access the facility on its west side. This would allow him quick access to the residential part of the facility without passing through the more industrial parts that he assumed were more heavily protected and frequently patrolled. Based on his previous reconnaissance and studying of overhead imagery, the ventilation tunnels appeared to be symmetrically arrayed around the facility. Plenty of options. None of them great.

He hoisted his pack out of the bed of his truck and started the trek toward the Casimir Institute property fence line. On the flat desert landscape, the fence line was visible ten minutes into his walk. He stood at the barbwire only thirty minutes after leaving his truck on the side of the abandoned desert road.

He took a flashlight and bottle of water from his pack before burying it in the sand outside the barbwire boundary. He hadn't penetrated this particular area of the perimeter prior to today and wanted to ensure he maintained plausible deniability in the event this area had remote sensors that the other areas he'd probed did not.

Jon ducked under the barbwire and walked directly toward one of the solar panels that stood slightly taller than the others around it. In Jon's research and reconnaissance thus far he'd found the taller solar panels were always an indicator of a ventilation shaft burrowed into the desert beneath it.

Once Jon located his entry point he wandered in a wide arc around the area looking for any evidence of security patrols, remote sensors or anything else that his trained eye indicated might compromise him over the next few days. As the sky began to brighten in the east, and having found nothing that threatened to upset his infiltration, Jon headed back toward the fence line to retrieve his gear.

Before putting his pack over his shoulder, Jon inventoried his gear one last time. He'd brought everything he could and planned for every reasonable contingency. But he was also careful to ensure it all fit in a standard backpack that wouldn't stand out if he needed to blend in once inside the facility. As he crossed back through the barbwire onto Casimir property, the reality that detection or capture now, with the equipment he now carried on his back, would make his intentions undeniable. He felt the thrum of adrenaline. He felt ready.

Once he had returned to the mouth of the ventilation tunnel Jon pulled the repelling anchor from his bag. He buried the disk and clamp in the sand, attached his carabiner and rope to it and pulled as hard as he could to ensure it would hold his weight as he descended the tunnel. He also piled as much sand as he could around the top of the anchor to ensure it wasn't noticed if someone happened by this area on patrol. Once he descended into the tunnel there was no removing the anchor and attached rope. *Here's to hoping this place is as abandoned and remote as it appeared this morning.*

He stepped into his climbing harness, said a quiet prayer and clipped into the repelling line attached to the anchor. With that done, he stepped backward into the dark and allowed the harness, rope and anchor to take his weight as he began his descent.

About a hundred feet down into the tunnel, as the light at the mouth began to shrink, Jon grew more confident on the conditions of the climb. The slope of the shaft was steep but not impossible. He'd used the repelling line to make the descent easier, but he probably could have scooted his way down the tunnel. Further from the desert sun, his eyes adjusted to the darkness. But the deeper he went the darker it would get. There was no evidence of lighting along this shaft. No indication that it was ever intended for a person to traverse.

Jon paused, stopping the payout through the belay and leaning back against the tension of the repelling line. He turned on his head lamp and swung his pack off his back so he could retrieve his night vision goggles. He traded the headlamp for the NVGs then clicked them down over his eyes. He turned away from the light at the top of the ventilation shaft before powering on the image intensifying green glow of the goggles.

Looking down the tunnel Jon learned nothing new. He'd continue his descent unimpeded for at least the next fifty to one hundred yards. He released the belay and resumed his descent.

Thirty minutes later Jon was beginning to think the repelling gear was a waste of space in his pack. He could have descended this tunnel without climbing gear with minimal risk. But just as he was starting to curse himself for his inefficient loadout, he saw what appeared to be a wall at the end of the shaft reflecting back at him in his night vision.

Jon closed the remaining distance quickly, anxious to determine if this was a dead end, which seemed unlikely. As he got closer to the wall the intensified image in his night vision goggles told him the tunnel likely turned and dropped straight down. This was a mixture of good and bad news. It wasn't a dead end but Jon had no way of knowing how deep the ventilation shaft went before arriving at the interior of the Casimir facility. But he knew how much rope he had. His pack was already starting to get lighter as the rope paid out on the trek so far. The rope he'd used up to this point wasn't a must have, but it would be a must have to repel vertically down the shaft in front of him.

Jon glanced back up toward the mouth of the shaft. It should be fully daylight on the surface by now, but he could barely see light from the tunnel opening. He was deep enough to use his headlamp to survey the area without risk of counter-detection. He removed the NVGs, powered them off and stowed them in his pack. He fired up the headlamp but didn't use it to stare down into the vertical ventilation shaft behind him. Instead he explored the sloped area around and above him, looking for a new anchor point for his repelling line. Finding nothing immediately, he began working his way back up the shaft, having determined that repelling vertically was only viable if he began that part of the journey with all fifteen hundred feet of rope he'd brought along on this adventure.

As Jon made his way back up the sloped section of the tunnel he surveyed it closely with his headlamp. About the time he had the rhythm of the upward climb on the thirty degree incline, Jon spotted what he was looking for - a seam between concrete sections of the tunnel. He drew a chisel hammer from his pack and started chipping away at the concrete around the seam, hoping to uncover a steel dowel running between the two sections that he could tie off to as an anchor. He hammered away for the next twenty minutes, until he ultimately found what he was looking for. He broke a chem light and tied it off to the dowel before continuing up to the top of the ventilation shaft.

Jon climbed up for the better part of the next hour, retreading his steps back to the mouth of the ventilation shaft. As he edged up toward the opening of the tunnel where he'd originally anchored his repelling rope, he felt a twinge of nerves. Doubling back over his previous path was risky. It increased the risk that someone would happen by to notice him; or worse, that he'd be making himself available for capture by someone that already noticed him.

Fortunately, when Jon emerged at the top of the tunnel his chosen section of desert was just as abandoned as it had been before dawn this morning. He quickly untied his rope from the anchor, dug the anchor out of the sand, and returned all the gear to his pack. He put his NVGs atop his head and his headlamp around his neck, ensuring either would be readily available as he made his way back down the tunnel without the aid of a repelling rope.

The climb down the second time around was slower than the first. Without the aid of the rope, and knowing that the tunnel eventually dropped down vertically, Jon wanted insurance against losing his footing - so he slowly scooted his way down the tunnel on his butt until he saw the glow of his chem light up ahead.

Once he'd rigged his line to this new anchor, he retrieved the chem light and stuffed it in his front pocket. He dropped his night vision into place, turned it on, and quickly made his way down to where the tunnel turned straight down into the earth. Jon scooted up to the edge, gave the repelling line a strong yank to ensure it would hold, then tightened the tension on the belay to ensure he had good control of the payout. He set his feet and leaned out over the opening beneath him, suddenly fully aware that any fault in his equipment or climbing technique could lead to him being injured and trapped (or worse) in a place where he likely wouldn't be found any time soon.

Jon eased off the tension on the belay and pushed away from the wall, beginning his descent. Once he had repelled down fifty feet, with no noticeable end point beneath him, he pulled the chem light from his front pocket and let it fall down the shaft. He watched the light fall for a few moments before he saw it bounce. But before Jon was able to get excited that the bottom was only a few hundred feet away, he saw the chem light abruptly change directions and continue bouncing downward as it disappeared from view. The tunnel continued further into the earth but something was obstructing it. Jon's heart sank. He knew a clean shot down the tunnel into the facility was a long shot but he'd gotten his hopes up with the success he'd had so far.

Jon estimated the chem light had fallen about three hundred feet before it had bounced around and he lost sight of it. He quickly repelled down to close the distance, but when he was somewhere around halfway there he could hear the electric hum that was going to interrupt his passage into the Casimir facility. As he descended the noise grew louder and he also detected the faint *vwump vwump vwump* of large fan blades cutting through the air. Jon stopped about ten feet above the noise that now consumed the space around him. He felt a slight breeze of air being drawn down into the tunnel beneath him and kicked himself for not having noticed it earlier in his climb. He'd been too excited and too hopeful to pick up on something so obvious. As he looked down through his night vision, Jon could see the shadow of the large induction fan blades beneath him. He switched off the NVGs and changed them out for his head lamp so he could get a good look at the fan and search the area for any ways he might disable it.

After powering on the head lamp Jon swung his gaze above, below and around him, trying to fully take in his surroundings. It wasn't until after the headlamp was on and Jon had begun surveying the area that he realized it was very possible that Casimir used cameras for remote monitoring of the operation of the fans. If they did have cameras employed here, there's a pretty good chance someone could already see Jon and might be dispatching security forces to apprehend him. Jon steadied himself with a deep breath, recognizing that if he was already on candid camera, there wasn't much he could do about it now. With renewed urgency he scoured the tunnel for anything that might indicate a security system or controls for the fan.

Finding nothing ten feet up from the fans he took a chance at lowering himself down further, ultimately dangling only two feet above the rotating blades. Glancing down again, Jon's heart sank as he realized there was another fan below the first. Worse, there was a large terminal box along the wall in the area between the fans. In order to disable either fan, Jon was going to need to figure out how to get to that terminal box.

Jon went to max tension on the belay and rotated his body to hang headfirst near the center of the upper fan and only eighteen inches above it. Jon scanned around, as close as he could get without concern of losing a finger or hand, and looked for ways to disable the upper fan. Jon wasn't an electrical engineer but was confident he could interrupt operations of both fans if he could get to the terminal box below. To get to the terminal box below he needed to figure out a way to mechanically disable the upper fan. The only vulnerability Jon found was the thick rubber drive belt that kept the fan moving. He could try to impede the travel of the blades to stop the fan, or he could try to cut the drive belt. Both had risk but since Jon was dependent on the repelling line he was hanging from, he decided to try cutting the drive belt first. Jamming something in the fan blades to allow him to get through would leave him at risk of having his rope cut (and his life ended) if the jamming device failed to hold against the fan's motor.

Jon flipped back upright and retrieved his knife from his pack. He opened the knife, took another deep breath while focusing his mind on the task at hand, and mustering all the confidence he could find. He rotated once again to the head first position, flipped open the knife, and extended his hand toward the fast moving drive belt.

At this precise moment, Jon was very aware of how exposed his face and eyes were to the potential consequences of contact between his knife and the thick rubber belt. The force of the belt could blow the knife from his hand. Jon tightened his grip as he extended his arm further. The contact of the blade with the rubber could throw shrapnel in his eyes. Jon shielded his eyes as best he could with his left forearm, continuing to extend his right arm so his blade would lightly impact the belt and begin to wear it down. A moment later, Jon's knife ate into the fast moving rubber; a moment after that Jon learned of another contingency he hadn't considered. The steel reinforced rubber drive belt began to throw sparks as Jon's knife tried to eat into the metal. Jon's left forearm screamed as the hot sparks bounced off his skin. Jon felt heat build in the knife handle as the blade began to glow a dull red. He was making quick progress, but not without a price. His entire body tensed as he prepared for the drive belt to give way.

When it did Jon was aware of a loud pop and a blinding pain above his left eye. As the fan began to slow, Jon took stock of his injuries.

His left forearm was freckled with small burns from the sparks that flew as he cut through the steel cable. His body ached from the tension he'd been holding over the last few minutes. But worst of all, his face screamed with pain, he felt warm blood running up his face and into his hair, and he couldn't see out of his left eye. He set his warm-to-the-touch knife on the center of the now static induction fan and felt around his left eye to determine the extent of the damage.

Fortunately, Jon realized the pain came from a gash on his forehead above his left eye. Not from the eye itself. He quickly flipped upright again and pulled the medical kit from his bag. He cleaned the blood from his eye, forehead and hair with clean gauze and applied pressure to the wound. With his free hand he rifled through the med kit in search of a way to close the wound. After a few minutes upright with the gauze pressed to his forehead he was able to staunch the flow of blood and apply a line of glue, followed by a series of butterfly bandages. Jon hoped the quick treatment would be enough to keep the wound shut and prevent the flow of blood from blocking his vision during the remainder of his descent into the underground facility.

Convinced he'd stitched himself up adequately, and having adapted to the pain of his newfound injuries, Jon gathered the knife and med kit back into his pack and lowered himself into the space between the two fans. Jon immediately pulled the Leatherman tool from the front pocket of his pack and went to work opening the terminal box in front of him. He quickly pried the cover of the terminal box open and studied the wiring inside. Jon took another deep breath and said a silent prayer, hoping that the three hundred feet of repelling line that he dangled from would provide adequate resistance against electric shock. Then, with his hand as steady as he could make it, Jon reached into the terminal box to snip the black positive wires that looked like they ran out to each of the two fan motors. Jon cut the first wire without incident and moved quickly to cut the second, refusing to allow himself time that might let his nerve waver. Once he'd cut the second he knew he'd been successful. The electric hum of the two motors faded and the fan below him began to slow.

Once the second fan had stopped spinning Jon didn't waste any time easing the tension on the belay and lowering himself below the fans. Once beneath the pair of fans and staring into the darkness of the shaft beneath him, Jon clicked off the head lamp and went back to his night vision goggles. He cracked a second chem light and waited for the chemicals inside to brighten it such that it nearly whited out his

NVGs. Then he dropped it down the shaft and counted in his head as it fell. Jon's count had reached thirteen before he heard, and barely saw, the chem light clatter to the ground. By Jon's rough math this put the distance to the bottom of this vertical shaft at around twelve hundred feet. Jon didn't waste any time thinking about how amazing it was that Casimir had built a facility half a mile underground. Instead he dreaded the idea that he might reach the end of his inventory of repelling line before he reached the bottom of the vertical shaft.

As Jon began to repel unimpeded down the shaft he paid close attention to the weight of the line that was paying out of his pack. As his pack got lighter over the next half hour, the glow of the chem light grew stronger in his NVGs. After what Jon estimated was an additional thousand feet of descent into the tunnel, he paused, planting his feet firmly on the concrete wall. He swapped his night vision for his headlamp again and pulled the remaining coil of repelling line from his backpack. He estimated about two hundred feet remained, and he prayed it was enough to reach the bottom.

He resumed his descent keeping the headlamp on so he could keep a close eye on how much line he had left. When he was down to six or eight feet of line remaining, his feet still not finding solid ground beneath, Jon stopped his descent and tried to stay optimistic. As he switched off the headlamp he could see the chem light below with his naked eye. That was good news. He made a fist with his left hand around the knot at the bitter end of his repelling line. With his right hand he slowly lowered himself by reducing the tension in the belay. He descended at a snails pace, in near total darkness, focused only on his hold on the belay and the growing light beneath him.

At the end of this careful descent Jon felt his left hand against the belay and his feet still above the ground. Jon stopped, dangling some unknown distance above the tunnel floor below. He turned off the night vision and flipped the goggles up on his forehead. After allowing his eyes to adjust, Jon estimated the chem light sat about ten feet beneath him. He could also see from the light coming off the chem light, that one side of the tunnel beneath him opened out to the side. Jon was going to have to disconnect from his repelling line and drop the ten feet to the floor below. He needed to land firm as there wasn't anywhere to roll to cushion the fall.

Jon reached up to grab the rope and pulled to put slack between the belay and the carabiner connected to his harness. After straining and fumbling with the carabiner for a few seconds he disconnected it and reached up to to grip the free hanging rope with both hands. He steadied his sway within the tunnel as he hung from the rope with a two handed grip. He looked down one last time at the floor below. No turning back now. If he let go of this rope there was no retreating back to the desert surface. He counted to three in his head and let go of the rope, putting a slight bend in his knee to absorb the shock of landing.

A moment after Jon had let go of the rope he knew he was falling too far. Just as he started to panic at the distance of the fall, Jon slammed into the concrete, heard a loud pop, and felt his joints and legs scream in protest. Glowing neon liquid spread over the floor around him as he instinctively went to the ground, desperately trying to take the pressure off his ailing legs. As Jon sat leaning against the side of the tunnel the pain in his right ankle occupied every synapse of his brain. He failed to notice the faint light coming from the opening in the side of the ventilation shaft. It required every ounce of focus to keep it together and to take stock of the focus areas for the pain that pulsed throughout his lower body.

Jon closed his eyes and tried to slow his panicking heart rate. The neon fluid on the ground wasn't his blood. He had somehow crushed the chem light in his fall. The pain in his legs was mostly in his ankles, particularly his right ankle. He rolled his right foot around. It hurt like hell but he still had mobility. Probably a bad sprain.

Jon Haynes took another deep breath and reminded himself he'd seen worse injuries in far worse places. He had to stay composed and keep moving forward. There was certainly no going back in this particular case. At least no one was shooting at him.

Having brought himself back from the brink of desperation, Jon opened his eyes. As he'd already convinced himself, he now saw clearly that the neon fluid spread out on the concrete floor was in fact from the broken chem light. His sprained right ankle throbbed but Jon now understood it wasn't just the length of the fall that had done it. His right foot had landed awkwardly on top of the chem light, causing it to burst, and rolling his ankle enough during the long fall to cause a sprain and some immediate swelling.

But as Jon surveyed beyond his injuries, he realized he saw more light now than he had since he dropped into the vertical part of the shaft. Right in front of him was a continuation of the tunnel about four feet in diameter at a very slight downward slope. He couldn't see the end of the tunnel from where he sat, but he could see enough light to know that it wasn't far away.

Jon gathered himself, stood up and tightened his pack on his back. He climbed head first into the near-horizontal section of tunnel ahead of him and pulled himself toward the light. As he crawled he tried to imagine what might come next. He might emerge into the waiting arms of Casimir security personnel. He might find that this tunnel terminates high above ground within the facility. With his climbing gear now left irretrievably behind, he'd be grateful for apprehension just so he didn't have to fall again. Or he might find himself where he'd planned to end up - near the residential area of the facility, able to infiltrate and remain undetected long enough to find Claire and sanctuary, until he figured out his next move.

As Jon crawled, the contact between his left forearm and the concrete served as a constant reminder of the burns he'd received earlier when disabling the induction fan. He had a closed but uncleaned wound on his face, burns on his arm that he now drug across the concrete, and a sprained ankle that he thankfully wasn't walking on at the moment. His forearm stung like hell. His face was throbbing. And Jon knew the ankle injury was serious because his right boot felt tighter with each passing moment.

But Jon Haynes reminded himself that he didn't know how to quit. He drug himself along the tight concrete tunnel refusing to stop and allow opportunity to feel sorry for himself. He agreed to take this job and this assignment. He had determined that now was the time to infiltrate the facility. He had chosen this ventilation shaft as the place where he'd take his shot. He knew the risk before he started. If he failed it was his fault alone.

Jon's focus on suppressing the pain of his injuries led him to hardly notice the ever-increasing light in the tunnel. Over the last half-hour he'd gone from climbing through darkness with a slight hue of light up ahead, to full daylight around him. He continued down until his progress was stopped by a steel grate that covered access to the ventilation tunnel. Jon had anticipated this contingency and calmly retrieved the tin snips from his pack.

Before he started snipping the steel to open his path into the facility Jon also withdrew a small set of binoculars to get a sense of what lay beyond the opening of the tunnel. Because of the slight downward angle of the tunnel he had to lay his face flat on the concrete in order to have a line of sight to the area outside it. What little he could see looked industrial. More importantly, he didn't see people. The opening was eight to ten feet above the ground, so he couldn't rule out that someone was nearby but outside his field of view. Once again, Jon came to the fairly simple decision that he had to carry on. There was no backing out due to uncertainty. He snipped the first piece of grating with a loud *twank. He listened for a reaction from outside the tunnel. Hearing nothing he continued, growing more confident with each cut that didn't lead to capture.*

Once Jon had cut away the center of the grate he pushed it free and set it on the side of the tunnel. He gingerly pulled himself through the opening, careful not to let his stomach or sides scrape against the remaining steel around the perimeter of the tunnel.

Excited, Jon scooted himself to the edge of the tunnel and, without thinking about the incredible risk of counter-detection, poked his head out to look down at the surface below. He was ten feet above ground. While he wasn't excited about jumping down from this height, he could see clearly in the light and was confident he could get down without exacerbating his existing injuries.

As Jon prepared to wiggle around in the tunnel to allow him to climb out feet first, he caught a glance up toward the top of the facility. Jon was awestruck. The ceiling near the center of the underground dome was probably a thousand feet above the floor. And Jon recognized the massive concrete tower extending up near its center. The massive dimensions matched the elevator access he'd seen in the above ground warehouse so many months ago. The ceiling was so bright and blue that Jon had to remind himself that he wasn't looking at Earth's natural sky. He'd never seen anything so incredible.

Jon shook off his awe long enough to finish rolling around to exit the tunnel feet first. In order to avoid further trauma to his injured ankle Jon lowered himself over the edge on his belly and then hung from the edge of the ventilation tunnel by his hands. This time he let go knowing he only had to fall about four feet. It hurt, but nothing like what had happened in the darkness of the ventilation shaft earlier.

The nearest structures looked like utilities and power distribution. Jon quickly made his way to a small structure next to a bank of transformers. He crouched between the perimeter of the dome and the small building confident that only someone patrolling the perimeter in this area could see him. He sat his pack down and dropped heavily on his ass; his back leaned against the building. He had a long way to go to find safety but he'd made it inside the facility, probably undetected, with minimal bumps and bruises.

CHAPTER ELEVEN

Jon chugged down a bottle of water and ate half an energy bar while charting his next move. Standing gingerly in an attempt to keep weight off his injured ankle, Jon peered around the edge of the small utility building to take in his immediate surroundings.

The first thing he noticed in peeking around the building were the power lines, running from the facility that served as his current fox hole, to a nearby four building compound. Jon tried to restrain his optimism. The compound ahead of him, directly across a hundred yard green space, might be the dormitories that Claire called home. But the only way he'd find out for sure was to casually make his way across the park and surveil the residential complex while convincing any onlookers that he belonged there. Easier said than done. Jon had a gash over his eye and a swollen face. He had burn marks all over his left forearm and a limp from his fall that was hard to hide. But his options were slim.

Jon stepped out from behind the utility shed and walked across the park area. He focused every ounce of energy he had on appearing to belong and suppressing the limp in his gait caused by his swollen right ankle. He tried to walk as though he knew exactly where he was going. Head up, shoulders back, confidence forced onto his face.

As Jon walked across the park directly toward the dorms ahead of him, he contemplated his response to challenge. He was an unknown in an unknown place. If someone stopped him he had no excuse that was potentially viable. He had no idea what comprised a common job down here. He could try to tell a would be inquisitor that he worked in utilities. They obviously had those. But if queried further he had no depth - no intel on how or where those functions were conducted. Jon decided, as he strolled through the park under the artificial morning sky, that he'd go with the utility man line. He also knew it wouldn't survive under second question scrutiny.

As Jon neared the dormitories he noticed people moving at the slow pace of morning. Some went to golf carts, some mounted bikes, and others just walked. Jon saw an opportunity. At this time of day he should be able to walk right into the complex and blend in with the morning bustle. A good plan, as long as the community wasn't so tight that the average morning commuter would stop the 'new' person in the neighborhood to chat.

Having cleared the park, Jon walked between two of the residential apartment buildings offset at a ninety degree angle from each other and found himself in a small courtyard. As long as he moved with intent across the courtyard he'd be fine. But this place was too small to linger. He'd stand out. Without becoming noticeable he tried to surveil the entire area, hoping to find an indicator that Claire's place, and rest, were nearby. Instead, his stomach dropped when he saw a six three, fit, sandy blonde man striding toward him with a small backpack slung over one shoulder. Jon normally wouldn't be intimidated by size or fitness, but the man walking toward him now wore a tight black t-shirt and khaki cargo pants; the same garb he'd seen on the sentry manning the massive gate in the warehouse above. Jon was certain the man ahead of him was part of the underground facility's 'real' security team. He did everything he could to keep his gaze straight ahead and avoid eye contact.

Jon's method seemed to be working. The guard appeared, like others in the complex, to be fresh out of bed and on his way to work for the day. Maybe he wasn't in security mode yet and wouldn't give Jon a second look. As the distance between them closed Jon was aware that he was quickly running out of courtyard. If something didn't change he'd soon be out in the open again, praying for a break before he was eventually apprehended.

Jon Haynes got his next batch of bad news as he passed shoulder to shoulder with the security beef. He noticed the man had an identification badge dangling from his belt. At the same time, there were three or four others in the courtyard within Jon's line of sight and he quickly realized that they wore similar badges, either from a lanyard around their neck, or a clip on their belt or collar. Jon had no such beacon that told others he belonged here and began to feel his pulse hammering in his ears. He was on borrowed time.

He passed the security clad man without incident but his senses were primed. He heard a change in the man's gait and could feel the man's eyes on the back of his neck as he walked away. Jon tensed, fighting the urge to flee. He fought every instinct and maintained his steady pace across the courtyard. He heard a conversation start up behind him.

"Hey Joe. You working the day shift today?" came a familiar female voice. Jon had no doubt who it belonged to. Claire had just struck up a conversation with the guard that Jon was certain was about to challenge him. He was so tempted to steal a glance, thinking this coincidence too good to be true. His fatigue and injury could be playing tricks on his mind; searching for a convenient way out. But Jon Haynes continued forward until he exited the opposite side of the courtyard. Casually he turned to the left to duck behind the adjacent apartment building and paused to catch his breath.

He focused his ear as best he could, trying to gather details of the conversation occurring behind him. But he was out of range, and whatever chance he had of hearing was drowned out by his racing pulse. He stood there a moment, gathering himself and trying to calm his frazzled nerves. He could tell the conversation had ended and heard the cadence of feminine boots on concrete nearing his position. He waited as long as he could stand, trying to let the woman he prayed was Claire Keen close the distance.

As the click of the heels approached the edge of the building, Jon started walking directly away, hoping to keep up appearances in the event it wasn't Claire.

"Hello Jon," Claire said as she exited the courtyard and strode up behind him. Jon glanced over his shoulder and confirmed his sincerest hopes. Then he breathed a massive sigh of relief as she took him by the hand and led him toward her second floor apartment.

CHAPTER TWELVE

Jon sat on the bed in the combination bedroom-living room of Claire's Casimir apartment. The relief of making it into the facility undetected helped with the pain in his arm, face and ankle. His fatigued body and mind were satisfied that he'd found rest and safety, at least temporarily.

Jon smiled as he watched Claire hustle between the kitchen and bathroom gathering supplies to tend to his wounds. She sporadically talked to him as she darted back and forth, but Jon's exhausted mind didn't comprehend any of it. He was settling into a satisfied bliss that can only be found at the restful end of total exhaustion. Sleep threatened to take him any minute.

"Take some Aleve and try to relax," Claire said to Jon, snapping him out of his trance.

Jon accepted the two blue pills and glass of water and quickly swallowed them down as Claire sat next to him on the bed and started fretting the wound on his head.

"What happened to you Jon," Claire asked, concern and a hint of irritation in her voice. "You look like you just left the battlefield."

"It's a long story," Jon replied. "I burned my arm and cut my face trying to stop a giant induction fan that would have otherwise kept me from making it down here. The swollen ankle was caused by the tunnel running longer than the rope I'd brought to climb down here." Jon chuckled quietly at his own misfortune.

"Oh my god, I hadn't even noticed the ankle," Claire blurted as she stood and headed back to the kitchen to put together a cold compress.

When she returned from the kitchen Claire instructed Jon to remove his cargo pants so she could see the extent of his leg injuries. "Pants off Haynes."

Jon slowly stood to comply. "No consideration for my modesty Miss Keen?" Jon asked sarcastically, barely controlling his delirium. Claire responded with only an expression, indicating that she was not joking and was not interested in Jon's playful banter. Jon kicked his shoes off and dropped trow to comply. As he stepped his left leg clear of his trousers and brought all his weight onto his right leg he winced and plopped back onto the bed. Claire went right into action lifting his right ankle from the floor and wrapping it tightly in the cold compress. Finishing, she looked up at Jon and smiled. "Does this qualify me as a field medic or something? I always knew you'd need me to rescue you."

She stood, crouched in front of Jon again, pressing a cold rag against the cut on Jon's eye, trying to clear away the dried blood. Face to face now, Jon stared into her deep green eyes. The combination of exhaustion, injury and relief at having found safe harbor made Jon feel slightly drunk. His inhibitions were low and he reached up to cup his hand around the base of Claire's skull to pull her into a kiss.

Claire responded favorably for a few seconds before she pulled back from the embrace. "That was nice, but you're injured Jon. You need at least some basic first aid, a shower, and some sleep. But mostly a shower." Claire wrinkled her nose with the last sentence.

"You're probably right", Jon acknowledged while simultaneously starting to work free the buttons on her blouse. "But like you said, I'm injured. I'm not sure its safe to shower alone." Claire popped him softly on the back of the head to indicate her disapproval of his advances. But Jon also took note that she didn't stop his continuing work on her blouse.

A moment later, Claire in her bra and slacks and Jon in his boxers and soiled black t-shirt, made their way to the bathroom in Claire's apartment. Claire lifted the shirt over Jon's head, careful to avoid the cut over his left eye. Jon immodestly removed the rest of his clothes with a mischievous grin before stepping into the shower. Claire reached in to turn on the hot water and, from the opposite side of the curtain instructed Jon to clean himself up. Jon soaped down quickly, hoping his cleanliness would be rewarded.

It was. A few minutes later Claire stepped into the shower behind him. They spent the next few minutes there, then transferred their activity to Claire's bed. An hour after the sequence had begun Jon was fully relaxed and let exhaustion take him into a very deep sleep.

***

Claire awoke two hours later, noticing the 'sun' was still high in the artificial Casimir sky. She let herself enjoy laying next to Jon for the next few minutes while she contemplated their next steps. Covert breaking and entering really wasn't her thing. She wanted to help. She wanted to keep Jon, and herself, out of trouble with Casimir. But she needed his expertise to chart the next move. She had a working knowledge of the facility and basic security protocols. None of these protocols would allow Jon to move freely outside her apartment.

As she lay next to Jon her thoughts started to run faster than she could keep up. Ultimately, every line of thinking ended with Jon being apprehended and her being implicated in his unauthorized entry. Maybe this would end with both of them unemployed. The idea of being thrown out of this amazing place a little over a week into her employment put Claire into a mild panic.

She rose from the bed, put on a robe and began cleaning around her apartment. Cleaning and organizing were Claire's go-to stress reliever. The minor problems of dirty dishes, laundry and floors were a welcome distraction that could temporarily push bigger problems to the fringes.

Claire kept herself busy with menial tasks in the apartment for the next few hours. Jon didn't even stir. She started to make noise as she worked around the apartment, trying to wake him. She started cooking dinner, hoping the aroma of browning meat or simmering sauce would roust him to consciousness.

She'd cleaned her small place nearly spotless and prepared a full dinner of spaghetti, salad, and garlic bread before she heard Jon groan and roll over onto his back. She peaked into the bedroom area from the kitchen and saw Jon rubbing sleep out of his eyes and glancing out the window to try and ascertain the time of day.

"Good morning sleepy head. It's nearly dinner time."

"Hmmmph. That bread smells amazing," Jon responded. Claire knew she should have started with the bread to wake him.

"What time is it?" Jon asked.

"Almost six in the evening", Claire responded. "I tried to be noisy and wake you earlier, but you were out cold. How do you feel?"

Jon swung his feet out of bed and onto the floor, still wiping fatigue from his eyes. He glanced over his shoulder at Claire. "Hopefully I look better than I feel. I feel like I fell down a ventilation shaft a few hours ago."

As Claire caught a fresh look at Jon's face she quietly hoped he felt better than he looked. His left eye had started to go black from the bruising around the laceration. And the burns on his forearm looked like a bad case of road rash.

"Come get something to eat," Claire said, pulling back a seat at her small kitchen table after she'd deposited the spaghetti, bread, and salad bowl at the center. "I'll get you some more pain reliever you can take with dinner."

Claire watched Jon with concern as he tried to comply with her suggestion. As soon as he stood to walk the short distance to the kitchen table, he winced as he put his weight down on his injured ankle. Claire stole a look at the ankle, which now, with a few hours of swelling, looked like a continuation of his calf that ran straight down to his foot. Claire winced silently, there was no way Jon was leaving the apartment unnoticed.

They ate. Jon did so gingerly at first, but his appetite won out over the pain. Claire watched Jon devour a heaping plate of spaghetti and then another. She tried to remain casual and work her way through her dinner. But she'd never seen this battle-fatigued version of Jon before. More of a recovering wounded animal of a man than the kind and confident one she'd come to know before. She was drawn to his masculinity, while a little apprehensive of the beast she saw lurking beneath the surface.

After finishing his second plate, and leaving no leftovers behind, Jon sat back in his chair with satisfaction spread across his battered face. Jon had hardly spoken during dinner, instead making a series of grunting and grumbling sounds that Claire chose to interpret as a form of male satisfaction with the food she'd prepared.

"You were hungry," Claire said, breaking the ice. "You want coffee or anything?"

"Black coffee sounds great. I can get it if you want," Jon replied. "You've already done so much," Jon said as he gestured to the decimated spread in front of them.

Before Claire could dissuade him, Jon was up rustling through the kitchen cabinets searching for the grounds.

"They're in a can in the cabinet above the sink," Claire offered. "Two level scoops is usually perfect, unless you prefer to eat your coffee."

"Thanks," said Jon retrieving the grounds and filter and continuing his task. "So, I'm thinking I get out there tomorrow and get some photographic evidence that I made it down here. Then I'll start working on my exit plan. Any ideas other than trying to take the big ass elevator out the front door?"

Claire bit back frustration. Jon looked like he'd been blindfolded and thrown into one of those ultimate fighting things. Did he really think he could just walk around outside? He could barely walk around inside.

Claire tried the non-assertive girlfriend approach. "Don't you think you should lay low for a while? Maybe let some of those injuries heal up a little? It looks like it hurts to walk." She decided not to mention how bad his face looked. He'd figure it out soon enough.

The rest and food seemed like they'd restored Jon's familiar confidence. Without turning away from his coffee making endeavors Jon replied, "I'll be fine. I've seen worse. Remember, I got shot off a mountain in Afghanistan not that long ago."

Claire's frustration now mixed with a little anger. Jon was borderline arrogant...and stupid. There's no way he honestly thinks he can pull off a tough guy reconnaissance mission in his condition. Hopefully its all for show.

Jon started the coffee and came back to sit at the table. As he settled into his chair he sighed, probably in relief at getting the weight off his swollen ankle.

"Claire, I can tell you're worried. I'm ok. Yeah I'm in a little pain, but if I keep eating these wonderful blue Aleve pills and use these ice things to keep the swelling down, it's really not that bad. The sooner I get out there and get what I need, the sooner I can figure out how to get out of here. My continued presence here is a risk to both of us." Jon smiled. Claire flared.

"I get it Jon. You're tough. Far be it for me to tell you how hard you can go or how much pain you can handle. But you need to go in the bathroom and look at your face. Unless you're going to let me slather your face in makeup there's no way that shiner is going to avoid attention if you take it out in public. And once your swollen quasimoto forehead gets someone's attention, your lack of security credentials will garner even more. If you go outside right now we're both screwed."

Jon cocked his head. "Seems like I hit a nerve. Sorry. Just calm down, I'm sure it's not that bad."

Claire almost saw red and would have completely lost it if Jon hadn't pushed back from the table to head to the bathroom. Claire stewed for a moment as she listened to him click on the lights.

"FFFUUUUCCKK," she heard from the nearby bathroom, the door still ajar.

Claire smiled in satisfaction.

Claire watched Jon limp back to the table with renewed humility.

"You're right," Jon said, eyes to the floor. "I can't go outside tomorrow, or probably for a few days after that. Let's forget everything I just said and enjoy hanging out together tonight. New plan tomorrow."

"Sounds great. I have the perfect idea for how to spend our evening." Claire went to her small DVD collection and pulled out her copy of America's Sweethearts, brandishing it and grinning ear to ear. "This movie is HILARIOUS."

Jon rolled his eyes, which Claire accepted as a gesture of reluctant compliance.

CHAPTER THIRTEEN

Jon spent the next day trying to relax while Claire was at work. He awoke when Claire did, but the throbbing from his face and ankle made it easy to stay in bed while she moved about the apartment in some sort of morning routine. Claire came over and kissed him on the undamaged side of his face.

"I should be back between four and five. There are basics in the pantry and fridge, so make whatever you want when you get hungry. Don't get any crazy ideas today. Stay inside and out of trouble." Claire paused, standing and looking at Jon as he lay in bed with his left eye swollen and hardly open.

"I love you Jon," Claire said, her tone shifting abruptly from instructive to loving.

Jon smiled. "I love you too. Thanks for taking care of me. And thanks for talking sense into me last night."

Claire smiled again at him, waved, grabbed her bag and headed out the door. Jon heard the deadbolt click from the outside of the apartment. He found it strange that they went with primitive deadbolts in such a high end facility. Why not spring for biometrics, or at least a card reader on the door. Everyone had a badge that probably included some kind of RFID chip. Jon paused, realizing his now rested mind was starting to catalogue the characteristics and vulnerabilities of the facility.

Energized, Jon hopped out of bed and limped into the kitchen to find a pen and paper to begin capturing his observations, questions and ideas. After a couple minutes rummaging through drawers and cabinets he had a pencil and a legal pad. He sat down and started thumping the eraser end against the pad.

Jon started writing feverishly, roughly outlining everything he'd seen since reaching the end of the vertical tunnel. He had three pages of observations and associated questions before he paused for the first time and realized he wanted coffee.

He took a break to get the coffee brewing and then sat back down, flipping to the next page in the legal pad. This time he drew a plan-view sketch of what he could recall of the facility outside this apartment. He used the apartment complex as a focal point and tried to draw things to scale. Because of the pain and the wound over his eye, his normally detailed memory drew fuzzy results. But he had enough for a basic sketch.

To the east (at least it seemed like east based on the tunnel he'd chosen to access), was a green park-like space, then the utility junction, then the perimeter. He tried to put himself back at his hiding spot at the utility station. What else was along the perimeter? He'd never looked behind him so that would remain a mystery for now. But ahead of him, to the north maybe, he drew in office buildings. Yeah, he was pretty sure there were a few four to five story glass exterior buildings. It would make sense if those were offices.

Jon remembered seeing the concrete tower that ran all the way to the top of the facility, so he drew it near the center of the paper. He paused to go pour a cup of the coffee that was almost finished brewing.

His mind was picking up speed but the tunnel vision he'd had yesterday wasn't allowing him to break through to see more of the facility. He stared at his mostly incomplete map then drew a big circle to represent the rest of the perimeter. The concrete elevator tower in the center.

Jon bit back frustration. His map of the facility was ninety percent blank and he wasn't learning anything new while hiding out in Claire's apartment. He flipped the page on the legal pad and continued to scrawl out questions and ideas.

He snapped out of his mania when he felt the sting of a drop of sweat rolling down through the cut on his forehead. He dabbed it away with a napkin, pushed back from the table, and started pacing the apartment. He went back to the table, started reading and re-reading his notes. He was at full tilt. He wanted to dart out the front door and start filling in the blank ninety percent of his facility map.

As Jon paced he wondered if this feeling in his gut and in his head was anxiety. That was something that happened to weak people. Jon was mentally strong. Capable and self-reliant. He didn't get anxiety attacks. Maybe he had a concussion.

Jon took a deep breath and fell back onto the sofa. He could keep himself to together and comply with Claire's instructions to lay low for today. But this wasn't going to last. Jon Haynes was a caged animal.

***

As Claire worked the key into the dead bolt lock of her apartment door her hand was shaking, just slightly. Part of her was excited to 'come home' to Jon Haynes in her apartment. Another part of her was certain that he was already gone, unable to constrain his instinct to get out of the apartment and go finish his mission.

But when Claire opened the door to her apartment she was surprised in a totally different way. Jon Haynes sat on the edge of the sofa, elbows on his knees and hands kneading his temples. Strewn all over the kitchen and living area of the apartment were legal pad sheets. Some contained haphazard lists, others drawings. Jon looked like he'd broken out of a mental institution and taken up squatting in her apartment.

"Hey," Jon said without looking up. "Why does your apartment only have windows looking down on the courtyard?"

Claire was concerned. "Um, because I'm on the interior side of the building."

"Ugh," came Jon's reply.

Claire realized she might have to figure out how to get Jon out of here sooner than she'd like. He probably needed to be evaluated for a concussion.

"Is everything ok Jon?" Claire asked gently.

"Yeah, it's nothing. I'm just not good at leaving things unfinished. I know what I need to do but I feel helpless to do it."

Claire sat down next to Jon on the sofa and rubbed his back between the shoulder blades. "We'll figure this out. It doesn't have to happen right away."

Jon continued as though Claire hadn't spoken. "I tried a memory exercise today. Something I used to do all the time after a reconnaissance mission. I tried to recall everything I'd seen on the way in here before you found me. I was hoping to piece together a plan without having to take the risk of exploring extensively outside. But between my blurry vision from the cut on my eye, and the hammering headache from the head injury, its all fuzz."

Claire was slightly relieved. At least Jon was acknowledging that he was injured. He wasn't crazy.

"I've only been here a little more than a week, but maybe I can help.

Ask me questions about this place, about the layout. You might be able to figure out a rough layout that gets you started. It's got to be better than just wandering around outside and begging to get caught."

Jon turned to Claire. She continued gently stroking his back; more of a soothing caress than a back rub. For a second she was nervous she'd said something wrong. That his machismo was going to reject her offer of support.

"Ok, I'll try anything in the name of progress," Jon replied, a sliver of hope returning to his voice.

For the next hour Claire offered Jon details of the parts of the facility she knew. Jon asked questions and continued his sketches and notes. He flipped back and forth between his day's worth of unanswered questions, scribbling faster and faster, getting visibly excited.

***

When Jon was certain he'd pulled every detail he could from Claire, he suggested they take a break. Claire sincerely wanted to help him. She seemed to recognize the caged animal sense of urgency he had about escaping his unauthorized hideaway. She was eager to give him what he needed. If he continued to press her tonight she was going to run out of accurate information and give him whatever he asked for. If you want it bad you might just get it bad.

"Why don't we stop for the night," Jon suggested. "This was really helpful and its given me some great ideas to focus my energy once its a little safer to go outside. Thank you."

Jon smiled at Claire and went to the kitchen to get a cold compress to continue working on the swelling over his left eye. As he walked back to the couch he realized he was ready to go. There would be risks, but he was trained to manage them. Trained to think and move faster. Trained to stay one step ahead of an adversary. Even an adversary he hadn't identified yet.

Claire and Jon sat in silence for the next few minutes until Claire excused herself to head to the bathroom to get ready for bed. Jon sat on the sofa for what felt like hours, waiting for Claire to return.

With one hand holding an ice pack over his eye, his thoughts drifted to Steven Pulling. What grand and mysterious purpose was served by this mission? Sure, Jon had found a security vulnerability, but now he was swallowed up by an underground compound with little prospect for escape. He could find his way to Pulling, surprise him with his presence, and report that someone could get in but wouldn't be able to make it back out. Was that enough for mission success?

"Damnit," Jon muttered, as he realized that even if Steven Pulling viewed his progress as success, Jon never could. Until he'd committed his full capacity to attempting a break out, anything less would amount to giving up. A complete effort, the proverbial one hundred and ten percent, was required before his conscience would allow him to throw in the towel. And why not? He'd get to spend a few more days with Claire while he figured out how that effort would be expended.

When Claire returned from the bathroom Jon rose and greeted her with a kiss. He then took his own, much shorter trip to the bathroom to ready for sleep.

He came back to a dark room. Claire was already in bed reading by a small lamp. Jon climbed in bed, kissed Claire on the forehead and tried to let sleep find him.

After two quiet but restless hours, Claire's lamp long since dark, and the soft rhythm of her breathing in his ear, Jon finally relaxed and drifted off to sleep with his next move decided.

CHAPTER FOURTEEN

Jon awoke the next morning to Claire's familiar bustle throughout the apartment. He forced himself to relax and remain in bed while she prepared for her day.

Thirty minutes later, her morning routine complete, Claire came over to him, as she had the day before. She leaned down and kissed him on the forehead. Jon reached up and pulled her to him by the back of her neck. He kissed her deeply.

"I love you Claire Keen. Have a great day. I'll see you when you get back. Don't be too long." Jon feigned a slight grogginess, stretching as she stood and looked down at him, smiling.

Jon lie back on the bed maintaining eye contact with Claire as she looked back at him on her way out the front door of the apartment.

As soon as Jon heard the deadbolt click he swung his feet to the floor, the faux lover-boy look immediately fading. He made his way to the bathroom, brushed his teeth and decided to let his two day beard remain. Next he started rifling through Claire's bathroom drawers. She wasn't the type to wear a lot of concealer, or any makeup for that matter, but he was sure she had something in reserve for special occasions. It took a moment but Jon found what he was looking for.

Jon had used disguises on a few occasions in his previous profession, so makeup wasn't a completely foreign concept. His work to conceal his black eye wouldn't pass heavy scrutiny, but it should be enough to prevent him being noticed by a casual passerby.

Next Jon dug around and pulled the only spare set of clean clothes he'd brought out of his pack. He donned a long sleeve brown shirt, jeans, and the same hiking boots he'd worn for the trip down the ventilation tunnel. Without allowing himself time to second guess his plan, Jon clicked off the deadbolt on Claire's front door and swung the door open.

As Jon didn't have a key to his voluntary prison in Claire's apartment, he only pretended to lock the front door behind him. While he did this he scanned his peripherals for any immediate signs of neighborly onlookers who would immediately notice he wasn't Claire. Seeing none, he relaxed slightly. The first major vulnerability was past. He casually headed to the stairwell at the end of the row of apartments.

Once he'd made his way clear of the apartment complex and was strolling across the park he'd crossed on his way in, Jon felt more confident. Out in the open he simply had to blend in. As long as he stayed far enough away from others he could prevent anyone from realizing he didn't have credentials. Avoiding interactions with security was a relatively simple matter of keeping his distance. He had the endurance and the will to explore the complex all day. If he stayed disciplined and remained unnoticed, his only constraint on this mission was ensuring he was home before Claire.

When Jon had nearly crossed the park he noticed something he hadn't on the way in. On this side of the utility outstation that had served as his only solace two days ago, he saw a wide trail that ran parallel to the complex outer perimeter. He tried not to let his hopes inflate too much. If this joggers trail circumnavigated the outer perimeter of the facility, he should be able to casually make his way around the entire underground complex and appear to be nothing more than an employee taking a refreshing walk on a day off.

Jon altered course to intersect the trail and head in the direction of the office buildings he'd seen two days ago. As he approached the trail he glanced back the other direction and breathed in a little more boldness as he saw no one behind him. So far the 'outdoors' of the facility were sparsely populated in the late morning. As Jon strolled confidently toward the office buildings about two hundred yards ahead and to the left of the trail, he reminded himself that the further he strayed from Claire's apartment the more likely he was to interact with actual Casimir employees, and potentially security personnel.

Jon passed the office buildings, avoiding direct observation of the glass faced buildings. There was no telling who was looking back at him, so best not to inadvertently give anyone a direct look at his face. By the time Jon had cleared the buildings he was convinced that he was standing next to the Casimir Institute headquarters. The cluster of structures consisted of four large buildings of similar architecture.

Each was four stories tall and the upper floors of each of the buildings was connected by a glass enclosed bridge; probably meant to allow upper management ease of transit between meeting places.

At first, Jon questioned why they hadn't built a single large structure to house the mysterious Institute's elite, but as he walked alone with his thoughts it occurred to him. The logistics of building in a place like this carried certain limitations. The larger the structure the more substantial the materials required. Building four modest structures down here was probably far more efficient than one large one.

The next hour of Jon's walk was uneventful. He did his best to look toward the center of the large open dome to take in the breath and detail of the facility. But nothing toward the center indicated a way out. And the perimeter only offered more ventilation shafts like the one that had tried to kill him on the way in. So far, the most promising way out was trying to escape via the front door - the monstrous freight elevator in the middle of the dome.

Jon continued along the path, slowly bending to the left around the campus perimeter. As he passed a large electrical distribution station that had obstructed his view for the last quarter mile, Jon saw the first disruption in the circular path around the facility. Directly ahead was a large, mostly concrete structure. Almost as soon as he saw it Jon registered a familiar low frequency hum that seemed to resonate in the base of his skull.

Undeterred, he continued forward, optimistic that this odd egg shaped building might be the key to his escape. All the structures he'd seen so far in the facility were built at least twenty five yards offset from the outer perimeter of the fantastic underground dome. This building, however, was built right up against the outer wall.

As he approached the big concrete egg Jon saw someone emerge from the structure and cross directly across the jogging path fifty yards ahead of him. The woman who'd emerged from the egg let the door swing shut behind her and Jon's trained ear heard the clink of a heavy door followed immediately by the metallic clunk of an automated lock clicking back into place. He also noted that the middle aged blonde woman wore a lab coat and moved with a purpose.

For a moment he followed her with his eyes. She walked directly toward the center of the massive underground dome. Jon let his eyes drift ahead to see where she was headed. He saw that the path she walked quickly opened up to a wider road and that road led directly to the massive lift housed in the concrete pillar in the middle of the

Casimir Institute facility. The door of the lift sat opposite the egg at the end of the road.

Without much internal debate Jon decided to stay the course and follow the trail around what he'd decided must be some sort of secure laboratory. He watched the door closely, concerned that another lab-coated Casimir employee might emerge as he passed. He was less than twenty yards from the door, the trail already bending around the curvature of the big concrete egg, when the door flung open again. Jon kept walking but glanced at his watch. It was eleven fifteen. Perhaps lunch time at the Casimir Institute.

Jon focused on keeping his gait steady. *Act like you belong here.* As Jon approached the door he tried to keep from tensing up. He passed the front door of the concrete egg without incident. Three steps later he heard muffled conversation just before the door swung open again behind him.

He was confident that he wouldn't draw attention with his back to the chatting group. He kept moving forward, trying to listen to their conversation. As he tried to focus his hearing on their words he was momentarily distracted by the strengthening of the deep hum. In that moment, it reminded him of his first time in the warehouse that sat overhead. Jon realized the hum had been there all along. He'd felt it since he left Claire's apartment. Maybe even while he was inside. But it wasn't until the door opened with him so close by that he felt the intensity change. It resonated in his chest and head. Something inside the egg was using a massive amount of energy.

Without looking, Jon determined the group behind him was probably three strong. One female and two male. Fortunately one of the males was loud. After the door clicked shut and the humming subsided significantly, Jon was able to pick up sound from the other two, but couldn't make out the words. Interrupting the other two, the loud-mouth exclaimed, "Well, Dr. Sawyer told me the candidates are all in place and we should be making the presentation within the week. Probably means we're working this weekend." Jon continued ahead with no idea what the loud-mouth was talking about.

Once Jon was past the concrete egg he found the first promising discovery in his search for an escape route. Construction equipment was staged near the perimeter wall and work had clearly begun on a tunnel. Jon searched his peripherals, and seeing no one, broke character from his absent-minded mid-morning walk around the facility, and stopped to study the tunnel project more closely.

The big concrete egg was set slightly into the exterior wall of the underground dome. The tunnel in front of him looked like it bent back behind the egg. But the presence of construction equipment told him that, regardless of where it led, this was not a finished project. It was unlikely to provide the escape from the underground that Jon was looking for. Jon mentally logged the project and continued on his way, not wanting to linger too long and draw attention.

A hundred yards ahead the landscape shifted to an industrial area. Jon saw power generating stations. He wasn't an expert but guessed they were geothermal. He saw large, fenced in transformer banks, and distribution lines running in all directions from what he'd assumed were three geothermal plants. There was some activity around the power stations, but for the most part it seemed to be a hands off operation. Nestled between the three plants was a small building that Jon figured to be the control station. Probably at least a few people on watch there at all times.

Once past the power plants Jon looked back to the middle of the dome. He was now directly across from the dormitories where his journey had started. The amount of space in this dome was amazing. It had to stretch at least three hundred yards further than the massive warehouse above, in all directions. The feeling was magnified by the LED embedded ceiling that simulated an endless sky. Jon knew he was indoors but it didn't feel that way.

Jon continued into the other half of the dome. Here he found two more groupings of buildings, likely more offices and probably more labs. He also saw something like a town center. There were a few modest storefronts. One looked to be a sandwich shop and the other resembled a twenty-four hour pharmacy. There was a larger structure in the center of the square. Given the amount of foot traffic near the lunch hour, Jon assumed there was probably a cafeteria inside. The building was probably some sort of employee social center.

As he strolled the perimeter jogging trail Jon considered walking through the 'town center,' but before he left the trail he reminded himself that there was nothing in that area that would help him escape the underground.

By the time the town square was over his left shoulder he'd made it nearly two thirds of the way around the facility. As far as his primary mission was concerned, Jon had seen more ventilation shafts, each perched ten feet above ground and probably built in the same configuration as the one that had beat the shit out of him on the way down here. He'd seen the incomplete tunnel behind the big concrete egg, and he'd seen the giant elevator. None of these stood out as viable routes to the surface. If he waited a few months, the under construction tunnel might lead somewhere. If he wanted to get caught he could try the elevator. If he had a death wish he could try to climb back up one of the ventilation shafts.

Jon glanced at his watch and registered that he'd been walking for over two hours. He needed to be back in Claire's apartment with his concealing makeup removed no later than four. Best not to assume that Claire wouldn't come home early.

As his stroll continued, Jon took heart in the fact that he was building a mental map of the facility. Even if this journey yielded nothing contributing to his escape plans, it at least was building his situational awareness. If he found himself in duress and evading security, he now had a much better understanding of the facility than he'd had when he woke up this morning.

Now directly behind the town square and the large galley/social center at its focal point, Jon, using the concrete lift tower as his primary aid to navigation, recognized that he was directly opposite the lift door and the big concrete egg all the way on the other side of the dome. There was nothing around him now. The town square was hundreds of yards away in the direction of the center of the dome. Behind him was the industrial and utilities part of the facility. Way up ahead was the residential area. Here there was nothing. Unclaimed real estate in this marvelous facility. As he continued along the trail he felt naked. There was no cover here and he was the only person anywhere nearby. It was probably uncommon for anyone to stray to this undeveloped part of the facility.

Jon lengthened his stride, anxious to get clear of this area before he drew attention. It felt like he walked in the open for hours, even though it was probably only fifteen minutes before he approached a small structure that stood outside the perimeter jogging path.

As he drew closer to the small outpost he saw a number of electric carts parked outside and thought the facility had the look of a miniaturized police station. Drawing closer still, Jon's breath caught in his throat when he read the sign outside the building from afar: 'CASIMIR SECURITY.' He was about to walk right in front of the security building. The one way glass around the small building gave him further pause. He could either walk right in front of the building, unsure who might be observing him - and his lack of credentials - from the other side of the glass. Or he could turn around. If someone was already watching him through the glass that was guaranteed to draw scrutiny.

Again, Jon decided the best approach was to appear to be on an innocent stroll around the complex. He walked right in front of the security building; calm, cool, and unflinching. He passed the building and waited to hear the door open behind him. Waited for someone to pop out from behind the one way glass and demand to see his Casimir ID. Nothing happened. He continued to open the distance between him and the security station, with each step growing more confident that he'd escaped notice..

After the adrenaline of passing the security building started to subside, Jon flipped through the mental catalogue of what he'd learned over the last four hours. Nothing he'd seen presented as a glaring escape route of choice. The best candidate he had was walking straight onto the lift and trying to make it to the surface without drawing attention. Hardly a sure fire strategy for success.

***

Joseph Bray tried to contain his excitement. Since leaving the Marine Corps two years ago he'd worked at Casimir racking up hours of boredom. The worst part was he'd been promised an exciting post doing security for a secretive one-of-a-kind organization. Instead he felt like an overpaid mall cop. Yeah, the pay was good, and the 'mall' was actually some sort of underground marvel filled with cutting edge computing and technology. But it wasn't like he was getting to do anything with all that tech.

But today was different than every other day he'd worked at Casimir. Two days ago he'd seen a suspicious character on his way to work. Just before he could stop him, maybe even bust him, he'd been distracted by his hot neighbor.

She'd never talked to him before. Sure they'd waved or smiled at each other from time to time. He'd introduced himself once. He always tried not to act too excited when he had the pleasure of small moments of her attention. But this time she'd struck up a conversation with him! Joe decided the chance to talk with the perky brunette trumped his desire to pop a potential intruder with a taser. Plus, what was the likelihood that the guy really was an intruder? Probably just some science nerd who'd hurt himself playing racquetball at the civic center. ID probably just in his pocket instead of clipped to his shirt like it was supposed to be.

But now Joe stared out the one way glass at the very same man who'd been wandering around near the apartment complex. It took a second to realize it was the same guy; when Joe had seen the man two days ago he was beat to shit, hobbling and bleeding from over his eye. Today he walked with confidence. It was the kind confidence only carried by a guy who's spent time in the military. Definitely no science nerd. Joe had no doubt that he was the same guy from the apartment complex. He remembered because after his hot neighbor left, Joe had fantasized about tasing the guy and cuffing him while pressing a knee into his back. And he was still walking around without security credentials.

Joe debated with himself. He could call it in right now from his small dispatch booth. Or he could watch this fucker to try and figure out what he was up to. Joe quickly chose the latter as it would be a far more interesting way to pass the time. He trained one of many cameras nearby on the man and followed him as he approached the apartment complex area.

The first fifteen minutes were uneventful, but as the possible intruder approached the apartment complex he seemed to scan his surroundings at a faster and faster rate. Joe recognized when someone was creeping around and trying to go unnoticed. He'd done it himself many times. A few times when following some of the more attractive female Casimir employees to the gym in the Civic Center.

Joe switched to a camera on the corner of the apartment building closest to the walking trail. The former military guy was definitely headed to the complex. He veered off the perimeter jogging trail and headed straight there. Joe switched cameras again and watched him enter the courtyard, then the stairwell up to the second floor. Joe lost visual for a moment until the man emerged from the stairwell and headed down the exterior walkway.

Strange. He was headed right toward Joe's apartment. Joe watched with increasing interest. He felt his heart rate increase. Then the man walked right past Joe's door and stopped at the next. He opened the door to the hot neighbor's apartment without hesitation, walked right in, and shut the door behind him.

Joe was lost in thought, staring at the apartment door through the camera for the next ten minutes before he realized he was grinding his teeth.

CHAPTER FIFTEEN

As he shut the door of Claire's apartment behind him Jon breathed a sigh of relief. He'd made it out of the apartment, circled the massive complex, and returned to base without notice. On the other hand, Jon felt anxiety still swirling in his gut. He'd made a full round of the facility and was no closer to escape. He could spend the evening obsessing over everything he'd seen, trying to find the key to getting back to the surface. Or he could see what Claire had in the pantry and start work on a romantic dinner.

Jon chose the latter and started digging through Claire's groceries. He found a few frozen tilapia fillets and decided he had his starting point. Like any good modern chef, he next located Claire's iPad and searched for tilapia recipes, hoping to mix and match available recipes with available ingredients.

As Jon searched he scrolled through a number of interesting recipes, mentally cataloguing those that he'd return to if he didn't find something better. Toward the bottom of the first page he saw a link to the Facebook page of a popular TV chef for a sweet and spicy tilapia recipe. Without hesitation Jon clicked the link. Instead of a Facebook feed, Jon saw a simple white page: CONTENT BLOCKED.

Curious, Jon went back to the search page and focused his search. He typed into the search bar 'sweet and spicy tilapia recipe.' The first result was the same Facebook feed that he couldn't access. The second was an Instagram post from the same TV chef. Jon tried that instead. CONTENT BLOCKED.

Back to the search results. The same TV chef, Jamie Stevens, also had a link halfway down the page to a Tweet that contained the same recipe. Jon clicked it, already knowing the end result. CONTENT BLOCKED.

This time Jon studied the nearly blank search page a little closer before moving on. The CONTENT BLOCKED notification was centered at the top of the page. Down at the bottom of the page Jon found the fine print: IP address blocked by CI security policy. Contact your administrator for access.

Jon wanted to cook Claire a nice dinner, but apparently the Casimir Institute would only allow him to do it without accessing social media. Jon filed this bit of information away and went back to the search results, locating a non-social media link to the same Jamie Stevens tilapia recipe. It was four o'clock and he needed to put his curiosity aside and get to work on the meal if he was going to appropriately surprise Claire when she came home from her training.

He checked the recipe against the available spices and got to work. Once the fish was in the oven Jon rummaged around for inspiration for the rest of the meal. Claire had a couple bottles of wine in the cabinet over the refrigerator, probably provided as some sort of housewarming by Casimir. Jon plucked a Dry Riesling from the modest four bottle selection, recalling that it paired well with fish.

Jon spent the rest of the fish-bake time prepping the table with the nicest flatware he could find in the apartment and a simple candle at the center. Last, he threw some green beans on the stove with butter and spices. The meal wasn't going to win any culinary awards, but he hoped it would serve as a token of his gratitude to Claire. The meal prep had also served to keep Jon's mind away from the anxiety associated with his current predicament. Last, he hoped the gesture came off as purely romantic. He could use a little passionate release to suppress the caged animal feeling brewing beneath the surface.

As Jon pulled the fish from the oven he heard a key slide into the lock at the front door. Perfect. He quickly shut off all the lights except the lamp in the bedroom and the candle on the table.

Claire opened the door and was obviously a little disoriented by the lack of light in her apartment. Jon watched anxiously as she paused for a second, trying to interpret what was going on.

"Hi," Jon said, breaking the silence.

"Hi," Claire replied smiling and setting her bag down on a small table near the front door. "What's this all about?" Claire asked as she walked toward Jon who stood near the stove.

"You've done a lot for me the last couple of days. I thought you could use a little special treatment," Jon said with a grin.

"Special treatment huh? What's for dinner?"

"I hope you don't mind. I found a recipe that looked good and cooked your tilapia fillets. There's also green beans and wine. I thought you might like something light. So we don't feel too full to enjoy the rest of the evening after dinner." Jon winked. Claire let out a small giggle in response.

Jon gestured to the table. "Sit down and relax. Let me pour you a glass of wine. Dinner's almost ready." As Claire headed to the table Jon moved just a little faster and pulled a chair out for her. He kissed her softly on the cheek as she prepared to sit. Jon felt the heat in Claire's cheek. He couldn't tell for sure in the dim lighting but he thought she might be blushing.

Next Jon grabbed the wine he'd selected earlier and poured Claire a glass.

"Do you need help with anything Jon?" Claire asked. "You looked like hell twenty four hours ago, now you're acting like my knight in shining armor."

Jon gave her a sly grin as he finished pouring the wine. "I feel much better today. I got this. You relax. I'd probably be in a holding cell in some dark corner of this complex if it wasn't for you. You deserve a little pampering."

Jon returned to the kitchen and finished his modest meal prep. He served one piece of fish onto each of their plates along with a helping of green beans. He glanced over his shoulder and saw Claire sip her wine while staring out toward the artificial evening settling in over the apartment complex courtyard.

Jon held a plate for each of them and made his way to the table. After setting Claire's plate in front of her, he sat down across from her at the small table. He poured himself some wine.

"Cheers," said Jon, lifting his wine glass, inviting Claire to lift hers.

Their glasses clinked, they both took a sip with eyes on each other, then started in on the dinner Jon had prepared.

The excitement of the day had helped Jon built up an appetite. He started to tear into the tilapia with his fork but paused, anxious to see if Claire enjoyed what he'd prepared. He glanced up at her in time to see her take the first bite.

"Mmmm," Claire groaned, chewing her first bite of fish. Jon's relief betrayed him as he let out a nearly imperceptible sigh that Claire didn't miss.

Claire looked up just in time to make eye contact with Jon. "It's good," she said. "Don't seem so surprised."

Jon returned her smile and they both ate and drank for the next few minutes. As they approached the end of their dinner the pace of eating was replaced with conversation.

"How was your day?" Jon asked.

"It was good," Claire responded. "I love this place. They made indoctrination sound like this scary thing." Jon smiled as Claire set her fork down and started to talk with her hands.

"Really its an experience. Everyday down here is mind-blowing. I walk outside in the morning and have to remind myself each day that I'm in a giant cave. Going to training each day is like attending a miniaturized Tech Crunch Disrupt. So much cool stuff that the rest of the world isn't even thinking about yet."

Jon scrunched his eyebrows, unfamiliar with the topic. Claire didn't notice.

She continued. "Today we had a seminar on AI predictive learning. These guys have processing power like nothing I've ever even imagined. They had a few people sit down to interface with the algorithm today to demonstrate how much it could predict about a person from a few minutes of question and answer."

Jon sipped his wine and waited for Claire to continue as she did the same.

"They picked me from the group to come up and talk to the interface. It was incredible!"

Jon smiled as Claire accelerated into the story of her incredible day, her hands a prop in the story she now recounted for him across the dinner table.

"It asked me maybe seven questions. I can't even remember them all. Where did you grow up? Where did you attend college? What do you like to do in your spare time? What motivates you? What is your area of expertise? Where do you want to be in five years? I answered as best I could in an auditorium filled with thirty of my peers. You wouldn't believe what this thing took away from my answers!"

Jon played along. "What? It must be good if you're this excited about it."

"It said: 'you have been overcome by human love.'" Claire imitated a machine voice, blushing and casting her eyes to the floor at the same time.

Jon stifled a laugh. "You're a nerd Claire. And that machine sounds pretty smart." Jon winked at her.

Jon took another sip of wine then stood and pulled Claire up from her seat. He kissed her deeply. "Smart machine," he said, breaking the kiss for just a moment before he re-engaged.

Eager hands roamed for the next few minutes until they were both undressed and had made their way across the short distance to the bed on the other side of the small apartment.

About twenty minutes later Jon and Claire lie next to each other tired and satisfied. Jon rolled from his back onto his side, propping himself up with his elbow.

"I love you Claire Keen," said Jon with a confident smile.

"I love you too," Claire said, returning the smile.

Jon slid his arm under Claire and pulled her to him, resting her head on his chest. "I left the apartment today."

Claire grabbed the sheet they were intertwined in and shot up straight, holding the sheet over her chest. "Wait, what!?"

Jon broke eye contact for a moment. "I left the apartment and walked the jogging trail that runs around the perimeter…"

Claire cut him off. "Jon, why?! I thought we agreed you were going to hold off until you were healed up. Until we could come up with a plan that didn't risk both of us getting caught."

Claire paused, scrunching her lips together, obviously trying to constrain her anger and frustration. Jon decided explaining himself wouldn't help right now. The smarter move would be to let her vent. Claire didn't say anything else. She pulled the sheet she was wrapped in the rest of the way off the bed and started to make her way to the bathroom.

"Claire, wait. I'm sorry. Let me explain," Jon tried. Claire didn't stop.

Jon sat alone in the bedroom trying to decide how to recover the situation. He should have kept his wanderings to himself. That was the original plan after all. Then a nice dinner, some wine, and some time in bed and he'd grown overconfident. Certain that Claire would subscribe to his superior logic.

Jon heard the shower running and realized Claire was intent on letting him sit and think about what he'd done. Half an hour later she re-emerged from the bathroom in pajamas that did not invite further intimacy.

Claire stood at the kitchen counter and stared daggers at Jon. She broke her stare and took a deep breath, probably trying to compose herself. "You should have talked to me about this first. You put my job at risk. A job I really like and really want to keep."

"Claire, I'm sorry, I..."

"Don't interrupt me. What would have happened if security picked you up? Did you think about that at all? Do you think you're out of the woods just because you made it back to the apartment? There are cameras everywhere down here. Security could knock on the door any second. They'll take you into custody and do whatever they do to unauthorized visitors down here. And I'll be fired so fast I might not have time to grab my toothbrush from the bathroom on the way out! Errgghh! Did you think about any of that!?"

Jon plastered on his most apologetic grimace. He sat in the bed but stared at the floor, ensuring Claire knew he was too ashamed of his actions to look her in the eye. Some of the guilt was honest guilt. He felt horrible at having upset her. He felt worse knowing that her anger and urgency was playing right into his plan. In fairness, he was playing this one by the seat of his pants. But he'd decided on this plan while prepping dinner about two hours ago. So there were probably still some contingencies he hadn't fully considered.

He gave Claire another long half minute of watching him stare guiltily at the floor before he responded. "I'm really sorry Claire, but what's done is done. Any ideas how to make it right? For what its worth I don't think anyone noticed me." Jon knew this last statement might not be true. He'd seen the one way glass on the outside of the security building. He'd passed only a few feet in front of the glass and it was possible he'd drawn the attention of someone on the other side.

"Didn't you hear me before Jon?" Claire asked, growing exasperated again. "They have cameras all over this place. On my first day of training I must have signed a thousand forms giving consent to video monitoring. The only placed they've promised big brother can't see is in our living quarters and inside bathroom and shower stalls. Everything else is fair game 'to protect our unique research and technologies.'"

Claire exhaled in frustration. "We have to get you out of here sooner rather than later."

Jon concentrated on looking guilty and ashamed. He tried hard not to smile. This scheme was a long shot and he felt bad for deceiving Claire.

As Jon walked the perimeter earlier in the day he'd decided a place this advanced likely had equally advanced video surveillance systems. They probably weren't using real time facial recognition or he'd have already been picked up by security. But depending on their protocols, they may have seen him, realized he didn't belong, and were just looking for an opportunity to grab him that would allow them to determine if he had help. If Jon was on the other side of the one way security glass, that's what he would do. He agreed with Claire. His escape timeline had to be short. He just needed her to be similarly motivated to make it happen.

Jon broke from his guilty posture, prepared to offer a solution to Claire's concern about the timeline for his departure. "Ok. But I didn't see anything during my walk that offered a way out. It seems like the only feasible path out of this place is through the front door. Right up the lift to the surface."

Claire stared the now familiar daggers at Jon Haynes before she responded. "Damnit Jon."

Jon was already smiling back at her.

CHAPTER SIXTEEN

The next morning Jon and Claire both woke early without the aid of an alarm clock. Claire had a sick feeling in the pit of her stomach. If this didn't go well she'd probably be headed back to Seattle, hoping she could land an entry level tech job. After the wonders she'd seen over the last two weeks at Casimir, the idea horrified her.

Jon flung his feet to the floor and stood, then stretched. Claire admired the definition of his back and hated that she was about to let him ruin her career.

"What happens now Jon? Do I go to work today and pretend like you're not about to turn this place upside down and get me fired?" Claire was trying her best to be stern as Jon turned around to face her while shirtless in loose sweatpants. She had a hard time staying mad when she looked at his boyish face and not so boyish body.

"Look, I know this isn't ideal. If it makes you feel better I'll tell them you had no idea I was an intruder; that I seduced you to convince you to harbor me in your apartment." Jon smiled ear to ear.

Claire blushed involuntarily. "I'm serious Jon. I'm a computer nerd. You're the Navy SEAL. How are you going to get us out of this?"

"It's not as hard as you think Claire. I've been in a lot of places I wasn't supposed to be. The best way to get past scrutiny is to act like you belong. Confidence goes a long way - assuming they aren't already looking for me."

Claire scowled. "What if they are already looking for you?"

Jon shrugged. "Then I'll get sent out of here in silver bracelets."

Claire grimaced at the mental image of Jon in handcuffs and her new job in shambles. She got up and headed to the bathroom to get ready. "You have about thirty minutes to think through your confident man plan while I get ready for work."

***

Joe Bray started his shift with a mug full of black coffee, a big lip of wintergreen Skoal, and by dialing up the same camera in the apartment complex that he'd used to watch the confident stranger walk into his hot neighbor's apartment yesterday.

Joe Bray hadn't slept much the night before. He laid in bed and couldn't stop picturing the ex-military guy walking in to his neighbor's apartment. From there his thoughts took him straight to the guy banging the hot neighbor. Next up on his mental playlist, Joe pictured himself busting into the apartment, tasing and cuffing the fucker, then spending some quality time with his neighbor while he made Mr. Confidence sit there and watch. Joe knew it was dark and irrational, but he didn't care. He was certain the guy didn't belong down here. And fuck him for showing up without authorization only to take one of the few available women that didn't weigh a deuce and quarter and spend her Saturday nights with Pepsi and Cheetos. Joe was going to bust him; sooner rather than later.

***

Thirty minutes later Claire emerged from the bathroom to find Jon fully dressed and pacing the apartment. He had a look of determination on his face that told Claire he'd decided on the next step. Claire wilted a little at the thought of not sleeping next to him tonight.

"You seem like you have a plan," said Claire, hoping the statement would come across as more of a question.

"Mmhhhmm," Jon mumbled back as he continued walking back and forth near the bed.

"Care to share?" Claire pressed, the slightest hint of irritation in her voice.

Jon abruptly stopped and looked up at her. "Sorry Claire, I was lost in thought. What's up?"

"Urrggghh," Claire grumbled softly. "I was noticing that you seem to have a plan. Do you care to share how you're going to keep yourself out of underground jail and keep me from getting fired?"

"Of course I do," Jon said, thrusting his eyebrows up twice in a faux gesture to invite Claire's curiosity.

***

Joe was grinding his teeth again. He knew the handsome stranger was still inside the hot neighbor's apartment. He hated that guy. He stared at the camera, waiting for something to happen. Then the door opened. His neighbor and her man friend walked casually down to the courtyard.

Joe didn't wait. He picked up the phone next to his work station and dialed the number he was certain would answer. On the second ring he heard a voice on the other end.

"This is Steven."

"Mr. Pulling, I have an issue to report."

***

Jon and Claire walked directly from the apartment to one of the Casimir carts parked along the side of the building. Claire was frustrated and nervous. Jon seemed so certain that everything would be fine. Claire was less optimistic, dread and jitters parked in her gut. There was no way this was going to work. As they prepared to split to opposite sides of the cart Jon squeezed Claire's hand. She felt a slight but immediate infusion of confidence.

Claire marveled at the simplicity and stupidity of Jon's plan. He really did like to keep things simple. After all her frustration and angst he'd agreed to outline the plan for her. She would drive him to a spot near the lift; the golf cart ride serving to make Jon appear to belong and prevent additional scrutiny as he walked toward the only exit from the facility. Once they reached the lift they would wait nearby until someone else was boarding. If possible Jon would board as part of a group but he'd take whatever he could get. The scrutiny placed on people departing the facility was significantly less than those trying to enter.

Claire hated the situation but knew it was better than the alternative of continuing to harbor her boyfriend in her apartment until they were caught. She parked the cart on a side street with a direct line of sight to the lift door. She looked at Jon to gauge his demeanor. He was locked on, staring at the approach to the lift, waiting for his opportunity.

Thirty minutes after parking the cart Claire watched the lift open to allow a tractor trailer into the facility. Once it emerged Claire saw that it contained the logo of the company that delivers the food regularly to the galley at the Civic Center. The truck turned in a wide arc to head around the central tower to deliver its payload at the Civic Center. When Claire glanced from the truck to Jon, she read his thoughts.

"When that truck leaves the Civic Center we need to get in line behind it at the lift," Jon said without turning to look at Claire.

They sat quietly, tense, for the next hour. When the truck re-emerged from the far side of the lift Jon squeezed Claire's hand in anticipation. "Lets go. Slowly," Jon said quietly.

Claire complied, easing the cart out onto the road and slowly accelerating toward the massive lift door. She took a deep breath, hoping to calm her frayed nerves. She needed to appear confident if they were challenged, not nervous and suspicious.

A few seconds later they pulled up behind the tractor trailer and Claire slowed the cart to a stop. The lone guard at the lift door walked around the back of the truck right in front of Claire and her fugitive. The guard didn't even glance at them. Maybe this was going to work after all.

The guard glanced down the passenger side of the truck and, seeing nothing interesting, made his way back up to the driver's window. Claire strained to listen to his conversation with the driver.

"Can you open the back so I can take a quick look?" the guard asked the driver. Claire couldn't hear the driver's response but he obviously planned to comply. The driver's side door opened and a heavyset man, with a beard he'd obviously been working on for years, dismounted the truck. The driver adjusted his jeans below his belt as he made his way to the rear of the trailer. The guard followed right behind him.

As the truck driver approached the rear of his rig he fumbled with a set of keys clipped to his belt and began working the lock on the trailer's door latch. Claire stole a glance at Jon. He was watching this mundane process with an intensity that made Claire nervous.

The basic inspection and associated boredom that took place in front of Claire over the next five minutes dulled her adrenaline, leaving her unprepared for what was about to happen.

The guard was obviously satisfied with the empty tractor trailer. He walked with the driver back toward the driver's side door and motioned to the camera above the lift door indicating it was safe to open the giant door and allow the truck to board the lift. The driver had re-mounted his rig and hadn't quite reached over to shut the driver's side door when Jon took a quick look around, then grabbed Claire's hand and pulled her to him for a short but passionate kiss.

"I love you Claire. I'll see you soon."

Jon exited the golf cart and closed the distance between it and the back of the tractor like lightning with no thunder. Claire was so fascinated with the way he moved, with speed and no sound, that it took her a second to realize that he'd just said goodbye and abandoned the plan they'd discussed. He quietly slid open the latch, cracked open the tractor trailer's rear door, and slid into the empty space behind it. The door came shut on the back of the trailer before the driver had shut his.

As the shock of Jon's sudden departure wore off she realized two things. One - she was dating a badass. Jon recognized the driver had forgotten to lock the empty trailer after the guard's inspection, and immediately seized the opportunity to use the truck as an escape vessel. *And he moved like a god.* Two - she needed to ditch her trip up to the surface. As a trainee she wasn't supposed to leave. Now that Jon was gone, the safest thing to do was stay down here and resume her normal routine.

Just as the truck started to pull forward through the open elevator door, Claire eased onto the gas pedal of the golf cart and turned the wheel to reverse direction back down Main Street. She would return to the apartment complex, hopefully unnoticed. Claire glanced back over her shoulder as the huge lift door started to slide shut. The tractor trailer was still visible and it's doors were still shut with Jon hidden inside. Jon Haynes was going to pull it off after all.

The trip back to her apartment was uneventful. A few minutes later she parked the car in the same spot she'd retrieved it from earlier. She climbed out of the cart and started back toward the inner courtyard and her apartment. As she entered the courtyard she saw her neighbor, Joe the security guy, leaning against the wall near the interior corner of the building. She waved and smiled as she passed, hoping to avoid conversation so she could get back inside her apartment before she lost her composure.

"Hi there neighbor," said the guard as Claire passed. In her peripheral vision she saw him push away from the wall he'd been leaning on.

Claire glanced quickly back over her shoulder, set on not stopping to chat. "Hi Joe, good to see you." She kept moving, but so did Joe, falling into step behind her.

"Where are you off to in such a hurry?" Joe asked. Alarm bells went off in Claire's head as she realized no one else was present in the courtyard in mid morning. Claire fought the urge to run. She knew Joe had a thing for her, and there was something in his eyes that suggested he might have a propensity for impulsive violence. He was probably the sort that held it together by a string. Low self esteem, seeking to overcompensate with an air of masculinity. The slightest provocation could set him off.

Claire had always tried to be nice to him but made sure she didn't do anything that might be perceived as flirtatious. Joe seemed like the sort that could get the wrong idea and become obsessive.

Claire took a deep breath and stopped to turn back toward Joe. Better to try and talk with him here than to risk him following her up the stairs and to her apartment door. At least she was in public right now. Even if no one else was around.

"I'm on my way back to my apartment. I have to get to work," Claire said, hoping to imply that she didn't have time to stand around and chat.

"Where you coming from?" Joe asked, stepping toward her.

Claire held her ground, resisting the urge to take an equal step back to maintain her distance. "I had some errands to run this morning before training. Nothing special."

"Who was the guy you were with?" Joe asked, a sinister smile spreading across his face.

Claire's saliva felt stuck in her throat. *Had Joe been watching her this morning? How much had he seen? Did he see Jon climb into the back of the tractor trailer at the lift?* She felt her pulse hammering in her ear.

"Just a friend from the training program," Claire lied. "I gave him a ride over to the Civic Center when I was out on my errands."

"Nice try neighbor," Joe said, stepping toward Claire again. He was now within arm's reach. "I know he's not in the training program. In fact, I know he's not authorized to be down here. I've been watching for the last few days and I know he's more than a friend. He was staying with you in your apartment." Joe paused, staring at Claire with a creepy smile that made Claire's stomach turn. Her skin crawled. Not only because of what he'd just said, but also because of the way his eyes darted back and forth from her face to the neckline of her blouse.

"Listen Joe, I'm not sure what you think you saw, but that guy is a classmate. Nothing more," Claire tried again, now desperate to escape the conversation.

With that, Joe reached to his right hip and suggestively placed his hand on the hilt of his taser. Claire noticed a bundle of plastic zip ties right next to the taser.

"I'm sorry neighbor, what was your name again?" Joe asked.

"Claire Keen," Claire responded quickly.

"Ok Claire, I'm going to give you one last chance to come clean about the guy you were with this morning. If you're honest I'll let my bosses know you cooperated. Maybe they'll look the other way regarding this little security violation."

Claire knew she was fucked. Her time at Casimir was over. But if she kept her mouth shut, maybe she could buy enough time to let Jon make it out undetected. Claire put on the most determined and defiant face she could muster. "I don't have anything else to say Joe."

"That's too bad. I feel like we could have been good friends Claire." Joe winked at her. *Gross.* "Instead, I'm going to have to call this in and take you into custody for questioning by our investigative branch. Turn around."

Claire reluctantly complied. But not until she saw Joe talking to his dispatcher in his shoulder radio. There was no way she was letting this guy put her in restraints until she knew someone else was on the way. When she heard the static laced reply of the dispatcher, she forced herself to push away her worst fears about Joe. Others would be here soon.

Once she was facing away from him, Joe pulled her arms behind her back, slid the zip tie cuffs over her wrists and pulled them tight. She fought the urge to flee when she felt his breath near the back of her neck. As he released her wrists he spoke softly near her ear. "We could have been such good friends Claire. Too bad."

***

Jon tried to contain his excitement as he heard a long low tone sound in the lift. Shortly afterward he felt himself accelerated upward. He had pulled it off. As long as he picked the right time to hop off the truck he was home free. Then he'd call Pulling, inform him of the success of his mission, and finally start working for the Casimir Institute in a more official, and normal capacity. He might even get back down there before Claire finished the training program. He felt a little guilty that he'd impulsively hopped into the back of the truck without giving her a proper goodbye.

It was completely dark in the trailer. Jon had caught a quick glimpse of the truck's contents when he'd opened the door to jump in. But now that he was inside with the door shut, he couldn't see his hand in front of his face. As a result of the deprivation of sight, Jon's other senses were heightened. He heard two low long tones sound outside the truck then heard the truck driver's door click open.

Jon's heart rate increased, facing the possibility that the driver might come back and take a look. Worse, he might come back and realize he'd forgotten to lock the trailer after the security inspection. If he locked it now, Jon would be along for the ride to this guy's final destination. No telling how far that might be, and Jon had no supplies to sustain himself if he ended up on a multi-day cross country trip.

Jon listened closely as the driver's footsteps fell on the lift floor. He heard him walking toward the rear of the rig, but then sighed in relief as his footfalls continued past the rear and up the passenger side. Growing more confident that the driver wasn't interested in his empty trailer, Jon split his attention between tracking the driver's relative location in the lift with thinking through his plan to dismount the trailer once it returned to the surface.

He could hop out as soon as he reached the top of the lift. That plan carried a lot of risk. He'd have to figure out a way to get past the guard manning the lift access, and find a way out of the above ground warehouse. If he stayed in the truck as it left the lift, his chances of escape were better, but he wasn't sure when he'd be able to hop out. If the driver headed straight for the freeway he could be stuck back here for a long time. As he spun options through his mind, Jon quickly decided that getting off in the lift was destined for failure. He'd have to stay with the truck as it left the Casimir campus and hope an opportunity to dismount presented itself.

As he finished this line of thinking he heard the driver's door shut again, followed quickly by deceleration of the lift. He listened as the lift door came open, then felt the truck rumble to life as the driver started the massive diesel engine. He heard muffled conversation between the guard and driver, but he couldn't make out the details over the low thunder of the diesel. Thankfully, he heard the air brakes on the truck release, and felt it pull forward to exit.

Ideally Jon planned to wait for the truck to stop anywhere outside the Casimir campus gate. If that happened, he could bail out of the truck and find his way through the desert to the spot he'd left his F-150. Any other solution probably involved either a long walk or an expensive cab ride. The closer to the Casimir campus he could dismount the big rig, the better off he'd be.

He felt the rig decelerate and stop again. Probably waiting for the campus front gate to open. He heard the hiss of the air brakes as the truck came to a full stop. He heard muffled conversation between the driver and someone else. Then the truck's diesel rumbled to a stop again. Not expected.

Jon's senses were on high alert but the conversation outside the truck had stopped. Jon heard footsteps approaching the back of the rig, but never heard the driver's door open. Jon's heart sank as he heard the footfalls stop directly outside the rear doors of the trailer. It sank further as the latch mechanism squealed and lifted to the open position.

Jon Haynes was temporarily blinded as light poured into the back of the tractor trailer when the door swung open. Jon squinted and shielded his eyes, trying to maintain his composure as he faced the shadow in front of him.

"Hello Jon Haynes," said the silhouette. Jon recognized the dry humorless voice. He strained his dark-adjusted eyes until he saw Steven Pulling standing in front of him.

Part Two

CHAPTER SEVENTEEN

Claire sat in a large room that was part briefing room and part college lecture auditorium. There was a lot of bustle in the lobby outside the room but only three other people seated in the space that could easily hold seventy. Claire sat on the aisle half way up the auditorium's ascending seating and waited with nervous excitement.

Victoria, her boss turned mentor, had assured her that this 'opportunity' represented a significant move toward the inner circle of the Casimir Institute. She'd be crazy to decline, especially given her recent transgressions with Casimir's security team. Accepting this opportunity was the only way her employment with Casimir would be allowed to continue.

Unfortunately for Claire, she was convinced that she'd only gotten this opportunity by selling Jon out to the Casimir security goons. As Claire was learning, the Casimir Institute treated its new employees much the same way the military treated new recruits. Certainly the Casimir program was much less physical. But the forced isolation was required until you learn and believed everything they wanted you to know. It had to happen before regular contact with the outside world was allowed to resume.

Her contact with Jon Haynes, renegade intruder, was completely unauthorized, and made her a significant source of intelligence on the weak points in Casimir's operation. Over the last few days she'd been frequently reminded of her failure in her duty to report unauthorized persons. With each reminder came renewed interrogation, demanding that she give up everything she knew about Jon's method of accessing the secure facility and his reason for doing it.

Claire had resisted at first, confident that Jon had escaped and completed his mission. A few days later Victoria Stein arrived.

Victoria pleaded with her to save her career and help the Institute understand how and why Jon had broken into the facility. Victoria's pleas went from impassioned to angry over the course of their ninety minutes together. Claire was too disoriented to understand the implications. She maintained her silence.

Later, none other than Steven Pulling had appeared in her interrogation room. He'd shown her a series of photos that depicted Jon being plucked from the tractor trailer, placed in plastic handcuffs, and put in an austere holding cell in the underground facility. Jon hadn't succeeded; there was nothing to protect. Claire had agreed to recount the details of Jon accessing the facility in exchange for her continued employment with Casimir. She left out the more personal details of Jon's time in the facility.

Her interrogation had finally ended two days ago. Despite repeated requests, Claire hadn't heard anything about Jon's detention or if he would be allowed to leave. She argued that Jon was a Casimir employee, carrying out his assignment as he'd been directed. Steven Pulling told her that she didn't have as clear an understanding of the state of play as she might think. Nevertheless, Claire tried to convince herself she'd done the right thing. On the one hand she was angry. Jon had shown up near her apartment. She hadn't asked him to come down here and find her, but she also hadn't dismissed the idea. As she poured over her rolodex of thoughts on Jon's capture, Claire couldn't help but wonder if she'd somehow been responsible for empowering him to break into the facility. On the other hand, Jon's fugitive presence in Claire's apartment for those few wonderful days added a tingle of excitement to her life that she didn't regret. And while no one had said a thing about it to her, she now found herself being offered an opportunity that she'd be 'crazy to decline.' It seemed almost impossible that all these recent weren't connected. She just wasn't sure how or why.

As she nursed this line of thinking other employees trickled into the room. There were now around a dozen sitting throughout the auditorium. No conversation between them, just a lot of nervous shifting and waiting. She scanned the room for familiar faces and saw a few. Unfortunately, while she recognized the faces from her time around the campus, she couldn't produce any names or enough about them to strike up a friendly professional conversation. So, she resigned herself to silence and tension. The only distraction from her anticipation was the low, throbbing, unavoidable hum. This wasn't the first time she'd noticed it. Since her first time in the underground facility she'd noticed the barely perceptible thrumming that emanated from this end of the facility. Once she had entered this particular building near the perimeter of the facility, there was no mistaking the increased strength of…whatever it was. She now had to deliberately focus on something else to keep it from snowballing her growing uneasiness.

When Claire thought time couldn't move any slower the door at the front of the auditorium swung open aggressively. Two Casimir security team members, in their now familiar black t-shirts and khaki cargo pants, entered the front of the auditorium with none other than Jon Haynes in tow. Trailing right behind them was the infamous Steven Pulling and a frail but oddly confidant man she'd never seen before. He wore a lab coat, thinning gray hair, and 1980's era metal wire frame glasses that seemed to be a fashion craze amongst Casimir management. The Casimir sentries led Jon to a seat right up front, pressed him into it and quickly withdrew from the room.

Claire felt her anxiety spike. She'd been a little jumpy before. But now she knew something serious was happening, with implications she didn't understand. Steven Pulling tilted his head to the side and muttered something to the man in the lab coat. The guy in the lab coat then took a seat right next to Jon, leaving Pulling alone at the front of the auditorium. Pulling scanned the room, as if he was taking silent attendance, then leaned on the podium.

"Congratulations to all of you," said Pulling, pausing for effect. "By nature of being invited here today you've been recognized by your superiors and this institute as being worthy of an opportunity that I can assure you is truly unique."

Another pause followed before Pulling continued.

"I know you're all probably anxious to learn of this unique opportunity and the details that you've been denied up to this point. Before I give the floor to Dr. Sawyer, let me assure you that this is not simply a unique opportunity. It is far more than that. In a few minutes my colleague is going to change your perspective on the universe you call home. He is going to present you with knowledge that you will find hard to believe. After today you will understand the reason for our security, secrecy and the colossal expense of this facility." Again Mr. Pulling paused for dramatic effect.

As far as Claire was concerned Steven Pulling's opening volley had the desired effect. Since her first moment in the underground Casimir

Institute facility, Claire was amazed. But despite her fascination with the facility she understood the enormous expense. And nothing she'd seen so far justified it.

Pulling continued. "However, before we move forward, we require certain assurances that you will protect this information. Many of you come from professional backgrounds that understand the sensitivity of national security matters. Let me assure you that the implications of releasing this information far exceed anything you've been privy to in your previous endeavors. So I'm going to ask you to go significantly beyond the bounds of a traditional non-disclosure agreement."

Pulling paused and reached under the podium to retrieve a small remote. He then pointed it at the projector hanging rigidly from the ceiling. A lengthy legal document appeared on the large projector screen at the front of the auditorium. Claire began to read it as Pulling resumed his monologue.

"Before you strain your eyes to review the document on the screen, allow me to summarize. This agreement effectively waives your thirteenth amendment rights. It isn't a permanent agreement, but in signing it you are agreeing to remain in the custody of the Casimir Institute until the advisory council determines that this precaution is no longer required. Each of you must individually determine that you wish to sign this agreement and agree to take on the responsibility to safeguard the information you are about to be entrusted with. An absolute sincerity in your intent to protect this information is the key to the advisory council deciding to restore your freedom in the future." Pulling paused to let the information sink in.

"Dr. Sawyer and I are going to step out of the room to allow you to read the document on the screen in its entirety. If you don't wish to sign it, you are free to leave and return to your previous area of employment at the Institute. If you have any doubts whatsoever about your ability to safeguard this information, I strongly urge you to take this opportunity to step out. If you have questions about the document, we'll address them when we return. However, if any of those questions are the linchpin of your decision to sign it, I encourage you to see that as a signal that you probably shouldn't."

Pulling motioned to Dr. Sawyer and they abruptly left the room through a side door.

Claire's stomach was in knots. She tried to thoroughly read the document but she wasn't an attorney. Her lack of experience with legalese and her frayed nerves made it difficult to comprehend. But after reading the words through three times, she had the gist. If she signed up for this 'opportunity' she was giving up her freedom until a group of people she'd never met decided she was safe to set free again.

Every synapse of her conscious brain ordered her to get up and leave the auditorium as fast as possible. But she couldn't get up. As if some subconscious and more powerful part of her mind knew she couldn't leave.

Her concentration was broken momentarily as two of the Casimir employees from a few rows in front of her abruptly stood together and left the auditorium. As they left Claire saw that Jon remained in the front row with no evidence that he was fazed by the proposition of indentured servitude for an unknown cause. Claire found herself oddly reassured by his calm demeanor. Over the next few minutes Claire saw a few others depart, but she hardly noticed.

Steven Pulling and Dr. Sawyer re-emerged through the same door they'd left and Pulling strode back up to the podium.

"Does anyone have any questions about the document before we move on?"

An awkward silence ensued. Reading the tension in the room, Claire could tell there were plenty of questions but no one brave enough to ask the first one.

"Ok. Then let's proceed. Beneath each of your seats you'll find a fingerprint sensor. When you're ready to sign, just press your right thumb to the sensor. Once all of you have signed, we'll move on to Dr. Sawyer's presentation."

Claire couldn't help but watch Jon down in the front row. In her peripheral vision she could see the other six remaining candidates groping under their seats looking for the biometric sensor. Jon reached down, retrieved the sensor, pressed his thumb into it without ceremony, and placed it back under his seat.

Without realizing it, Claire had retrieved hers too. She stared at it for a moment. She knew this was a major decision, maybe the biggest of her life. Despite the gravity of the moment she watched her thumb go to the sensor and press down firmly, defying the doubt she felt in her conscious mind. She still wasn't sure this was the right move, but it was done. No going back now. She replaced the sensor beneath her seat and fought the urge to flee the horror she'd just invited.

Claire waged an internal battle against her panic for what felt like hours but was surely only a moment. Then Steven Pulling pulled the microphone back toward him and resumed.

"Thank you ladies and gentlemen. I must admit I assumed that last part would be more difficult. Thank you for making it quite simple. I assure you your trust in the Institute will be rewarded shortly."

"With that, let me formally introduce Dr. Phillip Sawyer. He has earned PhDs from both UC Berkley and MIT. He has studied theoretical physics under some of the most prominent names in the field. I won't list them all here because, just as sure as you're sitting in this auditorium, they'd disown him as a distinguished understudy. Dr. Sawyer has accomplished what most physicists can only dream of. And as a result of his dedication he has largely been cast out from the mainstream; dismissed as a quack. But we have built the Casimir Institute around his ideas and theorems. The networks, nanotechnology and energy solutions that appear, on the surface, to be the basis of this Institute are all a means to an end." Pulling rose to a crescendo in his monologue before pausing to gather himself.

Steven Pulling was excited and animated in a way Claire had never seen before. It was cringe-worthy watching such an odd middle-aged man get excited the way he was now.

"Without further suspense, distinguished travelers, Dr. Phillip Sawyer."

An awkward applause ensued, largely fueled by the unexplained passion flowing from Pulling's introduction. The applause died out as quickly as it had begun and Dr. Sawyer approached the podium with a glimmer of sweat already forming on his brow.

"Welcome ladies and gentlemen. I'd like to echo Steven's gratitude for your willingness to sacrifice your freedom for a time in order to advance our species and our universe." Sawyer paused, shuffling through papers on the podium.

"Please bear with me for the next few minutes. I'm going to give you a bit of a PhD level lecture on the Casimir Effect. For those of you...most of you...without a background in theoretical physics, or at least some heavy post-graduate work, you will probably find yourself with an urge for caffeine, or maybe hard liquor. Rest assured, I'll get to the good stuff. But I need to lay some foundation or the rest of what I have to say and what I have to show you will come across as science fiction."

Dr. Sawyer then opened the binder on the podium and began to read a prepared speech.

"Everything about this facility, and in fact the Casimir Institute itself, originated from the founders' belief that the Casimir Effect was ripe with potential for technological advancement, commercialization and the advancement of our species. They believed that the Casimir Effect and its potential to harvest the effects of zero point, or negative, energy could make more advanced nano-electromechanical systems possible that would revolutionize countless industries. They believed that it might open the possibility of realizing advanced propulsion systems that could be used for deep space travel. And on the most aggressive, outer fringes of their dreams, they believed it might hold the key to faster than light travel through either the realization of an Alcubierre Drive or stabilization of a traversable wormhole. Two possibilities that would allow mankind to travel orders of magnitude deeper into our universe than previous generations had ever dreamed. Suffice to say the founders saw endless potential in harvesting the capabilities that might be resident in a greater understanding and harnessing of the Casimir Effect."

Claire felt as though she couldn't swallow. Her brain operated in overdrive as nervous adrenaline pulsed through her body. She tried to calm her runaway mind so she could catalogue the reason for her reaction.

Moments ago she signed away her freedom for an unknown end. Then Pulling referred to the group in the auditorium as 'distinguished travelers.' Now Dr. Sawyer was talking about faster than light travel into deep space. Claire felt a cold sweat on her hands and a panic in her stomach. She was not interested in being the first person rocketed into deep space. And her deepest fear was that she'd given up the ability to decide her own fate.

While Claire's mind raced Dr. Sawyer continued to trudge through his prepared speech. Claire tried to focus on his words but he was into the weeds where she couldn't follow him. Her composure hung on by a thin thread and her concentration wasn't any better. She caught fragments. Vacuums, parallel mirrors, acceleration, negative energy density. Nothing that brought the situation into focus. As far as Claire could tell Dr. Sawyer was laying out the physics behind a space warp that Claire was about to be involuntarily shoved into.

Dr. Sawyer paused, flipping to the next section of his speech.

"Hopefully most of you are still with me. I appreciate your patience as I get to the point. After all the theoretical physics and the experiments, the Institute initially focused its efforts on applying these theories to the development of advanced nano-mechanical devices. We determined that the materials required to embark on some of the more eccentric ideas didn't exactly exist yet and, contrary to what it might seem as you walk through this facility, the Institute didn't have an infinite funding source, yet. We either had to develop the technology to make the next steps possible, or commercialize some of our discoveries to continue to fund our research. We ended up doing a little bit of both."

Claire sighed in silent relief. Her fears of being launched through a wormhole into unknown parts of the galaxy were slightly relieved as Sawyer described the challenges and started to talk more about nanotechnology. She found herself focused on his remarks and waiting for the conclusion that would answer why she and the seven other people in the room were here. Particularly Jon Haynes.

Dr. Sawyer continued. "We were quite successful in working with DARPA, the Defense Advanced Research Projects Agency, to develop some of the nano systems. And fortunately, the Department of Defense pays well. Their funding allowed us to continue operations as a nanotech 'business' with enough cash reserves to continue researching and testing different ways to amass negative energy of sufficient density to realize our bigger ideas."

Sawyer paused to flip pages again.

"As the nano system development project with DoD continued we quickly realized that negative, or zero-point energy was able to be created in measurable quantities within the individual nano-mechanical systems we were testing. What we couldn't figure out was how to scale it up and generate this type of energy outside two nearly microscopic vacuum plates within the nanosystem."

Claire was getting lost again. The negative energy stuff seemed interesting and exciting but the concept was too hard to fully grasp. She tried to relax and let Dr. Sawyer get back to a point in the lecture that she could understand.

Sawyer continued. "The breakthrough came by accident. We were testing an interconnected series of the nano systems as part of an advanced microprocessor development. DARPA is always chasing the next leap forward in super computing power, so they were quick to suggest this potential application once we demonstrated measurable zero point energy. They were even quicker to classify the project. Once the project was classified things really picked up speed as there didn't appear to be an end to their funding stream.

"We continued at this breakneck pace for the next few years. Expanding our facilities, increasing our staff and building corporate expertise in computing and networks. With endless DoD funding we were becoming one of the most advanced computer hardware businesses in the country that no one knew about.

"The first time we really put a sizable number of our 'Casimir Chips,' as we'd started to call them, together to build the first prototype super computer, we made a discovery that changed our trajectory almost overnight. When we started bringing the prototype on line we detected zero point energy outside of the nano plates. That might not sound like a huge breakthrough, but remember, up to this point we'd never been able to generate negative energy other than between incredibly small plates separated by a few micrometers. If we could arrange a number of Casimir Chips in such a manner that we could concentrate, or focus, the negative energy, then perhaps we could get back to chasing our dreams."

Dr. Sawyer paused again, adjusted his glasses and looked up at the auditorium. He continued without the aid of his scripted remarks.

"Before I go on, let me explain a little of the Casimir Institute 'politics' that played out over this early period. During the time the Institute had been working with DARPA, the founders became split on the future vision for the Institute. Recall that initially, commercialization of Casimir Effect technologies was a core part of their vision. But so was development of deep space and faster than light travel. As the DARPA project continued and the Institute's makeup became more specialized in computing, those founders that were focused on deep space dreams became disillusioned outsiders. All the founders were excited about their progress but this particular group was starting to grow concerned that their dream would be lost as the Casimir Institute morphed into a defense company or supercomputer conglomerate. They tried to negotiate with their counterparts to divert some of their early profits into continuing to research their grander priorities.

"But the other 'faction' wasn't interested. In their minds the future of the Institute had already been revised. There were countless examples of technologies that had changed the world after emerging from similar efforts with DARPA. They argued that the Institute should throw its full weight of effort behind the supercomputer project in order to mature the technology as quickly as possible. Their goal was to transition to production for the Department of Defense where they would reap the rewards of sole source contracts and high profit margins.

"They argued that they had not left the true Casimir vision behind. While the supercomputer project was classified, the Casimir Chips themselves were not. As the Institute scaled production it would be able to develop other, unclassified applications for the chips based on the knowledge gained in the supercomputer project. These applications may just be the next game changer, the next desktop computer, internet, or smart phone."

Dr. Sawyer was getting visibly excited. He looked over at Steven Pulling seated in the front of the auditorium.

"Steve do you want to tell them what happened next?"

Steven Pulling shook his head and motioned for Sawyer to continue.

"Alright. A few weeks after they detected negative energy outside the Casimir Chips the small group of lofty-thinking founders made a proposal to the board. They proposed a split of the Institute, as it existed at the time. Specifically, they suggested an eighty-twenty split. After a few months of negotiation and many hurt feelings and broken friendships, they reached an agreement. The supercomputing business would continue on, with eighty percent of its cash resources, full rights to the supercomputing technology and subsequent contracts, the existing production facility, and the lucrative relationship with the Department of Defense. The new cell of the Institute would receive the under construction subterranean facility, full access to the Casimir Chips and access to the research performed thus far; particularly the configuration that led to detectable negative energy outside the chips.

"Twenty percent of the Institute's cash reserves might seem like a small amount, but when coupled with the nearly complete underground facility it was enough to continue for at least a few years without concern for cash in the bank. And the new supercomputing business was happy to be able to focus on its potential cash cow without the interference and distraction of ambitious scientists."

Sawyer paused as he flipped a few pages ahead in his notes, looking for the right place to jump back into the scripted part of his remarks.

"That's about the time when some really interesting things started to happen. The building you're in now was one of the first in the facility that was ready for use. The team built, with some iteration and a lot of frustration, its first attempt at concentrating negative energy from a conglomeration of Casimir Chips. They constructed two concentric spheres of Casimir Chips that could move relative to each other. Based on physics I won't get into, they believed this relative motion was necessary to steer, or concentrate, the negative energy in their experiments.

"It took a few iterations, but in a relatively short amount of time, this team had started to concentrate negative energy in the center of the sphere that was orders of magnitude higher than anything that had been done before. A few short months after constructing the device they were working on programming the spheres to move in a fashion that they believed had the best chance of opening a traversable worm hole; albeit one that they had no idea where it would lead."

Claire had returned to the now familiar feeling that she was choking on her tongue. She was sure that she was about to be told she was a guinea pig destined for deep space teleport. It took every bit of professional courage she had not to run for the exit.

Dr. Sawyer continued. "They decided to start small with their experiments by attempting to move inanimate carbon-based objects a small distance within the facility. Now remember, this was all based on a series of untested theories, but the scientists believed they had an algorithm that would allow them to predict how far they were 'launching' an object through the wormhole. They started with a few feet. Just enough to transport the carbon cube outside the sphere. But the experiments yielded nothing. The cube sat right where it started, or at least it appeared to do so." Sawyer glanced up at the auditorium with a foreshadowing grin.

"The team, approaching desperation as their funding pool dwindled, remained confident that they had the algorithm right. An object subjected to the concentration of zero-point energy that they were developing should be able to move through space, or at least be rapidly accelerated through it. They increased the 'distance' they were attempting to transport the object, to verify that they hadn't miscalculated and were simply failing to observe smaller movements. As a result, three years ago, in February 2020 the team of dreamers had a breakthrough they didn't immediately understand.

"As they attempted to move an object three hundred meters, to the other side of the underground cavern, they saw it disappear. Before the search for its ultimate location could begin, the object promptly reappeared in the exact same spot, three seconds after it had vanished."

Claire felt moisture on her palms. This was more science fiction, or magic, than science. Too unbelievable to be true. She glanced around the auditorium and saw an array of reactions. Some of her colleagues looked sick with disbelief, while others looked fraught with fear that they'd been caught up in a cult of the delusional. Claire wasn't sure whether to be frightened or to laugh at the ridiculous claim. She settled on fear as she recalled the contract she signed earlier.

Dr. Sawyer seemed to gauge the reaction of the room, like a comedian waiting to see if his jokes would score with the crowd. "I can see most of you are skeptical. We were too. We didn't know what to think at the time. We argued with each other over what we'd seen with our own eyes. After some debate we recognized we needed to better document our findings. We knew we could move objects, or at least cause them to disappear temporarily. Previously, we'd been so confident in our predictions that we'd assumed we would merely recover the transported object from its new location, or just watch it accelerate right into the nearest wall. Measuring the distance traveled would be all the documentation we needed. We hadn't considered the need to conduct detailed recordings of the experiments. Our arrogance seems ridiculous in hindsight.

"We re-arranged the sphere to add cameras and we added additional sensors to the object we were transporting to try and understand the forces acting on it when it disappeared. What we saw in our next experiment will hopefully make believers out of all of you."

Dr. Sawyer retrieved a remote from inside the podium and turned on a projector in the front of the room. The screen showed a high definition image of a dull gray cube sitting in the middle of a dome shaped chamber. The walls had an interesting texture that Claire inferred was the combination of Casimir chips and their interconnecting latticework. A timer in the lower left corner of the screen read 0:00 and was static.

Dr. Sawyer provided an introduction to the video. "I'll let this video speak for itself, but before I do, let me put it in context. These images have not been altered. The camera recording this video is mounted in one of four symmetrical viewing ports that were backlit into the sphere. They allowed us to observe the experiments without altering the symmetry of the overall device and the resulting negative energy field. Before we took this particular video our team had incrementally increased the energy density applied during our initial discovery. Each time we increased the density we observed a proportional increase in the time that it took for the cube to re-appear. In this particular test we were targeting a three-minute disappearance of the cube. So please be patient. I'll play the whole video at normal speed."

Dr. Sawyer pointed the remote at the projector again and the timer in the lower left corner began to advance. The auditorium was still and tense.

"Oh, before I forget, at the thirty second mark in the video you'll see an additional picture appear in the top right-hand corner of the screen. This was taken with a standalone camera mounted flush on the top face of the cube."

Claire watched, trying her best to remain patient and to keep an open mind. Just as Dr. Sawyer had stated, at the thirty-second mark a second picture winked on in the upper right corner, staring up at the top of the sphere lattice structure. Moments later the lattice of the sphere began to move in a dizzying pattern, rapidly increasing in speed until its texture seemed to vanish and give way to a smooth, polished stone-like surface. At the 1:23 mark the cube vanished from view on the main screen. Claire heard a few gasps sprinkled around the auditorium.

Dr. Sawyer cleared his throat. "Shortly you'll begin to see the texture within the sphere re-appear as it is shut down to allow our scientists to enter."

Claire wasn't surprised at what she'd just seen, given the preliminary briefing provided by Dr. Sawyer. But what happened next was...curious, particularly given what she'd been told about the synchronization of the two videos. Suddenly, as if blinked into existence, the likeness of Steven Pulling appeared, staring down at the camera in the top right corner of the screen. The clock at the bottom left read 1:40.

Claire tried to process what she was seeing. In the primary view on the screen the lattice of the sphere was beginning to come into view as the unit slowed to a stop. In this image there was no cube and no Steven Pulling. But in the small secondary picture in the top right corner, from the camera mounted atop the cube, Claire saw Steven Pulling bent down examining the cube while the lattice of the motionless sphere was visible behind him.

Claire felt the customary disquiet in her gut. She glanced at Dr. Sawyer. He wasn't watching the video, but rather the cadre of Institute select in the room, a smug half-grin spread across his wiry face.

Claire resumed watching the two disjointed scenes playing out on the two screens. On the main screen the lattice of the Casimir chip sphere came into focus as the unit slowed to a stop. No one was inside the sphere and the small carbon cube was nowhere to be seen. On the small screen at the top right, Steven Pulling crouched over the cube, his mouth moving as he recorded his observations verbally. This disjointed picture continued for several minutes.

At around the 4:00 minute mark Steven Pulling entered the sphere on the main screen. He walked directly to a spot near the center of the sphere and stood with obvious anticipation. He nervously twisted a college ring on his right hand with the fingers on his left.

By this point Claire had put the pieces together. The sphere was about to appear near Pulling's feet. Logically she understood this outcome, but practically she wasn't ready for it. As the clock in the corner rolled over to 4:23 the cube appeared, just as Claire knew it would, but she gasped aloud nonetheless. And she wasn't the only one.

A few minutes later the video ended and Sawyer pressed a button on his remote to shut down the projector and retract the projector screen into its storage location above the auditorium. "As I indicated earlier, that brain-jarring experiment occurred three years ago," said Sawyer matter-of-factly. "A lot has happened since then."

Sawyer resumed his professorial demeanor. "As with any discovery of this magnitude, it takes some time to fully realize its potential. We haven't achieved such a full realization yet but we have done some amazing things and opened opportunities that will shatter your understanding of the universe you live in."

"By sending an inanimate object three minutes into the future we'd proven a revolutionary scientific theorem. But we also recognized the practical utility of this capability was very limited. We immediately focused the entire organization on understanding exactly what we had done and how we'd done it. This understanding would be key to traveling further forward in time, traveling backward in time, and ultimately moving a human through time."

Claire felt unmoored from reality. She felt as though she was in a dream, but in that near conscious state where you know it's a dream but you can't quite wake yourself. She understood she was in this auditorium, but couldn't reconcile her presence with the fact that she was enrolled in time traveler boot camp, or that the laws of physics she'd previously taken for granted had been turned on their head. She took a deep breath and tried to remain focused; to understand the implications of what was unfolding in front of her.

CHAPTER EIGHTEEN

Jon sat in the front of the auditorium barely able to keep himself in his seat. *Time Travel!* An intense adrenaline coursed through him. He felt more amped now than any time before plunging into combat. His mind stormed with questions and his imagination was overwhelmed with possibilities. There were so many wrongs that could be righted if he could step back in time, knowing what he knows now. Not the least of which was the catastrophic end to his last mission in Afghanistan.

Jon had no less than a dozen questions threatening to burst from his lips when he realized Dr. Sawyer was continuing with the presentation. He tried to suppress the momentum of his imagination and focus on Sawyer's words.

"…a few months later, once we understood that our concentration of negative energy had connected two points in time rather than two points in space, we focused specifically on sending our time traveling cube backward in time.

"As we began to develop some viable theories on how we might reverse the effect we'd previously observed - to connect two points in time in the opposite direction - we found ourselves in the middle of a real-world science fiction debate. If we were successful, what sort of paradox would we create? What Pandora's box might we open? As the discussion, debate and arguments continued over the ensuing weeks, one particularly sticky question kept bubbling up. Could sending something back in time change the past and thus the present and future. What if the change meant we'd never make this discovery in the first place? Two distinct sides of this argument emerged. The first argued that we shouldn't test the ability to travel back in time. That it was irresponsible to risk changing the past without a full understanding of the implications. The other side argued that if we couldn't or wouldn't travel back in time then our monumental discovery had no real utility; no practical application to change the world in the sort of ways the Institute founders dreamed of when they broke off from the supercomputing business."

Jon felt his anticipation being replaced by frustration, even a little anger. Who cares about science fiction paradoxes? We could save lives, even prevent wars if we could travel back in time. Whatever consequences, whatever costs they had to face as a result were negligible when compared to the potential benefits.

Dr. Sawyer continued. "Ultimately, although not without damage to our previously unified vision for the Institute, the more compelling argument won the day. If we were unwilling to travel back in time, then we could never practically travel forward. Anything or anyone we sent into the future couldn't return. Any benefit to humanity that might be reaped from knowledge of the future could never be realized in the present if the traveler couldn't return. Even if we never went used the capability to go back from the 'present', we had to know how to move back in time to return from the future.'"

Jon began to feel a throbbing behind his eyes. Maybe the beginning of a migraine. Each time Dr. Sawyer spoke of the present he made air quotes implying, at least to Jon, that time was a more fluid concept than he'd ever had to consider before. It was a little too much to process. It made his head hurt. He rubbed his temples and tried to relax the tension in the base of his skull. As he did he thought of Claire. He fought the urge to turn around and steal a glance at her to see how she was handling all of this.

Jon focused on Sawyer's voice again. "Ultimately the answer to traveling back in time was simple, elegant, and symmetrical. We accelerated the concentric spheres at the same rate but in the opposite direction that we'd used for the three-minute future travel experiment. Our time traveling cube disappeared, just like before, but never reappeared."

"We had either successfully sent the cube back in time three minutes or stumbled into how to move things through space using zero-point energy. At this juncture there was no way to definitively prove either. We searched the entire compound for the cube just to be sure. And we certainly hadn't seen a cube appear in the middle of the sphere three minutes before the experiment. We were faced with a head scratcher that wouldn't be solved without reopening the time travel paradox discussions that nearly tore our research team apart a few months earlier."

Sawyer gestured toward Steven Pulling, who was still seated in the front of the auditorium. "So the founders, led by Mr. Pulling, directed the research team to focus our efforts on harnessing the power required to travel further forward in time. They set the goal at twenty-four hours; almost five hundred times farther than we had sent the cube up to this point. They also directed us to conduct experiments aimed at understanding the likely physical effects of traveling."

Jon listened intently as Dr. Sawyer's narrative accelerated. He spoke of massive capacitor banks, anxious moments awaiting a twenty-four hour movement of the now infamous cube through time. He spoke with excitement about sending plants and animals incrementally further forward in time to evaluate the physiological effects. All relatively successful experiments. No giant explosions or deformed mice that appeared hours into the future. But just as quickly as Dr. Sawyer's lecture had reached this thrilling peak, he stopped abruptly and ran a hand through his gray hair.

"Keep in mind it had been almost a year since our initial success sending the cube through time. Amidst all the experiments and excitement we had put a huge drain on our financial resources, mostly due to increasing our power output. When we first broke from the supercomputing business our leaders were confident we could fund operations for at least three to five years. But in the excitement of our discovery we had hemorrhaged cash with little regard and would be completely broke in six months if something didn't change. We temporarily suspended further experiments and stopped operation of the sphere all together."

Steven Pulling cleared his throat and rose from his seat at the front of the auditorium. "I'll take this part Phil."

Pulling stepped to the podium, trading places with Dr. Sawyer. "Over the next six months we didn't operate the sphere at all. We determined that we understood the physics, the power requirements and had a decent handle on how traveling through a negative energy wormhole was going to affect living things. Much of the staff was temporarily furloughed and the founders agreed to stop being paid while we charted the path forward. We slowed our financial outflow to a trickle. Just enough to keep the lights on."

"We debated endlessly in those months on how we would use this new-found technology to improve humanity and the world we inhabited. There was no shortage of ideas, most of them centered on sending people as far forward as possible to try and accelerate whatever technological advancement might exist years in the future. The thought being that we might bring back the next big thing; game changers on the order of smartphones or the Internet. We would simultaneously accelerate the improvement of the human condition while also putting the financial benefits of future technology squarely into Casimir Institute's coffers." Pulling paused as he let out an awkward chuckle.

"It was a frustrating time. These ideas were fantastic and would surely solve all our problems. At times we were practically drunk with the excitement of what we might find in the future. Some even supposed we might find the key to faster than light travel and bring it back to the present. But these were the dreams of the scientists in the group. We didn't start discussing practical paths forward until Dan Grayson, the Institute's Chief Financial Officer, became indignant in one of these fantasy sessions."

Dr. Sawyer let out a guffaw at the front of the auditorium. Pulling glanced over at Sawyer then smiled at the attentive candidates in the auditorium and adjusted his glasses. "I wish I could recount for you exactly how Mr. Grayson scolded the group of fanciful scientists, but I'll paraphrase. First, Dan acknowledged that he might just be a dumb accountant in a room full of geniuses. And for those that haven't met our CFO he is the prototypical accountant; certainly not prone to public demonstrations of emotion. But then he said something like 'If we nearly went broke sending mice and bricks twenty-four hours into the future, how in the hell do you all think we can afford to travel far enough ahead to find the golden goose? Unless the goose is going to lay an egg eight hours from now right outside our lab this is just a bunch of damn fantasy and we should all start looking for new jobs.' Then he sat down, flustered and a bit shaky. The reaction from the assembled group of scientific experts - a group of experts that had recently discovered time travel - was quite hostile at first. After some heated words were exchanged, the majority came around to Dan's point. We needed a more practical and less fanciful solution to our near-term problems.

"We all owe Mr. Grayson a great debt for having brought us back down to solid ground. What came next was so simple it felt like a slap in the face. It was the sort of idea that a kid might have after watching a Back to The Future movie. We'd send someone financially savvy one day into the future. He would sit down at a computer right outside the sphere and find the biggest movers in the stock market over the last trading day. Then he would hop back in the sphere using some predetermined settings that were provided by our cadre of geniuses, return to now and we would buy stock options that we knew would respond very favorably to the next day's market movement."

Pulling paused to adjust his glasses; a move Jon now realized was a nervous tic. Sawyer started to get up to return to the podium but Pulling gestured for him to keep his seat.

Pulling continued. "For the first time in months there was full agreement amongst the founders. One of us would go forward in time, gather valuable market information from 'tomorrow' and bring it back to 'today.' We were so bent on the good we would do for humanity by continuing our work, there was no debate on the ethics of our methods. We all agreed without discussion, that any harm caused by our time travel day trading would be wrought on Wall Street brokerage houses and they would hardly feel it. They took the wrong side of bets in the markets all the time.

"Given that he was our financial expert and the entire stock market scheme was his idea, there was little debate that Mr. Grayson would be the first person to travel to the future. He graciously accepted the nomination, as any of us would have.

"We spent the next couple weeks going over the details of how Mr. Grayson would execute the plan. We walked through our end of the operation in the present. How we would configure the sphere to ensure we sent him exactly where we wanted – to the close of the market the next day. We set up a computer terminal right outside the sphere chamber with high speed access to every market parameter you could imagine. Dan researched stocks and ETFs to determine the most recently volatile so that he could maximize the chance of quickly identifying the most profitable opportunities. We also spent a lot of time with Dan going over operation of the sphere. Dan had watched many of our experiments, but he was our finance guy. He'd never operated the system himself.

"Last but not least, and despite our successes up to this point, the entire group retained a constructive level of paranoia about the paradox we might create when 'present' Dan appeared instantaneously in the future. The team agreed that we'd schedule to have the building closed early the next day so that Dan from the present would encounter no one during his trip to the future."

Steven Pulling brushed thinning hair back on his head before continuing. "I wish I had an exciting story to tell about the first human traveling through time. But it went exactly as planned. In June of 2021 we sent Dan Grayson 26 hours into the future and he returned an hour later. He then sat at a computer armed with the most valuable stock tips anyone has ever obtained, and quickly solved all the Casimir Institute's financial problems.

"Since then we've expanded our reach and continued to learn more about the mechanics and dynamics of human time travel. We've been forward in time as far as we could manage and successfully returned travelers from months in the past. Each time we learned more, building our rule set and adding to our coffers. As you sit here today our potential and our resources are virtually unlimited."

Pulling dropped his hands atop the podium in an exhausted gesture. "So I thank you for your patience in listening to this combined history and physics lesson. I hope you are as excited as I am to move forward with us."

Jon tried to hide his amusement at Steven Pulling's 'excitement.' He'd delivered world shattering news of time travel and infinite financial resources. His demeanor indicated he could just as easily have been talking about the history of medieval European feudal farming.

Pulling abruptly stepped away from the podium and Dr. Sawyer returned.

"This concludes our presentation. I think we've given you plenty to process for one day. I'm certain you have many questions. Please trust me that they'll be answered in time. For now, please take the next hour or so to get to know your distinguished colleagues. We've put some basic snacks and drinks in the adjacent room for you to enjoy. Otherwise we'll see you back here at 7AM tomorrow. Bring an overnight bag. And again, thank you."

Dr. Sawyer gave a stifled wave to the group and he and Pulling abruptly exited the auditorium. The room was silent but Jon was starving, so he decided to lead the way to the hors d'oeuvres next door.

CHAPTER NINETEEN

Jon quickly found the unremarkable spread in the next room. It consisted of two super market meat and cheese trays, a vegetable tray, a pitcher of water, and a bowl of red punch. Jon set up shop next to the meat trays and occupied himself with people watching and appeasing his grumbling stomach.

The rest of the group trickled into the room over the next few minutes. With the exception of Claire Keen, Jon didn't see any faces he recognized. Although that wasn't unexpected. He'd only been inside the Casimir facility for a few days. Most of that time had been spent hiding out in Claire's apartment or under lock and key after his failed escape.

As Jon absently munched on the meat and cheese offerings he stole occasional glances at Claire, hoping to make eye contact and find an opening to talk about what had happened and to see if she knew why they were part of this group. Jon felt guilty for putting her in a situation where she had to choose between him and loyalty to her job. He wanted to tell her that he didn't fault her for telling what she knew of the story of how he got down here.

Right as Jon thought he was going to catch Claire's eye and invite himself over to his chosen spot near the punch bowl, his line of sight was momentarily blocked by a very attractive woman in her late twenties. There was a bold assertiveness emanating from her as she forced herself into Jon's line of sight.

"How are the hors d'oeuvres?" the woman asked, obviously to Jon. Jon was caught off guard for a moment. The woman had jet black hair and light brown eyes. She also had a very fit figure that Jon immediately attributed to an intense dedication to cross training, or possibly military service.

"They're fine, as far as Costco party trays are concerned. Nothing memorable," Jon replied. He tried to steal a glance around her to get another look at Claire, but the woman deftly adjusted her pose to remain in his line of sight. Jon wasn't going to get rid of her easily.

"I'm Denise. And you are?"

"Jon Haynes. Nice to meet you." Jon offered a handshake. Denise's grip was firm and in keeping with the confidence she displayed thus far.

"What brings you to the Casimir Institute Jon?" Denise asked with a hint of flirtatious intent.

Jon silently kicked himself for not preparing for this eventuality. Someone was bound to strike up conversation with him at some point and it would have seemed much more natural if he had a plausible story ready. But Jon was no longer sure what constituted plausible. He'd just learned that time travel had become plausible three years ago. He also wasn't sure of the status of his confidentiality agreement with Steven Pulling. He'd accomplished his initial assignment to gain access to the facility, and he'd been rewarded by spending the last handful of days detained in an apartment on Casimir's underground campus. Steven Pulling did nothing to intervene and instead had turned him over to a security team. In fact, the first time he'd seen Pulling since his arrest was when Steven walked into the auditorium about an hour ago.

Jon decided to proceed honestly and hoped he could get away with omitting most of the details. "I was hired as a security consultant."

Denise shifted her weight and looked at Jon suspiciously. "Security Consultant huh? Sounds fake. I think you're former military, probably special forces. Makes me think this whole thing is more than a science experiment. You don't need combat trained muscle for science experiments."

Denise, obviously sure of herself and willing to use her sexuality to her advantage, ran a hand down Jon's arm as she said this, inviting him to open up to her. Maybe everyone in this room was equally uninformed about the project they'd been invited into.

Jon really wanted to talk to Claire. Maybe she had some clue what was going on. If nothing else, he'd like to find out what she knew about his capture and the aftermath of the last few days. But before Jon could make his way over to Claire he had to shake the aggressive woman standing in front of him.

Jon clasped his hands together in front of him as he took an exaggerated step back, away from Denise. Then he looked her straight in the eye with a thin smile. "Excuse me for a moment Denise." Then Jon quickly sidestepped Denise and restored his line of sight to Claire. Jon's real smile broke as soon as he made eye contact with her. She was caught in a similar social net, sneaking a look at Jon as a lean youthful Asian man stood talking to her excitedly.

Claire glanced at Jon, glanced back at the man, then mouthed 'HELP ME' in Jon's direction when it appeared the Asian man wasn't looking. Jon was happy to have any excuse to escape Denise's attention and made his way over to rescue Claire.

Jon came in a little too hot and realized at the last second he probably appeared to be running from Denise and bull rushing the man talking to Claire. He pulled up at the last second and composed himself.

"Hi Claire, who's your friend?" Jon asked as casually as the situation allowed.

"What was your name again?" Claire asked, sneaking in a devious wink in Jon's direction as they worked together to throw the man off balance.

"Tim. Tim Nguyen," said the Asian man, clearly frustrated that Claire had already forgotten his name.

"What do you do for Casimir, Tim?" Jon asked, edging himself closer to Claire's side.

"I work on the business side of the Institute. Operations and Finance."

Jon saw that Tim didn't fail to notice Jon positioning himself closer to Claire. Jon was being sized up. "What about you? I don't think I caught your name," said Tim.

"Jon Haynes," Jon replied, extending a hand in greeting. "I'm a security consultant."

As Jon withdrew from his greeting with Tim he sensed someone else standing along his right flank. Then he felt fingers along his spine.

"Jon, you ran off so quickly. Introduce me to your friends." Denise had followed him across the room and was running her fingers along his back as she stood next to him.

Jon tried to casually ignore the gesture. "This is Claire Keen. She's a Network Engineer and a close friend. And this is Tim Nguyen. We just met." Jon immediately felt like a jackass. *Close friend? Idiot.* He felt Claire's gaze darting between him and the very attractive, very forward woman standing next to him.

The four stood in an awkward circle of silence for a moment before Denise broke the quiet. "Does anyone want to address the elephant in the room? What do we think is going to happen when we come back tomorrow?"

"I'm just a dumb ex-military guy," replied Jon. "But I'm assuming we're all about to become elite time travelers." Jon smiled at his own brilliance, then saw Claire's scowl deepen.

"Obviously," Tim replied. "But how does this work? Are we leaving for a few hours, a few days, a few months, forever? I think it's awesome but I'm not signing up to get launched into the future, or the past, without a better idea of what we're trying to accomplish."

"I think we already signed up," Denise replied. "Did you guys read the NDA we signed? It basically says that Casimir gets to subjectively decide when they're ready to let us out of here. I'm pretty sure if you try to negotiate the terms of your time travel deal you aren't going to build a lot of trust with management." She was running her hand along Jon's back again.

Claire stared daggers at Jon as she chimed in. "You guys are assuming way too much. Sure, they told us about time travel technology, and they've implied that we've been chosen - that we're somehow special. But don't you think they'll screen us a little more first? I mean, things - and people - change quickly. Just a couple days ago I was sure I was about to be fired. They probably want to make sure they really know us before they fully commit to us."

Jon understood Claire wasn't talking about time travel and the Casimir Institute at all. She was talking directly to him. First she was staring at Jon, then, worse, she was staring at the woman who was running her hand up and down Jon's back. Jon felt a little social panic. Denise was aggressive. He hadn't invited her attention but Claire was certainly holding him accountable for it. He needed to break out of his current position quickly or things were going to get very uncomfortable for everyone.

"Does anyone want something to drink?" Jon asked stepping away from the circle and toward the table with water and punch. Tim and Denise both tried to respond but Jon had already turned away and was walking to the table.

He grabbed a couple plastic cups, filled one with water for himself, then grabbed two more and filled them with punch. Someone would take them. As he turned around to make his way back, Claire stood blocking his path.

"What was that Jon? I asked for your help with that guy and you tell him we're *friends*? Then I have to stand there and watch some woman put her hands on you? You can tell people we're together. I'm not embarrassed; are you!?"

"Of course not," Jon replied too quickly. He stared down at his shoes, trying to formulate a response. "Umm, I got caught a little flat footed. That girl is aggressive. She's coming on to me hard, but she's after something. I probably let it go too long hoping I'd figure out her angle. Sorry Claire."

She stared at him with a disappointed girlfriend look in her eyes. He wasn't out of the woods yet. "Here, hold these cups of fruit punch." Jon took the two cups of punch he had grasped in his fingers and let Claire take one in each hand. "Let's go continue the conversation with our new friends."

As they walked back toward Tim and Denise, who had continued chatting in their absence, Jon threw an arm around Claire. When they were within about five feet, Tim and Denise glanced up at them. Tim's demeanor gave away his thoughts - Harvard whiz kid beaten out by former Navy SEAL brawn, again. Jon tried not to smile in satisfaction. Jon could tell Tim didn't have the self-confidence to remain a threat. Denise, on the other hand; she looked like she'd smelled sulfur. Her nose was wrinkled and the corner of her mouth curled in a look of repulsion.

Denise wagged her index finger back and forth between Jon and Claire. "So you two are an item?" She asked the obvious question while failing to hide a light roll of her eyes.

"Yeah," Claire said matter of factly. "Fruit punch?" she asked, offering the two cups of fruit punch, one to Tim and the other to Denise. Tim took the cup with a smile while Denise rejected it with a wave of the hand, her look of disgust abating but still present.

The conversation faltered for a moment as Tim and Denise processed their new social circumstance, now talking to Jon and Claire, the couple. Denise was the first to re-break the ice.

"Anyone want to guess at the purpose of sending eight of us through time? I have to admit, this whole thing kind of makes sense to me, but I still don't know what we're going to do in the 'future,'" Denise said, making air quotes.

Claire chimed in before Jon could. "This makes sense to you? What makes you say that? Nothing about this makes sense to me."

Claire wasn't being rude per se, but she was definitely using her body language to transmit her distaste for Denise and her opinions.

Denise smiled at Claire, then reached out and touched her arm in a sort of 'bless your heart' gesture. "I'm an electrical engineer and I've been here about six months. The Institute is obsessed with power output. Every project in my division is focused on increasing the power of our little micro grid down here. My boss won't stop talking about the goal of getting this place completely off the electrical grid. Today the ridiculous power requirements finally made sense. You're still in the indoctrination program right?" Denise was dripping with condescension, all of it directed at Claire.

Jon felt the slightest urge to flee before his girlfriend and pursuer started fighting in front of him. Jon silently thanked God as Tim stumbled into the fray.

"I know what you mean," Tim said. "I've been amazed at the way a research institute keeps cash coming in. Almost every investment they make is a winner. The losers are so small they seem intentional; just enough to keep the regulators' suspicions away. Now it all makes sense."

As Tim spoke Jon felt Claire tense, still bristling at Denise. He squeezed her opposite shoulder, hoping to release her building frustration. As she started to speak he knew his touch had been insufficient.

"Ok. So the Institute wants off the grid power, and they make tons of cash. That doesn't explain what they want from us. I'm a network engineer and I've worked here for a period that can be measured in hours. Jon's in security, Denise is an electrical engineer, and Tim's working on the business end of things." Claire shrugged. "Objectively, none of this makes sense."

Tim stroked his chin, clearly preparing to try to put it together. "Maybe they just need a new crop of time travelers to bring back technology and cash. If the fundamental goal remains deep space travel, both of those things would definitely help."

Tim was growing on Jon. The guy was thoughtful, maybe a genius. And he seemed less of a threat as soon as he knew Claire was spoken for.

Jon prepared to wade into the conversation but Claire cut in again. "Even if you guys have a purpose here, I'm not sure how Jon and I fit in. I know computer networks based on today's technology. What am I going to do in the future? And, why do we need Jon; a security consultant?" She glanced up at Jon, the fire momentarily fading from her eyes. "No offense."

"Maybe you two are the eye candy to keep the experts motivated," Denise responded sarcastically.

Jon felt Claire's tension coil up under his arm. He squeezed her tighter, hoping he could keep her from striking out at the black-haired instigator in front of them.

Jon finally got a word in to diffuse things. "Looks like the party's wrapping up and I don't think we're going to solve this puzzle tonight. It was nice to meet you both and I'm sure we'll see more of you tomorrow. Maybe we'll even get a few answers to our questions. We should probably go get some rest Claire." Jon said this, intent on implying that he and Claire would sleep under the same roof, even though that wasn't the case.

Tim responded first, extending a hand toward Jon. "It was nice to meet you. See you bright and early tomorrow," Tim said as they shook hands.

As Tim turned to shake hands with Claire, she broke from Jon's embrace. As Claire moved toward Tim, Denise moved toward Jon. Instead of a professional handshake she came in for a hug. Jon awkwardly maneuvered to a side hug, intent on avoiding further conflict with his girlfriend on this already weird, frustrating evening.

Jon took Claire by the hand and started to lead her from the room. Tim and Denise indicated they were going to stay and mingle with the other two remaining traveler candidates that were still hanging around. As they neared the door Jon spoke quietly to Claire.

"Well, that was interesting."

Claire glared at him.

CHAPTER TWENTY

The next morning Claire rose early to the sound of her alarm clock going off at 5:30. She'd planned to wake early, intent on being punctual for the day's events. As the alarm blared and she stood and stretched, she no longer thought of it as waking early, but rather relief that the restless night was over. She had hardly slept at all.

The previous day's revelations had turned her world, and her stomach, upside down. She was a relatively young and inexperienced network engineer! Yet now she found herself working for a secretive organization that had discovered how to travel through time. And all signs indicated they wanted her to be a part of it. She was uncomfortable with the idea, mostly because it was fraught with the unknown. But also because she couldn't understand how she was remotely qualified for this sort of assignment. Her thoughts were a runaway train for the last 18 hours. How on earth was she going to contribute to this effort? She knew computers and networks. Not quantum physics and nano-mechanical engineering. Was she an expendable guinea pig? Or a pawn in something criminal?

More than anything she wanted to understand why they needed to assemble eight 'lucky' people and then divulge such highly sensitive information to them, under the penalty of permanent slavery if they failed to demonstrate reliability and trustworthiness.

Claire Keen had tried everything to find rest and release the night before. After the presentation she'd followed Jon and the others into the anteroom only to find Jon being aggressively pursued by another 'lucky' traveler. Claire was irritated at first but Jon had redeemed himself to some extent. She'd held out hope that Jon would escort her back to her apartment and help her relieve the tension of the day. She'd also hoped they could discuss what had happened in the days since their capture during Jon's attempted escape. Instead, he had chivalrously escorted her to her door, informed her that Mr. Pulling had provided him separate accommodations for the night, and acknowledged they had a lot to talk about when things slowed down. Claire accepted his plan but had still awoken this morning frustrated on multiple fronts.

She shuffled to the bathroom to get ready. The familiarity of her elaborate morning routine helped slow the somersaults in her stomach. Claire found comfort in the predictable, unchanging tasks that anchored her morning. The same was true for the parallel pre-bed rituals that she performed. As she carried out her morning skin care regiment her thoughts drifted. Maybe the future wouldn't be so bad. Especially if she could return with the best new exfoliating scrub or purifying cleanser. They came out with newer, more advanced stuff every year...

Thirty minutes later, as Claire finished up in the bathroom, she heard a knock at the door. She shrugged into her bathrobe and went to the door. Through the peep hole she saw Jon Haynes, and she smiled involuntarily.

"Good morning Jon," she said as she opened the door. "Come on in. I'm still getting ready."

"Good morning to you Claire," said Jon, kissing her on the cheek as he walked past her into the apartment.

If it wasn't for the lingering uneasiness over their time travel field trip later today, Jon's appearance on her doorstep would have had her morning off to a great start. As Claire pulled clothes from her closet, she debated shedding her pajamas and strolling out into the living room/bedroom area where Jon waited. Then she'd jump him and relieve some of the stress that handed been hanging around since their capture.

Claire seriously debated this idea silently with herself for a few minutes before she decided the idea of a morning romp with Jon didn't outweigh the need to be on time to today's orientation. Their romp's had a tendency to run longer than planned. Claire smiled at the thought while she got dressed.

Once that task was complete Claire announced down the hall that she was almost ready. She heard Jon rustling around in the kitchen, hopefully brewing some coffee. Claire returned to the bathroom to pack the overnight back Steven Pulling had directed they bring along today.

When she was done she swung the bag over her shoulder and walked back to the kitchen. Jon greeted her with a travel mug filled with hot coffee. He held one for himself too.

"Ready Ms. Keen?" Jon asked with a smirk.

"Yes sir, I am. Shall we?" Claire was already feeling more dauntless since Jon had arrived. No matter the uncertainty that today carried, she was confident she could weather it as long as Jon was nearby.

***

Because they left so early, Jon and Claire decided to walk across the underground campus to the giant egg facility where the days events were set to take place. Jon tried to strike up conversation as they walked, but the nervous energy crowded out conversation. They walked the majority of the way in silence.

Once they arrived in the building they were directed by the staff to return to the auditorium they'd been in yesterday. This time Jon and Claire sat next to each other and watched familiar faces trickle into the room. By 6:45 the center of the front row had eight occupied seats.

The group waited in quiet anticipation, except for Denise. Unlike everyone else she seemed to think endless chatter would ease the tension in the mostly empty auditorium. Unfortunately for Jon, she'd found the seat right next to him, opposite Claire.

"Did you sleep well last night Jon?" Denise asked without waiting for a response. "I got great sleep last night, although I had to help it along with a couple glasses of wine." She laughed at her own comment.

"I've had worse sleep," Jon replied, trying to keep his response short in hopes that Denise would get the message and strike up conversation with someone else. She either didn't get the message or didn't care.

"How long have you two been dating?"

Great. Jon wished he'd stayed on the sleep topic.

"Umm. We've been together for about a month, with a few dates before that spread over another month or two," Jon replied, slightly nervous that Claire might interpret the timeline differently.

Denise pulled back slightly in mock surprise. "Young love. That's sweet," she said, condescension evident.

Jon glanced at Claire to gauge her reaction. There wasn't one. Claire seemed to be off in her own nervous thoughts, paying no attention to Denise. Jon grabbed Claire's right hand from her lap, squeezed it in a gesture of encouragements, then caressed the back of her hand with his thumb. She looked at him and gave a brief but sincere smile before she resumed her nervous thousand yard stare.

Denise rattled on, sure that the other quiet Casimir employees around her must want to know about her life. "I had a long term boyfriend; we'd dated about a year and I'm pretty sure he wanted to get married. Getting hired on by Casimir was a blessing. It gave me a way to end the relationship. I'm too young to get committed like that. Know what I mean?"

This was a trap Jon didn't intend to step into. He shrugged his shoulders in response.

Mercifully, the doors to the auditorium swung open and Dr. Sawyer walked in. He made his way over to the podium and fiddled with logging on to the computer. He pointed the remote at the projector overhead and turned it on, then flipped the button on the podium to drop the screen from the recessed storage area in the auditorium ceiling. Sawyer finally spoke as the WELCOME screen appeared on the projector in front of them.

"Good morning everyone. I hope you all slept well last night. We have a couple of big days planned for you." Jon was getting a little annoyed. Everyone around here was obsessed with the amount of sleep they got last night. Apparently it was the only available topic of casual conversation. Then again, there weren't any fluctuations in the weather to talk about down here.

Sawyer continued. "As soon as I can get this computer logged in you'll see your team assignments. You'll be paired off according to these assignments and we'll move over to the ready room, adjacent to the sphere, to give you a full briefing on today's events."

Jon watched anxiously as the elder Dr. Sawyer slowly navigated his way through the folder structure in search of the file he intended to display. When he clicked the folder titled 'Casimir Sphere' he had to enter a password before he could see the contents. In this folder there were only three folders:

Archive

Candidates

Experiments

Dr. Sawyer opened the Experiments folder and immediately clicked the only subfolder inside: 2023 Group 1. He then opened a .pdf file titled Team Assignments. Jon tried to push a way thoughts of helpless lab rats as he waited for the pdf reader program to open and display the file.

Once the file was displayed on the overhead screen the group collectively murmured at what they were reading. Denise let out a small squeal and squeezed Jon's arm. Jon quickly scanned the document:

<u>2023 Group 1</u>

Team A: Claire Keen & Tim Nguyen

Team B: Clarissa Smith & Paul Neidmeyer

Team C: Sarah Paul & Michael Johnson

Team D: Denise Steinfeld & Jon Haynes

Great. Jon didn't know exactly what they'd be doing yet, but whatever it was he was going to do it with Denise. He glanced to his left at Claire to gauge her reaction. She scowled at the screen. Jon wasn't sure if she was scowling at her assignment, or his. He didn't dare put her on the spot in front of Denise by asking.

Denise wasn't helping. Jon had barely finished reading the document when she piped up. "Looks like we're going to be spending a lot of time together Jon Haynes." She still had a hand on his arm. Jon rolled his shoulder to try and send the message that he didn't appreciate her touch. She didn't get the message.

"Alright," said Dr. Sawyer at the front of the room. "Pair off with your teammate and introduce yourself if you haven't already. Then follow me to the ready room."

Jon stood, thankful he could create a little space between Denise and himself. Claire also stood and started to make her way over to Tim who was seated at the other end of the row. Jon placed a hand on her shoulder before she could walk away. She turned and Jon put his hands on either arm.

"You good?" Jon asked her as they stood face to face.

"I'm fine Jon. I'm a big girl." She was definitely not fine. But Jon had learned that pressing the issue with a woman when she was 'fine' was always the wrong answer. Either Claire would talk to him about it in private after she had time to process what was bothering her, or Jon would dig it out of her when they were alone. For now, he tried to offer a reassuring smile as he squeezed her arms gently then dropped his hands. She turned and walked toward Tim, plastering on a smile Jon could tell was forced. Jon watched her walk away for a moment before turning back to face Denise.

Denise was going a hundred miles an hour as soon as Jon made eye contact. "Ready to go Johnny boy? I want to make sure we get good seats."

Jon tried not to react to the nauseating nickname she'd just assigned him. Hopefully it didn't stick. "Yeah let's go."

He was also excited to get to the ready room even if Denise was a damper on his excitement. He'd have to live with it for now.

The four pairs made their way the short distance out of the auditorium and over to the ready room. The entrance was opened via biometric lock that Dr. Sawyer activated. Past the door they walked down a short hallway and through another set of double doors.

The room they entered looked more like a locker room than a ready room, but looking around Jon knew they'd arrived. There were eight benches arranged like church pews. Four on each side of a center aisle. The first two rows had printed signs taped to them indicating which bench was for which of the four teams.

Before sitting, Jon did a three-sixty to take in his surroundings. At the front of the room there was a dark glass pane. Whatever was on the other side wasn't visible right now. On either side of the room were doors that led to locker rooms. The one on the left a women's locker room. The one on the right the men's room. In the back left corner of the room was a set of phone lock boxes.

Satisfied that he'd taken in all the small ready room had to offer he tried to make eye contact with Claire before she took her seat in the Team A row up front. She went directly to her bench and sat down without looking back at Jon. Jon sat down with a tinge of disappointment.

As the rest of the eight were shuffling around and beginning to take their seats, Dr. Sawyer strolled to the front of the room.

He cleared his throat. "I'm going to turn you all over to Kristen. She'll run you through the logistics for today and give you a short overview briefing. I'll be back when the real fun starts."

Dr. Sawyer gave a slight awkward wave and walked back out through the double doors at the rear of the room. An attractive blond woman, probably in her early thirties, replaced him at the front.

"Hello everyone. I'm Kristen Sprague. I'm the Sphere Operations Manager for this shift and will be giving you the orientation briefing. Before we get started I'd ask that you all power down your cell phones and store them in one of the phone lockers in the back of the room."

Jon complied, as did everyone else. They all pulled smart phones from their pockets, thumbed at them to power them down, then queued up at the back of the room to choose a lock box.

A few minutes later, everyone sat nervously on their benches and waited for Kristen to start the briefing. Jon was relieved. Since they'd walked into the ready room it appeared nerves were getting to Denise too. She'd finally gone quiet for the first time since Jon had met her.

"Ok, let's get started," said Kristen, returning to her spot at the front of the room. "Pay close attention. The details matter. If you have questions you should feel free to ask as we go."

"As you've all probably figured out by now, you're going to the future today. Specifically, you're taking what I like to call a familiarization trip to 2050. Your mission is pretty straightforward - experience time travel, stay out of trouble, and come back on time." Kristen chuckled at her own pun. Jon felt a smile crack on his own face.

"You've been separated into teams of two because it makes the logistics simple. We can only move two people at a time through the sphere so it ends up being a convenient way to arrange the logistics at your destination too. Even though you'll board the sphere in four separate groups, you'll all arrive at the same time."

The guy right in front of Jon shot his hand up with a question.

"Yes Mr. Neidmeyer," said Kristen.

"When you say we'll all arrive at the same time…umm." He adjusted his glasses and looked down at the floor, appearing to struggle with how to phrase the question.

"I get this one a lot," Kristen cut in. "You're all being sent to the same timeline. Maybe that's a better way to phrase it. Each pair will be sent a few minutes apart, but you'll arrive an equivalent amount of time after the team that went before you. Said differently, I'm going to send each pair of you exactly the same *amount* of time into the future."

Kristen paused to allow the possibility of a follow up question. Hearing none, she continued. "We've spent a decent amount of time in 2050 so let me explain what things are going to look like when you get there. You'll arrive in the same 'place' you depart from." Kristen made air quotes around 'place.'

"You'll find this same ready room, but there's an additional exit door that will provide you access to the surface. I won't spoil any more of the surprise. Just make sure you use that alternate exit rather than the main lift most of you used to get down here."

Kristen paused and looked directly at Jon, narrowing her eyes just enough that Jon knew that last remark was directed at him.

"When you get to the surface you'll find transportation ready for each of your teams. And don't worry, cars are still cars in 2050. They just have a few more bells and whistles."

Kristen smiled again. "When you get to your car… Oh, I forgot to mention that you'll find the keys to your ride on a hook near the door with each team letter labeled on it. When you get to your car, choose the first option stored in the navigation system. It will give you directions to your accommodations in downtown San Diego.

"Let's see, what else…right, the hotel is about sixty five miles from here. Don't go more than seventy miles from this facility while you're in the future. Also, make sure you're back no later than twenty four hours from when you left. Your return trip is pre-programmed with a unique ID to ensure its easy to get you back to now on the right timeline. You're not trained to operate the sphere yet so it's best if we don't find ourselves in a situation where you need to program a revised departure."

Kristen paused and scanned the room, probably waiting for hands to go up with questions. The guy across the aisle from Jon raised his hand. Once you spent time in the military it got easier to recognize others who had also. This guy was definitely military, and most likely special forces of one flavor or another.

"Yes, Mr. Johnson," Kristen said pointing at him to acknowledge.

"What happens if we get hung up and miss the twenty four hour window."

"It's best if you don't miss the window Mr. Johnson. Other questions?"

Jon watched Claire's hand go up.

"Yes Ms. Keen?" Kristen was well studied on her pupils for this demonstration.

"I'm not totally clear on why we're doing this. You want us to climb into a time travel machine, get launched into the future by a couple decades, make sure we don't get too far from the machine, and definitely get back on time. Seems like you're leaving out some important details. What's the catch? What's the risk?" Claire folder her arms across her chest as she waited for the response.

"Good question Claire." Kristen was still smiling in spite of the negativity Claire was transmitting with her glare and posture. "I guess the catch is the agreement you already signed. You are about to access a capability that governments would go to war to control. I'm a little surprised you aren't more excited. The risks…they're pretty minimal for this trip. Try to think of it as a paid vacation to an exotic place. I'm not asking you to do anything other than go, have an experience, try not to do anything crazy or noteworthy, and get back to the sphere before the twenty four hour point. Oh, and don't try to go find the future version of yourself to see how life turned out. We haven't fully explored this, but in general we try to avoid circumstances that would invite some sort of Back to the Future paradox. And who knows, the future you're headed to might not be the same one that we arrive at when Earth makes another twenty seven trips around the Sun." Kristen smiled, satisfied with the intelligence of her response.

Jon decided it was time to chime in. Mostly to let Claire know he was firmly in her skeptical corner. He raised his hand.

"Yes, Mr. Haynes."

"It seems like there's a lot you're not telling us. What happens if we're late for the return trip? What happens if we bump into our future selves on the street? Who's President in 2050? In my old job we spent hours pouring over intel about where we were headed to avoid surprises. Seems you're intent on keeping the surprises intact. Why?" Jon tried, probably unsuccessfully, to ask his pointed questions in as non-threatening a tone as possible.

Kristen Sprague was unfazed. "The surprise is half the fun Jon. I've told you the important things that will keep you out of trouble. Try to enjoy this. Once you acclimate to time travel itself we'll get you up to speed on the business of time travel. Or as you said, on the 'why' you're so interested in."

Kristen glanced around the room one last time, "Any more questions before we move on?"

After a short pause, Kristen Sprague was satisfied and began discussing procedures for the 'transfer.' Jon was surprised at how few rules there were. He was expecting crazy things, like no velcro, or no material with lint. Turns out the big time machine doesn't care about most of that stuff. The only items that had to stay behind were electronics.

There were no special clothes or fancy jumpsuits that had to be worn. Apparently 1960s fashion was back in vogue in 2050, so, they were going to show up looking twenty years behind the times. Not something that would stand out too much. Kristen even encouraged them to shop with some of the stipend that was going to be provided for their trip.

CHAPTER TWENTY-ONE

Once the Casimir staff had searched everyone's overnight bags for any electronics Kristen made her way back to the front of the room. "Team A, please grab your things and follow me."

As Claire and Tim Nguyen stood up, the lights behind the formerly dark glass came up revealing the Casimir Sphere in the next room. It looked exactly like the sphere Jon had seen in yesterday's video. The window was aligned with the viewing port, so most of the view was obstructed, but you could see into and across the sphere through a small rectangular area in the window.

Jon locked his eyes on Claire. He could tell by the rigid way she moved that she was terrified. He hoped she'd glance back at him so he could offer reassurance, or at least an encouraging smile. She started to turn to look over her shoulder but Kristen Sprague put an arm across her shoulders to lead her through the door that took them to an anteroom next to the sphere.

Moments later, the door to the anteroom clicked shut. A few minutes after that Jon watched Claire and Tim walk into the center of the sphere. Claire had her bag slung over her shoulder straining to act casual. Tim shuffled in with a backpack on, nervously pulling at the straps. They both came to stop at the center of the sphere and looked off to their right (Jon's left) at someone who was probably relaying final instructions.

Another minute later they both stood, shoulder to shoulder with arms by their sides as the sphere started to spin. At first it was difficult to see them as the concentric spheres spun slowly in opposite directions. But as the speed increased Jon realized he could see through the window again, like he was looking through the spokes of a fast moving bicycle wheel.

The familiar hum Jon had learned to associate with this building increased in amplitude. Jon worked his jaw to try and relieve the pressure building at the base of his skull. As the power of the humming reached its peak it abruptly faded. At the same time, Claire and Tim disappeared from view.

The sphere decelerated and eventually stopped, just as quickly as it had spun up a few minutes before. Kristen stepped back out of the anteroom.

"OK. We're ready for Team B. It will be about 5 minutes before the capacitor bank can recharge."

The next two travelers started toward the anteroom door with their overnight bags slung over their shoulders. They looked nervous, but not nearly as nervous as Claire and Tim had, probably comforted that they didn't see any agonized screaming or convulsing when Team A had been launched into the future. That observation certainly made Jon feel better.

Unfortunately, the slightly lowered anxiety in the room also ended the relative quiet of Denise Steinfeld. "That didn't seem too bad huh?" Denise asked Jon, wrapping her hand under and around his bicep.

"No, I guess it didn't," Jon replied. "Unless they emerged in the middle of a futuristic highway in traffic." Jon smiled, secretly hoping his comment would send Denise back into quiet nervous thoughtfulness.

It didn't. "I'm pretty sure, based on everything they've told us, that we end up in the same sphere in the same place, just at a different time. Not playing in future freeway traffic." She tugged at his arm in a flirtatious gesture, acknowledging his joke.

Apparently the fact that Claire and Tim hadn't had their faces melted off in the rapidly spinning time machine had given Denise the confidence to resume her full court press on Jon. She seemed slightly more empowered with Claire no longer present.

Jon and Denise sat next to each other and watched the sphere spin to life again. Just like when Claire and Tim departed, they watched team B depart in similar fashion. As Team B winked out of existence in 2023, Denise leaned over to talk softly in Jon's ear.

"What do you think it's going to be like in 2050?"

The question was legitimate, but Jon knew it wasn't motivated by Denise's curiosity. As she asked the question, breathing softly near his ear, her hand ran over his bicep, past the pit of his elbow, down his forearm, then back up the reverse path. She was using the adrenaline of the moment to try and create a physical connection. On the surface Jon was repulsed by her overt flirtation; flirtation that obviously commenced in force the moment Claire was not around. On another level, Jon's ego devoured the attention. He should have shut her down. He should brush her away and transmit a clear and unequivocal rejection. But he didn't. On some level he enjoyed the attention, and he hated himself for it.

Team C entered the sphere and disappeared into the future exactly as Team A and Team B had a few moments before. Jon breathed a silent sigh of relief when he and Denise were summoned to the anteroom for their final preparations.

They entered the small room where Kristen Sprague waited for them. Kristen stood with a pneumatic gun held by her side. She smiled at them as they entered the small room.

"You guys ready to go? Pretty exciting right?"

Jon thought the commentary seemed forced.

Kristen continued. "This should be pretty quick. I need to inject an RFID chip under the skin of each of your arms, then you're ready to make the trip to 2050. Any questions?"

"What's the RFID chip for?" Jon asked, skepticism evident.

"It's encoded with the itinerary for you return trip. That way, no matter what happens in 2050, when you return to the sphere, you scan your forearm at the control station and it knows exactly when to send you to get you home. It's for your protection."

Kristen stepped forward, wielding the chip gun. Denise winced and drew back a step. Jon played the hero and offered his left forearm to take the first injection. Kristin pressed the gun to the meat of his forearm and pulled the trigger. A short hiss of air issued and Jon flinched slightly at the pinch he felt as the chip was injected under his skin. Jon looked at Denise.

"Not too bad, just a little pinch."

Denise reluctantly held her arm out to receive her injection.

Kristen unceremoniously pressed the gun to her arm and depressed the trigger.

"See, not so bad right?" Kristen asked rhetorically. "If you're ready, you can step into the sphere now."

Jon led Denise into the sphere. As he stepped out of the anteroom into the sterile half sphere that was intended to launch him twenty seven years into the future, Jon felt his pulse quicken. Once he and Denise stood at the center of the sphere Kristen gave the final instructions.

"Arms by your sides. Stand still, relax, and I'll see you tomorrow."

Jon glanced at the door in time to see Kristen Sprague offer a forced smile and a thumbs up. Instinctively, Jon returned the thumbs up to signal his readiness. Kristen shut the door to the anteroom, leaving Jon and Denise alone in the sphere.

Moments later the sphere started to spin around Jon and Denise. As the sphere picked up speed Jon felt the opposite effect he'd felt watching in the anteroom. The hum he'd come to expect started to fade as the sphere accelerated. Once the sphere was moving fast enough that Jon could no longer make out the detail around him, there was no sound left in the room except for his pulse in his ear. He felt as though he was standing in a sensory vacuum.

Jon tensed as he felt a tingle run over his entire body; not painful, but not pleasant either. It reminded Jon of the static cling from a shirt right out of the dryer, except the sensation quickly spread over his entire body.

Jon squeezed his eyes shut, stealing himself to remain still and appear outwardly confident that this was all normal. Almost as soon as he closed his eyes he felt the tingle start to dissipate. He opened his eyes and relaxed his tense posture as he watched the sphere in front of him decelerating.

CHAPTER TWENTY-TWO

"Claire…Claire? Relax, it's over I think," said a voice nearby.

Claire didn't dare open her eyes. She held them shut so tightly she felt fatigue in the muscles in her face. She felt the same strain in her fingers and forearms as she realized she had balled her fists tightly into the fabric of her pants just below her hips where her hands had previously rested by her side.

Before the machine had started spinning Claire was nervous but ok. She'd taken a few deep breaths to fight back the nerves as the machine started to spin around her. But she'd lost her nerve when all the sound left the room around her. She'd closed her eyes, trying to escape, at least in her mind, when she started to feel an irritating tingle spread across her entire body. It took every bit of focus she could muster not to burst into tears and crumple on the floor in the fetal position.

"Claire? Are you ok?" the voice asked again.

As Claire's pulse slowed she relaxed her constricted facial muscles and opened her eyes. The sphere around her was no longer moving. In her peripheral vision she saw Tim Nguyen, right where he'd been when the massive sphere started spinning. But now, instead of looking straight ahead as Claire was, he was turned toward her looking on with concern.

Claire still hadn't snapped out of the terror induced trance until she felt a hand gently touch between her shoulder blades. It was a comforting feeling compared to the terrifying nothingness she'd seen and felt a few moments before. She let Tim's hand linger for a moment before she stepped to the side to put some distance between them.

"Yeah, I'm fine," Claire said in a slightly more clipped tone than she'd intended. She turned to face Tim in time to see him clumsily withdraw his arm.

"I think this is the future," Tim said. He walked past Claire toward the door that led back to the anteroom. Claire followed.

As they entered the anteroom Claire quickly noticed the only difference was that Kristen Sprague was no longer waiting there. Now more observant of her surroundings than before she'd stepped into the sphere, Claire noticed that one side of the room contained a complex wall to wall control console. As she stood looking at the dormant control console a subtle tone sounded and the main display at the center of the console lit up with red text flashing on a black background:

ESTABLISHING CONNECTION TO TRIP ID: T31723B
STAND CLEAR

The tone repeated at a faster and faster rate. Tim now stood next to Claire, staring in awe at the control console that had come to life without signal.

The control room door that led into the sphere slid shut on its own power and the familiar hum began as the sphere started to spin. Claire and Tim turned to watch, really just gawk, at the now closed door that led into the sphere. The persistent hum increased in amplitude and Claire rolled her jaw in a failed attempt to relieve the pressure she felt in her inner ear.

Just as quickly as the deep, disturbing hum reached a crescendo it started to ease again. The sphere slowed and the door in front of Claire and Tim slid open, revealing Team B standing dumbfounded in the center of the sphere. A tone sounded from the control console behind them and Claire turned to see a new message displayed in green on the console's main screen:

TRIP ID: T31723B COMPLETE

Claire couldn't remember the names of the two Team B members. If she did she would have called out to them, mostly in relief at knowing another pair of humans were here with her. Instead, she gave a mock wave in their direction, which got the attention of the woman standing closest to the door.

The woman stared back at Claire, dumbfounded with her mouth partly open like she was trying to speak but couldn't get the words to process. Claire interrupted the silence.

"Hello. I'm Claire, from Team A. Are you alright?" The direct question seemed to break the woman's mental gridlock.

"Yes. You went into the sphere right before we did. Are we… there?" asked the woman as she started toward Claire, the man behind her following quietly.

"I think so," Claire replied. "You should probably come into the control room with us. This whole thing brought itself to life and shut the door a few minutes after we got here."

The woman entered the control room right in front of her male companion. As she crossed into the control room she seemed to shake out of the daze she'd been in before and extended a hand in greeting to Claire.

"I'm Clarissa Smith, and this is Paul…" Clarissa trailed off.

Paul stepped forward next to Clarissa, offering a greeting handshake to Claire. "Neidmeyer," he said, finishing Clarissa's sentence. "Paul Neidmeyer. So, is this the future?"

"Not sure," Claire replied. "But I think so." Paul was lanky and looked like he spent a lot of time in a lab. But he seemed like a nice enough guy. Getting to know her peers was going to have to wait. The control console sounded the same tone Claire had heard about ten minutes before and the screen flashed red, just as before.

ESTABLISHING CONNECTION TO TRIP ID: T31723C
STAND CLEAR

Claire decided to make her way to the ready room so she could watch the sphere spin up through the viewing window. By the time she stood between the familiar rows of benches, the vibration at the base of her neck and the low frequency hum that crowded out all other thought was back. She looked into the viewing port and saw the two people from Team C appear from thin air.

Claire briefly considered going back into the control room to welcome the new arrivals to…wherever this was, but Tim and the two from Team B were still in the small control room and it was about to get very crowded. Instead, Claire looked around the ready room to try and get a sense of what had changed. At first glance, the only thing missing was Kristen Sprague. The lock boxes were still there and there was a door to a men's and women's locker room on either side. The double doors at the back of the room were still there too. Kristen had been pretty vague during the orientation, but Claire remembered her saying there was an alternate exit that they were supposed to use to get to the surface.

Claire didn't see another door in the room, so this alternate exit wasn't going to be obvious. She walked the short distance over to the double doors at the back of the ready room and gave them a shove. They were locked.

There was a biometric keypad next to the door so Claire tried pressing her thumb to the pad to release the lock. The light below the keypad flashed red, the pad issued an uninviting BEEEEEP, and the lock didn't release. She tried again with the same result.

She turned back to face the front of the ready room and found that Tim, Clarissa and Paul had all joined her, their attention on the sphere that was beginning to spin again. Claire assumed Jon was likely part of the next and final group that would arrive. But for the moment, Claire was more focused on the panic she felt at being trapped in this room.

Her eyes darted around the increasingly small space looking for the alternate exit she was certain Kristen Sprague had briefed them on earlier - technically 27 years ago if it really was 2050. She felt a surge of hope when she saw another biometric keypad, similar to the one next to the main exit doors, on the opposite side of the sphere viewing window from the control room.

As the humming of the accelerating time travel sphere pushed its way into her thoughts, Claire remained focused on investigating her newest discovery. She walked over deliberately, passing behind her three companions who were staring into the sphere as if in a trance. The humming reached its crescendo as she pressed her thumb onto the sensor on the keypad. The keypad lit up green. It might have beeped but the sphere's low frequency vibration blotted out all other sound. A pocket door slid open in front of Claire revealing a dark passageway that led out of the ready room.

The other three travelers in the ready room let out a simultaneous gasp. Claire spun, expecting that they'd watched her open this door. Instead they were staring into the viewing window of the sphere where Jon and Denise stood with eyes closed tight.

Claire's first impulse on seeing Jon in this strange twilight zone was to run to him. But before she could move over to the control room to get closer to him she was reminded of the desperation she'd felt only a few seconds before when she'd been nearly convinced that they were trapped in the ready room of the future. She was frozen in indecision.

As she watched Jon and Denise relax into the realization that their trip was over, Tim made his way over to her.

"Holy shit, you've been busy Claire!" Tim wasn't looking at her, but instead at the passageway open behind her.

"Um, yeah," said Claire, distracted still stealing glances at Jon and Denise exiting the sphere. "I just pushed my thumb down on the pad and it opened. I think it's our way out."

What are we waiting for?" Tim asked, excited. "These other guys will figure it out. Let's go see the future!"

The fear and adrenaline of the trip in the sphere had an odd effect on Tim. When Claire had first met him he seemed confident but reserved. Now he seemed almost recklessly eager to see what would happen next.

Tim didn't wait for Claire's response. He grabbed her hand in an unromantic gesture and quite literally pulled her into the passageway. Claire followed Tim's lead but glanced back over her shoulder just soon enough to see Jon, standing next to Denise, looking at the control console.

She hoped he'd turn and make eye contact so she could communicate nonverbally that she wanted him to follow. She felt safe with Jon. Instead she was headed out into the future with Tim Nguyen. Jon hadn't looked up before they were around the corner and headed down the mystery passageway.

As Tim and Claire entered the dark hallway, LEDs lining the edge of the floor and ceiling brightened to illuminate the passageway. The tunnel wasn't straight. Claire could only see forty or fifty feet ahead as the pathway curved ahead of her. She was no longer certain of her sense of direction but it seemed they were curving around the egg shaped concrete structure that housed the sphere, heading back into the bedrock that made up the perimeter of the Casimir underground facility.

Tim and Claire continued ahead for the next ten minutes. Claire found herself working to keep up with Tim. He no longer pulled her by the hand but his pace seemed to increase with every step. Occasionally he'd glance back at Claire to ensure she was keeping up.

The path ahead straightened to reveal what appeared at first to be a dead end. As Claire drew closer and more LEDs came up to light the way, she realized it was a ninety degree bend in the passageway. Tim and Claire closed the distance quickly. At this point they were both fully obsessed with finding out what waited for them at the end of the tunnel. The only sound that passed between them was the cadence of their clicking heels on the tile interspersed with slightly heavy breathing from their quick pace.

As Claire and Tim rounded the corner the end of this leg of the trip became clear. First, the path transitioned from tiled hallway with intelligent-looking recessed LED lighting, to a stone cave carved into the bedrock it penetrated. Lights hung overhead in no discernible pattern with electrical power cords strung between that looped down almost far enough to brush the top of Tim's head as he continued down the passageway. A mere thirty feet ahead of them the humble tunnel opened into a living room-sized cavern.

Claire and Tim increased their pace again, almost breaking into a run to cover the last ten yards. On the far wall of the cavern sat a plastic or glass bubble with two seats inside.

As they entered the cavern Claire stopped to take in her surroundings. Tim continued at the same pace, across the room, to investigate the transparent vessel. Claire quickly determined the two-seat orb was the only thing in the room. As she turned back toward Tim she heard a BEEP…BEEP…BEEP and a pneumatic hiss similar to what she'd heard when she opened the passageway door a few minutes earlier.

"I think this is our ride," said Tim as he climbed awkwardly through the face of the bubble that had slid open moments before. "Come on Claire, get in." Tim was already seated and looking around for the controls.

Claire made her way toward Tim to comply, but had doubts about his urgency. She tried to stall. "What about the others? Shouldn't we double back to make sure everyone finds their way here? Maybe we need someone else, not inside the bubble, to operate it. Are there any controls in there?"

There's nothing that I can see," Tim replied. "But I'm sure a couple brilliant Casimir Institute time travelers can figure it out." Tim smiled. "Didn't you say you were some sort of computer engineer? Surely you can figure out how to talk to this thing." He winked at her as she bent down to climb through the open hatch.

"I'm a network engineer. It's different." Claire shot Tim a look of irritation. He was still smiling. Claire couldn't help but crack a smile in return. Claire found this confident, eager version of Tim more attractive than the polished, overly kind corporate guy-version she'd met yesterday. This version of Tim seemed more authentic, she thought as she plopped down in the seat next to him.

"Ok, see anything that looks like the power on button…" Tim was cut off by a hiss of air and the shutting of the hatch in front of them. Once it slid shut there was no evidence a door had ever been there. Claire fought back a brief twinge of claustrophobia. Thankfully the bubble was transparent and she could still see the room around them.

Before Claire could decide if she felt trapped or not, a Mary Poppins voice filled the small space.

"PLEASE AUTHENTICATE"

As the british computer voice finished her request two translucent rectangles appeared on the glass. One directly in front of Claire, the other in front of Tim. It looked as though the previously clear glass or plastic had become fogged glass in this small area. It happened so quickly the change was almost imperceptible. Claire's eye was only drawn to it because of the heavy black outline that appeared around the fogged area.

On a hunch Claire pressed her thumb to the fogged glass. A few seconds after she did, her rectangle turned a light shade of green. Claire looked over at Tim and shrugged. Tim reached out and pressed his thumb into the rectangle in front of him. Just like Claire's it turned green a few seconds later.

The two rectangles now contained their stock Casimir ID photos. Claire and Tim were starting at their pictures in the glass when surround sound Mary Poppins returned.

"WELCOME ABOARD. PLEASE FASTEN RESTRAINTS. ONCE YOU'RE SAFELY BUCKLED IN, PLEASE SAY 'READY.'"

The voice was still booming inside the sphere, but the tone was less stern than when she'd demanded authentication a few moments before.

Claire and Tim both fumbled around in the seats looking for anything that resembled a seat belt. Tim found it first.

"Got it, you have to pull that tab between your legs," Tim said excitedly.

Claire felt around between her legs, found the small rubber tab Tim was probably referring to and pulled on it, gently at first, but nothing happened.

"You gotta yank on it," Tim said looking over at her. "There's some kind of mechanism that activates once you yank on the rubber tab."

Claire hurried to comply. Tim was so excited to get this bubble cart moving that Claire was worried he'd reach between her legs to pull the tab if she couldn't do it quickly enough on her own. She grabbed the rubber tab again and yanked up as hard as she could without losing her grip. She let out a quiet sigh of relief when she felt it click.

A small rod popped up from the slot the tab was attached to. That rod quickly telescoped open on either side to deploy a roller coaster-like padded restraint across her lap. The top of the restraint contained a slot with a nylon flap sticking out. Claire pulled it and saw it contained two small buckles on either side. She stared at it for a minute trying to decipher the complicated seat belt design.

She noticed Tim looking at her in her peripheral vision right before he spoke.

"You gotta pull the two shoulder straps down and buckle them in," Tim said matter of factly.

Claire looked over at him to find that he was fully buckled in. The nylon flap was pressed against his chest, held tightly in place by the connection to the lap restraint on bottom and two shoulder straps on top. Claire reached over her own right shoulder and pulled down the retracted shoulder strap. She buckled it in then repeated the process by reaching over her left shoulder. As soon as she clicked in the second shoulder buckle all the restraints tightened to ensure she was snuggly restrained to the seat. Claire let out a surprised "oooh" as the nylon centerpiece of the harness tightened in place over her chest.

Almost as soon as the safety restraints had tightened in place, Claire felt a surge of panicky claustrophobia creeping in. She wiggled nervously against the tight seat restraint.

"You good?" Tim asked impatiently.

"I'm fine," Claire muttered in reply. "But I still think we should wait here for a few minutes to see if the other groups show up."

Tim cut her off. "Why? It's not like anyone else is going to get into this bubble car with us. I'm guessing this thing is going to take us wherever we need to be and come back to get another team. The sooner we go, the sooner this thing gets back. Everybody wins."

"Take it easy. This is already weird and stressful enough. It's not going to get any better if we're at each other's throats." Claire was nearly pleading for Tim to constrain his aggressive side. She liked his forward leaning confidence, but now that things were moving he seemed irritable. Like he might lash out at anything that stood in the way of moving forward. It made Claire nervous; nervous that her only companion might be at best unpredictable, and at worst, totally unstable.

"Sorry," Tim responded to her rebuke. "I don't like being trapped below ground. I'd like to see some sunshine and whatever else might be out there."

"Ok. And you're probably right. If we take this trip now, we can wait for the rest of the teams at the other end." Claire paused and tried her best to offer a conciliatory smile to Tim. "Ready." Claire said.

"Ready!" Tim repeated, beaming.

"THANK YOU," said the British surround sound voice. "WE'LL BEGIN IN JUST A MOMENT. THIS TRANSPORT ACCELERATES AND DECELLERATES QUICKLY. IF YOU FEEL ANY MOTION SICKNESS, IT IS RECOMMENDED THAT YOU CLOSE YOUR EYES AND SIMPLY ALLOW THE FEELING TO PASS."

"Great," Claire mumbled, nervous bile rising in her stomach.

A few seconds later Claire felt a large metallic thunk beneath her feet. Then the bubble she sat in with Tim was lifted five feet above the floor. As they hovered midair, Claire watched the six other Casimir team members come around the corner at the end of the cavelike hallway. Jon and the other ex-military looking guy walked shoulder to shoulder at the front of the group. Claire resisted the urge to wave to Jon. She also resisted the urge to yell out 'STOP', in an attempt to get the intelligent machine to pause until she could talk to Jon and the others.

As Jon broke into a run, Claire felt guilt mixing with the nerves she already felt. Before Jon could close the distance further, the sphere spun Claire and Tim to face the wall of the small cavern. Almost as soon as they'd been turned to face the rock wall, it's face opened to reveal a dark, metallic tunnel.

The sphere made three beeping tones, then Claire was thrown deeper into her seat as the glass bubble rocketed into the tunnel and everything went black. The next five seconds felt like an eternity. Claire had never been a fan of rollercoasters. This felt a lot like one. She couldn't tell how fast they were moving but she felt the g-forces pushing her into her seat as they accelerated. Then it was replaced by consistent pressure against her chest from the restraints, indicating they'd reached their travel speed. It was dark outside the sphere but she knew they were moving very fast.

Just as she started to relax new g-forces pressed her down into her seat, making her feel twice her weight. In addition to hurtling forward in the dark Claire now had the sensation they were moving up too. With each passing second Claire grew more disoriented and a little more terrified. She closed her eyes and counted, trying to control her breathing and her runaway panic.

Claire hadn't made it to fifteen when the forces acting on her disoriented body shifted. She was pressed against her restraints, as though the sphere wanted to launch her both forward and upward. She fought a very strong urge to vomit.

When the acceleration shifted Claire had lost her mental count. All her attention was focused on willing herself to stay in her seat; on willing her restraints to hold her safely inside the glass bubble. Any mental bandwidth she had left was focused on keeping her small breakfast in her stomach. She heard a grunt followed by a wet slap next to her in the dark. Tim didn't sound like he was doing so hot either.

Claire's first feeling of hope came as she saw a growing light up ahead. It was the first time in the last fifteen seconds Claire had anything available to process visually. She was glad the darkness was nearing an end, but horrified at how fast they were moving toward the light. She didn't have time to process this newest fear before the deceleration that was pressing her firmly against her seat belt increased its intensity.

The sphere came to an unceremonious stop in a dimly lit room. More of a closet than a room. Claire thought for a moment she might pass out. This must be how pilots feel when they're launched off the decks of aircraft carriers. She took a deep breath and was assaulted by an acidic aroma.

"Uggghhh. That was rough," Tim said next to her. "Any chance you have a napkin or tissue handy?" He sounded like he had just woken up after a bender the night before.

Claire realized the stench filling their bubble was Tim's vomit splattered on the glass, chunks sliding down the curvature in front of him. She turned away and tried not to breath. She was a sympathetic puker and needed to get out of this horrible roller coaster sooner rather than later.

Almost as soon as the thought crossed her mind, the restraints loosened and the disappearing door from earlier reappeared and hissed open. Claire unbuckled her restraints with perfect dexterity and instinctively evacuated the sphere as fast as possible. Once she was standing outside the motion sickness caught up with her. She put her hands on her knees and heaved the contents of her stomach onto the floor of the tiny room.

Claire was grateful when the heaving subsided. She felt moderately human again. She looked back into the bubble at Tim. He was slowly unbuckling his restraints, his face ashen. Claire moved back toward the bubble to try and assist him but he waved her away, unclasping the final restraint and stumbling drunkenly toward the opening.

Claire offered a hand to brace him while climbing out of the sphere.

He took it without making eye contact and gingerly made his way to stand next to Claire in the tiny closet that marked the end of their ride on the world's most hateful roller coaster.

"We have to get out of here," Tim declared. "Your puke is rancid."

"Mine?" Claire spun on him. "You stunk up that tiny death trap we were strapped into. I almost didn't make it to puke out here." Claire wanted to kick him in the shin. "You know what, let's figure out how to get out of here before you make me get sick again."

Claire fumbled around in the dimly lit room, looking for anything that might be a door, a latch, whatever it took to get a little distance from Tim and the putrid scent of recycled stomach bile.

Claire's first thought was to look for a biometric thumb pad. So far those seemed to unlock everything in the future. But all the thumb pads she'd seen up to now had at least a dim backlighting that made them easy to spot. There was nothing like that in this little closet. She started to run her hands over the walls, looking for anything that might be the trigger that opened the way out. She was fighting the re-emergence of claustrophobic panic.

Things got worse when the transport bubble suddenly hissed as the door on the front came shut. Moments later the odd glass spherical departed back into the dark tunnel. Claire silently hoped it was headed back down to pick up Team B, or if she was lucky Team D. He'd figure out how to get us out of this latest trap.

As Claire ran her hands along the wall in front of her, she counted silently to try and distract herself from her fear. Then, right about waist level, she felt a segment of the wall that was slightly elevated compared to the areas around it. She ran her hand across it a couple times and determined it was a rectangle no larger than the palm of her hand.

"I think I might have found something," she said to Tim without looking back at him. He was still leaning over with his hands on his knees, probably trying to keep from vomiting again. Claire didn't wait for Tim to respond. First she pressed her thumb on the raised area. When that did nothing she pressed into it, hoping it might be some sort of button.

The panel moved with moderate pressure from Claire's thumb, and as soon as it was flush with the rest of the wall, the perimeter of the area in front of her hissed and started to move. Claire was initially disoriented by the drastic increase in light. She squinted and tried to shade her eyes but the room was brighter from all directions. Once the wall panel slid away and her eyes adjusted to the light Claire stood dumbfounded at the inside of an immaculate office lined with book shelves.

CHAPTER TWENTY-THREE

Jon climbed out of the transport bubble right behind Denise. When the sphere had finally come to a stop, Jon and Denise had thrown off their restraints and nearly climbed over each other to escape the putrid odors that filled the tiny space. Jon didn't have any trouble with the high g-force trip out of the underground facility, but clearly some of the previous teams hadn't fared so well.

Denise momentarily doubled over right in front of him in the dim, rectangular closet where their roller coaster ride ended. Jon considered stopping next to her to ensure she was ok, but he quickly realized the small closet they were in smelled almost as bad as the transport cart. He rushed to the long wall opposite the spherical transport and tried to find a way out. Light leaked in below the wall so he felt confident it was a door of some kind.

He heard Denise heaving behind him as he felt along the wall for any sort of latch or panel that might grant him freedom from the acidic-dairy smell of the closet.

"Huuggghhh," Denise heaved again, this time followed by a wet splat that Jon heard right behind him. She'd done well on the wild ride up here, for an engineer. But the lack of relief when she stepped out into this tiny room had claimed her nonetheless. The former SEAL in Jon briefly considered giving her shit about it. Just as he was about to ask if she needed crackers or ginger ale, Jon found a raised section on the wall. He pressed against it and watched the wall in front of him hiss and move clear to reveal an adjacent study.

Jon stepped out into the study with urgency, mostly to get a break from the smell of multiple flavors of vomit. Once he'd taken a few breaths of clean air, he doubled back to collect Denise. She was a mess, still doubled over, now only dry heaving.

"Are you alright?" Jon asked rhetorically.

Denise stood upright and wiped spittle from her mouth. "I'm fine. I would've been ok if this room didn't smell like puke too. I wasn't expecting that."

"Ok, well buck up. I think I hear the others." Jon walked out into the study and turned a slow three-sixty, taking in his surroundings. He was standing in a slightly futuristic home office. There was a large walnut executive style desk in the middle of the room. The walls, with the exception of the false one they'd just stepped through, were lined with books of every type and genre. Everything from thriller novels to engineering texts lined the shelves. Jon looked at a few of the titles. The collection appeared to be designed to provide variety and combat boredom.

Satisfied that he'd seen everything the office had to offer Jon started toward the door. Denise closed the distance and stood shoulder to shoulder with him as he opened the large wooden door that marked the only non-secret exit from the study.

As soon as Jon pushed the door open, he and Denise were greeted by six other people in various states of shock and recovery from the eventful ride up to this point. The two travelers nearest the door spun around from their position facing the other four. All six now looked at Jon and Denise, and initially didn't say a word.

"We're okaaayyy," Denise said. "Why so many solemn faces? You guys worried we're going to judge the many flavors of vomit you left behind in our transport?" She smiled with narrow eyes in a way that made Jon nervous.

Jon instinctively shifted to mission commander mode. "What have you guys figured out about this place so far?"

No one responded for a few awkward seconds. Then the other ex-military guy in the group spoke up. "Not much so far. Most of these guys got sick on the way up here so I've been focused on getting fluids back in them and making sure no one was going to pass out. From the little bit of wandering around I've managed to do, I'd say we're in some sort of safe house in the desert."

Jon walked toward the only person in the group willing to say a word. As he stretched a hand out to greet what he assumed was a fellow former operator, he allowed his eyes to flick over to Claire. She stood at the far end of the open concept kitchen. She looked a little sunken around the eyes, like she was recovering from a little dehydration and a bad case of motion sickness.

The former soldier with a shaved head and stubble gotee stuck his hand out to meet Jon's and offered a firm handshake. "Michael Johnson," said the soldier.

"Jon Haynes. Where'd you serve?" Jon asked, trying to build a quick rapport.

"Afghanistan with the Green Berets mostly. I was originally with the third special forces group out of Fort Bragg. Spent my last couple years in some other interesting places with the SOG."

Jon tried to maintain a blank expression. He was looking to confirm that Michael Johnson was former special forces. He'd confirmed it easily enough. But then Johnson had felt the need to establish himself by bragging on his work on joint CIA efforts via the Special Operations Group. In Jon's field that was the equivalent of telling someone you just met that you used to be part of SEAL Team Six. Interesting.

Jon introduced himself with much less detail. "Cool. I was with SEAL Team Five in San Diego."

Jon eyed the rest of the group standing around in the large kitchen. He sensed they could all use a few more minutes to recover. Jon started opening cabinets and the commercial sized chill box that was posing as a refrigerator. He found a lot of non-perishables; mostly protein bars and canned goods - a lot of canned goods. The refrigerator was also well stocked with strange steel water bottles. Jon pulled out as many as he could hold and set them on the large island counter at the center of the room. Hopefully all the sea sick looking travelers standing around in the kitchen would make use of them and start to re-hydrate.

"Drink up guys'" Jon directed the group. "It'll help."

Jon didn't wait for them to respond. He made his way toward what he assumed was the front of the building. As he left the large kitchen-dining room area he walked down a short hallway that led into a large foyer. To his left was a staircase that wrapped its way up to a second story. To his right was a sitting room. It's walls were lined with couches and chairs. In the corner of the sitting room was a desk that was home to a very advanced looking computer terminal that was currently powered off.

Directly ahead was a large ornate wooden door. Jon's first instinct was to stay inside and explore the rest of the house to see if there were any supplies that might come in handy. But right next to the door was a large pedestal with the now familiar thumbprint biometric sensors mounted to the side. Jon walked up without hesitation and pressed his thumb to the pad.

The top of the pedestal turned translucent as a green backlighting appeared from within. A pleasant tone sounded and a holographic image was then projected above the pedestal at eye level. The Casimir Institute logo spun in the center of the image. Jon read the bold text displayed in front of the logo, and for the first time was certain he was in the future: WELCOME TO 2050, JON HAYNES. Just below the greeting, smaller subtext read MEMBER OF TRIP T31723D.

The pleasant elevator music played for the next few seconds before the holo-projection shifted to display a count down timer and text indicating an orientation video was about to begin.

Jon was mesmerized by the depth of the holographic display and didn't realize that a few other travelers had heard the holo pedestal come to life and had walked into the foyer behind him to see what was going on.

Before Jon had a chance to turn around and determine who was behind him, a computer rendered man who looked to be in his early thirties materialized on the holo screen. Jon waited for the next part of the video.

"Hello Jon, my name is Alistair," announced the projected hologram in what Jon pegged as an Australian accent. "Who else do we have in the room?" As the holo projection asked the question it leaned to it's right, Jon's left, as though it was trying to see who else was in the room behind him.

"Umm..." The interactive man in the holo threw Jon off guard. He awkwardly stepped to the side to let the holo see the people in the foyer behind him. Jon's eyes darted between the holo pedestal and the rest of the people in the room. "Everyone, umm, introduce yourselves I guess."

Michael and Denise chimed in first, each exchanging awkward greetings with the projection. Each person attempted to introduce themselves, but it was clear Alistair already knew them all. For Alistair, the social exchange was a programmed formality. For the travelers in the room it was an awkward interaction with something un-human but much more than simple machine.

Reclaiming his awareness of his surroundings, Jon noticed Claire and Tim had made their way into the foyer too. Both followed suit and introduced themselves to Alistair.

"Hello Alistair, my name is Claire Keen."

"I'm aware Ms. Keen. Welcome." The projection of Alistair gave a welcome nod.

Jon watched as Claire nervously fidgeted with a small silver bracelet on her right wrist. He watched her hoping to make eye contact in a way that didn't draw the attention of the others.

It worked. Jon smiled at Claire and they both slowly moved toward each other around the other three that were huddling closer to the pedestal. By the time Jon stood next to Claire, Denise had taken up position right in front of the pedestal.

"Alistair, what is this place? What are you?" Denise asked. Jon wasn't paying attention to the response, if any from Alistair. As soon as Jon and Claire stood shoulder to shoulder, she leaned into him just slightly. Jon could feel her nervous tension. Instinctively, he put his right arm around her opposite shoulder. Claire responded with a deep breath and pressed into him a little tighter. Jon felt her relax under his arm, tension dissipating slightly. Jon smiled involuntarily, pleased that his touch made her feel safer. The moment was interrupted.

"Mr. Haynes? Mr. Haynes?" Jon looked up to see Alistair trying to see past Denise and get his attention.

Before he responded and broke contact with Claire he looked down to see that her face looked a little less gray than when he'd seen her in the kitchen. Her eyes, looking up at him now, were no longer sunken. Hopefully it was due to the water Jon had provided in the steel bottle she held in her hand. Jon felt pride swelling over his apprehension. A sizable portion of this Casimir group was inclined to follow him. And his inclination was to help them and figure out what to do next. Even better, he'd just confirmed he could non-verbally communicate with Claire to infuse her with strength and confidence. She trusted him.

Jon rubbed her arm firmly one last time before sliding away to make his way through the huddled travelers. A few seconds later he stood in front of Alistair with Denise on his right and Michael Johnson on his left. Claire and Tim presumably stood right behind them.

Alistair began speaking before Jon could acknowledge. "Where did you go Mr. Haynes? You triggered my introductory sequence and then rudely departed."

Jon was momentarily taken back. He was talking with a holographic computer persona with a sense of privilege.

"I apologize," Jon replied, selecting the humble approach. "This is all a bit much."

Denise chimed in, irritation toward Jon, Alistair, or both, coating her words. "I tried to ask him what he is and where we are. He said that he could only take questions from the 'primary user.'"

Jon glanced at Denise to see her arms crossed tightly across her chest. She stared at Alistair and tapped her foot. She was probably more irritated with the hologram than with Jon. It bothered Jon that he cared who or what Denise was mad at.

"Alistair, what is this place and what are you?" Jon asked gently.

"This is Hendrick House, and I am the host. If you'd like, I can provide you with a short orientation." Alistair's response seemed less sentient than their earlier interactions. As though Jon had triggered a recorded response.

"Yes, that would be great," Jon responded, oddly conscious of his manners with the hologram computer.

"Alright then. Let's begin." As Alistair said this, his image began to fade from the holo. It was quickly replaced by a computer generated image of a large residence in the desert.

The perspective of the image and it's holographic depth made it appear they were floating over the front yard, looking down at the front of the house from about eighty feet in the air. The image slowly rotated. In front was a large circular driveway with four modern-looking, identical luxury sedans lining the driveway. They reminded Jon of the Tesla Model S that was quite popular amongst wealthy Southern Californians in 2023. The house itself was set in a large shallow V-shape. The large front door sat in the apex of the V. The grounds around the house were well manicured with rock beds and a variety of cactus and desert flowers. As the image continued to rotate, Jon saw similar landscaping in the back of the house, coupled with a large portico that ran the length of the back of the V. From the exterior view, the house had all the trappings of a wealthy person's desert getaway. Beyond the grounds of the rear of the house was an endless field of solar panels.

The image rotated again, this time to directly over the house looking straight down at the roof. The roof evaporated from view to reveal a floor plan-type view of the second floor. Alistair resumed his narration.

"This residence was built as a base of operations, or safe house, for Casimir employees such as yourselves. The upper floor contains eight bedrooms, each appointed with the best accommodations available at the present time, and a few pieces of secure communications equipment that you won't find readily available elsewhere."

Jon leaned in closer to the holo projection, taking in the incredible detail. It wasn't like anything he'd seen in 2023. The image had depth and realism, like it was a realtime overhead image of the upstairs of the house. Four bedrooms (more like hotel suites) lined each leg of the V-shape of the house. In the center was a landing area and stairs that curled down to the ground floor. Jon realized the other four travelers bunched around him were doing the same thing. Denise even reached out to the touch the hologram, only to see her hand pass through it and the image shift.

"The lower floor contains a large kitchen and dining area as well as the study that disguises your access point. The other wing of the first floor contains a large common room. The center contains the foyer you are standing in now."

Denise let out a quiet gasp. "That's us…right now." She stepped back and looked up at the ceiling above. Jon saw a small figure in the holo projection do the same thing. Then he counted the five of them, in the projection, huddled around the pedestal. He counted the other three still lingering in the kitchen/dining area. The perspective reminded Jon of watching real time video from a high altitude, high resolution camera on board a UAV. The sort of thing, in a past life, that would be used to track a particularly valuable terrorist moving through a crowded urban area. If you zoomed in you could probably count the hairs on his head.

"Is this a live overhead image Alistair? How is that possible?" Jon asked.

Alistair's image re-appeared, smaller, in the corner of the projection, the house still occupying the rest of the holographic viewing area.

"It's not an image per se Jon. It's my real time rendering of the house. I'm fully integrated into the home and am updating its conditions in real time."

Jon had more questions but his mouth hung open. He looked around the foyer and into the sitting room he could see to his right.

"Can we access your information from anywhere in the house?" The question didn't entirely make sense but Jon suddenly had the urge to explore the house further, away from his huddled position around the pedestal. He wanted to maintain the ability to ask the intelligent host questions. He didn't want to 'log off' yet.

Alistair responded. "You may access me anywhere in the house Jon. Any other authorized user, once logged in, can do the same."

Denise quickly pressed her thumb to the biometric pad on the pedestal.

WELCOME TO 2050, DENISE STEINFELD flashed across the screen. The others followed suit as Jon stepped back from the crowd to return to the kitchen area. He went back to one of the cabinets he'd opened earlier and pulled out a protein bar. As he tore open the package he addressed the remaining three travelers that seemed to be having a little tougher time recovering from the trip up from the underground facility.

"Are you guys doing okay?" Jon asked the two women and one man left lingering in the kitchen. They had all founds seat and appeared to be in various stages of nervousness or sea sickness. "I'm Jon. Are you guys doing all right?" Jon recognized the man as Paul Neidmeyer, one of the few who'd asked questions in the ready room before they were shot forward in time. He'd seen the two women before but had no idea who they were. They also didn't seem too intent on offering.

"A little cold water and one of these protein bars will help if you're still feeling nauseas. Out in the front foyer there's a console you'll want to log into once you're feeling better."

The athletic black woman, Jon was pretty sure her name was Sarah, seemed to rally to the call of food and water. She went to the same cabinet Jon had been digging around in and retrieved a protein bar. With a mouthful of protein she decided to introduce herself to Jon.

"I'm Sarah. Sorry for the cold introduction before." She shook Jon's hand. Jon saw intelligence in her eyes but it was crowded out by a nervous uncertainty. She glanced down at her feet after briefly making eye contact. "I'm not a fan of roller coasters and that entire trip left me feeling lousy. Can you show me this console? My partners' an ass and he left me sitting here as soon as more interesting things started happening."

At that remark, Jon recalled that she'd been paired up with the shaved-headed tough guy Mike Johnson. No surprise that he left his partner as soon as opportunity presented itself.

Jon walked with Sarah to the console to find that Tim was the only one left standing near the pedestal and had just finished logging in with his thumbprint. The others had made their way into the large sitting room and were staring at a holographic screen projected onto the wall.

"Jon, come here, hurry," Claire called, beckoning him over to the sitting room. "Alistair just said he had more 'introductory material' to show us. Then this hologram screen popped up along the wall."

Jon abandoned his advisory role to Sarah, assuming she'd figure it out on her own. He made his way to the sitting room and found himself standing between Claire and Denise, as the rendering of Alistair appeared in the frame.

"Hello all," Alistair said in his distinct accent. "I'm pleased that you're finding your way around Hendrick House, but you really should get on your way soon. My understanding is that your current visit is introductory in nature and rather short in duration."

A cabinet opened to the right of the holo display. From Jon's vantage he couldn't tell what was inside.

Alistair provided the answer. "Here to my left, your right, are communications handhelds. One for each of you. I wouldn't recommend leaving this house without them."

All six of the travelers now standing in the sitting room started toward the drawer that had extended from the open cabinet. Just as Alistair had said, the drawer contained eight smartphone-like devices.

As the six stood in a crescent in front of the drawer Denise asked the obvious question. "Does it matter who takes which set? Are they unique to an individual?"

"They are not," Alistair replied. "Once you login in to one of them, the Pinnacle operating system will load your unique data onto the devices and they'll be ready for use. Data transfer rates are much higher than you're probably familiar with."

Alistair gave a slight wink and smile with his last remark. Jon wondered if that was a programmed expression or if the artificial intelligence of this house had the ability to feel and express complex emotions.

Jon hurriedly powered on the handset. As it powered up the handset displayed a cubical 'P' in the center. Once the startup sequence completed the handheld displayed a simple message: 'press right thumb to screen to authenticate.' Jon complied without hesitation.

Once he'd done this the handheld came to life. The touchscreen handheld looked a lot like a 2023 smartphone, with a much sharper and deeper display. Before Jon could explore the futuristic device further, Alistair started talking to them from the wall display again.

"Now that you are all getting acquainted with your handhelds, it's time to discuss transportation. Outside there are four sedans, one for each team. In order to make best use of your time here, I'd encourage you to depart now. Select the first option listed in the in-dash navigation and you'll find your way to your accommodations for the night. I'll see you back here tomorrow no later than zero nine hundred."

Jon slid the handheld into his pocket and looked around. The other five travelers were in varying states of awe at the advanced technology that surrounded them and the pieces they held in their hands. No one made a move toward the doors. Silently hoping that the assigned teams were more flexible now, Jon walked over to Claire and took her by the hand. Without drawing attention from the others, particularly Denise, Jon walked to the front door of the desert mansion, pulling Claire along with him.

"Jon, slow down. What's the rush?" Claire asked, breaking the silence. "I have to grab Tim before I can leave."

Jon followed Claire's gaze back toward the sitting room and saw that both Tim and Denise now noticed Jon and Claire's attempt at departure. Tim and Denise independently stowed their handhelds and started toward the foyer. Jon silently winced at his failed attempt to escape with Claire.

The four of them headed out the front door, led by Jon, to examine their transportation. Claire broke from the group and headed toward the first sedan in the line of cars in the driveway. "C'mon Tim. I'm assuming the first one is ours. Team A!" Claire walked around to the driver side then searched awkwardly for the door handle. Jon watched for a moment before Denise hooked his arm and drug him toward the last car in the static procession.

"She's probably right," said Denise. "It would make sense if they lined the cars up, Team A, B, C, then D."

Jon walked with Denise to the last car in the row. She took him to the driver's side door and stopped, as if waiting for him to open the door for her. Jon glanced back to his right, toward the front of the line of sedans, just in time to see Claire duck into her vehicle with TIm. She hadn't even looked back at him.

While Jon had been watching Claire, Denise had figured out how to open the car door. It swung open in an upward arc like a high end sports car from 2023. Denise squeezed Jon's arm affectionately and then bent down to take her seat. As she sat, Jon instinctively put his hand on the door to push it shut. As soon as he touched it, the door began moving to close on its own. As Jon walked around the front of the car in route to the driver's side door, Claire and Tim's car pulled away, moving down the desert driveway toward the mostly abandoned road a few hundred yards away.

Jon put his left hand near where a car door handle would normally be found on the cars of 2023. There was nothing there. But as he looked down awkwardly at the featureless car door, a key symbol appeared on the screen of his handheld and the door started to lift open. Jon ducked quickly into his seat, anxious to keep up with Claire and Tim.

He reached up to shut the door but it was already on its way closed. Then Jon looked around the oddly empty dash board area. From outside the car had seemed modern. Inside it looked futuristic. There were no gauges inlaid in the dash. Jon saw only one heads up display near the center, and given the small biometric thumb pad right below the screen, it was probably the primary interface for operating the car.

The steering wheel and pedals were also strange. They were present but recessed into the dash and floor respectively. Maybe they pop out when you start the car, Jon thought. He reached over and pressed his thumb to the pad below the heads up display. The screen lit up and various gauges were projected onto the bottom section of the car's windshield. Nothing happened with the steering wheel and pedals; they remained in their odd stowed position.

A three dimensional rendering of Alistair was now standing about four inches tall on the dash directly above the heads up display.

"Hello Jon. Please enter a destination on the screen below." Alistair gestured down to the heads up display as though he was aware he was standing over it. "You can choose a pre-programmed destination or enter one manually."

As Alistair gave these instructions the heads up display changed to show two pre-programmed destinations: The Manchester Grand Hyatt - San Diego, and Hendrick House. Below the short list was a manual data entry field. Jon recalled the instructions from Kristen Sprague back at the ready room and tapped the Manchester Grand Hyatt option.

"Fantastic," said Alistair. "Please fasten your seatbelts and we'll depart momentarily. In the event of an emergency, you can take control of the vehicle by pulling the red lever on the left hand side of your seat."

Jon looked down near his left leg and located the lever.

"Cool. Self-driving cars!" Denise squealed.

"Yeah, self-driving cars," Jon replied with nervous sarcasm.

CHAPTER TWENTY-FOUR

Claire was excited, if a little nervous, as the car pulled out of the driveway onto the main desert road…with no one driving. She glanced over at Tim who sat in the driver's seat wringing his hands together and squirming. He looked as if he was about to reach out and try to pull the recessed steering wheel from the dash.

Alistair's 3-D holographic image had just finished telling them how to take control of the car in the event of an emergency when he seemed to sense Tim's growing unease. "Try not to worry Tim; self-driving car's are common place in 2050 and have a much better safety track record than automobiles did in the early 2020s. In fact, since the introduction of the Pinnacle operating system to automobiles, the only accidents that have occurred were when human drivers decided to take control of the vehicle."

Alistair smiled. "Alright. The drive from here is about forty five minutes. I have a video that should bring you up to speed on what has changed since 2023."

As Alistair finished his brief introduction his hologram winked out and the sedan's windshield turned an opaque black, completely obscuring Claire's view of the road ahead.

"Holy Shit!" Tim exclaimed, instinctively grabbing again for the wheel in the dash and stomping his right foot on the nonexistent brake pedal.

Claire heard Alistair's voice over the speakers as the windshield shifted colors again and rolled an introductory scene.

"Tim, if you're concerned with your view being obscured I can display the view ahead of the vehicle on the dash in front of you."

"Um, yeah, ok," Tim responded with hesitation. As he did Claire watched a holo appear in front of the steering wheel recess.

The video introduction continued, but Claire was more intrigued by the hologram floating in front of Tim. When she looked at it from the passenger seat, she didn't see directly in front of the vehicle, but rather the perspective toward the opposite side of the road that she'd expect to see if she sat in the passenger seat and looked out through the driver's side of of a normal windshield. She leaned over, nearly putting her head on Tim's shoulder, and gasped as the perspective shifted until she could see the road in front of the vehicle. Claire was dumbfounded at the hologram that seemed to understand how to display perspective based on the location of the viewer. Before she could contemplate it further, or put together a question for Alistair, he began narrating the video displayed on the windshield.

"A lot has happened since 2023. The geopolitical landscape you remember has completely changed.

"Cas Computing, the other half, if you will, of the Casimir Institute, emerged as a powerhouse in the network and computing industry by the end of the 2020s. In your time, commentators were beginning to challenge Moore's Law and whether computing power could continue to grow exponentially as it had since the introduction of the computer over fifty years ago. In coordination with DARPA, Cas Computing built Ne Plus Ultra, a supercomputer that heralded a leap forward in computing power and efficiency that was unheard of. Initially, the Department of Defense closely guarded the capability. Some estimate it was online for as many as five years before information was released to the public. This supercomputer may have already been operational in 2023, but still highly classified."

The windshield turned 3-D movie screen showed an overhead image of a beautiful riverside campus. Claire recognized it but couldn't quite place it. Alistair continued as they 'flew' around the on screen campus.

"Ne Plus Ultra put previous record-breaking super computers to shame. It had just short of 2 exaflops of processing power. More amazing, unlike the previous record holder Summit, also built by the US government in cooperation with a computing company, Ne Plus Ultra needed less than 1,000 square feet of floor space, and pulled just over 1 Megawatt to operate at full capacity. By comparison, Summit, housed in the building next door at Oakridge National Laboratory, used about 13 Megawatts and took up an entire factory floor - 5,600 square feet.

"When Ne Plus Ultra was unveiled to the world, the creators from

Cas Computing indicated the machine was not always this fast or efficient. The Casimir chips gave it computing power beyond what had been available to previous generations of supercomputers, but the machine learning was the true source of the black swan-like leap forward. The algorithm, nicknamed Pinnacle, communicated with its creators on how best to optimize its hardware. It wrote its own software to redirect data and processes in order to maximize its potential. Pinnacle learned to optimize the zero point energy produced by the Casimir chips in order to realize gains beyond what the individual chips could provide and beyond what human engineers had been able to design.

"As this was happening, and the tech world's collective jaws hung open, Cas was negotiating with the Defense Department to move into commercial production on a smaller version of the Casimir Chip-based supercomputer that ran on a light version of the Pinnacle machine learning concept.

"In 2026 the first commercially available supercomputers were sold. Within two years companies like Apple, IBM, Dell, Microsoft and Google were racing to catch up and risked a complete loss of their market share. Cas Computing single-handedly revolutionized business and home computing. Even worse for the former tech giants, Cas Computing was making the software industry irrelevant. The Pinnacle operating system was capable of coding and debugging software with minimal help from its human user. The average computer user now needed no knowledge of computer science or coding languages. The user could tell his personal home supercomputer what he needed, and the Pinnacle algorithm would communicate with 'itself' on the web, find similar open source code, and use those code blocks to build whatever the user required."

As Alistair narrated, the windshield hologram shifted through images of massive supercomputers of old and press conferences where middle aged white men shook hands and gave smiling speeches. Then it showed big box stores filled with Pinnacle Computers with a Cas Computing logo stamped on the box. Then massive lines at the checkout, almost every cart holding one of the oversized computer boxes. Next, longer lines outside the stores clamoring to get inside and presumably buy their own Pinnacle. Claire felt the car accelerate. They were probably getting on the interstate. But she didn't care. Alistair's presentation had her full attention.

Alistair continued. "The Pinnacle cloud grew bigger and stronger.

As household use exploded so did the cloud repository of Pinnacle knowledge. As the world watched Pinnacle computers spread through the developed world like a prosperity pandemic, the Defense Department recognized a different opportunity. Ne Plus Ultra was orders of magnitude more capable than anything the world had seen before. As Pinnacle computers propagated into homes and businesses, Ne Plus Ultra became a sort of god machine that lorded over the emerging network. It was the leader of the new intelligent machine learning cloud.

"The Defense Department and the CIA's Special Activities Division paid an undisclosed, but sizable sum, to Cas Computing to backup the full repository of Pinnacle learning to standalone storage within the Oakridge Facility that housed the computer. They then paid Cas a large sum to pull the plug on Ne Plus Ultra with no promise that it would ever be reconnected. Ne Plus Ultra was physically disconnected from the rest of the world but still very much operational. And just to be sure, it was wrapped in a giant faraday cage.

"The project was codenamed Golden Javelin. The premise was simple. Could the world's fastest, smartest brain develop and implement a course of action that would bring about the end of great power competition? An end to the potential for major power competition and global war?"

Alistair filled the windshield with rendered images of world leaders shaking hands and nuclear silos emptied and decommissioned.

"Initially the computer had more questions than answers. After twelve months and no significant progress the simple question was posed to Ne Plus Ultra, now commonly referred to as NPU. What information do you require to provide a response to the original query? The answer that came back was simple: 'Everything you know. Not just what you're willing to tell me.' A couple months later the Golden Javelin team received presidential authorization to upload all available classified intelligence, net assessments, war game results, et cetera. Basically any data the United States government had on other nations, their centers of gravity, strengths and weaknesses, military might, both in numbers and capability, political vulnerabilities, even personality profiles on key leaders.

"Once all this data, much of it highly classified, was assembled in one place, it became easier to get into Fort Knox than Oakridge National Laboratory. A special military detachment was formed to provide security for the building that housed NPU. But the results were phenomenal and almost immediate. So phenomenal in fact, that despite all the sensitive information now accessible to NPU, it was reconnected to the outside world only two months later, eighteen months after the Golden Javelin project began.

"There were a few safeguards in place, to give the government bureaucrats confidence that their precious classified information would be protected. But even those safeguards were dependent on a certain level of trust that NPU would keep the data segregated - walled off from the prying eyes of the outside world. This decision alone represented significant trust in NPU from the military and intelligence communities. But it was determined that the proverbial juice was worth the squeeze."

Alistair showed archive footage in the windshield hologram first of a man in the Oval Office signing a document, then cut to an image of a half dozen men in a high-tech warehouse toasting with champagne flutes as one man pressed an over-sized cartoonish red EXECUTE button on a computer terminal.

"In a matter of minutes after Golden Javelin was set in motion, NPU disassembled the technological aspects of the Great Firewall in China. Even more impressive, it did it without the Chinese government noticing. NPU created an entire virtual world that played out on the monitoring terminals of the Chinese National Police and the Public Security Bureau. It was a remarkable plan. The veil of the Golden Shield Project was lifted from the Chinese public, while the government was thrust under a virtual veil created by NAU-generated synthetic Chinese internet activity. Chinese officials thought they were watching a continuation of the status quo - near total control of Chinese internet access, monitoring and surveillance of its citizens, and most important to party officials, protectionism of Chinese online trade. But in fact, the internet had gone completely open throughout the country.

"Word spread quickly via Chinese social media sites and word of mouth. The secret couldn't be kept from the Chinese government and monitoring entities forever. But the illusion only needed to work long enough for a spark to be lit amongst the billion strong Chinese populace."

The car windshield showed images of Chinese internet cafes bursting with users anxious to confirm the rumors for themselves.

"The average middle class Chinese citizen already suspected they were monitored, and self-censored most of their internet activity as a result. As word of the hole in the Great Firewall spread like an epidemic, self-censorship and restrained online speech ended seemingly overnight. Message boards, social media sites, and previously blocked online businesses saw a massive spike in Chinese traffic. The rest of the world quickly took notice of the change in China. Within two weeks media outlets throughout the world were reporting the massive breach."

Images of news anchors and commentators flashed across the windshield holo. Headlines like "The End of Internet Censorship in China," "One Billion New Online Customers," and "Breach of the Great Firewall" danced across the bottom of the holo as excited American and European news contributors tried to predict the outcome of these changes on everything from Chinese internal politics, the American stock market, and global trade, to the potential growth in the number of Netflix users.

Alistair's tone turned ominous. "Once international media attention arrived, the Chinese government took notice. When they couldn't see evidence of the change the rest of the world was talking about, they panicked. Senior party leaders ordered fiber optic connections in three key locations to be severed. In theory this was China's internet kill switch. The internet inside China would remain operational while the physical connection to the United States and Europe removed China from the global internet. Instead, the newly free internet in China became significantly more congested. There were still connections to the rest of the world, but the fiber the government had severed knocked the speed down significantly. The people rightly assumed the government was attempting to cut off their new found freedom and opportunity. The spark turned into a flame."

The hologram previously displayed on the windshield morphed into a fully immersive three hundred and sixty degree panorama in the car. Claire felt as if she was sitting in the middle of the Chinese government's compound, watching as the people closed ranks around her.

"Within a week, the world watched via Facebook Live as Chinese young adults marched on Tianamen Square, just as they had done in 1989. Only this time, when party leaders ordered the military to step in to quell the uprising, military leaders refused. On June 4th, 2029, forty years to the day after the Tianamen Square massacre, the military marched, with hundreds of thousands of civilians at their backs, into the Zhongnanhai complex in Beijing to remove the Communist Party from power. The Central Military Commission, usually chaired by the Communist Party Premier, was absolved, and the military declared that open elections would occur. First for the National People's Congress, then for a new President of China.

"One year after the toppling of the Communist Party of China, on June 4th 2030, free elections were held in China under a provisional constitution, and the first multi-party system of governance was established. Shortly thereafter, a trade and mutual defense alliance was penned with the United States, Japan and the Republic of Korea to ensure peace and stability in the Western Pacific. With the blanket of protection provided by Communist China removed, the North Korean government collapsed shortly thereafter. China, South Korea, and the United States were there to clean up the pieces together and the Korean Peninsula was reunified in 2032."

As Alistair narrated, the three hundred and sixty degree hologram rolled through images of Chinese citizens at the ballot box, followed by heads of state signing documents in an ornate room with media all around them. Claire felt like she was sitting in the middle of the media gallery.

"When the dust settled, focus amongst the media and historians shifted to understanding how this great change came about in such a short period. It wasn't long until investigative journalist Steven Goodard had put together all the pieces, identifying NPU as the key to knocking down the Great Firewall and triggering the events that followed. For the most part, the world celebrated the change. But Goodard's story contained more. It detailed the deliberate creation of Project Javelin. It detailed the special military detachment created to protect the data housed within NPU. Worse, it detailed the deliberate nature with which the United States government used NPU to undermine the Chinese Communist Party. It also revealed that the outcome of Project Javelin was exactly what NPU had predicted. There was no outcry from the new Chinese government. They'd sought this type of change unsuccessfully for decades. But the rest of the world was outraged. How else was the United States using this capability? What other nations, corporations, or groups was the United States targeting with this super machine?"

As Alistair continued a newspaper floated in the hologram. The giant headline read NE PLUS ULTRA, THE GOD MACHINE. The subtitle read 'How the US Government and Cas Computing Changed the World.'

"The pressure from the international community to cede control of the colloquial god machine was immense. Cas Computing started lobbying to make access to the machine internationally available - for the right price. The US military was strongly opposed, uncertain they could purge all the state secrets that had been catalogued for Project Javelin. But opposite the military and intelligence community, a significant portion of the U.S. population, as well as countless allies, argued that NPU could do more to protect the U.S. and other nations if the machine's capabilities were available to both governments and public interest groups. Ultimately, US politicians wilted under intense public and international pressure.

"In 2035, after a transition period, during which classified information was purged from Ne Plus Ultra, Cas Computing opened the doors to the super machine, fully integrating it with the Pinnacle cloud and allowing anyone with sufficient resources to request predictive simulation services from NPU. At the same time, Cas Computing changed its name to Pinnacle Computing, and continues to operate under that name today."

Claire felt the car decelerate and start to turn as if approaching a curve in a windy road. The hologram faded from the windows and Claire's breath caught in her throat. The car was flying down a highway exit ramp, hurtling toward a crowded urban area ahead. Claire felt the deceleration as she was pressed into her seat belt but was disoriented by the way the car in front of them seemed to decelerate at an identical rate, their bumpers only inches apart. She glanced out the rear windshield and saw an even scarier site behind her. A delivery truck of some sort filled her field of view. Worse, there didn't appear to be a passenger compartment in the truck. No driver. Just a giant automated box with an engine, presumably filled with groceries or other consumer goods, hurtling toward the urban area right behind Claire and Tim's ride.

"My god, this feels like a death trap." Claire looked over at Tim hoping for reassurance.

Tim didn't respond. His face had taken on a sickly grey color and she could see an infant sweat breaking out on his forehead. The knuckles on his right hand, which held tightly to his seat, were white.

"Welcome to San Diego and the year 2050. Remember, all cars are self-driving now and have been for some time. Any vehicle on the road is required to be connected to the Pinnacle cloud, ensuring they think and behave as though they are all part of the same transportation machine. Closer distances between vehicles really helps cut down on traffic congestion." Alistair seemed to sense the trepidation of his passengers. His tone was soothing and reassuring.

Claire relaxed, a little.

Alistair continued. "Shortly we'll arrive at the Manchester Grand Hyatt. One last thing before I drop you off. Remember earlier when I said that the geopolitical landscape has completely changed since 2023?"

"Yeah, the fall of the Chinese Communist Party seems like a pretty big change," Claire responded. She immediately felt embarrassed having replied to a rhetorical question from a computer. It just seemed so real.

"Well the bigger changes have come over the last fifteen years. Since Pinnacle made NPU available to the world, their profits have exploded. They are the most valuable company in the history of the world. Their net assets and annual revenue is orders of magnitude greater than that of the corporate titans of your time. But even more significant, they have influence that dwarfs any nation or political party. The world's problems come to the doorstep of Pinnacle. Governments, companies, and public interest organizations pay a substantial fee to have NPU solve these problems. With each request comes troves of information that feeds into the accuracy of the computations and simulations. With each solution, the Pinnacle cloud grows wiser in its own way. It is a benevolent machine, consistently delivering solutions that have made the world better and stronger. It creates far more winners than losers. But it has also become the de facto gatekeeper to international relations, conflict and even domestic policy within all nations that choose to make use of its capability. Nothing significant happens anymore that the Pinnacle cloud isn't aware of. And very little of significance changes without NPU and the Pinnacle cloud dictating how the change should occur."

As they made their way through downtown San Diego of the future, Claire was developing a crick in her neck. Many of the buildings she'd seen in her short time in San Diego back in 2023 still stood, and looked very much the same. But the skyline was now cluttered with additional skyscrapers twice as tall. At street level Claire noticed that probably half the vehicles she saw were like the delivery truck she'd seen on the offramp. No driver present at all. She saw driverless pizza delivery cars, large driverless tractor trailers, and even public transportation busses, filled with passengers, but with no one at the wheel. The speed at which everything moved in this crowded urban era was dizzying. And yet everything moved in such harmony, so in sync with other nearby machines, that Claire felt her trepidation receding and her confidence in the machines already growing. The algorithms behind this level of synchronization must be truly amazing.

The car pulled under a portico at their hotel and came to a stop. "I'll have the car back here to pick you up tomorrow at exactly eight o'clock so you're on time for the return trip. If you need the car at any point today or this evening, just ask for it via the personal assistant application on your handheld."

The doors opened and Claire and Tim both climbed out of the car with their overnight bags and handhelds. Claire started toward the doors to the hotel then glanced back to make sure Tim followed. He walked like a baby giraffe, on wobbly legs with the cold sweat from the car ride evident around his collar. Claire walked back to him, hooked her arm in his and drug him toward the doors.

"Slow down. I'm still a little woozy from that insane drive," Tim said glancing at Claire with something resembling resent.

Claire briefly thought about how quickly things had changed. When they'd first left the sphere Claire couldn't get Tim to slow down despite her pleas. Now she was the one dragging him along, anxious to see more. She briefly considered needling Tim about their sudden role reversal but decided against it.

"Sorry, I'm…um…excited," Claire said in response.

She was excited. How could she not be. Intelligent machine learning ran the world now.

CHAPTER TWENTY-FIVE

Jon and Denise pulled up in front of the Manchester Grand Hyatt as Alistair's presentation concluded. Jon was floored. Somehow over the last twenty five years, the United States had taken down their greatest peer competitor and then relinquished all the real power to a giant tech company. It didn't make any sense.

Driverless cars however, that made a ton of sense. Jon couldn't count the number of times some jackass had almost killed him or themselves on the road. Watching the busy San Diego streets move traffic quickly under the watchful eye of some super robot computer was a little unnerving, but Jon couldn't dispute that traffic jams were basically a thing of the past. And just think how much you could get done during a commute that wasn't consumed by gas, brake, honk.

As soon as Jon was out of the car and fully upright, his new shadow, Denise Steinfeld, was right on his arm. She seemed to revel in getting close to him, pressing her body into him. She knew he was unavailable and wasn't interested. It didn't stop her from trying to trigger every natural male instinct; instincts she'd clearly manipulated in other men before Jon Haynes. She had knowledge of her power and was intent on using it.

As Jon and Denise walked into the lobby of the Manchester Grand Hyatt, Jon felt like he was in a dream. He'd seen this hotel before. But he'd seen the version that existed almost thirty years earlier during a Navy SEAL Foundation event. The version he saw now was out of this world. Holograms were interspersed throughout the lobby. At the checkin counter it wasn't clear who was real and who was a helpful digital projection. Advertisements littered the space. Everything from spa treatments, to whale watching, and exotic car rentals were offered by people that seemed real, but that you could walk right through. Jon was approaching sensory overload. Denise on the other hand, was giddy, yanking at his arm and using the excitement of each new discovery as an excuse to press into him. Jon tried unsuccessfully to ignore it.

As they walked toward the check in desk, Jon saw a feature ad playing from a holographic projector in the center of the lobby. The projection was at least two stories tall and designed to get everyone's attention. Jon involuntarily stopped and stared. Denise followed suit.

An attractive red head stood towering over the lobby and asked a simple question: "Have you ever dreamed of being able to browse the web, to access the greatest compilation of information in world history, to pay your bills or to call home, all without lifting a finger? If you have, your dream has arrived."

The holographic woman was perfectly proportioned, and had a very attractive Australian accent. Jon was drawn to the image and her voice almost as much as he was intrigued by what she was offering.

"A Pinnacle implant offers every user the ability to be connected to the Pinnacle cloud all the time. Better yet, due to the neural mapping provided by Ne Plus Ultra, this connectivity has incredible functionality. With your Pinnacle implant, you'll be able to browse the web without the click of a mouse. Call up your browser with a thought, think of what you're looking for, and display it any way you can imagine. As a projection on a nearby wall, as a holo screen in the palm of your hand, or as your entire field of vision."

The hologram acted out what she described, holding a projection of a banking website in the palm of her hand, then displaying a recipe on the wall of a kitchen that materialized around her. A sort of holographic picture in picture appeared next to the woman. Jon was entranced as her eyes darted back and forth, as if reading but looking at nothing. The small picture nearby showed a basic web email interface. Her fingers twitched by her sides as she typed a response to an email that Jon quickly realized was projected in her mind as though she was seeing it throughout her field of vision.

The holographic infomercial continued. "Pinnacle implants are installed via precision robotics surgery, a pain-free outpatient process that can be completed in a little over two hours under very mild sedation. Pre-orders are being accepted now and implants will be available for install this November, making it a must have for this holiday season."

The hologram shifted to show the woman logging on to the Pinnacle cloud store and clicking a 'Pre-Order Now' link. Then she smiled seductively.

"Join me, in the future of the Pinnacle cloud."

"Cool!" Denise squealed, snapping Jon out of his focus on the massive holographic presentation.

"Yeah, pretty crazy," Jon replied with a hint of irritation.

"Let's go check in," Denise said, tugging Jon's arm in the direction of the counter at the head of the lobby.

Jon complied, following her toward the counter, one eye still on the massive hologram as it winked away from the attractive sales woman to a spinning globe that signaled a summary of the daily news was about to begin.

When they reached the counter Jon and Denise both noticed the subtle translucence of the brunette check in clerk - a holographic projection. "How's this gonna work?" Jon asked rhetorically to no one in particular.

Denise responded, "Be a good sport Johnny boy. I'm sure they know what they're doing."

"Welcome to the Manchester Grand Hyatt," the holo-clerk said. "Checking in?"

"Um, yeah," Jon replied awkwardly, not sure the protocol of talking to an automated projection of a person.

"If you have a reservation, please swipe your handheld over the screen in front of you," said the clerk.

Jon looked down in the direction she'd gestured. A moment ago he was certain the counter was nothing but high end grey slate. Now a recessed screen displaying the hotel logo and large text - WELCOME TO THE MANCHESTER GRAND HYATT SAN DIEGO - stared up at him from the counter. Jon retrieved his handled from his pocket and held it awkwardly over the screen, suddenly very uncertain if he had a reservation or a way to pay for it.

The screen showed a green circle with a large check mark. Then the clerk chimed in again. "Welcome Mr. Haynes and Ms. Steinfeld. You'll be staying in room 2312. The elevators are to your right across the lobby. Can I offer any assistance with your bags?"

"You've got to be shitting me," Jon breathed before he could stop himself. He bit his lips as though that would stop the words from having already escaped.

"Is there a problem sir?" asked the holographic hostess.

Jon quickly took stock of the situation. He was almost thirty years in the future. Alone and unafraid except for Denise and anyone from the other three teams he could make contact with; Claire hopefully. He had no wallet, no identification, no money of his own. Casimir obviously intended that he and Denise share accommodations. Maybe they had a reason. Maybe they were sadistically trying to ruin his fledgling relationship with Claire. Maybe this whole situation was fucked and he was going to end up stranded…or arrested…in twenty fucking fifty where the real Jon Haynes was over fifty years old. Probably best to go with the flow in this case.

"Uh, no, sorry," Jon stammered. His could feel his face flush under Denise's glare.

"I'm sure our employer would pony up the cash for another room if I'm cramping your style too much Jon," said Denise, indignant as she yanked her hand away from its prior resting place in the crook of his elbow.

Jon avoided eye contact. "No, no, I'm sorry. This is fine. Um, it'll be fun. Like a work retreat…get to know your colleagues." Jon knew he was a bad actor. Time to go all in to salvage the situation. Denise was the only other person from 2023 that he could talk to right now, and he might need her help at some point on this strange trip.

Without thinking, he threw his arm over Denise's shoulder, thanked the receptionist and nearly drug Denise toward the elevator. He forced the biggest smile he could muster. "Sorry about that. I assumed we'd have separate accommodations. It caught me off guard is all."

As the walked away from the counter the receptionist tried to interject but neither Jon nor Denise were listening as they walked away.

Denise narrowed her eyes at Jon as she scrutinized his sincerity. Then she appeared to accept his apology, sliding an arm around his waist and once again, pressing her curves a little too firmly into his side.

Jon was grateful they only had a few more yards to the elevator bank. He swung his arm clear of her shoulder and wriggled out of her grasp to hit the call button. One of the elevators opened immediately and they made their way to the 23rd floor.

When they arrived outside room 2312 Jon stared with uncertainty at the door and lock. That was when he realized he'd left the check in counter too quickly. He had no idea how to get into the room and certainly hadn't been given a key.

On a whim he dug the handheld from his pocket and hoped for a helpful message on the screen. Nothing.

"Try holding it up to the lock," said Denise. "Maybe it has, like, RFID or something."

Jon awkwardly held the device near the door handle, releasing the lock. He pushed the door open and held it for Denise to lead the way.

"Oh, this is nice," Denise breathed.

Meanwhile, Jon let out a silent sigh of relief when he saw two double beds.

Denise took a short lap of the room, running her hands along the drapes as she passed the window on the far wall. She stopped, then opened the curtains revealing a view of the downtown skyline and San Diego Harbor.

Jon absently walked over to take in the view. The skyline was familiar but different. This hotel, a trademark of the San Diego skyline back in 2023, felt like a small player now. Two massive skyscrapers flanked the hotel, leaving only the space in between open to view the harbor beyond.

Denise stepped back from the window. "I'm gonna check out this bathroom. It looks amazing."

Jon didn't respond. Denise stepped away and shut the door behind her. Almost as soon as she'd shut the door, Jon's handheld chirped and vibrated in his pocket. The message on the screen simply said 'view in private' with no sender information. Jon glanced over his shoulder to ensure the bathroom door was still shut. As he did he heard the shower come on in the bathroom. Now seemed like a good time.

He placed the handheld's audio tab behind his ear and pressed his thumb to the small biometric pad. Steven Pulling appeared in miniature hologram form, hovering above the screen in his palm.

"Hello Jon Haynes. I have an assignment for you."

CHAPTER TWENTY-SIX

As soon as Tim and Claire had checked in and made the elevator ride up to their room on the 23rd floor of the Manchester Grand Hyatt in the San Diego of the future, Claire realized she was exhausted from the insanity of the day. She hadn't really done much per se. She stood in a sphere and traveled through time, rode the worst roller coaster in history to the surface at the Casimir facility, took an educational trip in a self-driving car, and got a quick peek at downtown San Diego in 2050. But the mental strain of keeping her mind tethered to the present and her wits about her, especially when she considered that she'd woken up this morning in her Casimir facility apartment in 2023, left her feeling physically exhausted.

Claire let out a loud sigh as she flopped back on to the double bed nearest the window in the hotel room she was sharing with Tim. It was weird that Casimir, a company with sufficient resources to build a giant secret underground facility and send people into the future for the hottest stock tips couldn't spring for extra hotel rooms so they didn't have to share. Whatever. Maybe they had their reasons. And Tim had met Jon. He wouldn't dare try to make a move.

Claire shut her eyes for a moment. She took a deep breath and let out another sigh, attempting to clear her mind. When she did, the technophile in her emerged, reaching for the high tech handheld in the right rear pocket of her jeans. As soon as she thumbed the biometric tab to unlock the device the holo projector in the hotel room, directly in front of the bed, came to life. Her handheld and the holographic television both displayed the same message asking her if she wanted to link the devices while she was in her room. She tapped the green 'Yes' button on her handheld and immediately saw the contents of her handheld displayed holographically at the center of the far wall.

As Claire explored her handheld on the screen in front of her, she saw an option to stream a holographic television feed. Maybe a good way to shut off for a few minutes. She tapped the icon and the holo across the room displayed a local San Diego news feed that was rolling to a commercial break.

Claire reached up to the head of the bed, grabbing a pillow to pull under her head so she could comfortably watch the holographic news feed without straining her neck. As she settled into the pillow she took a deep breath right before her attention was snatched by the commercial now playing on the screen.

An attractive Australian red head was describing a networked neural implant that would allow its users to access the modern internet with their thoughts. They could browse inside their field of vision, or project an internet image on a conveniently located wall. No one else would see it, but from the user's perspective it was most certainly there. She watched the red head type an email by tapping out the keystrokes with her hands by her sides, simply twitching her fingers as the text appeared on screen. Amazing. Claire wondered how much it would cost.

As the commercial ended and the soothing Australian accent encouraged her to pre-order her Pinnacle implant, Claire was no longer tired. She fought a combination of excitement and uneasiness.

As more commercials continued to stream on the hologram, Claire thumbed the handheld again. She intuitively found her way to a search engine (the most common ones in 2023 were still alive and well in 2050), and searched 'Pinnacle Implant.' The search results were immediate and a picture of the Australian woman from the commercial was displayed in the thumbnail preview of the first link on the page. She tapped the link with her thumb and the screen of her handheld went black.

A moment later three dimensional text appeared to hover over the screen. 'For the best experience, please place your handheld on a nearby flat surface.'

Claire sat up on the bed and crossed her legs, placing the handheld on the bed right in front of her. As soon as she did the gorgeous Australian was projected right in front of her again, this time standing on a busy street corner, people brushing past her on either side.

"Welcome to the Pinnacle Implant Virtual Storefront. I'm Emily Brown, and I'll be your guide on this brief tour of this amazing new technology."

As virtual Emily finished her introduction she began walking toward Claire in the holographic projection. As she did, the projection wrapped around Claire's head, presenting a three hundred and sixty degree perspective, much like the one she'd seen projected by Alistair in the self driving car earlier. Claire had the odd sensation that she was going to bump into a virtual passerby on the street as she was thrust involuntarily backwards down the street as Emily walked. Claire craned her neck to the left to try and peek over her shoulder to see where they were going. As she did, a large mocha-skinned man in a suit brushed uncomfortably close to her left shoulder, walking the opposite way along the street. Claire knew it was only an image, a sort of virtual reality projected by her handheld. But she still flinched, sensing she was about to bump into the man as he passed by. She closed her eyes briefly and reminded herself that she was sitting still on her hotel bed.

"Pinnacle Implants represent a giant leap forward in the way we can interact with the rest of the world and with the Pinnacle Cloud. I can now check my email, messages, or social media; even take care of some online shopping or paying bills, all as I walk down the street, without burying my face in a handheld." As Emily said this, the projection rotated around so that Claire appeared to be looking at the street through Emily's eyes. The right side of her field of vision was then taken up by a translucent email client. As Emily clicked through unread messages, she continued to walk down the street, sidestepping pedestrians that walked in the opposite direction.

The street view faded. Claire now felt like she was sitting court side at a crowded basketball arena. Holographic players ran the court right in front of her. "Mobile computing and productivity will never be the same again. You can be anywhere, doing whatever you like, and always within reach of all the functionality of a full office suite."

As Emily said this, a desktop was projected across her field of vision. As she typed an email without the use of a keyboard, a video teleconference call came in. Then it opened in the top right corner of her field of view. A few moments later, the video conference call ended and the desktop winked out, revealing the basketball game that continued in the arena where Emily sat.

The holograph faded to black. Emily narrated from the black backdrop. "I've probably already convinced the workaholics that this is must have technology. For those of you that don't live to work, I'm not done." The hologram brightened to display a three hundred and sixty degree view of a sunny California beach. Behind Claire was the Pacific Ocean, endless sandy beach to either side, and gorgeous Emily Brown in a bright green bikini stretched out in a lounge chair in the front of Claire's field of view.

"I can do just as much from a long chair on the beach as I can from the office." Emily stared off into space while twitching her fingers, next to her thighs, typing something only she could see in her field of vision.

"And don't worry. When works all done I can still unplug, becoming unreachable unless I want to be." The hologram shifted to Emily's perspective. She was looking at a screen in the right side of her field of vision. The left side still showed the beach and the crashing waves of the Pacific Ocean. The top of the screen read 'PINNACLE IMPLANT SETTINGS.'

"From here I can use built in automation to screen calls, delay receipt of any messages, only allow incoming calls and messages from specific people, or simply unplug altogether."

A red button at the top of the settings screen switched to 'Power Off Pinnacle Implant.' The screen faded from view, revealing Emily's full view of the beach and ocean in front of her. Emily stood and walked toward the water. The perspective of the hologram remained in the lounge chair and Claire watched Emily walk gracefully into the surf and dive into an oncoming wave.

The beach image faded, as did the three hundred sixty degree hologram. A hologram of Emily Brown in business attire stood in front of Claire again.

"Financing in various terms is available for qualified customers, making Pinnacle Implants affordable for almost everyone. Installation appointments will be prioritized based on when you pre-order, so don't delay. A small portion of pre-order customers will be randomly selected to participate in beta testing of the implants. These lucky few will receive their implants free of charge and before they're available to the general public. Pre-order your Pinnacle Implants today."

Emily Brown and the hologram that carried her into Claire's hotel room evaporated. Then Claire noticed Tim had emerged from the bathroom and was standing near the end of the opposite bed, watching Claire with an intense curiosity.

"What was that? A hologram from your handheld? I didn't know they could do that. And who was the woman!?" Tim said excitedly.

"A saleswoman," Claire replied. "And a very convincing one." She felt an involuntary smile spread across her face.

Claire was just as infatuated with Emily Brown as she was with Pinnacle Implants. Something about that accent.

"Where did you find that hologram?" Tim asked, pulling his handheld from the front pocket of his pants.

"Just search Pinnacle Implants. You can't miss it." Claire watched as Tim frantically tapped away at his screen as he sat down on the end of the other bed.

The hologram popped up in front of him as he sat the handheld down on the bed, just like it had for Claire a few minutes earlier. Claire watched Tim get sucked into the Pinnacle Implant sales pitch, enjoying Emily Brown's Australian accent for the second time. Just as Tim's hologram when into a three sixty around his head, Claire's handheld chirped with a new message.

Her focus on Emily momentarily broken, Claire glanced down at the handheld to see white letters on a black screen. 'View in private.' Claire stood and quietly made her way to the bathroom. Tim didn't notice, now watching the basketball arena that holographically spread out around him.

Claire shut the door to the bathroom and tapped the message on the screen. The handheld directed her to 'Unlock with Thumbprint to View Message.' Claire pressed her thumb to the sensor at the bottom of the handheld. The handheld showed her a basic animated graphic indicating she should put the audio tab behind her ear to ensure the sound from the message was kept private. She stuck the tab behind her left ear and tapped the screen again.

A three inch tall version of Steven Pulling appeared above the handheld screen.

"Hello Claire Keen," said the holographic Pulling. "I have an assignment for you."

Part Three

CHAPTER TWENTY-SEVEN

Jon stood in partial awe at the three inch tall, but fully lifelike Steven Pulling that was projected above the screen of his handheld.

"Are you alone Jon?" asked the Pulling hologram. The sound from the audio tab felt as if it was coming from inside his head.

Jon listened to ensure the shower was still going and glanced over his shoulder to ensure Denise hadn't emerged from the bathroom. "Yes," he responded matter of factly.

"Very well," said Pulling. "I need to make use of your considerable skills in accessing another secure facility."

As the Pulling hologram paused, Jon wasn't sure if he was interacting with a pre-recorded hologram or if this was some form of futuristic teleconference where he was also a tiny holographic projection in the palm of Pulling's hand.

"Cas Computing, now known as Pinnacle, as I believe you're aware, has established a headquarters compound near your location. A few years back, the military shut down the Marine Corps Recruit Depot. Pinnacle swooped in to purchase the property and convert it to their West Coast headquarters. While the Ne Plus Ultra computer still resides at Oakridge National Laboratory, we believe significant server capacity is housed within two of the structures at this installation."

"Mr. Pulling..." Jon tried to cut in with a question but the Pulling hologram continued as though he hadn't spoken.

"Jon, Pinnacle is a problem. Access to this facility, particularly at this critical juncture in history, is vital to our understanding of the Pinnacle Cloud. In the safe in your hotel room you'll find a small computer peripheral, similar to a USB stick. Once you have the stick, your handheld will remotely receive the electronic key to a safe house a bit closer to the Pinnacle compound that you should use as a staging area for this mission. The address of the safe house is available in your handheld and is listed as St. Charles Place.

"I know we told you to stay with your partners during this training mission, but you are authorized to operate outside that constraint for this assignment. In fact, in order to carry out your mission, you must break contact with Ms. Steinfeld before you access St. Charles Place. She does not have a need to know. There are two doses of a potent sleeping pill in your hotel safe that you can use, at your discretion, to achieve this part of your objective."

Despite the vague but intriguing mission Steven was laying out for him, Jon's primary emotion was relief. It wasn't until Steven told him that he could break contact with Denise, that he realized how much her presence, and her barely veiled physical advances, were stressing him.

"Time is of the utmost importance here Mr. Haynes," said the Pulling hologram. "We need this access immediately. And you must finish and re-unite with your partner in time to make your return trip tomorrow, back to 2023.

"And one last thing Jon. Don't get caught. What you're doing is most certainly considered breaking and entering. We have put together a false identity for you, with all the necessary credentials staged at St. Charles Place. This identity should be good enough to get you through the front gate of the Pinnacle compound, but it will not hold up to more intense scrutiny if you're apprehended. And under no circumstances can your mission or associated activities be linked back to Casimir Institute. Good luck Jon Haynes." The Steven Pulling hologram evaporated leaving Jon staring at the black screen on his handheld which rested in the palm of his hand.

Jon returned the handheld to his right rear pocket and stared out the window for a moment, contemplating his next move. Once again, Steven Pulling had swooped in at the oddest of times and given Jon what appeared to be a highly questionable assignment. But Jon resolved to do it nonetheless. Partly to satisfy his curiosity, but also because it gave him an excuse to put some distance between himself and Denise, at least for a little while. He'd figure out the next steps once he got to the safe house.

Jon was snapped out of his thoughts when the water in the shower stopped. He quickly moved over to the closet, assuming it would house the safe that Steven had referred to in his message. He found the safe on the floor of the closet, as he'd expected. But the safe was unlocked, with a small card stuck to the door, giving instructions on how to set the combination and lock up your valuables.

He opened the safe nonetheless, hoping the tools Pulling had promised would be sitting inside. At first glance, the safe appeared empty. Jon's heart rate quickened as he tried to recall what Pulling had said. *Had he missed an important detail? Was there a different safe he should be looking for?* He didn't know how long Denise would spend in the bathroom, but he just heard the shower door open and shut. She was done showering and he might have anywhere from a few seconds to an hour before she re-emerged.

The closet was dark, but not so dark that he thought another safe might be hiding in it. He pawed his hand around inside the safe to ensure he hadn't missed any small objects inside. The inside of the safe was covered in a thin black felt, except for one spot near the back corner that felt like plastic. Jon grabbed the handheld from his pocket and thumbed the screen on. The backlighting from the screen cast just enough light into the dark safe that he could see the difference in the back corner. A small opaque thumbprint sensor, like a smaller cousin to the ones he'd seen at the Casimir facility earlier today, sat at the back of the safe. Jon pressed his thumb to it, heard a slight beep, and saw the familiar green backlighting appear in the sensor, indicating it had accepted his thumbprint.

The back wall of the safe slid away, revealing a compartment hidden behind the false wall. Inside the secret compartment Jon found what Pulling had promised. A small plastic bag with two purple pills and a thumb drive roughly two inches long. The connector on the end of the drive was different, smaller than a USB, but it obviously was meant to interface with a computer.

Jon stuck the thumb drive in one front pocket and the pills in the other. He pressed his thumb to the pad again, hoping intuitively that it would cause the secret compartment to close, becoming hidden again. He was right. The sensor turned green again, beeped, and the compartment slid shut. Jon pushed the actual door to the safe shut and stood. He then shut the closet door and turned to go sit on the bed and contemplate his next move. As he turned, now facing the bathroom door, Denise emerged, wrapped tightly in a towel.

Jon was momentarily frozen. He tried to form words to explain the awkward circumstance. Nothing. He also tried to keep his eyes from wandering over Denise's body, most of which was clearly visible. The towel seemed strained to contain her well formed chest and it ended just below her butt.

Instead of looking calm and cool under the uncomfortable circumstances, Jon forced his eyes away from Denise, darting from the floor to the far wall of the room. She noticed.

"What's the matter Johnny-boy. You were waiting for me by the door and now you're feeling bashful?"

Jon was not attracted to Denise, at least not in the way he was attracted to Claire. Physically, Denise was very appealing, but Jon also saw ugliness in her personality. And he didn't trust her. Unfortunately, his thoughts on her personality flaws were not outweighing his physical response to the surprise of her nearly naked with him in a futuristic hotel room. He felt a subtle animal tingle in his groin and she seemed to sense it as she took another short step toward him. Jon battled with himself, trying not to picture what Denise might look like if she let the plush hotel towel fall to the floor.

His eyes continued to dart nervously around the room as she inched closer to him. He had to extract himself from this situation now, or Denise might end up being more than he could resist.

Jon had an idea, and barely constrained the urge to run across the room to the dresser where an empty ice bucket sat on top.

"Um, are you thirsty," Jon said to Denise, while eyeing the ice bucket as though it was his only salvation.

"Sure, I could go for a drink," Denise replied. "Are you buying?" She smiled at him seductively and Jon saw his opportunity. By leaving to go get them a drink he'd diffuse the immediate situation and open up an opportunity for the next phase of his plan.

Jon took the opportunity to put space between himself and Denise, stepping over to the dresser to grab the ice bucket.

"Jon, I'm pretty sure the hotel bar has ice. I don't think you need that." She stretched her arms out wide and let out a relaxed sigh, which made her chest all the more pronounced. Jon almost winced.

"That shower really hit the spot," said Denise, walking over toward the closest double bed. Jon pressed himself into the dresser, desperate to ensure she couldn't create incidental contact with him. "I think I'll let you buy me a bourbon Jon. Hard day deserves a hard drink. On the rocks please."

"Sure," Jon replied, grateful for a clear path to the door. Jon abandoned the ice bucket and made for the exit, hoping his urgency to get out of the room wasn't too obvious.

As soon as the hotel room door clicked shut behind him, Jon breathed a massive sigh of relief. He hated the part of himself that wanted to ravage Denise. The idea made his groin tingle but his stomach clench. So far, his conscience was prevailing over his manhood, but he wasn't interested in sticking around to allow opportunity for that to change.

As he reached the elevator down the hall and thumbed the call button, Jon took a deep breath. He wasn't as hopeless as he felt. He shoved his hand in his pocket, finding the purple pills there, and considered his options. He didn't have an entire plan, but now that his libido was fading from the controlling position, he might be able to pull something together.

A few minutes later he stepped up to the lobby bar and tried to catch the bar tenders attention. It didn't take long as there were less than a half dozen other patrons. It wasn't quite lunch time.

"What can I get you?" asked the slim young man behind the bar.

Jon faltered for just a second, trying to recall what Denise had requested. "A bourbon rocks for me, and um, seltzer water with lime for my significant other."

"You got it, boss," said the bartender, grabbing a bottle from the shelf behind the bar and getting to work.

After a few minutes bustling around behind the bar, the young bar tender returned with Jon's requested beverages. Jon paused before grabbing the drinks, uncertain how he'd pay for them. On a wing and a prayer he grabbed his handheld from his pocket and watched the bar tenders eyes.

"Run it now or leave it open?" asked the bartender, looking at Jon's handheld in his right hand.

"Um, run it now," Jon replied, unsure of how to 'run it.' Fortunately, the bar tender glanced expectantly at the surface of the bar and Jon inferred that he should scan his handheld, much like he had when he checked into the hotel a little over an hour ago.

Jon held the device over the bar and depressed his thumb onto the scanner. A green check mark appeared on the surface of the bar and his handheld chirped, displaying a message that asked him if he wanted to tip. Jon tapped the icon for fifteen percent, tucked the handheld into his pocket and graciously grabbed the drinks off the bar.

"Thanks," Jon said, departing the bar and heading back toward the elevator.

"You bet," said the bartender to Jon's back as he walked away.

Jon said a silent prayer of thanks when the elevator door finally shut leaving him alone inside. He squatted down awkwardly and put both drinks on the floor of the elevator so he could retrieve the purple pills from his pocket. Jon opened the bag and dropped one into the caramel colored bourbon. The pill sank to the bottom of the glass and sat there, much to Jon's disappointment.

As the elevator approached the twenty third floor Jon retrieved both drinks and stood upright, waiting for the doors to slide open. Just in case he was joined by another passenger on the elevator, he strategically positioned his hand around the lower portion of the bourbon glass. The last thing he needed right now was a casual observer assuming he was trying to drug an innocent young lady for nefarious purposes. Although that wouldn't be technically untrue.

After exiting the elevator Jon walked quickly down the hall toward room 2312. Jon passed a small decorative table that held a floral arrangement. He briefly looked over his shoulder to ensure the hallway was still unoccupied. Once he was certain that it was, he sat the two drinks down on the small table.

He checked the bourbon glass again, hoping the purple pill Pulling had provided, had started to dissolve. A small bubble trail issued from the pill, but it was still very evident at the bottom of the glass. Jon was only a few doors down from the room he shared with Denise. He couldn't hand her a bourbon glass and hope she didn't notice the foreign material sitting at the bottom. So he stuck his finger in the glass and stirred vigorously.

Jon breathed a sigh of relief as the pill quickly started to break apart. He continued stirring, stopping every few seconds to let the bourbon settle and check for remaining evidence of the drug he'd put in the glass. He repeated the process for the next five minutes, eyes constantly darting up and down the hall, then back to the glass. Stir, settle, check. After what had to be twenty repetitions of the frantic process the pill was gone. A slight cloudiness had settled over the bourbon, but Jon was pretty sure it would go unnoticed.

Jon rolled his shoulders, relaxing the stress of the last few minutes exposed in the hallway as he prepared to drug his traveling partner. Then he picked up the drinks, focused on plastering a charming smile across his face, and strode the rest of the way down the hall to the door of room 2312.

He balanced both glasses in his left hand as he used his right to fish the handheld out of his pocket. Before he had a grasp on the handheld the door opened. Denise stood in the doorway, still wearing only the plush hotel towel.

"I heard you fumbling around out here and thought you might need help," Denise said, smiling with narrow eyes at Jon. She held the door open and stood just clear enough that Jon might be able to get through the door without brushing against her.

"I had it under control," said Jon, forcing an uncomfortable smile.

Jon turned to the side to pass through the doorway without making contact. The maneuver only served to invite her advances more. As soon as they stood face to face with Jon past the threshold of the door, Denise let the door swing shut and stepped toward Jon. She reached across the separation between them, which was less than six inches, and gently took the bourbon from Jon's left hand.

"What are you having?" she asked.

"Vodka and tonic," Jon replied. "I'm watching my figure." Jon smiled again, trying to break free of the entryway and put some physical distance between himself and Denise.

Denise smiled at his comment and lifted the bourbon to her lips. As she did Jon barely caught the 'oh shit' before it escaped his lips. A thin film of particulate was forming at the bottom of the glass, clearly visible when she lifted it to take the first sip. The dissolved pill must have started to settle since he stopped stirring it in the hall.

Jon sprung into action, desperate to ensure she didn't discover the foreign material in her glass. He acted without thinking.

"Let me take that for you," Jon said, grabbing the bourbon and setting it down, along with his water masquerading as vodka, on the nearby dresser. Immediately, he grabbed one of the two plush bathrobes hanging on the bathroom door.

"Here, put this on," Jon suggested with his best forced smile. "It'll be much more comfortable than that towel."

Denise smiled and turned her back to him, waiting for Jon to hold the bathrobe open so she could shrug into it. "Aren't you just the perfect gentleman all of a sudden Johnny-boy."

Before Jon had the robe fully open to drape over Denise's shoulders she pulled at the front of her towel, then released it to drop to the floor.

Jon's first instinct was too spin away to face the window. He quickly realized that wasn't an effective plan since he still held the bathrobe in his hands. The familiar heat in his groin returned as he instead stepped toward Denise and quickly held the bathrobe open, as a sort of barrier between him and her. Jon stared a hole in the floor between his feet, and thankfully, Denise slipped her arms, one by one, into the sleeves of the robe. Jon then set it over her shoulders and stepped back quickly to pick up the two drinks from the dresser.

Denise passed behind Jon, crossing to the far end of the hotel room nearest the window. While her back was to him, Jon dipped his finger in the bourbon again, giving it a quick vigorous stir in hopes that the contents of Pulling's sleeping pill would make its way back into solution.

With the two glasses back in hand Jon moved to follow Denise so he could get her back to drinking her sedative laced bourbon. She tied the robe into place, then glanced back at Jon and offered another very welcoming smile. This pill better work fast.

Denise took a seat in a leather chair in the corner of the room and kicked her feet up on the matching ottoman. Without a word Jon leaned down and put the glass in her hand. He sat a few feet away on the side of the bed.

"Cheers," said Jon as he tilted his glass of water back and downed half of it. Hopefully Denise would follow suit.

She did. Denise took a long pull on her glass and settled deeper into the chair.

"Are you trying to get me drunk Jon Haynes?"

"Maybe," Jon replied, winking in a way he was certain looked as awkward as it felt. If Pulling's sleeping pill didn't work fast Jon was going to have to either sleep with her or break into a dead sprint to escape the room. She seemed to take his every action as an affirmation of attraction. Denise was not concerned in the least with the possibility of physical rejection.

"What do you think of 2050 so far?" Jon asked. Trying to generate light conversation and buy time for the drugs to kick in.

Denise took another pull of her bourbon leaving her glass nearly empty. Thank god.

"It seems like things have worked out pretty well for the world. Global warming hasn't killed everything, nation's aren't constantly on the brink of war anymore, and some giant computer company basically runs the world. What could possibly go wrong?" Denise yawned and Jon saw a slight glassiness forming in her eyes. Optimism crept in. *This just might work.*

Jon tried to keep the conversation going. "I know right. The car robot told us all sorts of positive world developments and finished it off with the fact that a corporate giant is in charge now. I'm not sure what to make of that. And you saw that commercial for the internet brain implants. It's all a bit overwhelming."

Denise barely responded now. Her eyes grew heavy and her previously seductive posture had become languid. Seeing her drink effectively empty, Jon decided to swing for the fences.

"Do you want to lay down for a while Denise? We've got nowhere we need to be. Might as well get some rest now and we can go check out the town tonight."

Denise nodded sluggishly in response. Jon helped her up from the chair let her flop gently atop the linens on the bed he'd been sitting on. She was in dream land almost as soon as her head hit the pillow. Steven's pill had done the trick after all.

Jon grabbed Denise's bourbon glass from the chair and took it to the bathroom. En route, he downed the rest of the water in his 'vodka' glass. He dumped the remnants of bourbon and sleeping pills from Denise's glass down the sink then rinsed the glass.

Next he grabbed his handheld and thumbed his way to the personal assistant app. He pushed a microphone icon then spoke to the device as if it were a person.

"I'm going to need the car for an errand," Jon said awkwardly to the screen.

Alistair appeared on the screen. "Absolutely Jon. It will be outside waiting for you in less than five minutes. Is there anything else I can do for you?"

"No, that should do it," Jon replied. This technology was impressive. It was natural, like he was talking to a concierge. Jon stuck the handheld back in his pocket and stepped back out of the bathroom.

He walked over to double check that Denise was still breathing before he left. He heard her snoring softly before he was halfway across the room. Pulling's purple pills must be powerful stuff. He opened the door and hung a 'Do Not Disturb' sign on the outside handle before heading to the elevator and contemplating his next steps.

CHAPTER TWENTY-EIGHT

Claire stared in awe at the three inch tall Steven Pulling projected above the handheld in her palm.

"Are you alone Claire?" asked Pulling.

Claire said nothing for a moment, unsure now if she was watching a holographic recorded video of Steven Pulling or was on some sort of holo phone call with the real thing.

When she didn't respond after a few seconds, the Pulling hologram repeated.

"Are you alone Claire?"

"Yes," she replied.

"Good. You are being diverted from your training assignment. Please listen closely as every detail is important."

Claire's pulse quickened. She was so excited. Then she realized she'd failed to follow the first instruction - she wasn't listening.

"...fellow operative will use physical access to gain entry into the Pinnacle Cloud network. If things go according to plan this will happen in the next few hours. We will notify you when the tunnel is open. That's where your operation begins." The Pulling hologram paused.

Fellow operative? Claire smiled. A giant supercomputer effectively runs the world in 2050, and now Claire, the computer geek, is being called an 'operative.' The future is awesome. Claire tried to contain her giddy anticipation and focus on Pulling's words.

"You should break contact with your partner for this operation. He does not have a need to know. I'll leave it to you to accomplish this by whatever means you see fit at the time. If you need some assistance, I have provided a couple very potent sleeping pills. Only give him one dose at a time though." The Pulling hologram let those words hang in a way that made Claire a little uncomfortable.

She forced herself to shake off the trepidation and not miss a single word he was saying.

"Claire, this is a critical time in the history of Pinnacle, Ne Plus Ultra, and the world. A few months from now we expect that the architecture of the Pinnacle Cloud is going to fundamentally change. It will change in a way that appears wonderful for humanity in the moment, but will become catastrophic over time. It will also improve in such a way that its defenses are too advanced for us to penetrate. Suffice to say, it is critical that you get in now, today, quickly, extract the information we require, and get out."

Sensing a pause in his dialogue, Claire attempted to ask a question. "Sounds important. How is this going to w..."

Steven continued as though Claire hadn't spoken a word. "In your hotel safe you will find a laptop, along with the pills I mentioned before. This laptop has a custom-designed network mapping software developed for this express purpose. I'm confident once you map the network you'll see our area of interest - the interface between NPU and the cloud. Your laptop has a few other features that you'll find will help keep your activity hidden from the Pinnacle Cloud. Last but not least, the extraction of your data should be done through the special VPN client on the laptop. Ensure the data is fully uploaded to the secure Casimir server. As soon as it is, close the connection and get rid of the laptop. We're confident Pinnacle will not be able to physically locate you, but you can't be too careful. Good luck Claire."

With that, the Pulling hologram winked out of existence. Claire pulled the audio tab from behind her ear. As she attempted to fit it in the stowage location on the back of the handheld she found that she could barely contain the shaking in her hand enough to replace the audio device in its tiny storage slot. The adrenaline had her trembling. She was excited to be a computer badass in the future. She was terrified by how much she didn't know. Who was she up against? What would happen if she failed?

Once she'd replaced the handheld in the back pocket of her jeans Claire turned to the sink and mirror to check her appearance. Other than the slightly ashen complexion, probably brought on by the fear soaked adrenaline spike, she decided she looked good. As usual.

Claire splashed a handful of cold water on her face, dabbed it dry with a hand towel hanging on the adjacent wall, then took a deep breath. Satisfied she had it together, she stepped out of the bathroom back into the room she shared with Tim.

As soon as Claire walked out of the bathroom, Tim spun on her, smiling ear to ear.

"Those implants look amazing! Game changer. Can you imagine how productive people could be with access to all the capabilities of the PC in their office no matter where they are. The amount of things you could get done during a commute alone gives me a half hard-on… Shit. Sorry."

Claire bit back a laugh. She was infatuated with the tech of 2050 too. Just without the boners.

"Easy tiger," Claire teased. "Funny you mention hard-ons. A few people will get more productive with those implants, sure. But I'm afraid the bigger impact will be an explosion in porn viewership."

"Jesus Claire," Tim replied. "I guess you're the glass half empty type huh?"

"Not at all. Just a realist," said Claire, dropping into a seated position on the opposite bed.

"Personally I think the future is awesome," said Tim. "We should get out there and explore it. I mean, that's what they sent us here for right?"

Claire let out a sigh and forcibly scrunched her mouth, faking discomfort. "Yeah, I guess so. I still don't feel great. The tingle from the sphere, the hell ride on the elevator, and then the assault on the senses of the driverless car ride have all left me a little shaken up. I could use a nap."

Disappointment was immediately apparent on Tim's face. Perfect.

"But don't let me dampen your fun. Go right ahead. Explore the town while I rest a little. Maybe I can join up with you later." Claire tried to sound disappointed, cloaking her urge to get rid of Tim and pull the laptop out of the hotel safe.

"You sure you don't mind?" Tim brightened.

"Not at all," Claire replied, trying not to show her eagerness to have the room to herself.

"Um, ok. I'll have my handheld on me if you decide you want to meet up once you're feeling better." As Tim spoke he was already moving toward the door.

Claire laid back on the bed, hoping to ensure Tim didn't linger or change his mind about convincing her to come along. "Ok. I'll message you after I nap," Claire said softly.

She'd barely finished her sentence when the door clicked shut. Tim was gone. Claire forced herself to stay stretched out on the bed for a few minutes to ensure he wasn't going to return. Every muscle in her body was tense. She could hardly constrain her urge to fetch the laptop Pulling promised was waiting for her in the hotel safe.

After what felt like half an hour but was probably less than two minutes, Claire stood from the bed and walked to the hotel door. She looked through the peep hole to ensure Tim was gone. Seeing nothing she threw the deadbolt to ensure there wouldn't be any surprise entries.

Claire walked to the closet, assuming the hotel safe was somewhere inside, and nearly threw the door open. As expected, a small rectangular safe sat in the far left corner. Claire's heart sank a little when she saw that the door of the safe was ajar. It wasn't locked.

She crouched down and opened the door to look inside. It was empty. She dropped onto her butt and sat cross legged staring into the empty box. She felt a twinge of panicky stress building in her chest. Had she somehow checked in to the wrong room? Was the other operative still executing their mission, possibly for no reason? She needed to get word to Mr. Pulling. Something was wrong.

Claire reached into her back pocket and drew out her handheld. As the screen came to life she looked for a list of pre-programmed contacts. When she found the contacts application, the only names on the list were the other seven travelers that had stepped into the sphere earlier this morning.

She briefly considered sending Tim a message, then dismissed the idea immediately. The Steven Pulling hologram had told her clearly that he did not have a need to know. Then she stared at Jon's name. He might know what to do. She tapped it, calling up the message application.

'How's everything in your neck of the woods?' she typed on the screen. She made a disgusted face to herself. What was she hoping to accomplish with a corny greeting message? She deleted the text and stared at the blinking cursor in the empty field.

Claire cradled the handheld and stared into the open, empty safe. It was a plain cube with black felt lining all sides. Completely bare. Except…

Claire leaned forward to examine a small area in the back corner. It didn't absorb all the light the same way the rest of the black felt did. Probably just an area where the felt had been rubbed bare, exposing some sort of plastic material beneath it. She extended her arm into the safe and ran her thumb over the bare area to make sure her eyes weren't playing tricks on her.

"Whoa!" Claire exclaimed as the safe beeped and the area under her thumb lit up green. Following the electronic beep she heard the click of a small latch releasing. The front edge of the bottom of the safe popped up, just slightly. Claire lifted the lip of the bottom panel, exposing a hidden compartment beneath a false bottom. Perfectly fit into the compartment was a laptop and two purple pills in a small plastic baggie.

Adrenaline now coursing through her, Claire scrambled to get her fingers under the laptop to pop it out of the compartment. Hesitating for a beat, she pocketed the pill baggie in the front pocket of her jeans. Once she had the laptop in hand she flung the screen open and mashed the power button while she walked over to the nearest bed in the room. She hopped onto the bed, crossing her legs and sat the laptop on the bed in front of her.

While she waited for it to start up, Claire finally took a second to actually look at the machine in front of her. It didn't seem much different than a high end laptop in 2023. It was lighter despite being a little larger. And above the screen, where she was used to seeing a self-facing camera, there was instead some sort of LED strip that stretched the full width. Otherwise, the keyboard didn't seem to have any differences and the trackpad looked and felt just like a computer from her time, almost thirty years ago.

Once the computer finished it's startup sequence the screen went black. Displaying only a single line of white text: 'Please Authenticate.' Claire put her right index finger on the trackpad to attempt to wiggle the mouse to see if other options were available. Almost as soon as she touched it the computer made a rejecting 'bump' sound. The text on the screen shifted: 'Invalid Entry.'

All she'd done was touch the pad. Claire remembered the last time she'd been asked to authenticate. It was at Hendrick House and the key to authentication had been her thumbprint. She twisted her wrist awkwardly to press her right thumb to the trackpad.

The backdrop of the laptop screen turned a shade of green and displayed new text: 'Welcome Claire Keen.'

Awesome. The screen shifted to display a boot sequence, probably for the operating system. Claire fidgeted anxiously while she waited for the process to run its course. She took a couple deep breaths and watched a nearly empty desktop come into view on the screen.

The background was a soft, almost baby blue. There was a standard application bar at the bottom (that hadn't changed much), and a single folder on the desktop. The title of the folder was a convoluted series of letters and numbers: M31723A.

Claire clicked on the folder to view its contents. There was an executable file for a program called cMap. It's icon was a dark blue eye. Below that was another executable for Casimir SecNet with an icon that looked like a mail dropslot. There was another application called MagWipe and, finally there was a simple text file titled 'read me first.' She clicked it and began reading:

"Hello Claire Keen. Welcome to 2050. As you know by now, we have a very important assignment for you. Congratulations. Later today you'll be notified on this laptop and on your handheld when it's time to get to work. When that signal arrives, you'll see a new network available within the cNet application - The Pinnacle Cloud. You should map the network as best you can, as quickly as you can. Focus your efforts on the interface between NPU and the Pinnacle Cloud. Our entry point, if successful, will provide you access virtually anywhere on the cloud, right up to the doorstep of NPU. There are likely a significant number of instructions coming from NPU to the cloud and an equal number of data streams from the cloud back to NPU. Characterize them as best you can. You'll need to work quickly as we don't expect our entry point to be permanent. Catalogue everything you see and send it back via the Casimir SecNet application. I'm sure you'll find it very intuitive. Once the SecNet application indicates a successful upload, run the MagWipe application. After that it really doesn't matter what you do with the laptop, although we'd prefer you destroy it. Take some time now to get familiar with the cNet application - we have provided a few sample virtual networks fully contained within the laptop for you to utilize to get familiar with the software. Best of luck. We're counting on your expertise."

Claire could hear her pulse in her ears as she read the text file three more times to make sure she hadn't missed a single detail. Then she closed it and opened the cNet application.

Once she had the application opened she found her way to the files for the training networks. She opened the first in the list and was unimpressed. It looked like it was simulating an intranet for a medium sized company. There was a central server that housed all the shared files and about forty other nodes that were probably people's individual workstations. It was all displayed two dimensionally, just like the software she'd used in 2023. Nothing too glamorous, although it did move faster through the network than she was used to. She wasn't sure if it was because the laptop and software were more capable or because the network was 'fake,' housed entirely within the laptop she was working on.

Claire looked over the entirety of the very simple network. Then she zoomed in around the central server section of the map. As soon as she used the zoom functionality, another icon appeared on the screen. It was a big button, centerline, at the bottom of Claire's screen: Virtual Topology.

She clicked it and the LED strip above the screen lit up. A moment later she was enveloped in a three hundred and sixty degree hologram, projected by the laptop. She was in the network - virtually.

She fumbled to reach for the trackpad on the laptop, that was now obscured by the hologram. Failing that, on a whim, she put a finger up to the hologram in front of her and swiped to the left. The holographic image moved with the swipe of her finger. *Incredible.*

For the next half hour Claire immersed herself, walking along the links of the network, learning its behavior, its character. The hologram made everything so real; exactly the way she'd pictured it in her mind. Only now, the technology and the hologram allowed her to walk about inside it.

Claire felt herself getting lost in her element. The immersion was so complete she had to take a deep breath and remind herself she was still sitting on the bed in her hotel room. She forced herself to leave the application, reminding herself that it wasn't a real network.

Once she entered the Quit command, the hologram quickly retreated back into the LED strip on the laptop. Claire was back in her hotel room; back to reality.

She took a deep breath. In her conscious mind she knew she'd just explored a fake network, but it all seemed so real. She'd never melded with a computer like that before. She drug her finger along the trackpad to the Casimir SecNet application to continue her research and preparation.

Once the application booted up Claire thought it looked a lot like a standard file transfer protocol program. She navigated the menu options, trying to figure out how to connect. She found the login selection and saw the familiar 'Please Authenticate' screen consume the laptop. She pressed her thumb to the trackpad and was quickly logged in.

As she delved further into the file transfer client Claire felt a tingle of fear and stress rising in her chest. It was the most complicated file transfer path she'd ever seen. Any data uploaded via this application was routed through a daisy chain of servers unlike anything Claire had ever seen. The cloak and dagger nature of the data routing made Claire's chest constrict. You only covered your tracks like this if you were doing something illegal.

Claire had been messing around with computers since she was a preteen. And like any computer savvy kid, the temptation for illegal activity was very real. Opportunities arose to make a little money or even to embarrass an online bully. But Claire had always steered clear, intent on turning her love of computers into a real, legitimate profession.

She closed the laptop and returned it to the hidden compartment in the bottom of the hotel safe. She needed to think, and get some rest if she was going to go through with the mission. With the computer stowed she headed for the door, planning for a stop at the hotel bar. Something strong would help her sleep.

As she walked down the curved hotel hallway her mind bounced back and forth between excitement and dread. Even though she only walked for a few minutes, by the time she reached the elevator she'd flip flopped back and forth at least ten times on whether she'd proceed with the assignment. Adrenaline and nerves had her brain working at an overclocked speed. She really needed that drink.

Claire had been so deep in thought as she approached the elevator that she failed to notice Jon Haynes standing and waiting for the same elevator. She almost bumped into him before she clicked back into reality. He was smiling at her.

"Hey you," she said, forcing a little too much excitement into her tone.

"Hi," said Jon, his smile fading. "Everything ok? I watched you come down the hall. You looked like you were off in your own world. For a second I thought you were gonna walk right into me."

Claire felt her face flush as she scrambled around in her head to find words. She wanted to tell Jon. Get his thoughts; his advice. But she was pretty certain she wasn't supposed to say anything to anyone. Her mission was 'need to know,' whatever that meant. Worse, he might try to talk her out of it, or into it. She had to make this decision on her own. No leaning on handsome Jon Haynes to bail her out of a tough decision by giving her the answer. Worse, if it was illegal, she didn't want to drag him into it. He'd already had his fair share of trouble with Casimir.

Jon's eyebrows raised, and a thin smile returned to his face. "Well?"

Shit. She still hadn't answered. She was frozen in place, thinking about her answer. Like an invalid.

"Sorry. I've got a lot on my mind. 2050 is awesome, but its a lot to process." She felt self-conscious. She was rambling.

"Anything in particular bothering you?" Jon asked.

He was good. If she didn't turn the conversation in another direction quickly she was going to tell him everything.

"No. Tim left an hour or so ago to explore the city. I'm headed down to the bar to grab a drink and take advantage of the quiet room to catch a little nap." She struggled to maintain eye contact, nervous that her eyes would give away that she was withholding something. If Jon pressed, she'd fold like the legs of a cheap plastic table.

"Ok," Jon replied, although he didn't seem to buy it. "Mind if I join you? I'm headed out to do a bit of exploring myself, but I'm not in too much of a hurry."

"Sure," said Claire as she felt the muscles in her face smile for real this time. "Where's your partner?"

"She's grabbing a nap too," Jon replied, breaking eye contact with Claire.

Claire hardly noticed. She was glad to have Jon to herself. Even for a few minutes. She did her best to suppress all thoughts and concerns about her upcoming assignment and the underlying decision. She was going to spend time with Jon. A little distraction would be good for her.

As the elevator arrived he dropped an arm over her shoulder and flashed her a knee-wobbling smile. Maybe she would invite him to 'break in' her hotel room while Tim was out. A little physical exertion would definitely clear up her mental space and make it easier to get to sleep for that nap.

She nestled in a little closer to him as the elevator descended.

As the elevator decelerated she decided to begin her campaign. She turned her face up toward his, closing her eyes slightly, inviting him to kiss her. She expected a casual peck on the lips. What she got in response was a little more.

Jon swung his arm free and twisted to face her. His hands made their way to the base of her skull as he kissed her deeply. Initially she was caught off guard and let her hands drop to her sides. As she returned the kiss she let her hips sink toward him as she put her hands around his waist. The kiss went on for somewhere between a minute and thirty. Jon eventually pulled away gently but Claire couldn't find the strength to open her eyes.

"Excuse us," said Jon. *That was odd.* Claire opened her eyes to see Jon, hands still in the hair at the back of her head, looking to his left at the elevator door. She turned, following his gaze, to find a family of four standing outside the elevator and the two adults looking very uncomfortable. When Claire saw the fanny packs on the two older members of the group and smirks on the faces of the two teenagers, she brought a hand to her mouth to stifle a laugh.

Jon grabbed her hand and led her past the dumb struck family and out of the elevator. Once they were into the open lobby he brought his arm back over her shoulder and laughed out loud.

"I'm guessing that fanny pack couple hasn't kissed like that in years," said Jon, smiling at Claire.

"Nope. But I think their kids might have been taking notes." Claire returned the smile as Jon led them to the lobby bar.

As they walked across the lobby and entered the bar, Claire couldn't help but feel like her winging-it plan to get Jon back to her room was on track. They didn't talk as they crossed the lobby, but Jon held her in a way that broadcast that she was his.

As they stepped up to the bar, the red-headed man serving drinks looked at Jon. "What are you having?"

Always the gentlemen, Jon looked to Claire for her to order first.

"Moscow Mule," said Claire without forethought. "Double the Moscow while you're at it."

The bartender gave her a slight eyebrow raise in response. "You got it," he said before looking at Jon. "And for you boss?"

"Just a water for me."

Claire's head snapped over to Jon so fast she almost injured her neck. So much for her plans to get him a little buzzed and lure him back upstairs. She probed. "Water? Got somewhere important to be later?"

Jon went from relaxed and casual to uncomfortable as he stammered out his response. "Nuh…No. I was just, um, going to drive the car. I'm not totally on board with the driverless car thing yet."

Claire wasn't buying it. Something was on his mind, but she was more disappointed that he had plans to be somewhere other than her hotel room.

The bartender had their drinks ready quickly as things were relatively quiet in the hotel bar at mid day. As soon as he slid her drink in front of her she grabbed it and took a long pull while Jon awkwardly paid for the drinks by swiping his handheld across the bartop.

With his water glass in hand Jon took a seat at the bar stool in front of him. Claire followed suit. They both sat silently for a moment, waiting for some distance from the bartender as he made his way around to the few other patrons.

"What do you think of 2050 so far?" Jon asked, twisting toward her on the stool.

"It's awesome!" Claire responded immediately, momentarily forgetting her frustration with his sobriety. "If the history video they showed us is accurate, the threat of war is over and a giant computer is essentially making all the big decisions. What's not to like?"

"What if that computer isn't one of the good guys?" Jon said as he stared down into his water glass.

That hit a little close to home, thrusting Claire back into the turmoil of the decision she had to make sometime in the next few hours. She took another deep gulp of her drink and felt a warmth in her face as the alcohol took hold. She looked down into her glass and saw her drink was nearly empty already.

Claire barely noticed as Jon gulped down his water and sat the glass on the bar. He rubbed her arm then stood from his stool.

"Are you leaving already?" Claire asked, a little too loudly. "We just sat down."

"Sorry," Jon replied. "I can't get into it right now but I have to run."

"I thought you said you were going to look around town. That you weren't in a hurry." Claire huffed out a breath and realized the alcohol had dulled her restraint. She took a deep breath, trying to regain control.

Jon leaned in and kissed her on the forehead. Insult added to injury. She wanted to slap him. But she took another deep breath, and another sip of her drink, leaving only the ice in the bottom of the glass.

"I'll message you later," Jon said, obviously trying to make his exit. "Even if Denise and Tim are with us, it would be fun to hang out."

Claire wasn't so sure. But she went with it anyway. There was nothing she could say at the moment that wouldn't either embarrass her, make a scene, make Jon really uncomfortable, or all of the above.

"Sounds good. Let me know when you're free," said Claire, forcing a smile in response to his fatherly kiss.

Just as quickly as they'd arrived at the bar, Jon was gone. She watched him climb into the waiting sedan under the hotel portico before she turned back to the bar. Fortunately, the bartender had returned.

"Can I get another?" Claire asked as she wiggled her glass in front of her face.

"Sure thing," said the bartender as he went to work.

Moments later he slid her another double Moscow Mule in a bronze mug.

"Should I start you a tab?" he asked.

"No, I should probably go," Claire responded as she swiped her handheld over the bar top to pay. "Supposedly I have work to do later today." With that she tipped her glass at the bartender, took another sizable gulp and spun to walk back toward the elevator.

She could feel the flush in her cheeks and a little wobble in her step as she made her way to the elevator. The alcohol had freed up a certain 'fuck it' mentality that she reveled in for a moment. Until she remembered that she had a major decision to make. Trust the benevolence of the Steven Pulling hologram and go through with her assignment, or trust her own instinct and never again touch the laptop that was hidden in a secret compartment in her hotel safe.

Claire punched the call button for the elevator without any more clarity than she'd had when she left her room a half hour before. When the elevator arrived she mashed the button for the 23rd floor and continued making quick work of her very potent drink.

By the time the elevator arrived on her floor she was drunk, by all definitions. She'd have no problem getting a little sleep. It happened fast. She wondered when she'd last eaten anything. She exited the elevator and made a left to walk down the hall to her room. She made a mental note to drink a glass of water before she laid down. Nothing would be quite as bad as waking up to a huge decision and an important assignment with a hangover.

A few minutes later, her drink nearly empty again, Claire clumsily thrust her handheld against the lock on the door to her room. The door beeped and clicked open. She kicked her shoes off right inside the door, downed the rest of her drink, and made a straight line for the closest bed. She sat her empty glass on the nearby nightstand and flopped onto her back.

She felt the room spin a little and considered getting up to use the bathroom. Instead she rolled onto her side and slid an arm underneath one of the pillows. As she started to drift off to sleep she half dreamt about walking around inside a virtual computer network. She was an operative now and 2050 was awesome.

CHAPTER TWENTY-NINE

Fifteen minutes after he'd climbed in the car outside the hotel, Jon's ride ended on a side street in a run down residential area.

"My instructions dictate that I not go any further Jon. You'll have to walk the last half mile to your destination," said Alistair.

Jon hadn't expected that, but it made sense. If he was supposed to be discreet it probably wasn't a good idea to park the driverless, cloud connected car in the driveway of his secret hideout. *Why hadn't he considered that?*

Jon climbed out of the driver seat of the car and started walking, unsure of which direction he should go but certain he wanted to put distance between himself and the car. He pulled his handheld from his pocket and thumbed it on, planning to call up the map application. As he looked down at the handheld he heard the car whir to life. He fought the urge to turn around to see where it was going, but ultimately failed. He looked over his shoulder in time to see that the car had already made a u-turn and was accelerating along the reverse route, heading out of the neighborhood.

Jon looked back down at the handheld and saw that his destination was just four blocks north; he was walking west. As he dropped the handheld back into his pocket, he decided to continue down this street, in case any onlookers in the adjacent houses had seen him get out of the car. Once he reached the end of the block he'd go north a block and then switchback his way to St. Charles Place. Doubling back each block would take longer, but it would also flush out anyone who might be watching or following him. He walked as casually as he could over the next half hour, resisting the urge to double check his location on the handheld. He needed to look like he belonged in the neighborhood. Just a guy out for a lunch time stroll.

When Jon arrived at the address for St. Charles Place, he was underwhelmed. The place looked like a dump. But it fit right in with the other houses on the street. Before he walked up the driveway to the front door he stopped and quickly looked up and down the street, doing his best to ensure no one was watching him and hoping no one would see him enter.

Once he'd decided he most likely wasn't being followed, he quickly made his way to the door. The front door had some sort of smart lock, similar to what he'd seen on the hotel room door. He grabbed his handheld and swiped it in front of the lock. The lock lit up with a yellow LED and his handheld chimed. Jon looked down at the screen and found the familiar direction: 'Please Authenticate.' As soon as he depressed his thumb to the biometric pad on his handheld, the LED on the door lock turned green and Jon heard the satisfying kathunk of the dead bolt sliding free.

Jon pushed the door open, stepped across the threshold and quickly shut the door behind him. He reached for the deadbolt to lock it behind him, but before his hand was on the lock he heard it thunk into place as the LED on the interior side of the lock turned red.

Satisfied that no one was going to surprise him by entering the house, he started exploring the small space. The interior was just as underwhelming as the exterior. He stood in a very basic living room that contained only a dingy beige sofa. From his position near the front door he could also see into the small kitchen that probably hadn't been updated since the house was built in the previous century. To his right was a hallway that likely led to bedrooms and a bathroom. To his left, off the kitchen, was a door that probably lead to the small one car garage Jon had seen from the outside of the house.

Jon went to the kitchen and started pulling out drawers and opening cabinets, hoping to find the identification documents Pulling had promised, or any other supplies the Casimir Institute might have staged for his use. As he went through the kitchen he found nothing but a few pots, pans, plates and basic utensils. They all carried a thin layer of dust that indicated they hadn't been disturbed in quite some time.

Satisfied the small kitchen didn't contain what he was looking for, Jon made his way down the hall. The bathroom was bare, containing only a toilet, a pedestal sink, and a shower-bathtub combination with a dingy curtain. He continued down the hall to check the bedrooms.

It didn't take Jon long to determine that the house only had one bedroom. In it was a full bed with scratchy sheets that looked like they'd been borrowed from a seedy low budget motel. Next to the bed was a nightstand with two drawers. Jon pulled the top one open and felt an initial surge of excitement. He grabbed the device sitting in the drawer and spun it around in his hands, inspecting it.

After a moment his excitement faded. The device was an old, dusty, low tech ebook reader; it looked old enough to have been manufactured before 2023. The battery was dead so on the off chance it did contain valuable information, Jon wasn't going to be able to access it anyway. He dropped the reader back into the drawer, deciding he'd come back for it if he happened upon a charger during his search.

His search of the rest of the bedroom yielded nothing. Not even a change of clothes. He made his way back down the hall to check the garage next.

As he stepped into the garage he flipped the light switch near the door. The garage contained nothing but at least ten years worth of dust. When he shut the garage door behind him the slight breeze stirred up the dust and sent him into a fit of sneezing.

Once Jon had stopped the sneezing blitz he pulled his shirt up over his mouth and nose and went back into the house. He pulled a cup from the kitchen cabinet and stuck it under the faucet to get a glass of water. Thankfully, just before he took a swig, he glanced down into the cup. The water within had a slight brownish yellow tint. He was probably the first person to turn on the faucet in years. Jon dumped the water down the sink and turned the faucet back on, hoping that running the sink for a few moments would flush it enough that he could retrieve drinkable water.

Jon left the faucet running and walked back into the living room, then plopped down on the old couch.

"Damnit!" Jon exclaimed as he kicked up a small dust cloud from the sofa. He yanked his shirt back up over his mouth and nose hoping to avoid another bout of sneezing. He failed.

After the second fit of sneezing had subsided Jon was in need of a kleenex. Certain he wouldn't find any untainted by the pervasive dust in the house, he used the bottom of his shirt to wipe away the snot hanging between his nose and mouth.

Jon made his way back to the kitchen, his second battle with the dust making him more intent on getting that glass of water. He filled the glass and took a long drink without bothering to look at the color.

It had a slight coppery taste but one glass wouldn't kill him.

After he'd downed the glass of water he cupped his hands under the faucet and splashed water on his face. He could feel his eyes trying to water. Something in this dusty house was trying to trigger an allergic reaction. He leaned over the sink and looked up at the ceiling, letting the water drip down his face.

When he opened his eyes he saw the access to the attic in the ceiling in the middle of the living room.

Jon didn't hesitate. He pulled his shirt back up over his nose and mouth, then gently drug the sofa to the middle of the room. Climbing up on the sofa he grabbed the short string hanging from the attic access and gently pulled it toward him. He shut his eyes just in time to avoid the next bout with the years of dust built up in the safe house. It cascaded down on him as he pulled open the attic door.

He climbed off the sofa and pushed it away with his foot while continuing to pull open the access from above. The attic access door had a typical fold away ladder attached to the inside. Jon gently unfolded the ladder and climbed up the first two steps. Once there he bounced slightly to ensure the ladder would carry his weight before he ascended further.

As he reached the top of the ladder, his head poking into the dark attic, he was pretty sure he'd found what he was looking for. A large trunk straddled two of the ceiling girders. Jon ensured his shirt was still tight over his mouth and nose, then reached out to start dragging the trunk toward the opening.

The trunk was heavy but Jon was fairly certain he could handle it down the ladder. Worst case he'd be able to slide it down the steps and endure the ensuing dust storm.

After five minutes of grunting, battling the weight of the trunk, and squinting against the attic dust, Jon had the trunk on the living room floor. It was the only thing in the house that didn't seem like it had been here, undisturbed, for at least two decades. Jon quickly found the smart lock on the front of the trunk. Now instinctive, he held his handheld in front of the lock and watched the lock turn yellow. He then pressed his thumb to the handheld's biometric pad and watched the lock turn green and the trunk lid pop off the lock. He swung the lid the rest of the way open and began sorting through the contents.

On one side of the trunk sat a neatly folded security uniform and a pair of boots. Sitting on top of the uniform Jon found a security badge and matching driver's license with his photo on both. He picked up the badge and ID to inspect them closer and laughed out loud. The badge was attached to a lanyard and read:

Mark Johnston
Gateguard Security

Somehow the same identity he'd been given on his first visit to the Casimir Facility back in 2022 was being recycled for him to use nearly thirty years later. And from the same fake company. That seemed bold.

He sat the identification materials down next to the trunk and pulled out the uniform to set in a pile on the floor. At the other end of the trunk was some sort of futuristic handgun and two boxes of ammunition - one with green trim and one with red. Jon left the gun in the trunk for now. He wasn't quite ready to find out he was going to have to kill to accomplish his task.

The next item sitting in the trunk was a pair of tactical glasses. Jon picked them up and found them heavier than he'd expected. The wraparound lens appeared to be a sort of composite material. Too heavy to be plastic, but certainly not glass either. It looked like the glasses housed LEDs on either side. He slid the glasses onto his face and found they fit perfectly. He then reached up to fiddle with the LED on the right hand side. His finger found an intuitively placed button on top of the section of the glasses that housed the LED. As soon as he pressed it a strong red light emanated in what ever direction he faced. Not quite night vision goggles, but it would help him see in the dark without trashing his night vision. He pressed the button again and the red light extinguished. Next, he reached over and pressed the other button, located in the same location but on the opposite side of the glasses. He squinted against a very bright light projected in front of him. Apparently this light served as a standard flash light mounted to his glasses. After he turned the white LED off he ran his hands over the rest of the frames, looking for any other features. Finding nothing, he pulled the glasses off his face and set them atop the uniform items piled next to him on the floor.

He went back to the trunk and pulled out the only item remaining, other than the weapon and ammunition. It was a small rectangular pouch with a zipper running along the outer edge. Jon unzipped it and unfolded it on his lap. What he saw was an elaborate lock picking kit. It contained the traditional tools to mechanically lift the tumblers in a good old fashioned deadbolt lock, but it also contained a handful of electronic tools. The most intriguing among them was a flat black device with the front side completely covered by a smartphone-like screen. It looked a lot like one of the handhelds Jon and his fellow travelers had been issued, but was only a third the size. Jon rolled the device around in his hand, inspecting it for any indication of how to power it on. It contained only one button on the side. Jon depressed the button and the small screen directed him to 'hold near lock.' Jon stared at the device dumbfounded. *Was lock picking now also done completely by computer? Skill no longer required?* Before he had time to be disappointed in the obsolescence of one of his many special operations acquired skills, the text on the device started flashing and then the screen winked out. Jon decided he'd mess around with this gadget more later and replaced it in the kit.

He continued to go over each of the contents of the kit, intrigued by a half dozen small plastic discs in the mesh pocket in the back of the pouch. They seemed fragile and potentially important so Jon left them alone, electing not to take them out for further inspection.

Jon zipped shut the lock pick kit and dropped it on top of the uniform, alongside the tactical glasses. He returned to the trunk and was about to pick up the handgun to get a feel for it, when he noticed a pouch mounted on the side of the trunk closest to him. He reached in and withdrew a large, thin tablet. It reminded him of a larger version of an iPad from the 2020s.

He sat back down and began to turn the tablet in his hands, looking for a way to power it on, while also growing hopeful that it might contain information that clarified his mission; particularly why he needed the high tech pistol still resting at the bottom of the trunk. He found a thumbprint sensor near the bottom on the front of the tablet, similar to the sensor on his handheld. He pressed it and the tablet came to life. First his name flashed across the screen in green text. His name quickly faded and white text appeared: 'Place Tablet on a Flat Surface within Three Feet of User.'

Jon twisted his torso ninety degrees away from the trunk and gently laid the tablet down on the dingy carpet in front of him. Almost as soon as he'd set the tablet down he was face to face with Steven Pulling.

"Hello Jon. Welcome to St. Charles Place. Sorry it isn't a more inviting environment, but we needed to get close to the Pinnacle Headquarters while avoiding notice. Since you're watching this projection you obviously found the gear we left for you. Please pay close attention as I go over the contents of your kit and the details of your assignment. At the end of the presentation I'll also provide instructions on proper disposal of this tablet."

Pulling faded from view in front of Jon and was replaced by a three hundred sixty degree view of the street. Jon felt as though he was standing on a street corner, looking toward a guard shack that sat next to a road leading into a large gated facility.

"This is a model of the entry point to the Pinnacle Headquarters compound, less than a mile from your current location," said Pulling's voice, even though Jon could no longer see him. "The exterior gates are manned by the same company you work for, Gateguard Security. In 2050, Gateguard is a real private security firm that specializes in corporate security. They have been under contract with Pinnacle for the last ten years. And the best part - they are a shell company, established by the Casimir Institute for purposes just like this. When we started the company in 2035, we never actually planned on it being profitable. But here we are. I digress."

Pulling paused as the hologram carried Jon across the street and then face to face with the guard manning the entry point. Jon saw a first-person shooter style view in the hologram as an arm extended to show security credentials to the guard.

"Welcome back," said the virtual guard as he handed him a small radio and a key. "Your cart is parked on the back side of the shack."

Jon watched as the hologram advanced around to the back of the shack, then climbed into the electric cart. "Johnston checking in," he heard in surround sound.

Pulling resumed narration as the virtual cart started driving along the perimeter of the headquarters campus. Jon fought a slight sense of vertigo at the motion he saw but didn't feel. "Checking in to your shift should be pretty simple. Your shift manager is expecting a new employee, Mark Johnston, for the swing shift this afternoon. Once you have your radio and your patrol cart, the rest is fairly straightforward. Patrol the campus, respond to any calls on the radio, and take the opportunity to get the lay of the land."

The virtual view of the Pinnacle campus evaporated and Jon was staring at Steven Pulling again. "Keep in mind that, as a Gateguard employee, you don't have access to the majority of the buildings on site. You can access the lobby of the main building - the thirty story building in the middle of the campus - but can't get to the upper floors unless granted access to respond to an incident. The same holds true for the other research and server buildings scattered across the headquarters complex. Access is compartmented, even for Pinnacle employees. Security within the individual facilities is provided by Pinnacle security personnel, heavily supplemented by AI surveillance. As far as we can tell, a single Pinnacle employee is responsible for multiple buildings at any given time."

The Pulling hologram gestured toward the trunk. "Let's quickly review the contents of the trunk. Hopefully the uniform and credentials serve an obvious purpose. In addition to the uniform and access badge, your handheld contains a backdoor that will shift the embedded ID from Jon Haynes to Mark Johnston. We've tested the false ID capability extensively and are confident it's foolproof. After you've left the safe house, on the way to the campus, tap your thumb to the sensor three times to open the backdoor. You'll see a virtual switch on the screen. Swipe it to the alternate position and your handheld ID will shift. When your mission is done and you've left the facility, reverse the process and you'll be Jon Haynes again."

Jon tapped the thumb sensor as described. The screen illuminated with nothing but a virtual switch and his name at the top of the screen.

Pulling's holographic projection continued the presentation of the trunk's contents. "The glasses appear to be standard issue eye protection. They are not. There are red and white LEDs to provide additional lighting if necessary, but the real trick comes when you swipe your finger across the top of the frame. Go ahead and put on the glasses." Steven paused, staring at Jon.

Jon grabbed the glasses from atop the pile of uniform items and slid them in place.

"Do you have the glasses on now?" Steven asked robotically.

"Uh, yeah," Jon responded, surprised at the question from a pre-recorded presentation.

"Very good. Go ahead and swipe your right index finger across the top of the frame, from left to right."

Jon complied and his field of vision was filled with a detailed translucent map, presumably of the Pinnacle campus. A red dot was illuminated in the interior of one of the buildings.

After a short pause Pulling continued. "As you've probably guessed, you're looking at a virtual map of the Pinnacle campus. The red dot indicates the location of the three servers where we need you to install the program from the peripheral. When you're on the campus, your position will be indicated with a blue dot. I shouldn't have to emphasize that its very important you keep these glasses in your custody at all times.

"Next is the handgun. Weapons are not authorized for Gateguard employees working at Pinnacle facilities. So keep it hidden, don't leave it behind, and only use it in case of an emergency."

Jon reached in to the trunk and withdrew the gun along with the two boxes of ammunition.

Pulling continued. "I'm certain I don't have to tell you much about how to use the weapon we've provided. Technology in this area hasn't changed much over the years. A few important differences worth noting - first, the gun can only be fired by you. The palm of your hand provides a unique signature that the weapon is programmed to recognize. This is standard in 2050 and a significant contributor to reductions in gun violence. Second - It is capable of firing lethal and non-lethal projectiles. The red box contains the lethal and the green box, the non-lethal. There are two clips in the trunk. I'll leave it to you to organize your ammunition in a way that will prevent confusion in the middle of a crisis. Just know that while the green rounds are non-lethal, they aren't without consequence. They still use gunpowder for projection but are rapidly slowed using advanced aerodynamics. The outer shell separates from the projectile and leaves only a dart, containing a potent tranquilizer that travels to the target. If you need to use these to eliminate a threat that you don't intend to kill, make sure you don't shoot them in the face. The dart will leave a considerable mark wherever it strikes. You should also know that the recipient of a green round will be unconscious within about ten seconds and will remain that way for two to four hours. Then they'll awaken with a considerable hangover and possible memory loss."

Jon started loading the ammunition into the provided clips. He put the red rounds in one and the green in the other. He made a mental note to load the clip filled with green rounds into the weapon and figure out somewhere accessible on his person to hide the other.

"The one final piece of equipment we need to discuss is, what I like to call, the breaking and entering kit. Most of the instruments in this kit you're probably already familiar with. I'll highlight the electronic lock pick. It's one of my favorites. Hold this device up to any electronic lock and it will rapidly decipher the means of encryption and attempt to authenticate. Once it does this for the building you're attempting to access, you'll still need to authenticate with a thumbprint. That's what the plastic discs are for. Put one over your thumb and press it to the thumbprint scanner. The lock pick device will be emulating the handheld of the building manager. If our intel is correct, you should be on your way after that. Oh, and Jon? Don't lose control of the electronic lock pick. That technology does not exist in 2050.

"Now that we've covered your gear, I have a little more to say on the conduct of this operation. You must insert the peripheral device we provided you in one of three principle servers located in building 31 of the headquarters complex. Take some time during your shift to get an understanding of the pattern of life, particularly around that building. We suspect very little activity after working hours, but given that this facility houses the servers that ferry all data in and out of the complex, there is a high likelihood of a twenty four hour physical presence in the building.

"You are permitted two, twenty minute breaks during your shift. You should use one of them to carry out your mission. Ensure you leave your handheld and your cart a safe distance from the building. The location of both these items are likely tracked continuously by the Pinnacle Cloud while you're on the campus."

Jon wished he could pause the presentation. He felt like he needed to be taking notes as Pulling continued to get more specific about the task at hand.

"Once you have located the set of principle servers, plug the peripheral into any open port on any of the three. This server cluster performs a shared function and any location should do the the trick. Once the peripheral is plugged in you'll see a green light illuminate indicating our access program is being uploaded. The upload should take three to five minutes, and when complete, the green light will begin blinking rapidly. At that point it's safe to remove the device. As soon as the program is uploaded an encrypted message will be transmitted to our other operative, indicating your task has been completed and the Pinnacle server is accessible.

"Don't leave the peripheral device connected under any circumstance. Once the program is uploaded you must take it with you. If Pinnacle were to gain possession of the device, they likely will be able to reverse engineer its contents and learn that we were behind the wall of the protected portion of the cloud network."

The Pulling hologram let out a deep sigh. "Alright, I know that was a lot to process, but I trust you got the gist. We're relying on you Jon. Get to work. Your shift starts at fifteen hundred hours."

Jon glanced at his watch. It was already fourteen hundred, or 2:00

PM for the non-military types. He felt a flush of nerves as he recognized there was no time for advanced reconnaissance. He was going to have to jump right in to this one.

"Oh and Jon, one last thing. Put this tablet in the bathtub and cover it with water. Chemistry will do the rest."

The Pulling hologram winked out leaving only the large black screen of the tablet behind.

Jon picked up the tablet and walked to the bathroom. As he started the water he tried to catalogue everything he'd just learned. Mark Johnston of GateGuard Security, special glasses with hidden maps, gun with non-lethal bullets, special servers in building 31, USB device with super secret program, leave nothing behind, don't fuck it up.

Once there were a couple inches of water in the bathtub, Jon tossed the tablet in and waited for something to happen. After half a minute of watching the high tech piece of gear sitting at the bottom of the tub, he contemplated retrieving it to destroy it himself. Just before he could reach into the water to grab it he heard a loud pop. The tablet separated into at least a dozen individual square pieces and those individual pieces began to dissolve like Alka Seltzer tablets. He stood dumbfounded for the the next few minutes until nothing but bubbles and particulate remained.

Thank god ISIS didn't have this sort of technology back in the 2020s. Forcing himself to accept what he'd just seen, he reached into the tub and pulled the drain plug. A minute later there was nothing left other than wet ceramic.

Jon returned to the living room and donned the Gateguard uniform. Next he carefully placed his gear on his person. He placed the breaking and entering kit in the pocket of the black GateGuard Security cargo pants. He tucked the gun, with the non-lethal round-filled clip inserted, in the back of his waistband. He put the extra clip in the opposite cargo pocket of his pants and put the glasses atop his head. He went back to the bedroom, where there was a full length mirror on the closet door, to inspect himself and ensure none of his illicit cargo was obvious. Satisfied, Jon headed for the front door.

Once he was out on the street, walking toward the Pinnacle HQ, he flipped down his glasses, anxious to study the map of the compound. As he flipped them over his eyes he found that they'd tinted in the bright afternoon sun. Satisfied that he now fit in even better, walking outside on a sunny San Diego afternoon, he slid his finger across the top of the glasses to call up the map. When the green map popped into view he was momentarily disoriented and stopped in the middle of the sidewalk to regain his bearings. He peeked over top of the glasses to ensure no one had noticed his awkward pause. The residential street was empty so he spent the next few minutes committing as many details as he could about the complex to memory. He swiped the map clear of his field of vision and continued toward the front gate.

Next he reached in his pocket and withdrew his handheld. As Pulling had instructed earlier he tapped his thumb three times on the sensor. The switch appeared and he quickly swiped it to the right. The switch moved to the opposite position and the name at the top of the screen now read 'Mark Johnston.' Seemed simple enough. Hopefully it worked.

Fifteen minutes later, as he stood waiting at the crosswalk across the street from the front gate, Jon pulled out his handheld. He thumbed on the screen to check the position of his car. It was comforting to know he had an alternate escape plan available if things went south.

CHAPTER THIRTY

When Jon crossed the street to enter the Pinnacle campus, he found two guards in a shack clearly meant for one. The guard nearest the window was wearing a black uniform with the Gateguard logo, identical to the uniform Pulling provided for Jon at the safe house.

The guard looked him up and down then said, "You must be new. Credentials?"

Jon pulled the Gateguard badge with his photo on it from the front pocket of his pants and handed it over to the guard. The guard pulled it in through the window and scanned it at a console in front of him.

While Jon was waiting for whatever sort of check in process was occurring, he noticed the second guard running down a checklist attached to a clipboard. Since Jon was arriving for his shift, maybe he was also witnessing a shift change at the guard shack.

After a few moments of staring at the console and intermittently tapping at the screen, the guard returned Jon's badge through the window.

"Welcome aboard Pinnacle H-Q, Mark. You're just in time. I'll radio Clint, the dayshift patroller you're relieving. He'll come get you from right here behind the shack. Feel free to take a seat while you wait."

"Thanks," Jon replied, accepting his badge and clipping it to his collar similar to what he'd seen on the two guards in the shack. He walked past the shack and found the bench on the back side. Sitting, he decided the wait for his counterpart would serve as the start of his reconnaissance.

As he looked out at the portion of the campus he could see, a long road stretched out directly from the shack. At the end of the road was a chain link fence, probably marking the end of the campus property. He'd only been sitting there a moment when he heard the roar of a jet engine and watched a plane lift off the runway on the other side of the fence. The San Diego airport, exactly where it was back in 2023.

To the right of the road Jon saw an area with clusters of trees, walking paths, and a few smaller side streets. Through the trees he thought he could see large residential homes. Maybe officer's quarters from back when this compound was still a recruit training depot for the Marines. He made a mental note; it was interesting they hadn't knocked the homes down and converted that part of the property to something more functional for Pinnacle's operation.

On the left hand side of the street, directly across from the green space and residential areas was a long rectangular building four stories tall. The center front entrance of the building was decked out with ornate carved pillars and an archway. The end of the building nearest Jon bent back at a ninety degree angle, the structure continuing at least another hundred yards in a direction perpendicular and away from the street. That leg of the building cut off Jon's view of what was behind it and he was tempted to slide a finger across the top of his glasses to check the map. Instead he convinced himself to hold off, reserving that feature for use when he was alone.

Far behind the short building along the street Jon sighted a towering building that had to be at least thirty stories tall. Recalling his virtual briefing from Pulling, he pegged it as the main headquarters building.

As he finished eyeing the only particularly tall structure on the campus he saw an electric cart approaching on the road with a Gateguard uniform clad man behind the wheel. A minute later the cart stopped right in front of the bench where Jon was seated. The cart wobbled as a very tall man, probably in his late twenties or early thirties, with a noticeable paunch protruding over his belt, climbed out of the cart and walked toward Jon. The man's hair was an unkempt dirty blonde bowl that threatened to droop over his eyes.

"Hey there chief, you must be Mark," said the tall man.

"Yep," said Jon, cringing at the greeting, while standing to shake the man's hand.

"I'm Clint. I work the day shift and am sure glad to see you here. Let's go." Clint turned right back toward the cart he'd just dismounted and continued talking to Jon over his shoulder as he walked the few short paces.

"It's a good thing the weather's so nice. Everything else about this place bores me to tears. I'll be honest buddy, they keep a lot of security around here, and nothing ever happens."

Clint plopped back down into the driver's seat of the cart and Jon followed suit on the passenger side.

Clint kept talking as he pulled the cart into a u-turn to head back into the Pinnacle campus. "It's customary around here when we get a new guy for the off-going guy to take him on a round. Just to give you a feel for the routine. For the most part we get to operate independently, so it helps to have someone show you the ropes before you're off on your own. 'Course it also means I have to stay a half hour later today; but it's a fair trade if you promise to show up on time each day. Last guy that had your job was always late and full of nothing but horse shit and excuses."

"Well I used to be military and take pride in being where I'm supposed to be when I'm supposed to be there," Jon replied, taking on a slight bubba accent to endear himself to Clint.

"Oh yeah?" Clint said turning to look Jon over again. "What'd you do in the military?"

Damnit. Jon had brought it up in the interest of small talk, but he quickly decided it wasn't a good idea to give any details about his real military service, especially since his entire career happened nearly thirty years ago. "I was a grunt in the Marines for three or four years."

"No shit. I didn't realize the Marines were still around after they downsized the military all those years back."

Jon tried not to let his frustration with himself show on his face. Clint might be right. The Marine Corps might not even exist anymore. Jon needed to be less sloppy or he was going to end up drawing very unwanted attention from his peers.

"Who lives in the houses over there?" Jon asked, changing the subject.

"Not sure. I think a couple of them are kept ready for executives visiting from out of town," Clint replied. "I think one of 'em is decked out as a security outpost for the Pinnacle security guys. I sometimes see guys coming and going from a distance. That street's not on our patrol route though, so I've never paid it much attention."

As Clint finished responding to Jon he shifted his demeanor and tried to take on a teacher to pupil tone. "Ok, see this display here in the dash of the cart?"

"Sure," Jon replied quickly, shifting his attention to focus on whatever intel Clint was about to unknowingly provide him.

"The yellow bar highlights the route they want you to patrol. Each round should take you about an hour, although no one seems to care if you're a little faster or slower. If you see something that you want to check out closer - someone who doesn't seem to belong; that sorta thing - call it in on the radio before you get too far off your route. Nine times outta ten dispatch will consult with them and you'll get waved off to continue your route."

Clint's multiple references to an unnamed 'them' caught Jon's attention and he bit back the urge to pry for more information.

"To be honest with you bud, that's pretty much it. Drive the route, call in anything out of the ordinary on your radio, and check it out unless they tell you not to. Pretty boring. On the good side, you get a couple half hour breaks during your shift. I used to be a swing shift guy when I first started, and if I remember right, they were typically at around 6 PM, right after most of the Pinnacle employees leave for the day, and the second is somewhere between 9 PM and 10 PM, just when the nighttime boredom is getting so intense you feel like you might not make it through to the end of your shift."

Clint turned the car to the left, onto a secondary road, after they passed the long four story building. Once they made the turn, Jon had a clear sight line to the base of the tall headquarters building. It was surrounded on all sides by a massive parking lot that was about three quarters full of cars, many that looked a lot like Jon's sedan.

As Clint drove Jon down the road that sat about a hundred yards south of the southern perimeter of the massive lot, Jon had his best view yet of the majority of the installation. The north end of the parking lot was lined with one and two story u-shaped buildings that looked like old military office buildings. Probably serving the same purpose for Pinnacle now.

Closer to Jon, adjacent to the road on either side, were six H-shaped buildings, each four stories tall. Jon recognized them as military barracks. Three sat along the north side of the road and the other three were offset in a checkerboard pattern and sat on the south side of the road. Running near the road, between the tops of the buildings, Jon saw heavy duty electrical lines. Large utility pipes jutted up out of the ground near the base of each building before making a ninety degree elbow and entering near the base of the first floor.

As the cart approached the first building Jon could hear the hum of electrical transformers and noticed pump houses near the utility penetrations. He wasn't an expert but he knew that this level of cooling and power input wasn't part of the original setup for the Marine Recruit's barracks. The heavy duty utilities must have been added by Pinnacle after they bought the property. Jon guessed the former barracks had been converted to server farms. His finger itched to call up the map inlaid in his glasses. One of these buildings might contain his objective.

Jon took in every detail he could as they passed the six converted barracks buildings. He assumed these were among the many buildings Gateguard employees couldn't access.

As the cart approached the end of the road, Jon grew self conscious about how much he'd been focused on his surroundings at the expense of conversation with the more 'experienced' security guard in the seat next to him. He looked over at Clint and found his counterpart already looking at him.

"Pretty heavy duty stuff huh?" asked Clint rhetorically. "You big into knowing all about how the cloud works?"

"Um, I guess," Jon replied hesitantly.

"I've heard some folks spend their whole life trying to figure it out. I sometimes wonder if I'm driving around the answers to all their questions in my cart here each day." Clint tapped the steering wheel thoughtfully. "But I ain't no computer whiz, so who knows."

Jon changed the topic as Clint turned the cart to the left again, now heading north along the east side of the large rectangular parking lot and towering headquarters building. "Where do you go to get food around here? During your breaks I mean."

"I usually bring food with me. Way better use of time than standing in the cafeteria lines with all the white lab coat Pinnacle folks. During my breaks I park my cart way over there on the far side of the campus. There's a little finger of San Diego bay that reaches right up to the edge of the property. I park there, stare out at the water, watch the planes take off overhead, and munch on a PB&J. My favorite part of my shift."

"Sounds nice. Um, where is that cafeteria you mentioned?" Jon asked.

"There's one in the lobby of the HQ tower," said Clint, pointing at the tall structure in the middle of the lot. "The other one's a little smaller, but also less crowded. It's in that building over there," said Clint, pointing at one of the many small u-shaped buildings north of the large parking lot.

Jon strained to follow his finger, but couldn't make out which building he was pointing at.

"Don't worry Mark. You ain't gonna go hungry. There are signs over on that street. You'll see when we get closer."

"Ok, good. Guess I shoulda' brought some food for my first day," Jon said with a smile.

"You'll learn," Clint replied. "Oh, if you look over here to your right, there's another place to avoid."

Jon followed the new direction of Clint's finger and saw a single story building on the far side of the road. He immediately recognized it as an old base movie theater.

"That's the rec center. One of the few places, besides the cafeterias, where they let us lowly security types hang out in the same place as the Pinnacle employees. I've only gone in there once, but I think it's a sort of cloud cafe. One of the front gate guys goes in sometimes on his break. The Pinnacle guys use it to access the cloud for personal business, entertainment; that sorta thing. Apparently that's a no-no inside all their secure buildings."

"Good to know, thanks," Jon replied. *Interesting.*

As they were passing the old converted base movie theater, Clint slowed the cart at an upcoming crosswalk. A man and woman, each donning a white lab coat, stepped out into the crosswalk, exiting the theater and probably heading back to their primary place of work. Once the pedestrians were clear, Clint accelerated the cart as Jon tried to track where the coeds were headed, without being too obvious.

A moment later Clint pulled the cart to the left again, this time down a road that ran along the northern edge of the giant parking lot. As Jon looked to the south he finally understood the original reason for the massive concrete expanse. On the southern perimeter, unnoticed before because he'd been distracted by the server farm buildings, was a long set of old parade reviewing stands. Pinnacle had built a massive headquarters tower in the middle of what used to be the parade ground back when Marines were trained here.

As they traveled down the northern side of the lot, Clint pointed out a number of buildings, including the cafeteria. Jon feigned interest as he continued to try and track the two pedestrians out of his peripherals. He thought he saw them headed toward the easternmost barracks-turned-server building, but eventually lost them behind the parade stands.

When Jon turned his attention back to what was ahead of the cart, he saw they were approaching what had to be the back side of the ornate building he'd seen on the first street when he'd entered the base. The building was much longer than he'd realized before. After one leg of the building ran back away from the street, it flared out in another ninety degree leg, making it a five part structure overall. Stretched out straight it would run at least six football fields long. The center of the structure was equally ornate on the back side as it was from the front, with sculpted granite and marble columns surrounding the double doors to the entrance.

As the cart advanced Jon glanced down at the map on the console of the security cart. The road they were on was about to dead end, into the northern-most leg of the ornate four story building. They'd be forced to turn left again, passing near the back side of the structure.

Once they'd made the turn, Jon's adrenaline really kicked up. He sighted a narrow side street just off to his right. Jon glanced down the road and saw an automated gate with some sort of scanner housed in a stand next to it. On the opposite side of the street from the scanner was a large red sign with white text:

'Building 31
Restricted Access
Authorized Personnel Only
Beyond This Point'

Clint didn't seem to pay any attention to the more restricted area to their right. Jon waited a moment, hoping he'd offer some information. Instead the cart continued ahead in silence as they approached the west end of the same street they'd driven down earlier; the one that had taken them past all the server farms. They had effectively circled the block that contained the old parade ground and HQ tower.

As Clint prepared to turn right, and Jon sensed his guided tour was nearing an end, he couldn't help himself. "What's with the extra security at Building 31?"

"No Idea," Clint said with emphasis, as though he expected the question. "I don't know a single Gateguard guy who's ever been in there. In fact I could probably pick out the faces of the half dozen Pinnacle people I see going in and out of there on a regular basis. Seems to me that place is locked down tight. I've also never seen a Pinnacle security person go in there either. My guess is they use some sort of automated security system, but that's just a wild ass guess."

Jon remembered Building 31 from his last Pulling hologram briefing. His target was somewhere inside it. He resisted again the urge to consult his map, choosing instead to study all he could about the building as they made their way around it's perimeter.

Moments later they were headed back up the main road and Jon could see the guard shack a few hundred yards ahead.

Clint started to wrap things up. "Well that's pretty much it bud. Got any big questions for me before I punch out for the day?"

Jon had two; he'd figure out the rest on his own. "Yeah, you said most of the Pinnacle employees are gone by six. Does it get pretty busy before that, you know, when everyone's leaving?"

"Honestly, it's been a couple years since I did the swing shift, but if it's anything like when everyone rolls in between seven and eight in the morning, then yeah. It's probably a little bit of a mad house in the parking lots and on the road leading off the campus."

"Got it," Jon replied. "One more question about the, um, chain of command. You said if I want to go look into something - to deviate from the route - I need to call dispatch and then dispatch talks to someone else? Who's giving them instructions?"

"Boy is that ever a great question," Clint said with a guffaw. "There's a bunch of theories but I don't think anyone actually knows shit." He smiled big and looked at Jon as he slowed the cart on approach to the guard shack. "Hell, some of the guys think they're getting their instructions from an intelligent computer instead of a person. Morons."

After everything Jon had seen since arriving in 2050, the possibility didn't seem too far fetched. Especially not at a facility run by the company that brought about a revolution in artificial intelligence and networked machine learning.

"Well thanks for the training intro," said Jon, stepping out of the cart to circle around and shake Clint's hand.

"You bet chief. She's all yours," said Clint, smiling with the relief of the end of his workday, and gesturing to the driver side of the cart.

"Wait, that's it?" Jon asked. "I don't have to clock in or something?"

"Nope. You've got a handheld on you right?"

"Of course," Jon replied, rubbing his finger over the device in his pocket.

"Then as soon as I leave the campus, with you here, the system will recognize that you've taken the watch and that I'm gone for the day. Easy peezy."

"Hmm. Cool," Jon said, forcing a smile and departing wave at Clint who was already on his way out the gate toward a nearby parking lot. Jon silently hoped his Pinnacle ID as Mark Johnston, imprinted on his handheld, was foolproof. Otherwise this might be a short mission.

Jon pulled the cart into a u-turn and glanced down at the dash console for his first patrol route assignment. The yellow line highlighted a series of roads that were further out on the perimeter of the campus than what he'd just driven with Clint. Jon stifled a sigh. All he really wanted was to get closer to Building 31, especially around five in the afternoon when the place started emptying out for the night.

CHAPTER THIRTY-ONE

Claire opened her eyes slightly, assessing her surroundings and trying to recall the reason for the throbbing pain she felt in her forehead. She was laying on a comfortable bed, atop the bedding, staring at a beige wall with a framed photo in the center. The photo looked like a shot of the San Diego skyline, just a little…different.

When Claire rolled over to take in the rest of her surroundings she saw Tim Nguyen, her Casimir partner, sitting on the opposite bed and watching holo videos. The tide of Claire's mind shifted back to consciousness. She worked for Casimir, she was in the future; in 2050, and she had an important assignment.

Tim noticed Claire's stirring. "You snore when you sleep Claire," he said without looking away from his holo videos.

"Sorry," Claire replied groggy, "I was out cold. What time is it?"

Tim didn't respond, now swiping at the holograms in front of him, searching for something else to watch.

Claire swung her feet to the floor and stood next to the bed. As she did, the headache throbbing within her forehead rolled around, bringing the pain around to her temples and the back of her eyes. She also felt a nauseating vertigo sensation. She bit back the urge to vomit and took a deep breath.

The urge to either lay back down or vomit now under control, she turned back toward the bed to grab her handheld. As she leaned down to grab it she had to grit her teeth against the spinning feeling that seemed to intensify each time she moved. The vertigo was quickly overtaking the headache as her primary concern.

Claire palmed her handheld and gingerly made her way to the bathroom. She shut the door behind her and looked herself over in the mirror. Her hair was a mess and she had dark puffy circles under her eyes. She winced at her own appearance, then turned on the bathroom faucet and splashed water on her face.

The cool water felt amazing. Until Claire raised her head from the sink to let the water run down her face. She was caught by a quick surge of vertigo that caused her to wretch and vomit bile back into the sink. Graciously, the vomit seemed to carry some of the nausea down the sink with it.

With the faucet still running she stared into the mirror. Realizing her discomfort and appearance had all the markings of a hangover - something she hadn't experienced in at least a year - she grabbed her handheld to check the time.

She'd been asleep for four hours! A surge in adrenaline, followed by a quickening of her pulse helped her forget about the hangover. A new terror crept up in her gut. The message directing her to access the Pinnacle network could come at any moment. Instead of being poised for the call, her head was cloudy from the booze of a few hours ago. Worse, Tim was lounging around in the only place she'd considered using to get the solace and isolation she'd need to carry out her assignment.

Claire splashed water on her face again, then waited for the surge of nausea. When it didn't return she spent the next few minutes considering her options as she put her hair back in place and wet a washcloth. She held it to her face, trying to force down the circles under her eyes and ease the headache that had settled in behind her eyes.

She considered contacting Jon. Maybe he could help her figure out how to get rid of Tim. She opened the messaging application and stared at the blinking cursor. If she was going to use Jon's help she'd have to recruit him without letting him know why. She decided to reach out to him cautiously, not yet sure how, or under what premise she'd ask for his help.

'Hey, what are you up to?' She hit send without giving herself a chance to second guess it.

When a few minutes passed without a response, and without any of her own revelations about what she'd say if Jon did respond, she set the handheld on the bathroom counter. Claire reached into her front pocket and rolled the small bag containing Pulling's purple pills around in her fingers.

Claire took a deep breath. She couldn't afford to wait for Jon to respond. She couldn't afford to sit around hoping he'd help her without questioning why. She had another idea. She didn't like it, but the stress of knowing her call to action could come at any moment made waiting for a better plan intolerable.

She turned off the faucet, grabbed her handheld, and slid it into the back pocket of her jeans. Claire looked herself over one last time in the mirror, deciding she'd cleaned up as much as she could under the circumstances. She was silently grateful her look wasn't dependent on layers of makeup or hours in front of the mirror.

Claire emerged from the bathroom and found Tim still engrossed in holo videos projected from his handheld.

"Are you ready to get out of here and show me the town in 2050?" Claire asked, approaching the bed Tim was sitting on. She put her right hand on her hip and tried to come off a little flirtatious. It was enough to get his attention.

"Huh?" said Tim, as he clicked off the hologram from the handheld and wheeled around to look at her.

Claire smiled, satisfied with the minimal effort required to get his undivided attention. "I was about to ask if you wanted to escort me down to the hotel lobby to have a drink and plan out our evening."

"Um, yeah, of course." Tim fumbled with the handheld as he climbed to his feet, clearly eager to go get that drink.

Claire followed him out of the room and down the hall. Tim chattered in excitement the entire way there. By the time they reached the elevator Claire felt her headache returning. He wouldn't shut up.

"...so I searched for a coffee shop nearby. Not only did it give me all the coffee shops, but it showed the wait times, menu favorites, and other related establishments the cloud thought I might be interested in, including a bakery and a book shop that served coffee."

Tim hit the call button on the elevator and didn't miss a beat.

"When I got into the coffee shop the cloud knew I was there. It showed me the menu for the place I'd just walked into and two e-coupons for first time customers!"

Claire was desperate for Tim to shut up, but she also wanted coffee now. Thankfully, the elevator arrived only a few seconds later. Tim led Claire into the elevator with a hand on her back. She fought the urge to spin away from his touch.

"Anyway, once I decided what I wanted I ordered it right from my handheld while I stood in the line. Then I just paid with my thumbprint and stepped off to the side to wait. So efficient. How are companies not doing things like this in 2023?"

"Sounds awesome," said Claire feigning fascination. To be honest, as much as she wanted Tim to be quiet and give her a chance to get her headache under control, it did sound pretty awesome. She thought of all the times she'd stood in line at her favorite coffee shop in Seattle, knowing exactly what she wanted, but stuck behind someone asking a dozen questions about whether or not the milk was actually from free range cows.

As the elevator started descending to the lobby, Tim didn't stop.

"Once I had my coffee and sat down; that's when the really cool stuff started."

Claire rolled her eyes, caught herself, then glanced at Tim to be sure he hadn't noticed. He didn't. He was too absorbed in his coffee shop blabbering.

"I put my handheld down on the table - what seemed like a regular coffee shop table. As soon as I did, the surface of the table came alive! In giant letters it said 'WELCOME TIM NGUYEN.' I spent the next hour totally engrossed in the top of my table. Apparently its called a PUSH Terminal; Pinnacle Universal Simplified Hyperterminal. And they're all over the place now. Restaurants, bars, department stores, even little boutique coffee shops have them. I was so fascinated I spent half the time researching the terminal itself."

The elevator dinged, signaling their arrival in the lobby. As the doors slid open Tim moved to place his hand on Claire's back again. She moved just fast enough out the door to keep it from happening.

As they crossed the lobby en route to the bar, Tim closed the distance to walk shoulder to shoulder. Claire took a deep breath as Tim continued on about the PUSH Terminal.

"The whole experience was so immersive. When I searched for articles about the PUSH Terminal a holographic sphere hovered above the table. When I expanded the sphere it was actually a giant ball - more like a web - of articles and videos related to what I'd searched for. I could narrow the search and watch the sphere become more transparent as the number of results were filtered. I almost don't know how to describe it. It was so intuitive. Like I was swimming in the cloud."

Tim's last statement caught Claire's attention. "Do you think the hotel bar has a PUSH Terminal?" Claire asked Tim as they entered the bar.

Tim's eyes lit up with the recognition that he'd said something that had interested her.

They walked up to the bar and Claire was surprised to see the same fair-skinned red-haired bartender from earlier in the afternoon.

"Back for another Moscow Mule miss?" asked the bartender, smiling.

Claire instinctively glanced down at the bar top, avoiding eye contact with either Tim or the bartender. She wondered if the bartender realized how drunk she'd been a few hours before.

"Um, no. I'll have whatever he's having," said Claire, motioning in Tim's direction.

"What'll it be boss?" asked the bartender, shifting his attention to Tim.

Claire felt Tim's eyes on her as he considered his drink order. "How about bourbon on the rocks. That good for you Claire?"

"Sure," she responded too quickly.

"What's your brand?" asked the bartender.

"Why don't you pick it for us," Tim stammered. Claire suddenly had the impression Tim wasn't a bourbon drinker. Maybe he was trying to throw a false masculine vibe.

A moment later the bartender returned with a bottle of Basil Hayden's. As he grabbed two glasses and dropped a large ice cube in each, Claire felt the warmth of nostalgia. She felt pretty confident the bartender had selected the same bourbon Jon Haynes had been drinking their first night together. She glanced toward the front door involuntarily, wishing he'd walk through the door and save her from Tim Nguyen.

As her thoughts were drifting away to Jon Haynes, the bartender pushed the drinks across the bar to them. "Cheers!"

"Thanks," Tim replied as he swiped his handheld across the bar top to pay. "Do you guys have a PUSH Terminal in the bar?"

"Of course mate. Just put your handheld down on the bar top." The bartender walked away to tend to customers on the far side of the large rectangular bar.

Tim set his handheld down and Claire saw the bar top light up with the same welcome message Tim had described earlier. Tim pulled a chair back from the bar and took a seat. Claire followed suit, pulling her's close to him to watch him navigate the terminal.

Claire sipped her bourbon and immediately thought of Jon again. He had good taste.

"What should we search for?" Tim asked her.

"The history of Ne Plus Ultra," Claire replied too quickly. In her peripherals she saw Tim glance up at her, but was unable to pull her focus from the terminal. "Sorry," said Claire sheepishly. "Computer nerd fascination I guess."

Tim entered in the search she'd requested. Almost instantly the flat terminal transformed into a tangled sphere filled with the search results. The more prominent articles were in larger windows at the front of the sphere, but behind it, with incredible depth, were other more obscure articles.

Instinctively, Claire reached out to the holographic sphere and swiped a finger at it, left to right. In response, the sphere spun slowly on its axis in the direction she'd commanded. Amazing. Claire reached out her index finger and touched the sphere to stop the spinning. Then she brought her thumb and forefinger together. When she opened them, as though performing the reverse of a pinching motion, the sphere expanded in front of her.

Claire felt Tim's eyes on her as she manipulated the incredible holographic web search results. She looked at him. He was smiling. "What?" she asked with her best attempt at a friendly return grin.

"Nothing. It's just, you might be nerding out on this harder than I was."

"Well, you were right. This is amazing."

Tim sipped his bourbon and Claire saw him bite back discomfort as he swallowed. He set the drink down on the bar top.

"I'm going to go use the restroom. I'll be right back," said Tim as he pushed back from the bar.

Claire was glad he didn't grab his handheld and break up her fun. As he walked away she continued exploring the tangled sphere of search results, constraining herself against diving all the way in.

Suddenly, as if an invisible hand had slapped her across the face, Claire recognized her opportunity. She looked up from the PUSH Terminal just in time to see Tim pushing the door open to the men's room. Next she glanced right and left, looking for any attention she might be receiving from the half dozen bar patrons or the bartender.

Reasonably confident no one was paying her any mind, Claire reached into her right front pocket where she'd left Pulling's purple sleeping pills. She opened the small plastic pouch with her hands under the bar. She withdrew one of the pills and palmed it in her left hand while returning the bag to her pocket with her right.

Without hesitation she dropped the pill into her bourbon glass. As the pill sank to the bottom of her bourbon her eyes darted to the bartender. Still at the other side of the bar. Then to the bathroom door. Tim wasn't on his way back yet. Looking back at her bourbon glass, Claire saw a small trail of bubbles coming from the purple pill at the bottom of the amber liquid. This was not happening fast enough.

Claire picked up the glass as though she intended to take a sip. Instead she swirled it vigorously while holding the glass just below her nose. The pill fizzed more aggressively but was still very obvious at the bottom of the glass.

She set the glass down again in front of her and scanned the room again. The bartender was still preoccupied, but Tim had just emerged from the bathroom and would be back alongside her in a few seconds. She stuck her finger in the bourbon glass and stirred as hard and fast as she could without causing the drink to cascade over the side.

Once the liquid had settled Claire saw only bubbles and a very fine particulate. Time to take her chances. She swapped her glass with Tim's and went back to browsing the search results in the holographic spherical web in front of her.

"You were one hundred percent right about these terminals," said Claire as Tim returned to his seat at the bar. "They're amazing. I could do this for hours," she said as she quickly expanded and contracted the ball of search results in front of her. She reached over and picked up her drink, holding it out in front of her at shoulder height. "Cheers."

"Cheers," said Tim, grabbing his drink (formerly Claire's) from the bar and gently clinking her glass.

Claire withheld a satisfied smile as he took a long pull. Claire sipped her bourbon, enjoying the warmth and hair-of-the-dog effect it was having on her lingering hangover from earlier.

"So what's next Tim," said Claire, suggestively tipping her glass toward him, hoping to entice him to take another drink.

Tim complied, taking another gulp of bourbon before he responded. "I watched a holo video earlier today about a company near here that has immersion rooms. We should check that out."

Claire took another small sip of her drink before responding. "What's an immersion room?"

Tim drank again, to Claire's satisfaction. "From the video I saw, it's like an escape room, but it's all virtual, so the things you can see and do are much more..."

As Tim trailed off he rolled his lips back and forth over each other. He stared off blankly at the other side of the bar, his eyes glazed, with a look that said he was trying to remember what he'd been talking about a moment ago. He hadn't drank enough to be drunk yet. Claire assumed the sleeping pill must be taking hold.

"That sounds like fun Tim. Let's go back up to the room and finish our drinks."

"Naw," Tim said with an obvious slur added to his speech. "We just got here. And I wanna go to the immersion room."

"Me too," said Claire hooking her arm in his. "But first why don't you see me back to our room so I can freshen up." She looked up at him and smiled, pulling herself in close. She felt a pang of guilt at her provocative methods, but the increased dilation in his eyes and the thousand yard stare told her she needed to get him out of the bar quickly. If she couldn't get him up to the room she'd be dragging her sleeping partner through the lobby.

"Fiinne," said Tim, his slur becoming more exaggerated.

Claire felt his body weight shifting against her in a wobbling pattern as they walked out of the bar. If she didn't hold on to his arm he might crash to the floor.

As they crossed the lobby en route to the elevator Claire felt Tim's pace slow. She looked up at him and smiled the biggest, warmest smile she could muster. What she found was that in addition to his steps dragging, his blinking was becoming more exaggerated, his eyes staying shut a little longer each time. Claire decided to drop the flirty act and drag him to the room as fast as possible.

Claire pressed the call button on the elevator and waited with her zombie-like partner for what felt like an eternity. As they stood waiting, Tim's weight seemed to shift in larger and larger proportions. Claire slid her arm around his waist in a more intimate embrace to try to be sure he wouldn't go down for his nap right in front of the elevator.

She tried not to think about the chain of events that might unfold if he fell right here. She could try and tell people he'd had too much to drink and she was taking him upstairs to let him sleep it off. But if anyone asked, the bartender would certainly fail to corroborate their story. He'd only served them one drink.

Claire had to shuffle her feet in reverse to rebalance Tim as he nearly fell backward.

As the situation deteriorated, she started to think the elevator might never come. She glanced at the stairwell door adjacent to the elevators. Tim wasn't a big guy but there was no way they'd make it up twenty three flights of stairs. Her mind raced through the nightmare scenario of Tim falling onto the marble lobby. She played out different versions in her mind's eye. Claire wasn't much of an actress but she'd need to become one quickly if she couldn't keep Tim on his feet.

Then her heart sank like a stone. Tim's bourbon glass - the one with Pulling's purple pill dissolved and floating around in it - was still sitting on the bar. He hadn't finished it a few minutes ago when she drug him out of the bar. She could see clearly in her mind exactly where he'd left it and how much of the poisoned drink was still in the glass. She also pictured the bubbles and particulate that she'd been afraid were going to give her away before he started drinking it. As the elevator chimed its arrival Claire found herself wondering if incarceration in 2050 was any better than it was back in 2023.

Luckily the elevator was empty. Claire nearly hefted Tim forward to walk him into the elevator and prop him up as best she could in the back corner. On the way, she reached back to tap the button to send them to the 23rd floor.

As the elevator began its ascent, Claire let out a deep breath. Now that Tim and her were clear of the lobby she guessed that her chances of talking her way out of trouble using the 'he drank too much' story were much better. Still, she desperately hoped no one joined them in the elevator on the way up.

The elevator continued its providential trip to the 23rd floor without a single stop. As the door slid open Claire tried to use her arm around Tim's waist to heft him forward and out of the elevator. He hardly budged. Next she grabbed his hand and pulled it behind her head, draping his arm over her shoulder.

With her right arm around his waist and her left hand pulling on the wrist of the arm that was wrapped around her shoulders, Claire managed to get Tim moving forward and out of the elevator.

"Are you tryin to take uvantage of me Mizzz Keen?" Tim slurred as they lumbered together down the hall.

Claire cringed. Tim's hand, the one Claire had gripped at the wrist to keep his arm over her shoulder, was entirely too close to her breasts. Incidental contact as she drug him out of the elevator seemed to be the trigger that brought on his sloppy advances.

"You need to sleep Tim," she responded as she tried to pick up the pace.

As they arrived at the door of their room Claire carefully removed her right arm from supporting Tim at the waist. She then went to retrieve her handheld from the back pocket of her jeans. But before she could, Tim used his arm, wrapped around Claire's shoulder, to pull her toward him. Claire looked up at his face in time to see that he was coming in for a kiss. He was trying to make a move.

Claire turned her face away causing Tim's kiss to land awkwardly between her ear and cheek. She continued trying to dig the handheld out of her pocket, precariously trying to unlock the door before Tim could try to kiss her again.

Once she had the handheld in her palm she strained to pivot their two bodies toward the door so she cold swipe at the lock. As she did, Tim's opposite hand came up to her face, gruffly cradling her cheek to try the kiss again. Deciding she'd had enough, Claire stepped back. At the sudden loss of support ,Tim's eyes widened as he fell forward into the hallway.

Claire recoiled slightly at the dull thump Tim's body made as it flopped onto the hall carpet. She swiped her handheld against the lock and swung open the door to their room. She held the door slightly ajar with one hand and considered turning back to kick Tim in the ribs as repayment for his advances. Unfortunately she couldn't hold the door to the room open and get in good position to put some power behind her strike. Then she remembered that the only reason Tim was in this condition was the unnamed drug she'd applied to his drink half an hour ago. As she took a deep breath to recalibrate herself she heard the rumble of a soft snore coming from his position on the floor. He was out cold.

She stopped down and hooked his legs in each of her arms, both right below the knees. Then she leaned back with everything she had and drug him through the door into their room. The process was not quick. She only moved him a few inches at a time and every pound of his slight frame was dead weight.

When she had him almost all the way into the room, she cringed again as the door, which had been propped against his shoulder a moment earlier, swung into his jaw, connecting with a hollow thud. He'd feel that when he eventually woke up.

Claire gave one last heave, with everything she had, and drug Tim the rest of the way through the door. It swung shut immediately, once his head had cleared its path. Claire was panting from exertion and almost didn't hear the chime from her handheld that had been returned to her back pocket. But she did feel the vibration.

Retrieving it from her pocket, her fingers tingled as she read the

message on the screen:
'PINNACLE NETWORK READY FOR ACCESS'

CHAPTER THIRTY-TWO

Jon diligently followed his console's prescribed route for the first few hours of his shift. He did it in spite of his frustration that whoever was dictating the security patrols hadn't taken him anywhere close to building 31 again. He'd mostly been doing laps east and north of the former parade grounds turned HQ tower.

On the bright side, Jon had found a half dozen places to park his cart within a couple blocks of the cafeteria Clint had showed him. Given that the security 'them' that Clint had described earlier were able to track his handheld and the location of his cart, he'd need to put some distance between himself and those items if he was going to carry out Pulling's mission.

Jon was just wrapping up a route on the east end of the complex when he passed another access gate. This one was obviously an alternate entrance, probably used for additional access during peak hours back when this place had been a Marine Corps training base. Now it looked abandoned, with the extra gate permanently closed and the guard station forever unmanned. Pinnacle probably didn't have enough people coming and going from this complex to need an additional access point. The gate wasn't just closed, it was chained shut. But the gate itself was only eight or ten feet tall and wasn't topped by razor wire like the rest of the fences that marked the perimeter of the campus. Jon filed this away in case things got hairy later in the evening.

As he passed the gate and continued along the road that paralleled the fence line, Jon heard the now familiar tone from the cart's console indicating a new patrol route had been loaded. He smiled at his good fortune. The new route would have him continue along the northern perimeter fence of the campus and then follow a small road that would take him just north of Building 31 before he'd re-emerge on the main campus access road inside the front gate.

Jon glanced at the time displayed in the corner of the console's screen. It was 4:45 in the afternoon. If he timed his trip just right he could be near Building 31 at 5:00 when people started filtering out for the day.

He pulled the cart to the side of the road and swiped his forefinger across the top frame of his glasses, calling up the campus map. He saw the blue flashing dot indicating his current position along the perimeter road. But the focus of his attention was on the red dot blinking in the northernmost wing of Building 31; the section that his current patrol route would have him pass shortly. Based on the location of the red dot, within its particular wing of the building, Jon guessed it was probably inside a door about halfway down the building's main corridor. If he could get into the building through a side door at the northernmost end of the building, he might be able to get in and out, undetected, minimizing the amount of time he was forced to walk the halls of a building that certainly had plenty of internal surveillance.

Jon swiped the map away and slowly pulled his car back onto the road. Earlier, Jon had figured out that the cart could get up to around twenty five miles an hour, but for now he crawled along at just over ten, watching the console and trying to time his arrival at his point of interest.

Ten minutes later, Jon shifted in his seat, trying to quell the build up of nervous energy. The road he'd been following near the fence line curved away from the fence and toward what Jon recognized as the northern end of Building 31. He was still too far to see any detail on the side of the building, but he slowed the cart further to give him as much time as possible to study it as he passed.

Moments later he was close enough to make out an automated security gate, exactly like the one he'd seen on the back side of the building during his initial tour with Clint. It was preceded by a small access road that branched off the road Jon was following. He was less than a hundred yards from the intersection and racked his brain for an excuse he could call in to dispatch that would allow him to stop.

As he drew even closer, Jon saw the outline of a heavy metal door on the closest side of the building. He hoped it could serve as his entry point. With that in mind, he decided not to stop. He'd wait until it was dark to get closer to the potential entrance. He stared at the door as the road drew ever closer to the end of the building. Unfortunately, he was still too far off to make out any details about surveillance equipment or, particularly, the locks on the door that he'd need to breech. He passed the intersection, crawling along now at less than five miles per hour. He saw the same large red sign along this access road that he'd seen earlier on his tour with Clint:

'Building 31
Restricted Access
Authorized Personnel Only
Beyond This Point'

He was boring in on the end of the building so intently that he didn't notice the cart drifting to the right side of the road until he heard the churn of gravel under the tires and he felt the cart lean to the right as it started crossing onto the shoulder. Jon jerked the wheel to the left to return to the road and resumed his inspection of the building, approaching the point where the road passed closest to the building.

Back on the road, Jon looked back again toward his objective. When he did, he instinctively slammed the brakes on the cart, bringing it to a stop in the middle of the road.

A man in a white lab coat had just emerged from the door and was walking to one of the two cars parked in the lot behind the security gate. Then Jon had an idea and reached for the radio on his shoulder.

"Dispatch, this is Johnston, over," said Jon as he held the talk button on the radio.

"Go ahead Mark," crackled the radio a moment later.

"I, uh, request permission to check the door closest to my location. I just saw one of the Pinnacle employees exit and it looks like the door didn't fully shut behind him."

"Standby," came the reply from dispatch.

"Roger."

While Jon waited for dispatch to come back he watched the lab-coated man climb into a sedan, which, Jon assumed, would then back itself out of the parking spot. Using it's connectivity to the cloud and self-driving features, the sedan would then ferry the man through the front gate and back to his home, all while making the experience quick and infinitely safer than the fallible driving skills of humans back in 2023. Jon stared at the console in his cart, not wanting to draw the attention of the man in the sedan as he passed by on his way out of the facility. As Jon stared down at the console and watched the sedan pass in his peripherals, Jon wondered briefly what people in 2050 did with all their free time during their automated commutes. If people hadn't changed in the last thirty years, then they probably spent too much of it watching porn.

Once the sedan passed him on the road, Jon shook the random distraction from his mind and went back to studying the door to the building. He was only about fifty yards from it at his present location. He wasn't certain, but he thought he could make out a black box next to the door. Jon hoped it was the automatic lock he was equipped to penetrate.

Just then Jon's radio crackled to life again. "Mark, that's a negative on checking that door. They say they checked their system and its secure. Resume your route."

"Roger," Jon replied after he'd depressed the talk button. *Damn.*

As Jon pulled away frustrated, he reminded himself that the last ten minutes had prepared him significantly more for his assignment than everything else that had happened over the last two hours.

When Jon reached the intersection with the main base access road, he could see that the end of the work day was descending on the campus. Cars were lined up from the stop light outside the main gate, back through the gate and all down the road that ran in front of Building 31. Jon sat patiently in the cart and waited for an opportunity to turn left across the traffic.

He sat there through two cycles of the stoplight outside the campus. The traffic behaved like a slow moving accordion. Each time the light turned green, the cars stretched out slightly as the one in front accelerated and the next recognized it was time to move forward. Then, as the light cycled back to red the accordion shrank back down, each car settling slightly off the bumper of the one in front of it. The same thing happened back when cars were driven by humans, but what he watched now was so much more organized. The cars behaved as part of one system rather than a bunch of disparate systems - the humans behind the wheel - behaving independently and simply reacting to each other.

Jon was so fascinated with the process that it took him a moment to notice, on the third cycle of the light, that the car to his left had deliberately stopped short of the car in front to allow room for him to cross the outbound lane.

Instinctively Jon waved his gratitude as he pulled the cart into the turn. But when he glanced at the driver's seat through the windshield he saw a woman working distractedly with a laptop across her lap. Had the network of cars in traffic granted him passage? *Impressive.*

As Jon drove his patrol cart in the lane opposite the stop and go departing traffic he was fascinated to look through the windshield at the 'drivers.' The ones he could see had their faces buried in a handheld or larger tablet-like devices. About every third car had a tint over the front windshield making it impossible to see inside. Jon assumed they were engrossed in something more elaborate, similar to the holographic history presentation Alistair had presented during his ride in from the desert.

As he approached the end of the line of waiting cars he felt an odd nostalgia as he realized road rage was probably a dead language in 2050.

***

An hour later Jon continued to follow the yellow highlighted route dictated by the console in his Gateguard cart. The campus had gone quiet again after forty five minutes of departing commuter activity. His current task had him circling through the residential area and passing down the narrow road that ran along the small sliver of waterfront that was part of the campus.

Looking southwest over the water of San Diego Bay and out toward the ocean, Jon saw the sky beginning to turn an angry shade of red-orange as the sun passed below the hills of Point Loma.

Jon slowed the cart to appreciate the view. The Southern California sky seemed clearer than he remembered it. He glanced down at his watch and saw that it was just past eighteen hundred. It would be dark soon, and he should be due for a break.

The thought of making his move with so little preliminary reconnaissance made his heart rate increase. As he pressed his foot on the accelerator to continue through the green residential area of the campus, Jon pondered the worst case scenario. When he was a SEAL he'd used the same tactic to help him visualize how he'd get out of a bad situation, or how he'd know when to accept mission failure and shift his attention to saving the lives of his teammates. He never accurately predicted the way things might go wrong, but the exercise of thinking through the best ways out of a bad situation were valuable repetitions for his mind.

There was no activity in the residences that Jon could see from the street. The large houses either served only for decorative purposes, or they were currently vacant. He continued back toward the main access road, anxious to see his next assigned route when he reached the end of the current one in under half a mile.

A few minutes later he eased on the brakes as he approached the stop sign at the intersection with the main campus entrance road. As soon as his cart had stopped two dings emanated from the console. He glanced down to see the map replaced with 'Check In with Dispatch for Shift Break Number 1.'

Across the street and to his right Jon could see the opulent front facade of Building 31. Directly ahead was the northern leg of the building that represented his evening objective.

Jon considered calling in to dispatch to report that he was taking his break. But then he remembered that Clint had said the breaks were only twenty minutes long. He couldn't afford to waste a single minute of that time. He mashed the accelerator, crossed the main campus entrance road and continued past his previous reconnaissance area.

As the road bent back toward the perimeter fence line he'd driven along earlier, there was one additional side street he hadn't explored, but that ran into the more densely populated part of the campus near the cafeteria. He took the shallow right turn and headed for the dining hall.

As he approached the set of buildings Clint had pointed out earlier, he slowed and tried to read some of the small signs set off from the road closer to the buildings. Realizing they were difficult to read because of the oncoming darkness, he flipped the switch next to the steering column that energized the cart's headlights. They didn't help.

Once Jon sensed he was close to the cafeteria he squeezed the talk button on the radio on his shoulder. "Dispatch, this is Johnston, checking out on break."

"Roger," came the quick reply. "See you in twenty."

Jon jerked the steering wheel to the right into a narrow alleyway between two of the single story buildings. Once he had the cart out of view of the street he'd departed, he killed the lights and stomped the brake pedal all the way down to set the parking brake.

He quickly unclipped the radio from his shoulder and tucked it in a compartment in front of the passenger seat of the cart. Next he shoved his hands into his cargo pockets to inventory his gear. He felt the B&E kit, right where he'd placed it before leaving the safe house. Then, just to be certain, he pulled the ammunition clip from the opposite cargo pocket and looked at the rounds in the magazine. They contained red bands, indicating lethal ammunition. He re-pocketed the clip and reached around to the back of his waistband to place a re-assuring hand on the grip of the pistol that he'd confirmed was loaded with non-lethal rounds. Last, he pulled the Gateguard polo shirt over his head and stuffed it into the passenger side glove compartment. He'd decided a few hours earlier that trying to access Building 31 in a Gateguard uniform was a bad idea. It would only serve as a billboard announcing he wasn't supposed to be there. Once the uniform polo was tucked away, he re-situated the pistol in his waistband one last time to ensure it was concealed by the t-shirt as best it could be. The bulge felt obvious, but Jon hoped the darkness would obscure it.

Jon was out of the cart, down the alley, and already two blocks away from his parking spot when he stopped dead in his tracks. He still had his handheld in his pocket. He glanced at his watch and saw that he was already three minutes into his miserably short break. He didn't have time to waste returning to the cart to put it back, but he couldn't continue on with it in his pocket and risk that Pinnacle could track his location as he entered Building 31.

Jon tossed the handheld in the bushes that ran along the sidewalk, doing his best to take a mental snapshot of the area so he could find it when he returned.

With the handheld no longer on his person, Jon picked up the pace. He was only a block away from crossing the street that ran along the east side of Building 31. He cut quickly across an open grassy area that allowed him to shorten the distance he had to cover to reach the northern area of the building that contained the door where he intended to attempt his entry.

He was now closer to the door than he'd been on his earlier patrol, but it was also darker now. He squinted to try and make out any cameras or other security that might be situated to monitor his entrance of interest. When he was less than fifty yards out and still unable to tell, he altered his trajectory to approach the building from around the corner, shielding him from any potential monitoring near the door until he could get a better idea what he was up against.

Jon broke into a jog for the last thirty yards as he arced around to the corner of the building. As soon as he reached it he stopped and leaned with his back against the painted concrete wall. If anyone had seen him running up to the building he was already caught. Once he was against the wall he surveyed the area, hands in the pockets of his cargo pants - trying to appear nonchalant, as though he belonged. Fortunately, this side of the building was not well lit, and he didn't see a single person in any direction he looked. The campus, at least outside the buildings, was abandoned at night.

As he settled in to his temporary surveillance post, Jon was pleased at how excellent a spot he'd chosen. As he leaned against the wall, directly in front of him, less than a hundred feet away across the grass, was the backside of another small building; part of the long row of administrative buildings that ran along the northern edge of the HQ tower parking lot. To his right was a well lit, covered walkway that ran between the admin building and the north wing of Building 31. And to his left was the grassy field he'd just crossed. Jon was also surprised with the lack of physical security on the exterior of the building. Where someone obviously needed the right access to drive a car up to the building, someone on foot only had to walk across the grass.

Confident he hadn't been noticed yet, Jon walked over to the corner and peeked his head around, to get a better look at the door. It wasn't the best vantage point. In order to avoid detection by any cameras that might be there, he allowed only a few inches of his face to extend out past his wall of sanctuary. The door was less than fifty feet away. There were two flood lights positioned above the door. One projected out to illuminate the small parking lot, a parking lot Jon noted was now empty. The other flood light cast a bright circle around the area of the door. There was also a surveillance camera above the door, pointed out toward the parking lot. While he wasn't exactly sure of the field of view of the camera, he was fairly confident he could avoid it if he stayed very close to the wall as he approached the door. The last detail he could make out was a box at eye level next to the door. It was probably the lock he'd need to defeat to get into the building. Out of caution, he assumed it had a camera too; probably used to see who was badging into the building.

Conscious of the short time he had available, Jon mentally assembled his plan to get through the door. He called up the map on his glasses to take one last look and gauge how far into the building he needed to go before he started opening doors looking for the server room. Next, he reached into his cargo pants pocket and withdrew the breaking and entering kit. He unzipped it quickly, opened it and pulled out the electronic lock pick, hoping Pulling's intel was right. He couldn't afford to linger under the flood light outside the door for long. He also pinched one of the small plastic thumbprint discs between his thumb and forefinger. He palmed the two items he hoped would get him through the door, zipped the B&E kit shut, and dropped it back in his cargo pocket.

Without hesitation, Jon rounded the corner and walked casually toward the door. As he walked his left shoulder brushed along the concrete wall. He tried to stay as close to it as possible to avoid detection by the camera, while not appearing too suspicious to anyone who might be watching him through the windows of any nearby buildings. He also tried not to tense as he stepped into the bright light in front of the door. Jon stalled before stepping in front of the electronic lock. It was slightly below eye level. There was probably a camera, or worse, facial recognition that needed to be defeated to release the lock on the door. Jon took the plastic thumbprint from his palm and pressed it into place on his right thumb. Then he took a deep breath.

Guessing that if there was a camera it was probably above the big pad in the middle of the mechanism, he draped his left arm across the top of the black box as he stepped in front of it, hoping to obscure any view of his face Next he pressed the button on the side of the electronic lock pick. The screen lit up yellow and showed a cartoon graphic indicating Jon should hold the back of the device against the handheld reader. He did as indicated. As soon as the lock pick was within range of the reader the screen turned a shade of greenish-yellow. White text appeared on the small screen: DECRYPTING

The text pulsed, fading in and out, indicating the device was processing its task. Jon felt exposed. An individual eternity passed with each cycling of the text on the screen. In the meantime, without moving his arm from its resting place along the top of the electronic box, Jon searched for indications of a camera. He silently prayed that if there was one, his arm was obscuring its view. He also risked a glance up at the larger surveillance camera he'd seen perched above the door. When he couldn't see the lens of the camera at this angle he felt confident that a set of eyes wasn't on him.

After what was probably a few seconds, but felt like hours, the screen on the electronic lock pick abruptly turned red and the text turned solid: DECRYPTION FAILED, PLEASE TRY AGAIN.

Jon's instinct demanded he break off and devise a new plan. But something in his gut kept his feet planted and his arm draped over the top of the lock box. He pulled the electronic lock pick away from the lock and the screen turned yellow again. He quickly mashed the button on the side of the device and the screen went black. Another deep breath and he pressed it again. The yellow screen returned, now with the instruction graphic displayed. He pressed it against the face of the lock reader again.

The device repeated the same process again. After a minute of decrypting the screen on the device turned bright green with white text: DECRYPTION SUCCESSFUL. Jon exhaled as he dropped the electronic pick in his pocket, careful not to remove his left arm from atop the box.

As soon as he'd pulled the lock pick away from the display he saw another set of instructions displayed on the lock panel: WELCOME MICHAEL HALL. PLEASE AUTHENTICATE.

Jon delicately pressed his right thumb, covered with the plastic false thumbprint, against the smaller pad below the screen. Seconds later it issued a satisfying beep, and the heavy electronic lock on the door thunked its release. Jon Haynes was through the door before he had time to think about what might be on the other side.

As the door clicked shut behind him and the lock thunked back into place, Jon found himself standing at the end of a dimly lit hallway. Both sides were lined with doors spaced roughly ten feet apart. Probably individual offices. The only light in the corridor was from recessed lighting at floor level along both sides. The building was probably closed down for the evening.

Jon started down the hallway, planning to examine the doors midway down the right side of the hall to try and find the server room. He glanced down at his watch. He had just over ten minutes before he was expected back from his break.

When Jon was about ten feet from the exterior door and continuing down the hall, the overhead lights all came on at once. He hesitated briefly, taking an awkward stutter step. His adrenaline went from a normal high - the kind Jon was used to feeling during any operation, providing a boost in focus and energy - to the red line. His mind went into overdrive, calculating if he could escape back out the door before a pursuer, bursting from one of the many side doors in the corridor, was able to apprehend him. He fought a panic that urged him to turn and flee. Fighting down his nerves, Jon rolled his head around between his shoulders, forcing the tension down. He fought to appear casual. It was his only chance to stay on mission. If he started running, it would only draw attention. And who knows, maybe no one had seen him. Maybe the building was energy efficient and he'd just triggered the motion activated lights.

Once he coached himself back to calm, he was already almost half way down the long corridor. Just ahead and to his right, there was a set of double doors with a larger spacing between them and the adjacent rooms. It was also the only set of double doors Jon saw in the entire corridor. And it was near the midway point of the corridor on the correct side. Jon felt a surge of the good adrenaline, confident he was honing in on his target.

Jon angled toward the door, trying his best to appear that he belonged and knew where he was going. The placard next to the doors was made of simple gray plastic with raised white text: SERVER ROOM SIX, AUTHORIZED PERSONNEL ONLY.

Shit. It was probably locked. Jon resisted the urge to grab his breaking and entering kit from his pocket. Instead he pushed the handle on the door to check it. It offered no resistance, swinging open into the server room.

The room was dark, illuminated only by LEDs interspersed throughout rows of servers that spread out twenty feet to Jon's right and left. The area immediately around the door, within its swing radius, was lower than the rest of the room. Jon could see dimly lit stairs that led to the the raised server room floor.

Jon stepped clear of the door, allowing it to shut behind him, darkening the room further. Before he moved up the stairs to begin exploring the row upon row of servers, he called up the map in his glasses. Unfortunately, the scale of the map put his blue dot and the red dot of the server cluster of interest right on top of each other. Based on the map in his glasses, he was probably in the right room, but he'd be here all night trying to pinpoint the correct server to load the data stick into.

On a whim he pinched his thumb and forefinger together and touched them to the outside of his glasses. Then he spread the two fingers out over the front of his glasses, making the standard 2023 smart phone zoom in motion. As he did, the image in his field of vision grew, creating distance between the red and blue dots.

As he zoomed in there was no detail to the building's interior that appeared. Casimir probably didn't have intel on the floor plans or layout of the servers. Yet somehow they knew exactly where the servers of interest were located.

Jon decided to leave the map called up in his glasses. It was translucent enough that he could see to walk between rows of servers to bring the blue and red dots closer to each other, zooming in further if required as he got closer. But as soon as he stepped onto the stairs to climb onto the raised server room floor he was hit with a blinding light.

"Fuck," Jon exclaimed, surprised for the second time since entering Building 31 by an unexpected transition from dark to light. He'd convinced himself once before that the lights were motion activated. He decided to do the same now, gulping down his panic and pressing forward.

Once atop the raised floor he hung a left and walked two rows down. Then he stopped briefly and zoomed in again on the map inlaid in his glasses. In the full fluorescent light of the room his map was more difficult to see, but he could still make out the blue and red dots as they got closer to each other. He turned right, zooming in twice more as he made his way down the chosen row. He was two thirds of the way down the row when he couldn't zoom in any further to separate the different colored dots on his map. He was right on top of the target servers.

To his right all the servers were lit with intermittently blinking blue LEDs that seemed to dance synchronously with the rest of the servers on that side of the aisle. To his left were three cabinets that stood out with an array of colors flashing in patterns that were too complex for him to process. Jon swiped his finger atop his glasses to clear the map and inspect this spot more closely.

Once the map disappeared Jon knew he'd found his spot. With his field of vision clear, he could see a plastic door in front of the colorfully blinking group of servers. As he inspected the cover he located a small latch and lock on the far right hand side. He didn't waste any time pulling out the B&E kit in his cargo pants' pocket.

Thirty seconds later he had the cover open and the lock pick back in his pocket. Next he scoured the set of servers looking for a port that looked compatible with the peripheral stick Pulling had provided. Jon tried not to panic when his initial scan of the front of the servers didn't reveal an interface that seemed to fit.

He glanced nervously down at his watch to check the time. As he did he noticed a glint of silver metal amidst the flat black of the servers and surrounding chassis. He bent down to inspect it further, forgetting about the time remaining on his break. When he did he found a shiny silver handle attached to a thin section of the server cabinet.

Jon, still squatting in front of the cabinet, grabbed the handle and pulled it gently toward him. Nothing happened. He felt around for a latch or button that would release this section. He found nothing and started to check the time again. But before he looked at his watch he had an idea. He tapped the right side of his glasses to turn on the bright white LED to get a better look.

As soon as he did, he saw the shadow of a small thumb switch next to silver handle. Leaving his light on he pushed the switch to the side with his right hand while pulling the silver handle with his left. The drawer slid toward him, revealing a black keyboard with white backlit keys. At the top of the keyboard was a peripheral port that looked to be the female companion to the stick Jon clutched tightly in his hand.

Jon wasn't sure how much time he had, but it was definitely short. Without hesitation he plugged the stick into the port atop the keyboard. The light on the device turned green, just as the Pulling hologram said it would during his briefing a few hours earlier.

Based on Pulling's brief, Jon expected the process to take three to five minutes. While the light shone from the stick now plugged into the keyboard, Jon looked at his watch. His break was set to end in less than five minutes. There was virtually no chance he'd make it back to his cart to check in with dispatch. No turning back now.

He watched the light on the data stick like a pot of boiling water. The minutes were agonizing. He hardly noticed the burning in his thighs as he remained squatted in front of the server's keyboard. As soon as the green light flashed, indicating the completion of his mission, Jon was poised to remove the stick and make haste back to his patrol post.

After what seemed like an eternity, the light on the stick went from solid to a rapid flashing. Jon stuck his right hand out to grab the stick, but before he had it in his hand time stopped again.

"Don't fucking move," came a shaky voice from over Jon's shoulder.

His adrenaline shot through the roof and he focused every bit of his energy on slowly wrapping his hand around the stick to pull it from the keyboard.

The voice over his shoulder, even more shrill than before chimed in again. "Who are you and what are you doing in here?"

Jon let out a long slow breath, calming himself before he made his next move.

CHAPTER THIRTY-THREE

Claire's pulse was already elevated from straining to drag Tim into the hotel room. Once she read the message on her handheld and realized it was go time, her heart was beating so fast she was worried she'd have a heart attack.

She took a deep breath and slid the handheld into her pocket. Then she sat on the end of the nearest bed and tried to slow her breathing. A moment later, thinking she had it together, Claire lifted her arms, bent at the elbow and looked at her hands, palms up. They were visibly shaking. She had to get herself under control.

But she also had to get to work. She stood and made her way the few steps over to the closet that contained the safe she'd explored earlier. Before she could get the door open she had to reposition Tim's lifeless body to get his legs clear of the path of the closet door. She grabbed his feet and heaved them in the direction of the bathroom, creating just enough space. Then she knelt down, opened the safe door and thumbed the biometric scanner at the back. Just like before, the bottom of the safe popped open and she quickly withdrew the laptop.

Once she had the laptop in her hands she felt strangely confident. Her pulse was still making a racket in her ears but holding the laptop and preparing to take on her task - her mission - gave her a rush that left confidence in its wake.

Claire hopped onto the bed and sat cross legged with the laptop in front of her. She flipped the screen open and mashed the power button. As soon as the computer finished booting and asked her to authenticate, she pressed her right thumb to the trackpad just like she'd done a few hours earlier. A moment later she saw the baby blue background and the folder titled M31723A. She opened it, then opened the cMap application from within. Just as predicted by the read me file from earlier, a new network was available within the application. Pinnacle Cloud was displayed at the bottom of the short list, in bold text with a green dot next to it. Claire clicked the network.

A two-dimensional network topology diagram filled the screen almost immediately. The screen was packed with nodes and the links between them. Even more links ran off the screen out of view. What Claire was looking at now was orders of magnitude larger than the training program she'd walked through earlier.

She stared at the diagram for a moment, trying to orient herself. It was made more difficult by the fact that nodes winked in and out before she could get a true sense of how they tied into the hierarchy. Near the edges of the screen it looked similar to the hierarchy of a cellular network, with smaller nodes connected to base stations which tied back in to the terrestrial network. But it wasn't that simple. The smaller nodes, which Claire was ready to assume were individual cell phones, also intermittently carried other nodes back to the base station. Maybe cell phones, or handhelds, in 2050 were smart enough to allocate excess bandwidth to other devices nearby in order to boost the range and processing power of the base station. Claire knew from some of the research going on back in the early 2020s that those types of data streams and spectrum sharing were complex and fraught with security risks.

Claire was starting to get the picture, but the cutoff image indicated there was much more to see. She used the trackpad to zoom out on the 2-D image. The screen quickly became cluttered as the individual nodes became indistinguishable and the base stations started to look like tiny stars in the sky. But Claire could still differentiate the large data carriers - probably fiber optic lines - that gathered up entire regions of data and began to merge toward a larger highway of links that ran off her screen.

She panned to the right, watching as more and more main line links joined together near the center of the screen. The further right she went, the more the data highway widened. She continued to pan right, following the widening highway until it terminated at a massive node - a server farm maybe? Similar superhighways of data departed the main node in three additional directions. Claire got excited. She might have found the hub of the Pinnacle Cloud.

She zoomed in slightly on the 2-D image but was disappointed when she couldn't draw any additional resolution on the intersection of the four digital superhighways. Thinking back to the scale of data she'd been viewing when she started, she tried to imagine how much information this hub was processing. This was more than a server farm. It had to be a massive network hub, the likes of which didn't exist in 2023. And it's internal architecture was protected such that she couldn't determine it from this vantage point.

Claire zoomed back out and followed a different connecting line. She watched as the highway of data flow narrowed and the spiderweb of interconnecting links expanded out in different directions. As she continued to pan up and follow the increasingly dispersed and narrowing highway, she was becoming convinced that she'd already found the Pinnacle Cloud's singular hub - *maybe it was NPU.*

She continued to pan up to see how far the links would disperse before becoming unrecognizable amidst the sea of data running out in every direction. Instead, she saw links start to pour back in to the fiberoptic highway. She increased her pan rate and watched the links converge again, just like they had before. The highway grew wider and wider. She panned faster and faster, swiping the trackpad faster than the laptop could process. Then she arrived at another of the massive junctions. So much for finding the primary network hub.

Claire zoomed in on the hub, expecting the same result as before. A second later she'd confirmed it. The massive network hubs had an internal architecture that was intentionally masked such that she couldn't investigate it.

Claire zoomed out and reversed her tracks, panning back in the direction she started. She passed the first super node from a few minutes before, then continued retracing her steps. When her screen hovered over an area where the super highway of data dominated the screen but the giant hub was no longer visible she grew anxious. It was going to take some time to find her way back to exactly where she'd started.

She took a deep breath and brushed a few strands of brunette hair out of her face. She decided to try shifting the program into the three dimensional mapping mode she'd used earlier in the training network. She tapped the trackpad to zoom in as far as possible, then the laptop emitted an irritating 'bump' sound. Text appeared at the bottom of the screen, accompanying the sound: "Three Dimensional View not Available. Return to Point of Origin."

"Damnit," said Claire under her breath. She rolled her head between her shoulders trying to ease the nervous tension that was building in the back of her neck. She was supposed to minimize her time roaming around in the Pinnacle Cloud. She'd already wasted ten minutes and found nothing. And she wasn't sure she could find her way back to the 'Point of Origin.'

On instinct, she closed the cMap application then checked the laptop's task manager to ensure the program had stopped running. Once she'd confirmed the program was completely closed, she opened cMap again and selected the Pinnacle Cloud from the list of network options.

A few seconds later she was hovering over a two-dimensional image of the familiar cluster of nodes and base stations she'd seen when she'd first logged on. Hopefully this was the 'Point of Origin' she was supposed to return to. She pinched her fingers together on the track pad, then spread them apart, instructing the program to zoom in on the area at the center of her screen.

Almost immediately the LED above the laptop screen danced with light and Claire was swept into the middle of a three hundred and sixty degree hologram. She stood in a dense cluster of nodes and could almost feel the data moving feverishly in and out of the area. She commanded the program to move her toward the perimeter, to an area of less intensity, so she could try to understand where she was in the network hierarchy.

When she approached the edge of the cluster she stood astride a link that shot straight out into the openness in front of her. She quickly determined the cluster behind her was somewhere mid-way up the network's food chain. About a hundred yards ahead of her, or what appeared to be a hundred yards in the holographic projection, the link that ran as a straight line between her feet then exploded out in thousands of directions. Without moving from her current position she followed one of the minor branches. Barely perceptible in the distance she could see the minor branch arrive at a bright node then branch out again in more directions than she could count from her far off vantage point.

In all her experience Claire had never seen anything like this. Networks were built by men, with structure that had a clean hierarchy. With permanently established links between components. What she saw now was nothing similar. The network spread out like the veins in a massive leaf. But the veins weren't static and they didn't all lead to one branch. The organization of the veins shifted before her eyes as the network actively re-organized itself to optimize the data flow. It would take years for a single person to map this network if it were static. It would take hundreds of years to understand the algorithms that governed it's shifting structure.

Researchers in the 2020's would kill for this level of intelligent network. One of the greatest plagues to the resiliency and security of large networks in Claire's time was the lack of redundancy at the higher echelons in the network. Failure of one major switching station could take down an entire section of the network. And the only way to restore it would be to repair or replace the busted component. The net she stared out now was not just redundant; it used it's built in redundancy to make itself faster, re-arranging itself almost instantaneously to adjust to shifts in loading.

Claire was tempted to leave her current location and get lost in the wilderness of the adaptive cloud that spread out in all directions in front of her. She had to force herself to stay put. Her assignment was to map how Ne Plus Ultra interacted with the Pinnacle Cloud. She didn't know where to begin, but logic told her that Pulling picked this specific access point for a reason. There had to be some significance to the tangled cluster behind her.

She turned ninety degrees and walked the perimeter of the cluster. As she made the trip around she saw at least six more links similar to the one she'd inspected before. Galaxies of links and nodes spread out in all directions. It was all amazing but nothing stood out as unique or different from everything else. The entire network behaved as though it was being directed by the same brain, but she couldn't see where the instructions came from. She needed to change her perspective.

Claire walked away from the hub along one of the major links. Just before she turned back she noticed a transparent haze surrounding her. She had the distinct impression she was in the center of a bubble. She could see outside it but she knew inherently that she couldn't penetrate the bubble to interact with anything. Like she was quarantined from the network she was exploring.

Looking back over her shoulder the entire cluster now fit in her field of view. She twisted the holographic projection one hundred and eighty degrees to comfortably look back and study the bright mess in front of her. A few seconds later everything made sense.

A thick gray link extended from the top of the cluster, giving Claire the impression of an upside down tree. The solitary link was the trunk and the infinite expanse that she stood on now was the branches and leaves. But the 'trunk' never reached the 'ground.' It simply disappeared into blackness. Claire knew it was significant when the trunk seemed to come alive for a moment. A surge of color flowed from the blackness above, down into the network cluster. The same surge, or brightening, that came down the trunk into the large node passed out beyond it. It was almost imperceptible, but Claire saw the brightening as the pulse of color was distributed throughout the expanse around her. She was reminded of a heartbeat and the ensuing push of life sustaining oxygenated fluid that moved through the body.

Just as quickly as the trunk link had brightened, it returned to its dull gray base state. Claire wasn't one hundred percent sure that this trunk was her point of interest - the Ne Plus Ultra interface with the Cloud - but it was the most interesting thing she'd seen so far.

Now very aware of the translucent bubble around her, Claire made her way back into the cluster while keeping her view fixed on the trunk line. She needed to determine where it entered the dense node, and she might not be able to figure it out from inside. But despite her best efforts, once she was into the cluster, she could no longer see the trunk that was so prominent from a distance.

She walked to what felt like the center of the dense activity. Then, hoping the network mapping program would play along, she swiped her hand from top to bottom within the hologram hoping to rotate her perspective. The program complied. Suddenly what had been above her was now in front. She advanced to the 'top' of the network cluster, trying to locate the trunk. She reached the permitter and looked out at nothing. Really she looked up at nothing. It was as if the grey trunk had disappeared as soon as she'd come close enough to touch it.

Claire looked out at the rest of the Cloud in the distance. With her perspective rotated it gave her a slight sense of vertigo. Before she could get her bearings her attention was drawn to a flash of color that materialized directly in front of her. Without hesitation she moved toward it as fast as the cMap program would allow her. The hologram moved ahead, the ball of color growing in front of her. But as she glanced to either side it appeared she was departing on a shuttle, the network below her growing more distant as she moved up. She wasn't certain if the ball of color was growing, or getting closer as she advanced upward.

The question was quickly resolved as the ball of color grew exponentially faster. It was moving toward her at an incredible speed. Before she could process what was happening she was engulfed in color. It happened so fast. She almost didn't notice that the path of the color was diverted slightly as it passed around her protective bubble. Then the area in front of her was black again and her bubble no longer perceptible. She quickly reached out to the hologram and spun her perspective a hundred and eighty degrees. She now faced down.

What she saw made her mouth hang open involuntarily. As soon as the burst of color had passed around her bubble it rocketed down to the 'surface' landing at the node where Claire's experience on the network had begun. When it hit the node it burst outward, bringing something akin to life to everything it touched as it propagated outward at inconceivable speed.

From her former perspective Claire thought the network seemed like an inverted tree. When she saw the trunk feed its branches and leaves she was reminded of the heart beating in a living creature. But from this elevated perspective, there was a god-like quality. Whatever was carried in the pulse of color was absorbed like precious droplets of water in the desert. The entity Claire couldn't see, but was beginning to suspect was NPU, breathed life into the Pinnacle Cloud with its data…it's words and instructions.

Even though Claire couldn't see it, she was sure that she was standing astride the grey link that carried the digital god-bread. There was only one logical thing to do now. She spun the holo back through a one-eighty, facing upward again. Then she moved forward. She wouldn't stop until she reached whatever resided on the other end.

As she scrolled ahead over the next few minutes, advancing upward into the black expanse, Claire felt a tickle of foreboding. She hadn't been to church in years, but she remembered a Bible story from her childhood about people trying to build a tower to heaven. Their objective was to reach God, but instead they were pitched into confusion and chaos. Their language was confounded and a once unified people were scattered all over the world and destined for cultural and physical conflict. Claire wasn't worried that she was about to be stricken down by God, but she did have the slightest sense that her exploration above the plane of the normally trafficked Pinnacle Cloud was likely to draw attention at a minimum, but possibly consequences as well.

Despite her misgivings, Claire pressed forward. She was a time traveler on a mission and wasn't about to abandon her task on the basis of a tingle of worry. She'd spent the last few days swamped with tension and nerves. Her thoughts were probably totally natural given the daily-increasing level of stress she'd been under.

Then suddenly the hologram stopped. Claire tapped in front of her, trying to resume her upward advance toward the source of the earlier colored light. Nothing. Then she fumbled for the trackpad on the laptop that sat in front of her on the physical bed in her physical hotel room. Once she'd found it she tapped on the pad. Still nothing.

Recognizing she wasn't going to be able to move further forward (up really), she spun around to take another look at the network expanding out below her. Once she twisted the perspective she recognized how far above the network she'd traveled. She felt like an astronaut in orbit, looking down on a digital version of Earth. Claire saw the same collection of digital superhighways she'd seen in the two dimensional mode earlier. In the distance she could see one of the massive, impenetrable nodes that sat astride the intersection of multiple data superhighways.

From her high vantage, the dense cluster she'd emerged from appeared directly in front of her (below her really) as a bright light in the distance. Claire took a deep breath, appreciating the digital equivalent of her space station view. She needed to penetrate, or at least understand, the stop above her. But it was hard not to appreciate the massive expanse below.

Claire reached toward the holo to spin herself back around. But before she flicked the hologram, everything around her exploded in color and light. Her bubble was engulfed in a bright rush, so intense Claire felt like she was being flushed downward. As quickly as it began, she was no longer surrounded in the colorful burst. She watched it race out in front of her, as though she was watching a fired bullet from a seat inside the barrel of a gun. An instant later it hit the node below. Then Claire watched it break apart, spreading outward at breakneck speed over every part of the network she could see from her orbital perspective.

As the light spread outward, Claire discovered yet another detail about the pulse that fed the network. Once it's spread seemed to dim at the furthest outskirts that Claire could see, a faint blue light traveled back. At first it appeared like an echo of the stronger outward pulse of light. But as Claire watched, the blue return gathered strength. It fed into the data superhighways, growing in intensity. Soon Claire watched the blue pulse travel down the data mega-highway like a ball of furious plasma. Then, when it hit the giant node in the distance, it shot upward into the virtual sky. Just as soon as it had gathered it winked out into nothingness directly above the huge hub on the horizon.

She had to know what sat perched high above the topology of the network. What was the source of the colorful burst, and what was gathered in the strengthening blue ball of light that returned to the air from another node in the network? Claire spun back around, pointing the face of the hologram up again. Like before, she tried to advance forward, toward the source of the colorful data burst. Nothing happened. She tried everything she could think of over the next few minutes. She tapped the hologram in front of her, trying to investigate the empty space in front of her. She tried reaching toward the hologram with her hands together, then moving them apart in a gesture that she thought might logically direct the program to zoom in. Still no change. She was stuck.

Trying to think like a computer, Claire had one more idea to try. She waited, as patiently as she could, never taking her eyes off the center of the holo directly in front of her. It seemed like forever until another burst of colored light appeared in front of her. When it did, she was immediately engulfed and had to squint against the abrupt change from darkness to all encompassing light. But Claire was ready. She immediately reached out, again attempting to advance the hologram. This time it responded, moving her protective bubble forward into the onrush of light and color.

When the burst of color receded, everything had changed. Instead of the blackness of the virtual sky, Claire was surrounded by pure white. She had the sensation of being in a rectangular room. The walls and floor so brilliantly white that she struggled to differentiate the walls from the floor and ceiling. The faintest lines were present along the edges of the room. They were the only feature present that kept her from thinking she stood in a sea of infinite white. She could no longer make out the bubble around her position. All she could see was the intense white of the walls that surrounded her on six sides.

There was one exception to the white emptiness of the room. Directly in front of Claire, and small enough that she had the urge to pinch it between her fingers, she saw a small black cube that appeared to float at the room's center. Without thinking she advanced the hologram closer to the suspended object to investigate it further.

Almost as soon as she started moving, the infinite white was interrupted as segments near the center of each of the walls ahead, to her right and left, and above and below all opened revealing the blackness of the network 'outside.' Before she could fully process the change, the formerly white walls of the room turned a brilliant shade of blue. Then the cube at the center of the room pulsed with an unexplained energy. As it did, the blue walls around lost their color, fading back to the pure white they'd possessed a moment before. Now the cube itself glowed a deep blue. It all happened so fast. Claire had the sensation of sitting in a room with all the lights on at the moment of a power surge. The change happened so quickly she wondered if it had really happened at all. Maybe it was an illusion created by the blink of her eyes.

But Claire was able to push away her doubt as she recognized that the formerly black cube at the center of the room still held a fading blue glow. She continued advancing toward it, intent on investigating the inanimate object that glowed in front of her.

As Claire closed the distance to the cube she recognized the room was much bigger than it seemed when she'd entered. And the cube was much larger. As she moved forward the cube grew larger. With each passing second the cube seemed to absorb the blue color, slowly returning to black, as it had been when she first entered this space.

When Claire finally stood next to the cube there wasn't a trace of blue left in it. It appeared as though the cube, which Claire's estimated to be as tall as she was, had absorbed the blue into its interior. The flat black surface of the cube seemed to absorb everything. It's surface didn't reflect the intense white of the room or offer even so much as a glare of light. It was a deep black that drew Claire's eye into it's depth.

Claire maneuvered around the cube, looking for any deviation in the smooth black surface or any indication of how it interfaced with the room or the vast Pinnacle Cloud outside the walls. Before she could finish the exam the cube seemed to become aware of her presence. It pulsed red momentarily and then Claire found herself in a virtual hail storm. Red pellets assaulted the front of her bubble that faced the cube. When they impacted her protective sphere the pellets spread over the surface like splattered paint.

Beginning to panic, she maneuvered to the adjacent side of the cube to move out of the storm. But it followed her. Claire's view was becoming obscured as the red paint like substance spread over the surface of her shell. And since she didn't exactly understand the nature of the bubble that contained her, she wasn't excited to find out what happened if it was penetrated. The network was aware of her presence and the cube seemed to be trying to interrogate her and break through.

Claire decided she'd had enough. She quickly entered the quit command and saw the LED generated hologram retreat into the strip above the laptop screen. With a trembling hand Claire reached for the trackpad, copied the cMap file that had recorded her activity, and pasted it onto the desktop of the laptop. Then she force quit the cMap application, hoping to sever any connection she might still have to the Pinnacle Cloud.

She took a deep breath, trying to calm down and think. She drug the trackpad over to the Casimir SecNet application and opened the secure file transfer program. While she waited for the program to establish a secure connection, she wiped sweat from her forehead with her shirt sleeve. *What the hell just happened?*

Claire tried to dismiss her unease and process what she'd just seen in the hologram. The whole experience was virtual but it felt so real. She'd anonymously walked around on the network. She was fairly certain she'd then accessed a normally walled off portion of the network while it established a short duration connection to send data out to the cloud. Once inside the protected part of the network she was pretty sure she'd seen the connection re-established to receive return data back from the network. Then a few minutes later, the black cube seemed to notice that someone or something was inside it's secure enclave and tried to interrogate it, attack it, or drive it out.

The cube was undefinable. Claire couldn't place it's role in the network under any traditional hierarchy that she understood. The closest analogy she could think of was of a god lording over the universe below. But this god clearly didn't want to be approached, and certainly did not react kindly to being seen.

As soon as the Casimir SecNet connection showed a green stoplight, indicating it was active, Claire drug the cMap file into the drop space and watched the progress bar grow with green as the data began to upload.

Claire anxiously watched as the green bar slowly advanced as the data was uploaded. It felt like it was taking hours. Every second that ticked by was another one Claire used to replay the virtual events in her mind. The more she thought about it, the more concerned she became. The cube lorded over the entire network. On the bright side, she was almost certain she'd interacted with Ne Plus Ultra. And there was a better than even chance that she'd mapped exactly what Pulling had asked her to - the interaction between NPU and the Pinnacle Cloud. On the downside, even if it wasn't NPU she was certain it was an intelligent machine. And it had seen her - or at least it had seen her small bubble of anonymity. Had it seen her long enough to backtrack how she'd accessed the network? Worse, could it track her physical location?

The progress bar crawled forward as Claire's pulse climbed. She fought the urge to shutdown the laptop and bolt out of the hotel room. She glanced at Tim, realizing if someone was coming for her, they'd surely find him unconscious in possession of the laptop. Eventually they'd wake him up and he'd point to Claire as the likely culprit.

The green bar passed the fifty percent mark. Claire climbed off the bed and began pacing, her eyes darting back and forth between the slow advance of the data upload and the door of the hotel room. Her nerves and pessimism drove her toward despair. She was sure the door was going to burst open at any moment.

Claire rubbed her clammy hands together and forced herself to take a series of deep breaths. She tried to convince herself she was freaking out for no reason. The Casimir Institute could send people through time. Surely their technology ensured her anonymity remained intact. Everything was fine. She could finish the data transfer, wipe the laptop hard drive, find a way to get rid of the laptop itself, and then wait for morning to arrive when she could escape to the sanctuary of 2023. Everything was going to be fine.

The progress bar finished it's slow crawl across the screen and was replaced with a rectangular message window: TRANSFER COMPLETE. Claire quickly opened the MagWipe application and clicked through the commands to begin wiping the laptop. Another creeping progress bar appeared, indicating this was also going to be a slow process too.

"Arrrgghhh," Claire growled in frustration as she hopped off the bed. The alarm bells in her head were all going off. She needed out of this room. She felt the walls closing in around her and she shut her eyes to stave off a panic attack.

CHAPTER THIRTY-FOUR

"I said, who the fuck are you and what are you doing in here?" came the nervous voice.

Jon had the data stick closed in his right hand and slowly pulled it from the keyboard. From his squatted position he brought his shoulders slightly forward, imperceptibly shifting his weight onto the balls of his feet.

"Security told me to take a walk through the building. Said they had an abnormal alarm somewhere in here," Jon lied.

"What? Let me see your credentials," said the shaky voice behind him.

Jon twisted slightly to his right, still poised on the balls of his feet. He brought his left hand toward his pocket, feigning to grab his 'credentials' to present to his accuser. He took the opportunity to drop the stick in the pocket of his cargo pants.

Jon fiddled in his pocket for another few seconds, positioning himself for his next move. Then, before Squeaky saw what was coming, Jon exploded up from the floor, leading with his right shoulder. He landed his shoulder against the solar plexus of his accuser. Squeaky let out a breathy whimper and immediately buckled at the waist, heading for the fetal position.

Jon didn't hesitate. He dropped into a dead sprint for the double doors. In a few seconds he was back in the main corridor, turning to his left and sprinting for the same door he'd used to access the building. Moving with reckless abandon he blew through the exterior door and emerged into the floodlight outside, then slammed face first into a very surprised technician trying to badge in outside the door.

Jon took the brunt of the hit as he went nose first into the side of the guy's head. Jon's eyes watered at the blow to the bridge of his nose.

"Whoa, are you ok?" asked the lab coated Pinnacle employee.

Through his teary eyes, Jon eyed the handheld in the man's hand.

"Yeah, I'm ok," said Jon. "Sorry for bum rushing you there. I'm in a bit of a hurry."

Jon turned to walk away.

"Hold on. I didn't get your name. What division do you work for?"

Jon turned back toward the man. The tone of his question was more accusatory than inquisitive. Jon wasn't going to talk his way out of this. And the longer he stood outside the door under this floodlight, the greater the chance that Squeaky would get himself together and emerge from the building to identify Jon as his attacker in the server room.

"I'm with, um…"

Before the man in the lab coat could register what was happening, Jon had drawn the pistol from his waistband and put a non-lethal round directly into the man's chest. The effects were immediate. The man's eyes rolled back eerily just before his legs buckled beneath his slight frame.

Jon moved quickly toward the downed scientist, hooking his arms under the fallen man's armpits to prevent him from bashing his head into the concrete on his way down. Jon drug the scientist out of the field of the floodlight and laid him gently on the nearby grass adjacent to the building.

Then he broke to his right, resuming his sprint. He looked down quickly at his watch. He was five minutes late to check back in from his break. Then he heard a giant voice over the campus public announcing system: "Security violation. Security violation. All personnel shelter in place. Security personnel muster with dispatch immediately." Any chance of drifting back into his cover as a security team member was over. His radio was in his cart and his handheld was in the bushes multiple blocks away.

Moments later Jon was a couple blocks from where his cart was parked, near where he'd ditched his handheld earlier. He briefly considered his options. The handheld was a liability. By putting it on his person he might compromise his location and allow Pinnacle to track him as he left the campus. But he also needed it to affect his revised escape plan. He could switch to his actual Cloud ID, but that carried its own set of risks.

He stopped near where he'd dropped the device earlier and leaned into the shrubbery on all fours. He felt around in the bush until he felt the cool glass amidst the leaves and dirt. Without examining the device, Jon dropped it into the front pocket of his pants and continued running in the direction of his stashed security cart. He had to move fast. His best chance at escape required being outside the security perimeter before the lockdown was fully implemented and before he was identified as the culprit.

Jon broke into a dead run again. Recalling his earlier patrols, he now had a plan in mind. Two blocks later he stopped at his previously abandoned golf cart and grabbed the radio from the front seat and the Gateguard Security shirt from the glove box. He flipped the shirt inside out and slipped it over his head, assuming even a minor change in appearance might delay someone recognizing him. He clipped the radio to his shirt near his right shoulder. It was another vulnerability that could be used to track him, but it would also allow him to listen in on any communications between security forces that might be looking for him.

Stepping out of the alley Jon glanced up and down the street. Seeing no activity he decided to try and lower his profile by walking to his egress point. The chatter on the radio indicated the Gateguard team was focused on shutting down access at the main gate. Jon smiled as he walked in the opposite direction.

He continued his casual stroll along the dark street, estimating no more than ten minutes to the exit at his current pace. Then the radio crackled to life again, adding to his sense of urgency.

"Johnston, this is dispatch, over."

Jon stopped mid stride, waiting for more over the radio.

"Mark Johnston, this is dispatch. Report your location, over."

Jon fought the urge to resume his sprint to the exit. He reached for the radio and depressed the talk button.

"This is Johnston, I'm three minutes out from the main gate," said Jon into the radio on his shoulder.

Jon kept walking, hopeful that he'd bought himself a few minutes before the rest of the security detail realized he wasn't coming. But the more he thought about it, he realized that his deception was probably futile. It might temporarily mislead the humans at dispatch, but it was useless against the Pinnacle AI that probably had his handheld pinpointed. As soon as he became a suspect his exact location would be immediately known to all his would be pursuers.

The thought of an intelligent computer vectoring in forces to hunt him down sent Jon Haynes back into a run. He couldn't be more than a half mile from freedom. Properly motivated, he could cover that distance in less than two and a half minutes.

Then he saw it. The abandoned gate at the east end of the complex. Jon pumped his fist when he got closer and saw that it was not guarded as part of the security lockdown. He slowed his near-sprint to a jog so he could pull the handheld from his pocket and implement the final part of his escape plan.

He tapped the thumb sensor three times to call up the backdoor ID-swap switch. He flipped it back to the left, converting his handheld ID from Mark Johnston back to Jon Haynes. Then he quickly powered down the device, hopeful that if he was being tracked by Pinnacle security they wouldn't get enough Jon Haynes location data to recognize that it was exactly the same position as what had been Mark Johnston moments before.

When the device was off he sped back up to a near sprint, angling to his left, directly at the facility's locked back gate.

A minute later Jon lept onto the gate, jump starting his climb to the top. As he scaled the chain link it seemed too good to be true. The locked, but moveable section of fence that represented the former vehicle gate wasn't topped with barbwire. It was ten or twelve feet tall, so it posed a bit of a fall risk when he swung over to the other side. But Jon was well equipped to deal with such a simple obstacle.

Within a few seconds he was on the ground on the opposite side without incident. He then walked casually along the sidewalk, headed back in the direction of the dingy neighborhood that was home to St. Charles Place. His new vantage outside the gate was infinitely less nerve racking. He couldn't be sure, but he figured the Pinnacle AI security watch probably stopped at the fence line. Unless the security forces spread their search outside the boundaries of the campus, Jon was probably close to home free.

He reached into his pocket and powered his handheld on again. Once the boot sequence was complete he quickly tapped in the commands that would direct his car to meet him just inside the neighborhood a few blocks away. Immediately, the handheld screen shifted to show him a map that included his location and the car's location. The car was already en route and would get to the rendezvous before Jon would.

There was light vehicle traffic on the road that Jon followed back toward the neighborhood. He desperately wanted to run the remaining five blocks so that he could cross the main road and duck quickly into the neighborhood, securing his escape. But he held back on the off chance that Pinnacle security was looking outside the fence line for anything suspicious.

Even though it was only a few moments it felt like an eternity. Jon spent the entire time trying to keep a calm, casual posture. But his mind ran on overdrive and his eyes darted in every direction, constantly scanning for threats or any indications that he'd drawn the attention of the alert security forces inside the campus.

He finally arrived at the stoplight one block down from the main entrance to the Pinnacle campus. Two hundred yards ahead he could see two security vehicles blocking the main gate and a bustle of activity around the guard shack. But they were all Pinnacle vehicles. No indication that they'd called in local authorities. Maybe they were trying to keep the breech quiet. *Strange.*

Jon crossed the street, entering the quiet and dimly lit neighborhood. He breathed a sigh of relief, walked another block into the residential area, then broke in to a casual jog.

A short two blocks later he hung a left and saw his ride waiting a hundred yards up ahead. He closed the remaining distance quickly and hopped in the driver's seat of the car. As soon as he shut the door, the avatar of Alistair appeared, hovering in holographic form over the dash.

"Where to Mr. Haynes?"

Jon hadn't really thought about it.

"Back to the Manchester Grand Hyatt," Jon quickly decided.

"Very good Mr. Haynes. How was your evening?"

Before Jon could answer he was distracted by the ding of his handheld signaling a new message. He pulled it from his pocket.

Just as Jon had begun to relax following his escape, his pulse was jolted high again. The urgent message was from Claire.

CHAPTER THIRTY-FIVE

Claire paced at the end of the bed in her hotel room with nervous anxiety. As she did, she kept glancing back at the slowly advancing progress bar for the MagWipe application. For the last half hour, the program had been slowly working to remove any trace of her work inside the Pinnacle Cloud. All the while, Claire had racked her brain trying to think of what to do next. She needed to get rid of the laptop. She also had a feeling that staying in this hotel room was a bad idea. If her worst fears were right, the supercomputer NPU had detected her inside protected parts of the network. There was no telling what Pinnacle might decide to do about that. There was also no way to know how much the smartest, fastest computer in the history of the world had been able to learn about her during her short encounter. Claire shuddered again at the thought. Pinnacle, or worse the actual authorities, might be on their way to get her right now.

She glanced over at the computer again just in time to see the progress bar finally full. As soon as the process reached one hundred percent, the screen went black. Claire stopped pacing and approached the laptop to try and validate that all traces of her work had been permanently removed. She mashed the power button and waited to see what would happen.

A few seconds later she smiled for the first time since logging off the Pinnacle Cloud in a terrified hurry. The laptop showed a boot disk error. The blue screen of death. The hard drive was dead. It wasn't perfect verification but it was good enough for now. It would take a computer lab and a skilled technician to dig inside the machine to ensure the data was really gone, and Claire didn't have that kind of time.

Claire quickly closed the laptop, tucked it under her arm and headed for the door. As she stepped over Tim's unconscious body, her nascent plan was taking shape. First get rid of the laptop, then find someplace else to stay until she was certain no one was coming for her.

As the door clicked shut behind her, Claire felt a slight pang of guilt at the drugging and abandonment of Tim Nguyen. If someone did come looking for Claire, especially after Tim awoke, he'd be very surprised and have to talk himself out of a situation he knew nothing about. But carrying him away with her was impractical. He had done nothing wrong; he'd come out okay.

Claire made her way toward the elevator as steady and calm as she could manage. Her mind raced, franticly grabbing for an idea to get out of the current situation and to restore her feeling of safety. While she'd wanted out of the confines of her hotel room more than anything a few seconds earlier, the new nakedness she felt in the hallway of the hotel's twenty third floor brought a new feeling of terror and exposure. If she couldn't find a way to at least trick herself into feeling safe again she was going to have a nervous breakdown.

Claire reached the elevator bank and hit the call button. In a moment of clarity, without realizing it was happening, Claire withdrew her handheld from her back pocket. She opened the messenger application and typed a message to Jon Haynes: 'Are you back in the hotel? I need to see you.' She tapped the send button before she could second guess herself.

Just as she'd sent the message to Jon, the elevator signaled it's arrival and the door slid open. Claire tensed, suddenly afraid her would-be captors were going to be on the other side of the door, ready to charge out of the elevator car and arrest her. Instead the elevator was empty. Claire stepped inside and mashed the button for the lobby.

The elevator descended, stopping three times during the trip to allow additional passengers aboard. Claire hardly noticed. Half her brain was occupied with figuring out how to ditch the laptop and choosing a safe place to spend the rest of the evening. She decided she'd exit the south side of the hotel and walk the few short blocks to the water and simply drop the laptop into San Diego Bay. After that, she considered calling the car and having Alistair take her back to Hendrick House where she could lay low until it was time to head back to 2023. Tim would figure out how to make his way back when he came out of his drug induced coma.

Claire didn't notice the declaration of the elevator as it arrived at the lobby. She snapped back to reality when it chimed its arrival and the door slid open. Because she was the first in, she ended up the last out. She followed the six other passengers into the lobby at the back of a dense, shuffling cluster. As the group in front of her dispersed throughout the lobby, Claire got a better view of her surroundings. She glanced over at the check in desk and nearly swallowed her tongue.

Three men in black suits stood in a cluster in front of the check-in clerk. Two were talking to the clerk intently. From a distance, the clerk seemed to respond to their questioning by frantically banging away at the keyboard behind the counter. The other black-clad man stared into the distance with glazed eyes and a thousand yard stare.

Claire stopped in the middle of the lobby. Her former resolve to walk the few short blocks to San Diego Bay and ditch the laptop faded. The staring man suddenly trained his gaze on Claire, looking toward her but not really at her. Her feet took on a lead-like quality. Indecisiveness gripped her. Claire was suddenly certain the three men were looking for her. The man with the thousand yard stare turned slightly his eyes now looking directly at her, but still retaining an eery lack of focus. Then the two that were interrogating the check-in clerk also turned to look in Claire's direction.

Claire panicked. Cutting her gaze away from the men, she spun around and made her way back to the elevator. She tried to walk casually, but her calves burned as she quickly strode toward what seemed to be her only respite. Claire was intensely aware of the laptop tucked under her arm. She had to get rid of it.

When she arrived at the elevator bank a few seconds later she tapped the call button half a dozen times, as though pressing it more would force the elevator to arrive faster. Claire fought every fiber of her being not to look back toward the lobby to see if the three black-suited men were pursuing her.

After an agonizing eternity, the door slid open. Claire stepped in, pressed the button for the twenty third floor, then impatiently pressed the 'Door Close' button repeatedly until it began to slide shut. Before the door slid shut she looked up and saw the three men in suits making a bee line toward the elevator bank. *Shit.*

Claire's mind raced as she willed the elevator to move faster. She could barricade herself in the hotel room with Tim, but if the goons following her already knew who she was, they almost certainly knew which hotel room she was in. And the one guy with the unfocused eyes made her skin crawl. He was looking but not really seeing. Like he was blind but their was something feeding into his vision.

Then Claire's heart really sank. She remembered the Pinnacle Implant add she'd seen when she first arrived at the hotel. They were only available on pre-order. If that's what the guy was using, then the three black-suited pursuers were definitely Pinnacle. And they had high end AI to help them find Claire.

As the elevator ascended she pulled out her handheld, anxious to power it off and remove it as a means of being located. The elevator slowed and signaled it's arrival at her floor. Claire walked out of the elevator and turned down the hall toward her room. At the same time, with the laptop still tucked under her left arm she fiddled to pull her handheld from her pocket so she could shut down it's connection to the cloud and power it off. But before she could tap in the commands, she noticed a new message had come in a few minutes ago, probably when she'd been panicking to escape the lobby.

It was from Jon: 'On my way back to the hotel now. What's wrong?'

Claire stopped dead in her tracks a few doors down from her room and stared at the message. Jon would know what to do. Time to be honest and put all her cards on the table.

Claire rapidly typed her response: 'I did a mission for Pulling. Some sensitive network mapping. Think I got discovered. Now there are three guys after me in the hotel. Need help. I'm going to lay low in my hotel room until you get here. Hurry.'

She tapped the send button and continued the last few steps down the hall to her room. Trusting Jon had enough information to find her and help her figure a way out of this, Claire started tapping through the commands again to shut down the handheld. It seemed like a long process. Much more complicated than shutting down a smart phone back in 2023. But then again, there was not supposed to ever be a reason to be disconnected in 2050.

Again Claire stopped the shutdown process when she reached her hotel room door. She needed the device to unlock it.

"Hey Claire, how's your day going?" came a familiar voice from down the hall to her left.

Claire turned in the direction of the voice and saw Denise shuffling toward her, rubbing her right temple with her hand. Then Claire had an idea.

"Not so great, um, Tim's been passed out for the last few hours and I could really use some company," Claire lied.

"Come on then," said Denise, motioning Claire down the hall

toward her room. "I've been out for a couple hours too. I'm not sure when Jon will be back but I could use a few minutes to relax. My head's pounding."

Claire smiled with relief. The anxiety of being pursued was still there, but she thought her chances were infinitely better if she holed up in a room other than her own. And Jon would eventually come to her rescue.

As Claire walked through the door of Jon and Denise's room, she finally finished shutting down her handheld. She walked across the room and took a seat in the chair in the far corner. Denise followed and sat across from her on the bed, swinging her legs up and laying back into a stack of pillows.

"So Claire, what do you think of 2050 so far?" Denise asked as she continued massaging her temples.

Claire rolled her eyes in irritation. She hadn't come here looking to make friends with Denise. While she suppressed her irritation she silently prayed Jon would walk through the door soon so she didn't have to make small talk with Denise. Regardless of what else was going on, Claire knew that Denise was a wolf in sheep's clothing and would try to steal Jon from her if she could.

"It's pretty cool I guess. Different. I won't be sad to head back home tomorrow," Claire finally responded.

"I think it's…" Denise's response was cutoff by three heavy knocks on the door.

Denise glanced at Claire, confusion on her face. Jon wouldn't knock. His handheld was coded to open the door. Then Denise swung off the bed and headed toward the door.

Claire's stomach was in knots and she felt a cold sweat returning to her palms. Without thinking Claire followed a few feet behind Denise. But as Denise approached the door, Claire cut into the bathroom and shut the door, clicking the lock on the knob once it was shut.

"Who's there?" Denise asked.

"Hotel services," came the reply.

With shaky hands driven by fear and adrenaline, Claire shut the bathroom drain and turned on the water in the bathtub. She had to ensure the laptop was destroyed, regardless of what happened next.

The running water masked most of the sound of Denise's conversation outside, but Claire hoped she wouldn't open the door and it would all go away. She watched the tub fill slowly. When there was about an inch of water at the base of the tub she sat the laptop under the faucet. She let the water run.

The sound of the water and her tightly shut eyes almost let her escape the shitstorm that seemed to be swirling. Then the wheels came off the wagon.

"What the fuck!?" Claire heard Denise yell over the din of the water and through the bathroom door. Then a full throated scream. Next Claire heard two loud spits of air driven by metal. She fought the urge to vomit as she heard something heavy hit the floor right outside the bathroom.

Tears filled her tightly shut eyes. She knew what had happened but refused to believe it. When she finally opened her tear-streaked eyes and looked toward the bathroom door, she saw pooling blood leaching under the door and onto the bathroom floor. *Where was Jon?*

A moment later the door shuddered. Then again. After the second pulse against the door, Claire instinctively huddled into the small space between the toilet and the tub. The water continued to run, dulling her sense of sound. The third crash against the door was the last. The jamb gave way as splinters of wood sailed into the bathroom and the door swung open violently. One of the suited men she'd seen in the lobby stumbled into the bathroom behind the swinging door. The other two stood behind him, shoulder to shoulder. All three stared down at Claire in her frightened defenseless position. Behind them Denise lay lifeless on the floor, her blood continuing to slowly advance from the saturated carpet onto the tile of the bathroom floor. Claire screamed involuntarily as tears streamed down her face.

The man who blew the door open walked over calmly and shut off the water in the bath tub. He grabbed the laptop from the tub and held it up, waiting a moment for the water to drip off. Without a word, the man pulled a towel from the rack above Claire's head, sat the computer on the bathroom counter and began to gently dab away the water.

Then the man with the thousand yard stare stepped forward into the bathroom. He still had the same glaze in his eyes, looking directly at Claire, but also looking at something else no one could see.

"Claire Keen, you are under arrest for illegal access to the Pinnacle Cloud. Please come with us."

Claire knew she had no choice but to comply, but she also couldn't bring herself to move.

CHAPTER THIRTY-SIX

As Alistair accelerated the car to leave the dingy neighborhood and ferry Jon back to the Manchester Grand Hyatt, Jon sat in the driver seat, staring at his handheld. His hand shook with nervous energy.

Jon read Claire's message again: 'Are you back in the hotel? I need to see you.'

He wanted to believe it was a message born out of love, or raw physical desire, but Jon's gut told him something was wrong. That Claire needed help. This wasn't a booty call, it was a cry for help.

Jon tapped his reply: 'On my way back to the hotel now. What's wrong?'

As soon as he'd sent his message he sat the handheld on his lap and watched the scenery of San Diego harbor pass to his right as Alistair accelerated onto Pacific Highway. Claire's message made Jon forget temporarily that he might be a fugitive on the run. He had no idea whether or not Pinnacle had pegged Mark Johnston as an alias of Jon Haynes. If they had, they were probably on the way to take him right now. He might get dropped by a massive Pinnacle security detail as soon as he stepped out of the car at the Grand Hyatt, the Pinnacle Cloud aware of his destination as soon as he'd told Alistair where to take him.

But none of that risk seemed to matter now. Claire might be in trouble. Based on her message, he inferred she was in the hotel and needed him now. The bulge at the back of his waist band reminded him that he could fight his way through any problems when he arrived and give Claire whatever help she required.

Jon closed his eyes to try and slow his racing thoughts of what might or might not happen when he returned to the hotel. He took a deep breath, fighting to clear his head of the thoughts that assumed the worst possible outcomes - more loss of people close to him.

Then his handheld chimed another message. It was a response from Claire: 'I did a mission for Pulling. Some sensitive network mapping. Think I got discovered. Now there are three guys after me in the hotel. Need help. I'm going to lay low in my hotel room until you get here. Hurry.'

Shit.

His worst fears were being realized. A network mapping mission from Pulling? Jon's gut told him there was no way this was coincidence. Pulling had sent him into a server room to upload some sort of computer program. And Claire was being pursued because of a botched network mapping mission she'd been assigned by the same shadowy guy.

Jon punched the dash of the self-driving vehicle. "Damnit!"

Deep down, Jon wanted to smash Pulling's wire-rimmed glasses into pieces against his face. But beating down a middle-aged balding covert puppet master wasn't going to solve the mess he was in now. Why couldn't Pulling play them straight up? Why not be honest from the get go about what they were doing and why?

During his time in the Navy, Jon always felt the SEALs, or at least the people pulling the strings, had a tendency to only reveal the bare minimum to facilitate getting the job done. But the SEALs were never dishonest or misleading when it came to telling an operator that he was about to go down range and into harm's way. Not only did they say 'you might die today,' but they also told you everything they knew about who you were up against - how they were armed, their defenses, even where they likely slept inside the den of bad guys. Pulling offered none of that. He'd sent them unknowingly into the lion's den with no context, intel, or even a basic understanding of the risk they were accepting for themselves or, more importantly, for the people they cared about.

Jon contemplated trying to contact Steven Pulling, but quickly dismissed the thought. He didn't trust him. While Jon knew nothing of the power struggle happening below the surface of the current circumstances, he knew in that moment that he wouldn't open himself up to be manipulated further by Steven Pulling. Jon was going to have to solve this problem himself.

The battle raging in Jon's head was interrupted when he realized he hadn't responded to Claire. He knew how he was going to fix this, but Claire still needed reassurance. Jon typed his message: 'Sit tight. I'll be there in five. Everything is going to be fine.'

He sent the message and an error message immediately appeared on his screen: MESSAGE UNDELIVERABLE. USER OFFLINE.

Jon unleashed his frustration on the dashboard again. This time Alistair took notice.

"Mr. Haynes, I must urge you not to damage the vehicle. My processing is very sensitive. Damaging the vehicle places you and passengers in nearby vehicles at risk."

"Shut up," Jon yelled back, brooding at his lack of control over the current situation.

Jon stared out the window again, breathing slowly in an attempt to release his frustration. The vehicle left the freeway and screamed down the offramp into downtown San Diego and toward his hotel.

Focused on the task before him, Jon pulled the weapon from his waist band to take stock. He ejected the magazine containing non-lethal rounds and verified the count. Thirteen rounds remained. He was down two following his escape from Building 31. In his right cargo pocket he carried a magazine filled with fifteen more traditional, lethal rounds. After a short mental debate, Jon slid the non-lethal mag back into the gun and racked the slide back, putting one into the chamber to ensure he was ready to respond the moment he stepped out of the vehicle.

As the car pulled into the portico in front of the hotel, Jon tried to control his pulse and breathing. He took a deep breath. Seeing no party of would-be-assailants waiting for him, he leaned forward and slid the weapon back into his waistband.

The car came to a stop and Jon stepped out of the car. "Stay close Alistair," Jon said, patting the dash before he shut the door. Jon ignored the muffled response from the car's artificial intelligence. He was wholly focused on making his way through the lobby and up the elevator to find Claire and rescue her from her distress.

As he entered the lobby he fought the urge to break into a dead run for the elevators. He walked quickly but did his best to appear casual. With his peripheral vision he looked for anyone that might be watching him or moving to follow him.

When he reached the elevator enclave and mashed the call button, he calmly turned to survey the lobby behind him. Nothing seemed out of place. If someone was tailing him they were doing a fine job.

The elevator dinged on arrival and the door slid open. He quickly pressed the button for the twenty third floor and then repeatedly pressed the 'Door Close' button, willing the elevator to get moving.

After an eternity, or a few seconds, the door slid shut and the elevator accelerated upward. Jon shifted his weight nervously between his heels and the balls of his feet, again willing the elevator not to stop. Willing it to carry him directly to his destination without delay.

He felt deceleration as the LED above the door indicated he was passing the twentieth floor. It came to rest at the twenty-third, the chime sounded, and the door began to slide open. When it was just wide enough for Jon to fit through, he turned his body sideways to exit. Then he was running at a dead sprint to Claire and Tim's room.

When Jon was still a few doors down, he slowed his sprint and called out. "Claire! Claire?" Nothing.

He stopped in front of her room and banged on the door, despite trying to knock gently. He waited, trying to slow his pulse and catch his breath. Still nothing.

He banged on the door again. This time he gave up on being gentle and hammered the door four times with the back side of a closed fist. "Claire, if you're in there, open up. It's me, Jon."

He waited a moment, then banged on the door again. Maybe a little harder than the last time. "Claire!"

Jon backed away from the door. He was going to have to shoulder it open. It had only been minutes ago that Claire was messaging him. The fact that she wasn't responding put a knot in his stomach. Jon hated to think what he might find on the other side of the door once he'd knocked it down.

Then Jon heard the click of the lock releasing from the inside. The door pulled back into the room to reveal Tim Nguyen standing in the doorway. He looked like he'd just woken up from a hard night of drinking. A little dried spittle spread from the right corner of his mouth onto his cheek, his hair was disheveled, and he had serious bags under his eyes.

Jon didn't wait for an invitation, pushing right past Tim into the room. "Claire?" Scanning the room quickly he turned back toward Tim, trying to keep his temper in check.

"Where's Claire?" Jon asked with more accusation in his tone than he'd intended.

"I don't know," Tim responded as he walked over to sit down on the end of the bed. "I was out cold on the floor until you started banging on the door. What time is it?"

Jon ignored the question. "She messaged me. She's in trouble. What happened?"

"I don't know. The last thing I remember we were getting a drink in the hotel bar. I'm not even sure how I made it back up to the room. But something's not right. I feel hungover, like I drank the bar dry, but we only had one drink and I don't think I finished mine."

Jon recognized the symptoms. He'd inflicted the same on Denise a few hours earlier. Suddenly he remembered Denise was probably still unconscious down the hall. Maybe she'd seen something. Hell, maybe Claire was hiding out in Jon and Denise's room.

"Come on," Jon said, charging out of the room with the same deliberate intensity he'd had when he came through the door a few moments before. As Jon opened the door and stepped into the hall, he glanced back to see Tim following gingerly a few steps behind him. Jon held the door just long enough for Tim to follow him out.

Then he hung a right and made his way down the hall toward the room where he'd left Denise unconscious a few hours ago. Tim followed, falling further behind as Jon strode deliberately down the hallway.

When Jon reached the door to his room he quickly swiped his handheld in front of the lock and pushed the door open. The door only opened a few inches before he met resistance. Something malleable was blocking the door. He pressed into the door harder to clear the obstruction. As soon as his nose crossed the threshold, Jon's heart sank to his knees. He smelled blood. And based on the strength of the odor, there was carnage on the other side of the door.

He eased his press on the door and squeezed through the gap. With his right hand still holding the door ajar for Tim, Jon found the source of resistance. Denise lay crumpled on the floor inside the door. Her head lolled to the side with two dime sized red holes in her forehead. Blood saturated the laminate that covered the room's entryway floor, and bone and red-grey pieces of brain matter spread in an arc out into the room, indicating Denise had been shot by someone standing with their back to the door.

As Jon stared down at Denise's lifeless body, Tim squeezed through the gap in the door and came shoulder to shoulder with Jon.

"Oh my god. What the fuck!?" Tim exclaimed, leaning forward and clutching his head between both hands. Then he wretched, bile splashing onto the floor between his feet.

Jon hardly noticed. He stepped over Denise's destroyed head to look through the room. His stomach was in knots, terrified he'd find Claire in a similar condition. But he quickly confirmed Denise was the only one in the room. *Now what?*

He flopped into the chair in the far corner of the room. Then he pulled his handheld from his pocket and rolled it around in his hands, trying to think of how he might find Claire.

He opened the message application and stared at the last message she'd sent him. He tapped on her name and the application switched to show the details of her Cloud profile, which were pretty sparse. At the bottom of the screen was a simple button which said 'Location Services.' Jon tapped it and the handheld screen transitioned to a two-dimensional map view. At the top of the map, black text faded in and out: Searching.

Jon waited impatiently. He leaned forward, staring at the handheld hoping the device would tell him where to find Claire. After thirty seconds of searching, the text at the top of the screen shifted to a steady black: User Offline.

"Damnit!" Jon exclaimed as he threw the handheld onto the carpet and laid back in the deep hotel lounge chair.

Where would he even start his search. Based on the time since her last message, she was probably somewhere nearby. But her captors, or Claire, had shut down her handheld. Even if she was still somewhere in the hotel it would be like looking for a needle in a thirty story haystack. And he had just under twelve hours until he needed to be on his way back to Hendrick House for the trip back to 2023. But who was he kidding; he wasn't leaving 2050 until he found her.

Jon leaned forward in the chair massaging his temples. Thinking. Digging for something that he could use to find Claire. He tried to stack all the details of the last few hours on top of each other into an organized structure but it all felt out of reach.

Once again Pulling was in the middle of it all. Jon had been sent on a mission that didn't go according to plan. He'd had to drug his time travel partner, then he'd been caught with his hand in the cookie jar during a breaking and entering op where he'd plugged a mystery stick into a well protected server.

Somehow, around the same time, Claire had been sent on a mission too. She'd been tasked to do network mapping - something Jon didn't understand in the least. It was all intertwined for sure. Jon was pursued, Denise was dead, Tim was drugged and Claire was gone.

Jon wasn't sure talking across time was even possible, but he didn't know what else to do. He selected Steven Pulling from his contact list and started typing a message, his dialect slipping back to the clipped and direct reports he was accustomed to making in the military. He also kept it vague, increasingly certain that anything he did on his handheld could be traced and used against him by Pinnacle and its supercomputers.

'Mission complete with complications. One member of Team D is KIA. One member of Team A is missing, likely captured, location unknown. Request guidance or additional support to find missing Team member, and permission to transport body of Team D member back home on scheduled return trip.'

Jon re-read his report and quickly hit send before he had time to think through all the reasons he shouldn't try to contact Steven Pulling.

He stared at the handheld for the next few minutes, willing the message to travel through time. Willing Steven Pulling to respond with the miracle clue that would help him get Claire back. Each passing second whittled away at his already slim optimism. Jon thought back to the briefing from Kristen Sprague right before they'd hopped in the sphere to travel to the future. He tried to envision every word she'd spoken, looking for some sliver of information that would jumpstart his brain into figuring out how to find Claire.

Then he had an idea. He grabbed his handheld off the floor and tapped his way to the 'Location Services' option for another of his contacts. The Pinnacle Cloud returned two results. Neither of the locations was too specific, probably to prevent stalkers from sneaking right up behind anyone that shared their location with contacts on the Cloud. One of the large translucent dots covered the block occupied by the Manchester Grand Hyatt. The other was a few short miles away, a block off Sunset Cliffs Boulevard in a cluster of four-plex condos in nearby Ocean Beach. Jon pump his fist in subdued satisfaction. It was a long shot, but it was the only thread he could think to grasp.

He popped out of the chair, fueled by the optimism of his hail mary idea.

"Tim, let's go. Follow me," Jon said as he strode directly to the door, irreverently stepping over Denise in the process.

"What are we doing?" Tim asked as he fell in behind Jon who was already stepping through the door.

"We're going to talk to someone who might know how to find

Claire. I'll explain on the way."

"Jon, wait. We can't leave Denise here. We walked into the scene of a murder. We have to tell someone." Tim stood in the doorway, holding the door open, pleading with his expression for Jon to come back in the room.

Jon pursed his lips in frustration. Each second he wasn't looking for Claire might be letting her get further away and harder to find. "Tim, we'll sort all that out later. There's nothing we can do for Denise right now. But Claire is out there somewhere and we're going to do whatever it takes to find her."

Tim's resistance softened and he stepped into the hallway to follow Jon. As soon as he did, Jon turned and resumed his determined pace toward the elevator while also tapping at his handheld to summon his car to the front of the hotel.

As they approached the elevator bank, Tim asked, "Can you at least tell me who we're going to talk to? I just left the scene of a crime with you. We're stepping out on a windy corner here, and I think I deserve to know why you think this is the right call?"

Jon hit the elevator call button and looked at Tim, surprised at the sudden fortitude. "I looked myself up in location services and got two results. One here in this hotel, and another a few miles away in Ocean Beach; a place where I always dreamed I'd retire."

"Wait, so we're gonna go see…"

"Yep, we're going to talk to Jon Haynes of 2050. Maybe he knows what happened to Claire."

"Oh shit," Tim muttered as he followed Jon into the opening elevator.

CHAPTER THIRTY-SEVEN

It was just after eleven o'clock when Jon and Tim turned off Sunset Cliffs Boulevard to circle the block. The source of the signal from future Jon hadn't moved since Tim and Jon left the hotel. Between the lack of movement of the signal and Jon's own knowledge that he loved this neighborhood, he felt confident his future self lived somewhere very close by.

As the car made a right to bring them onto the next street, Jon saw a dim lamp shining above four mail boxes near the street. Behind the mail boxes was a small gravel lot and a four unit apartment building. Two units at ground level and two second story units.

"Alistair, stop right here," said Jon, reaching for the door handle. He was out of the car before it had completely stopped. Jon crossed in front of the stopped car and headed straight for the mail boxes. Tim climbed out of the passenger side to meet him.

"Bingo," Jon said looking at the mail box. The lower left box, was labeled '1823 Cable St. Unit A.' Beneath the address the door was stenciled with 'J. Haynes.'

Jon headed for the door before Tim stopped him. "What about the car Jon?" It was still stopped in the street.

Jon kept walking toward the door for unit A while tapping the commands into his handheld that would send the car to find a place to park or loiter until he was ready to leave. When he was done he pocketed the handheld, now halfway across the gravel toward the door to the apartment he called home in the future. This was definitely not the way he pictured his Ocean Beach retirement.

Jon had imagined he'd finish his adventurous professional life in at least an upper middle class income status. He wanted to live near or on the San Diego waterfront. Instead it looked like he'd settled into a shitty apartment only a few blocks but quite a few income brackets away from his dream. Hopefully this was only an interim stop on the way to his dream retirement home. In 2050 Jon Haynes would only be fifty three years old. Plenty of good earning years left. When Jon was only a few steps from the porch that led to the apartment's front door, his thoughts were interrupted by Tim.

"Wait. Have you even thought about what you're going to say?" Tim said in a sort of shouting whisper. Jon turned to see that Tim had only made it a couple steps past the mailboxes.

Tim motioned for Jon to come back toward him, apparently afraid to get closer to the apartment building and afraid to speak loud enough that Jon could hear him clearly. Jon sighed at Tim's reluctance but took a few steps in his direction nonetheless. Tim was right after all. Jon hadn't even considered what he'd say when he met the twenty-seven-years-into-the-future version of himself. Tim also walked toward Jon and a few seconds later they stood no more than three feet apart in the center of the gravel lot.

"What do you think I should say?" Jon asked, impatience coating his tone.

"Nothing. I still think this is a horrible idea. This is the one thing they warned us not to do. Have you considered all the ways this might go wrong?"

"It's already gone wrong. Denise is dead and Claire is missing. The way I figure, it can only get better from here."

"Ok, I see your point. But what if it can get worse? What if meeting your future self creates some sort of paradox that you can't control?"

"If it helps me find Claire it's worth it. Either come with me or wait here." Jon turned and walked back toward the porch of Unit A. He wanted Tim's help but he wasn't willing to waste another minute waiting for him to come around.

Seconds later Jon was standing on the porch facing the front door of the apartment. He tapped his knuckles on the door gently.

He waited a few seconds, listening for someone in the house to approach the door. It was late, but most people were still awake at eleven. He heard the porch creak and turned his head to see that Tim had decided to join him.

Emboldened he knocked again. Louder this time. Still nothing. Then he closed his fist tightly and rapped the meaty side of his hand hard against the door three times. "Mr. Haynes, we really need to speak to you. We know you're in there."

A few seconds later he heard a metallic screech and a clang from the other side of the door. It reminded Jon of the sound made by an old recliner when the footrest was slammed shut. He heard footsteps approaching the door. Then the click of an old style dead bolt being unlocked. No fancy Pinnacle Cloud locks in this building.

Before the door opened, Jon heard a gruff voice from the other side of the door. "This better be good."

The door opened into the apartment and what Jon saw next caused his mouth to hang open. He was staring at his own weathered reflection. Except this version was easily thirty or forty pounds heavier. His eyes were surrounded by heavy puffy bags. His dirty white t-shirt rested on a substantial paunch, and the skin on his cheek bones and across his nose was highlighted by visible veins and a bumpy red texture that Jon intuitively decided was caused by years of hard drinking.

Before Jon could manage to say anything, the fat weathered version of himself that stood in the doorway in front of him reacted. "Oh fuck," mumbled the man in the doorway, shaking his head and looking down at the porch.

Jon tried to respond but couldn't find a single word. His mouth still hung open in disbelief.

"It's today isn't it," said future Jon. "It's March 17th and it's happening all over again isn't it?"

"I'm sorry?" Jon replied, still staring dumbfounded at the destroyed version of himself, almost thirty years older, that stood in front of him.

"I stopped paying attention to the calendar, but I knew this day was coming. I've always been too stupid to heed a warning."

"You've been expecting us?" Jon asked, his voice cracking slightly as his mouth went completely dry.

"Of course," said future Jon. "But there's nothing I can do for you. It's already happened, so leave me the hell alone and let me sleep." The older version of Jon began to shut the door in Jon's face.

"Wait, what's already happened? Is Claire okay? Don't you want to help us save her?"

The older version of Jon stopped the swing of the door. He stared at Jon through the small remaining crack, his eyes narrow and bloodshot. Jon suspected the man was drunk, on some sort of drugs, or both.

"You can't help her. We tried that twenty seven years ago. Now leave me alone." Future Jon stepped back from the door to finish shutting it in Jon's face.

In a surge of adrenaline Jon decided he wasn't taking no for an answer. He struck his left hand and left foot out, preventing his future self from shutting the door. Then before the older man on the other side of the door cold react and gain leverage, Jon shouldered the door all the way open. He caught future Jon off balance and the push sent him tumbling backward onto the floor.

"Get out of my apartment!" bellowed the elder Jon Haynes as he struggled from his back to his side, trying to regain his feet.

Jon was shaking from the adrenaline. He took a few steps into the apartment and now stood directly over his future self. Now in the apartment he registered the smell of bourbon, stale beer, and marijuana. "You ended up like this because you lost her. I'm not leaving until you tell me what happened, and I'm not going to repeat your mistake. Now get up off the floor. You're embarrassing me." Jon offered a hand to his older, fatter self.

Once future Jon was back on his feet, he grunted, walking away from Jon toward the dilapidated sofa in the living room. "What do you want to know?" he asked without turning around.

"Everything," Jon replied. He followed his future self into the living room and sat in a dusty creaky chair across from the worn sofa that future Jon now occupied.

"Alright, well I think by now you know that asshat Pulling never once told you the truth. He had plans all along to send you and Claire to do his bidding in 2050. I think he always assumed the mission you were sent on was pretty risky. But he also figured you'd be able to think or fight your way out of trouble. Since you're sitting here now I'm guessing it worked out same for you as it did for me twenty seven years ago."

"But Claire's mission was actually the more dangerous of the two. And Pulling made it seem pedestrian; important but very low risk. He gave the impression that the Casimir network protocols were undetectable and that Claire would be invincible against the Pinnacle's attempts to trace her physical location. And somehow Pulling never considered how the risk profile might change if Pinnacle found out that the access program had been uploaded in the first place."

Jon hung on every word the washed out 2050 Jon Haynes said. The last words hit him with a freight train of guilt. As he'd suspected, but tried to ignore, his inability to remain undetected when he uploaded the program in Building 31 had directly contributed to Claire being captured.

"Anyway, enough about the asshole Pulling. Let's see, what happened next. Oh right, when I realized she'd been taken and the other girl had been killed, I went into overdrive. I searched all night, trying to ping her location with my handheld every ten minutes. I tried to message Pulling, begging for some sort of direction on what to do. He never responded. I went back to the Pinnacle campus, thinking maybe I could find answers there. Instead I found Pinnacle security waiting for me."

"They let me on the campus. They let me think I was going to break into Building 31 the same way I had earlier in the evening. It wasn't until I was trying to hack my way through the lock on the side door a second time that I realized it was a setup."

Jon winced at what the older man was saying. He'd been tempted to act on the same desperate plan before coming here instead.

"Of course I fought my way out. I emptied the magazine of non-lethal rounds into the team of six Pinnacle guys that showed up outside Building 31. When I ran out of non-lethals I had to use live rounds to get off the campus. I still remember thinking I was home free as I headed for the abandoned back gate I'd used earlier that night. But this time they knew. A mix of Pinnacle guys and Gateguard rent-a-cops swarmed me as I tried to leave. I killed every one of them without remorse. Even if they didn't know what had happened to Claire, they stood in the way of me finding her."

Future Jon Haynes paused and shook his head in disgust. He was obviously lying about the lack of remorse.

"After I'd escaped the campus for the second time, I retreated to Hendrick House, thinking I might have time to regroup, make contact with Pulling to get better information, and make one last run at finding Claire. Instead, when I got to Hendrick House, Pulling had a team of Casimir guys waiting for me. They put me down and the next thing I knew I was back in 2023."

"So you never found Claire?"

"I didn't. Pulling put Michael Johnson in charge of a team to go back and get her. They went in old school without Cloud ID's. They went in the middle of the night, back into Building 31, killed every Pinnacle employee they saw, and tore the building apart until they found her."

"Where was she?" Jon asked, standing as though he was about to burst into motion to go get her.

"Easy young fella. You need to hear the rest of this."

Jon sat back down, tension in every fiber of his body.

Future Jon held up his hand. "I'm going to tell you where they found her, but you have to promise you won't move until I'm finished."

"Fine. Promise."

"She was two doors down from the server room I'd broken into earlier. Right there in Building 31 like I'd suspected all along." The older version of Jon paused, rubbing his hands against his chin.

"So, where is she now? The Claire of 2050, I mean." Jon was at the edge of his seat.

"She's not. She was dead when Mike Johnson's team found her."

"Wait, what?"

"Yes you naive fuck. She was dead. And not just dead by a clean bullet through the forehead like Denise. Claire was tortured." The older Jon Haynes let his words hang, staring daggers at the younger.

"Oh god," Jon groaned. He looked up and asked a question he hoped his future self wouldn't answer. "When you say tortured?"

"She'd been destroyed. Not mutilated or flayed, but worse. They found her with a prototype set of Pinnacle Implants installed. Her eyes were wide open, pupils dilated and filled with blood. Her mouth was frozen open in a look of complete agony and horror. And taped to her chest was a data stick similar to the one I'd used to upload Pulling's program in Pinnacle's servers.

"Mike Johnson watched the video file that was stored on the stick. It was a recording of Claire's perception of the forced immersion into the alternate reality projected by her implants. They tortured her in a totally immersive virtual reality. And because of the implants, it was a virtual reality she couldn't terminate. She was trapped. Imprisoned physically by Pinnacle in a room in Building 31. Worse, she was a prisoner inside her own mind. A computer told her what to see and what to feel. The worst part was it was working. She was starting to give up information about her access to the Cloud but went into cardiac arrest before coughing up Casimir's real secret. It makes me sick to think about how much pain she must have felt."

"Oh god," Jon groaned again.

"They never let me see the video personally. I was pretty mad about that at first, but as the years have gone by and the pain has dulled…"

Jon noticed the mention of dulled pain caused his older self to glance over at the quarter bottle of bourbon sitting open on the nearby end table.

"…I guess I'm grateful that I don't have the images burned into my mind. The knowledge that it happened is painful enough."

The 2050 version of Jon Haynes was no longer talking to the younger. He was talking to himself, slipping into some sort of self-administered therapy session. He'd probably told himself these same things many times before.

But for the Jon Haynes from 2023, this was new, raw, terrible information. He wasn't willing to accept it. It wasn't just the loss of Claire that threatened to push him over the edge with rage. The idea that a company could develop a product, pitch it as a world changer, and at the same time use it as a way to torture someone from within their own mind. These people were worse than the religious zealots Jon flushed out of caves in Afghanistan in his past life. If there was one hair out of place on Claire's head, they'd pay for it in ways Jon hadn't dreamed up yet.

The younger Jon Haynes couldn't sit around any longer. "I mean no offense, but it seems like you could have done more with what you know now. I'm going to go get Claire. Any final words of advice?"

The older Jon groaned and lifted himself from the sofa. But instead of extending a hand to shake Jon's or offering any words of advice, he reached for the bottle of bourbon he'd been eyeing earlier. "Nope. Good luck and all, but I've seen this movie before." The older Jon Haynes took a long pull of the bourbon and headed down the hall toward his bedroom. "I assume you can let yourself out," he said without looking back.

Tim watched the older Jon walk down the hall with a look of shock on his face. But 2023 Jon motioned a 'forget about him' gesture and put a hand on Tim's shoulder to lead him toward the front door. As Jon was about to step across the threshold of the shitty apartment and leave his future self behind, he had one final question. "Hey, even if you couldn't save Claire, why didn't you stay with Casimir and try to stop Pinnacle from rolling out the Implants?"

Future Jon stopped and turned to look back at Jon, shaking his head before he took another pull of bourbon. "I can't believe I was ever so naive. Time is a giant machine. It turns at the rate it chooses. It consumes whatever it chooses. It destroys whatever it chooses. Just because Casimir figured out how to move through time doesn't mean they can do a damn thing to change how it turns out. Regardless of any heroics you pull off tonight, you'll have done nothing more than move a few chairs around on the deck of the Titanic." Future Jon didn't wait for a response. He tipped the bottle at Jon and shut the dilapidated door that led to his bedroom.

Jon looked at Tim, who stood next to him by the front door. "I guess I didn't grow up to become an optimist."

CHAPTER THIRTY-EIGHT

As soon as Jon and Tim were back in the car, Alistair asked for their destination.

"Sorry Alistair. We're going to have to do this trip the old-fashioned way."

"I don't understand Jon. No one drives in a major city without assistance from the Cloud. It's considered dangerous," said Alistair, concern in his artificial voice.

Without responding to Alistair, Jon pulled his handheld from his pocket and powered it off. "Tim, turn off your handheld. If this is going to work they can't see us coming."

Tim's face was ashen, but he complied, resigned to trust the former soldier turned compatriot.

"Okay," said Jon. "Alistair, I need you to tell me how to disable the car's Cloud connection."

"I strongly advise against that Mr. Haynes," Alistair replied. "The vehicle's Cloud connection is for your safety and the safety of other motorists. My control of the vehicle can only be overridden in the event of an emergency."

An emergency. This situation satisfied the parameters of an emergency as far as Jon was concerned. He reached for the recessed steering wheel in the dash, pulled down the tab to release it, then drew it toward him. A more stern robotic voice replaced Alistair inside the car.

"Emergency user override activated."

Jon gripped the steering wheel but still sat in front of the dingy apartment complex. He tapped his way through the menus on the large in dash display looking to assure himself that the car was no longer connected to the Cloud. After a few minutes he navigated his way to the 'System' menu and manually turned off every connection the vehicle had to the outside world. The dash was glowing with alarms and warnings, telling Jon he was recklessly disconnected from the Pinnacle Cloud and now in serious danger.

Satisfied he'd severed every smart connection and was now driving nothing more than an overpriced golf cart, Jon pushed the accelerator and drove the car away from his future apartment.

After a couple turns he was back on Sunset Cliffs Boulevard, making his way to the freeway that would take him back to the Pinnacle HQ compound. Thankfully, there were very few cars on the road, so the fact that he didn't have a smart internet connection controlling his movements, was less likely to raise alarms.

A few short minutes later Jon exited the freeway and pulled off the main road into the same beat up neighborhood he'd visited earlier when he'd begun his mission from St. Charles Place. This time, he simply pulled the car over on a low traffic side street to talk Tim through the next phase of the plan.

***

A few minutes later Tim was behind the wheel. He dropped Jon a few blocks from the unused back gate and drove off, turning to follow the fence line toward the spot Jon had directed. Meanwhile, Jon ran for the gate. He sprinted with reckless abandon, confident that any interest he drew in the next few minutes was going to be overcome by the next trick he had up his sleeve.

Jon quickly scaled the fence, and dropped to the ground on the Pinnacle HQ side of the boundary. He didn't waste any time continuing toward Claire in Building 31. He ran until his legs and lungs were on fire. Even then he didn't relent. He didn't have long to get to Building 31 and the timing was going to have to be just right for him to get inside.

***

Tim's palms were sweating on the steering wheel of the normally automated sedan. From the moment Jon suggested going to visit his future self, Tim had serious reservations about what they were doing.

The Jon Haynes of 2050 had described a horrible series of events that transpired. What would happen if he and Jon changed that timeline with their actions? Worse, the current timeline had Claire killed and no mention of Tim. If he stuck to Jon's plan now, there was a non-zero chance that he'd end up in some secret room, tortured with virtual reality aided by artificial intelligence.

He shuddered and considered turning back. After coming to a stop at an intersection, he glanced down at his watch. Jon was depending on him to carry out his part of the plan in the next three minutes. There was no time to waiver. In or out. Now or never. The light turned green. The sweat on Tim's palms had spread to his forehead. He wondered if this was what a nervous breakdown felt like.

Gripped by anxiety, Tim turned the car to the right, headed back into the shabby neighborhood and away from the spot he'd assured Jon he'd arrive at in exactly…two minutes from now.

Tim made a quick left turn two blocks off the main road, then he slowed the car to a crawl, contemplating what to do next. He'd turned coward and was about to leave Jon high and dry. He should at least stay close and provide Jon an escape route if he managed to ever leave the fence line of the campus, with or without Claire.

He stopped the car along a quiet residential street lined with shabby duplexes. His mind was racing, but he was gripped with fear and inaction. He slammed his hands against the steering wheel in frustration.

***

Jon slowed to a walk a hundred yards from the north end of Building 31. His pulse was elevated and he was breathing heavily, but he'd also just finished a half mile at a dead sprint. He smiled imperceptibly, satisfied at the benefits of putting in the time to stay in shape after life in the military. Without moving his head or adjusting his gait, he scanned the area around him for any signs that he'd been noticed. It was very quiet on the Pinnacle campus. As he walked across a grassy area adjacent to the building he glanced at his watch. *One minute.*

He leaned against Building 31, around the corner from the same door he'd broken into hours before. Hidden in the shadow of the back side of the building he pulled the weapon from his waistband. He quickly released the clip and verified he still had plenty of non-lethal rounds. Hopefully it was enough to fight his way out with Claire, without having to take any lives. He slammed the magazine back into the gun then pulled the slide back gently to verify one round remained in the chamber.

He glanced at his watch again. Any second now Tim should be creating the diversion that Jon hoped would open the door for him. Jon took a deep breath, shrugged his shoulders to release the building tension, and poked his head around the corner to check for activity near the back entrance to Building 31.

Not only was the entrance quiet, but the bustle of activity Jon had expected to flare up after Tim's grand entrance hadn't happened. Jon waited, trying to remain patient. Maybe Tim had been held up at a light. He was only a couple minutes late.

Five more minutes passed as Jon hid in the shadows. His doubts swelled. What if Tim had been apprehended before he could create the planned chaos? Worse, what if he'd decided to ditch Jon and Claire altogether? Each second Jon waited he felt a growing tightness in his chest. There was definitely an upper limit to his patience, especially now that he knew what the future held for Claire if he didn't intervene.

Jon reached down into the pocket of his cargo pants and wrapped his hand around the B&E kit he'd used earlier. He was certain the Pinnacle AI would see him coming if he tried to break in using the same method he'd used a few hours earlier. But if another option didn't present itself, Jon was going to get desperate enough to try it and see if he could get lucky a second time.

After another three minutes with no diversion Jon gave up on waiting. He crept along the north side of the building as he pulled the B&E kit from his pocket. Better to try something that was likely to fail than to stand fast and do nothing at all. This time Jon stood in front of the pedestal and did nothing to hide his identity from the camera. He placed the small device in front of the electronic lock and waited. DECRYPTING...

Jon took a deep breath to control the surge of adrenaline. The text flashed slowly on the device. Jon had seen it before and knew the process would be painfully slow. Every muscle in his body was tense. He held the device against the electronic lock and waited.

DECRYPTION SUCCESSFUL

He pulled the device away and dropped it back in his pocket. If the Pinnacle AI was watching, he didn't have much time. *Where the fuck was Tim?*

WELCOME MICHAEL HALL. PLEASE AUTHENTICATE.

Jon slipped a fingerprint cover onto his thumb and pressed it to the pedestal. This was stupid. His impatience was going to get him caught. Any second now Pinnacle security was going to surround him and ensure he never got to Claire.

While Jon was waiting for the thumbprint authentication to complete, he was startled by the giant voice. "Security violation.

Security violation. All personnel shelter in place. Security personnel muster with dispatch immediately."

The announcement repeated a second time. By the time it was complete Jon had stopped paying attention to the electronic lock he'd been trying to defeat a few moments ago. Instead his attention was drawn to a commotion on the other side of the heavy door in front of him. As it grew louder he recognized the sound as two sets of heavy footfalls running toward the door.

He instinctively stepped to the right to ensure there was room for the door to swing open to his left. A second later the door burst open and two Pinnacle employees stumbled onto the concrete pad. Both pulled up, surprised to see Jon standing right next to the door. Jon, meanwhile, stepped forward to catch the large door before it clicked shut. Immediately he knew he'd moved too soon.

"What the hell are you doing?" asked one of the men. "Everyone badges in on their own credentials. No piggybacking. Let me see your handheld."

"Of course. Sorry about that. I guess the second security violation of the night just has me a little rattled." Jon feigned ignorance as he reached toward his pocket to present his handheld, but instead pulled the pistol from his waistband. He put a non-lethal round in each man before they could register that he'd drawn a weapon. And he did it all without letting the door to Building 31 click shut.

***

Tim slowly opened his eyes. The first thing he was aware of was wetness on his face. The second was the taste of iron in his mouth. He blinked, trying to clear his vision. When that didn't work he wiped a hand across his eyes. Blinking again, he could see but everything was blurry. He blinked rapidly then saw the back of his hand smeared with red.

His heart rate jumped higher as he recognized the moisture oozing down his face and the taste in his mouth was from his own blood. He frantically wiped his face with the front of his shirt, fighting a losing battle against panic. His shirt came back even bloodier than he'd anticipated.

"Oh god," Tim moaned weakly.

He blinked again and was slightly relieved that he could see clearly out of his right eye. But the left wasn't improving. The lid felt heavy. He gently touched his fingers to the eye and confirmed it was swollen, almost fully shut. He felt around to try and find the source of blood.

"Shit," he winced as his fingers grazed the deep cut along his eyebrow.

Without anything handy to stop the flow of blood he leaned his head slightly to the left and pulled his left sleeve up to hold it against the cut.

With that settled, at least temporarily, he scanned his surroundings, trying to determine the extend of damage to the car and the rest of his body.

The last thing he remembered before waking up with the cut over his eyes was violently hopping the curb. He was probably five or ten minutes late by the time he'd finally mustered the courage to go through with Jon's plan. He'd made up some of the time by running two stoplights on the road adjacent to the perimeter of the Pinnacle campus. Unfortunately, when he finally hopped the curb to hit the fence a few hundred yards down from the campus entry post, he was going too fast. Tim was pretty sure the right front tire had blown which jerked the car hard to the right and rammed him into the fence more directly than he'd intended.

Overall it could have been a lot worse. The deflated airbag hung loosely from the center of the steering wheel in front of him. Probably the source of the cut on his eye. And other than the cut and some soreness in his neck, he seemed to be in ok shape.

Blinking again, he looked outside the car for the first time. His stomach tightened into a knot. Three black clad Pinnacle guys stood in front of the hood of the car. Another stood at the driver side door, and a fifth stood along the passenger side. Fear and adrenaline screaming through his veins, Tim mashed the 'Start' button on the console in front of him. Nothing happened. He pushed it one more time, hoping. But he got the same result. The car was dead.

"Get out of the car," came a muffled voice that belonged to the large Pinnacle employee that stood outside his driver side door.

Tim didn't have much choice. He already tried to flee but the car hadn't started. He definitely wasn't going to be able to climb out of the car and outrun these guys. Best to comply and hope that he had enough security personnel distracted to give Jon a fighting chance.

He pulled the handle on the door to open it. As soon as he did, the security man waiting on the other side yanked the door fully open and quickly had a hand around Tim's left arm just above the elbow. The Pinnacle man pulled him roughly from the car.

Tim felt stiffness throughout his back and lower body. If he made it to tomorrow he was going to be sore.

The security guy who'd drug him from the car maintained a vice-grip on Tim's shoulder as another guy from in front of the car walked over and started patting him down. Tim had been careful to empty his pockets before setting out on this idiotic mission. The guard quickly found the only item he'd deliberately kept on his person.

"Why is your handheld off?" the guard ask gruffly, sticking it too close to Tim's face. "Did you think you were going to get in here undetected?"

The guard fiddled with the handheld. Tim saw the light from the backlit screen reflected on the guard's face as he powered it on. Tim leaned forward to try and see what he was doing, but the other guard, who still had hold of Tim's arm, spun him around aggressively.

"Turn around and put your hands on top of the car," said the guard that held his arm.

Tim didn't really have a choice. As he said it the guard pressed him forward into the driver's side of the car before releasing his arm.

"How did you end up crashing through our fence?" asked one of the guards from behind him.

Tim started to turn around to answer.

"Don't. Face forward and keep your hands on the roof of the car. How did you end up crashing through our fence?" the same voice asked again.

"I...don't know," Tim stammered. "I think I must have blown a tire or something."

Tim watched as the guard on the other side of the vehicle stooped to inspect the wrecked wheel on the front passenger side of the sedan.

"What's your name?" asked the guard behind him who'd taken on the role of interrogator.

"Mark Johnston," Tim blurted. "Look, just give me back my handheld and I'll go call a cab or something. I'm sorry to have interrupted your evening, but it was just an accident. I'd offer to fix your fence but I'm sure Pinnacle can afford it more easily than I can." Tim's head was pounding and he wasn't sure how much longer he was going to be able to remain standing.

"Mark Johnston? Hey Mike, isn't Mark Johnston the Gateguard Employee who disappeared during the security violation earlier tonight?"

"Yeah, that sounds right," said the guard on the passenger side of the car. "But they said he was a built white dude, not a skinny asian."

"Check his Cloud ID," said the interrogator.

"Yeah, I'm working on it," said the other guard from behind Tim. After a few seconds of silence, the same guard spoke up again. "He's not bullshitting, this thing belongs to Mark Johnston. And it's the same Mark Johnston that works for Gateguard."

"Call this in Jim," said the interrogator to one of the security guys still loitering in front of the crashed sedan.

Tim watched as the guard, evidently named Jim, walked a few steps away from the car while he spoke into the radio handset on his shoulder. Nobody other than Jim spoke for the next few minutes, and Tim couldn't make out the details of the conversation.

The guard named Jim turned around a minute later and walked back toward the car. "They want us to bring him in."

"Roger," said the interrogator. "Looks like you're coming with us Mark."

"Wait, you're arresting me? Can you even do that? Aren't you guys private contractors or something?" Tim was putting on an act, but the concern in his voice was genuine.

"You illegally entered a sensitive private facility. And we have an arrangement of sorts with the local authorities. So, you're not being arrested per se, but you are coming with us. Whether you do it willingly or not is up to you."

Before he'd finished speaking, the interrogator guard pulled Tim's hands from the roof of the car and tucked them behind his back. Tim felt plastic slide loosely over his wrists before it was cinched tight with a tug from the guard.

Next the guard put a firm hand on Tim's shoulder and pulled, indicating he should stand, taking his weight off the car. "Our ride is over there on the road," said the guard as he guided Tim to turn to his left and walk forward.

As Tim walked away from Jon's destroyed car he saw a black van with flashing yellow lights parked in the streets less than fifty yards ahead. One of the guards jogged ahead of the group and opened the back door to the van.

Tim tried to swallow but his mouth had gone dry as he recalled what 2050 Jon Haynes said about the way Pinnacle had dealt with Claire Keen.

***

Jon felt a slight twinge of guilt as the two Pinnacle employees fell like wet heaps of warm meat onto the concrete in front of him. One of them landed on his shoulder without incident. The other went down face first and the sound of his forehead hitting the concrete reminded Jon of the hollow thump that a watermelon made when dropped on a hard kitchen floor.

The last time he'd used one of the non-lethal darts he'd caught the victim to soften the fall caused by the fast acting drug. He didn't do that this time. Primarily because he couldn't risk giving up his hold on the door that was going to get him into Building 31. But also because he felt no remorse at having put the two men down. In the moment, he knew he would have shot them with lethal rounds if they'd been loaded. For all he knew, these guys might have just come from the room where Claire was being held - maybe even tortured.

Once both men were down, Jon stepped through the door and let it click shut behind him. He didn't waste any time, running down the hall, past the server room, coming to a screeching stop two doors past it. The door was unlabeled. Jon pushed down on the latch, but it was locked. He considered stepping back and shouldering the door, but thought better of it. The door looked to be solid metal and would probably do more damage to him than he could do to it. But there wasn't time to debate strategies with himself.

He closed his fist and banged hard on the door three times. He waited for a response, or the sound of someone coming to the door. Nothing. He banged on the door again. Harder this time.

A voice came from far behind the door. "This part of the facility is off limits. Authorized personnel only. Move along please."

Jon's adrenaline responded before his brain could. His heart raced. The voice he'd just heard may belong to the person that would eventually kill Claire. He considered kicking the door off the hinge, confident he could in the moment. Then he had an idea.

Jon yelled back at the door. "Sorry to bother you sir, but on account of the second security violation tonight we've been directed to make face to face contact with every person on the campus. Please open the door. I won't take much of your time."

"Move along son," came the response. "I assure you I'm exempt from any security protocols. The entities actually in charge are well aware of where I am. And I am well aware fo the security protocols."

"I have to insist sir," Jon replied. "I can't leave this building until I've talked with everyone in it."

"I'm done talking to you," said the voice from the other side of the door. "If you like your job here, you'll move on."

Jon pursed his lips. He thought for sure his little white lie would get the door open and give him a chance to get inside. On the bright side, he seemed to be getting under the skin of the mystery guy on the other side of the door.

He balled his fist and banged it on the heavy door incessantly. BANG...BANG...BANG...BANG...BANG...BANG. Then he yelled into the door again, a little louder than before. "I have an assignment and I'm NOT LEAVING until it's done."

At first he heard nothing. No response from the arrogant man on the other side of the door. BANG...BANG...BANG, he rapped on the door again. Then Jon heard the man's voice, this time much closer to the door.

"You moron. I hope you enjoy unemployment. You're fucking done here and anywhere else connected to the Pinnacle Cloud."

Based on the proximity of the voice Jon sensed the man was right on the other side of the door. He drew the pistol from his waistband and stepped back from the door to ensure he had room to fire it.

The handle on the door moved slightly and he heard a heavy deadbolt lock click free. The handle moved further and the door started to come open, stopping when it was only open about an inch.

"What'd you say your name was, son? I want to make sure the right guy gets fired in the morning."

Instead of answering the threat-laced question, Jon launched himself into the door. He felt a moment of resistance and a cry of pain as the person on the other side was knocked to the ground. Then the door swung wide. On the floor in front of him Jon found an overweight, middle aged bald white man with a greying goatee. He wore khakis and a polo mostly covered by a lab coat.

Every fiber of Jon Haynes wanted to pull the man up by his collar and beat the soft flesh on his face with a closed fist. Instead he fired two non-lethal rounds from his pistol into the man's flabby neck. The bald head lolled back immediately. Jon wouldn't be getting any intel from him.

Jon stopped long enough to shut and lock the door behind him. Then stepped over the fat unconscious man-in-a-lab-coat and followed the short hallway ahead of him. The ceilings in the room were high, but there were shorter dividing walls that kept Jon from seeing into the center of the space. The hallway made a ninety degree turn to the left just ahead. Once Jon made the turn he saw that the room opened up another ten yards ahead of him. It seemed that the short walls were meant to keep someone at the door from seeing what happened inside.

Jon broke into a jog. "Claire! Claire!?"

He reached the end of the view-obscuring wall and saw the makeshift lab. "Oh my god," he nearly blubbered as he saw Claire, in the center of the room, unconscious on a reclined exam chair. Jon sprinted across the room to her and immediately took her pulse. Her heart rate was slow but her pulse was strong. She'd been sedated.

Jon looked around, trying to get a sense of what was happening in the room before he arrived. There was a table next to Claire's chair with various medical instruments mounted on it. Jon wasn't sure what most of them were. But there were two silver disks with sharp needles protruding from one side. The disks looked like the silver tabs he'd seen behind the ear of the people in the implant advertisements.

Without thinking about it further, he pocketed the small devices. He was preparing to pick Claire up off the chair to carry her to safety when he realized she had an IV in her left arm. He frantically followed the hoses, afraid her sedation might be more significant, but found saline at the other end.

Jon was no doctor, but he knew battlefield medicine and was confident he could remove the IV without issue. Once he'd done that he was ready to carry Claire out of the building and away from the Pinnacle campus. But there was a better than even chance he was going to have to fight his way out and it would definitely be more practical if Claire was moving on her own.

He went to a cabinet on the far wall of the room and started rifling through various basic medical supplies. Then he found what he was looking for and quickly made his way back over to Claire.

Once he was next to the exam chair again, he cracked open the small vial and held it under her nose. The smelling salts would bring her back to consciousness if the sedation wasn't too strong. Claire's face scrunched and her head reflexively turned away from the ammonia Jon was wafting just below her nostrils. Jon followed the motion of her head, keeping the noxious salts right below her nose.

After a few more pained expressions (in any other scenario Jon would have found the expressions hilarious) Claire opened her eyes and screamed her way back into consciousness.

"Stop it! Stop it! Let me go!" Claire said as she came out from under the sedation.

Jon stepped back, giving her a moment to get her bearings.

"Claire, it's me, Jon."

Claire looked with unfocused eyes in Jon's direction. Her pupils were dilated and she probably couldn't make out the detail of his face.

"Jon? Did they get you too? Where are we?" Claire blinked her eyes hard, trying to bring the room into focus.

"No Claire, they didn't get get me. We're at Pinnacle computing's headquarters and I'm getting you out of here."

Jon saw the glassy lack of focus fading from Claire's eyes. She started to stand and Jon closed the distance to help her out of the chair. Before her feet reached the floor Jon positioned himself on her right side, wrapping his left arm around her back and under her left arm. As Jon had suspected, the sedative was still very much active in Claire's bloodstream. Her legs wobbled and tried to give way when she stood. Fortunately Jon was already there to brace her. The only thing keeping her awake was probably a combination of the salts he wafted under her nose and the adrenaline surge she'd just received when she realized Jon was there to break her out. As soon as the excitement died down she'd probably sleep for another couple hours.

"Let's get out of here," said Jon, smiling at Claire as he brought her right arm up onto his shoulder to stabilize her further. "We probably don't have much time before they figure out what I'm up to, and I'd prefer to not have to fight my way out."

Claire nodded her consent and Jon walked her out of the room the way they'd come in. As they rounded the final corner in the makeshift hallway to head for the door, Claire stopped in her tracks and stared at the unconscious form on the floor ahead.

"That's the guy," said Claire. Jon felt her pull weakly in the opposite direction.

"He's out cold Claire. You don't have to be afraid of him." Jon tried to gently pull Claire forward, encouraging her to continue walking toward escape. But her feet were planted.

"He said his name was Dr. Flores. That he was going to make me experience pain that I couldn't even fathom. That if I didn't tell him how I'd gotten into the nerve center of the Pinnacle Cloud, he was going to torture me in the worst possible ways without leaving a scratch..."

Jon interrupted her rambling when he felt a cold sweat start to break on the arm draped across his shoulders. "Claire, you're ok. I have you. Do what I say and we'll get out of here. None of them will ever hurt you again, I promise." Jon hoped he could keep the promise.

Claire looked at him, still a little glassy, but more herself. Jon could feel the tension of nervous adrenaline in her body as she trembled slightly with each step forward. But Jon kept her moving forward. Eventually, he felt her start to carry her own weight on her legs. He pulled her to the right to step around the body of Dr. Flores but Claire resisted, pulling out of Jon's grasp.

Before Jon could change direction to keep hold of her, she took a strong step forward, drew her right leg back, and kicked the unconscious Dr. Flores squarely in his half open mouth. Jon saw it happening in slow motion. Fortunately, when he saw Claire's leg come back as though she was about to kick a field goal, he closed the distance behind her. As soon as her foot connected with Flores' face, Claire's opposite leg gave out and she started crumpling to the floor. Jon hooked his arms through her armpits and took the weight that her legs decided they couldn't carry.

"Whoa, you've got more strength left in you than I thought," Jon said sheepishly as he cringed from the wet thud Claire's shoe made against Flores' face.

Jon re-situated Claire so that he could continue to help her walk out of Building 31. But this time he ensured that he also had access to the weapon in his waistband. Once they walked out of this room and back into the main hall of the building, anything could happen.

As Jon hooked Claire's arm over his shoulder again and prepared to open the door, he took one last satisfied glance at Dr. Flores. Despite her weakened condition, Claire had jarred a few teeth loose and left Dr. Flores drooling blood onto the tile.

Once they'd stepped past the unconscious doctor, Jon clicked the deadbolt free and opened the door toward him. Still balancing Claire, he leaned out into the hallway and checked to his right and left.

Somehow the building wasn't swarming with Pinnacle security. Maybe Tim's diversion had worked. It was time to get the hell out of here. Now all Jon had to do was figure out where they were going and how they were going to get there.

CHAPTER THIRTY-NINE

Once Jon was into the hallway with Claire and heading back for the side door he'd entered through twice before, his sense of urgency started to build. He walked faster and faster down the hall, nearly dragging Claire as they approached the door.

Jon stopped at the door and ensured he could still reach the handgun in his waistband. He drew it, then shouldered the door open. He breathed a sight of relief when the two guards still lay unconscious on the concrete, right where he'd left them a few minutes earlier. No one else was around.

Satisfied there was no immediate danger, Jon put the gun back in his waist band and gently lowered Claire to sit on the concrete step outside the door. He needed to think quickly. The security AI had to have figured out what Jon was doing by now. The only advantage he had left was unpredictability. How could a computer figure out how Jon was going to escape the campus when Jon hadn't figured that part out yet.

Jon walked the couple steps to the two unconscious goons he dropped with non-lethal tranquilizer darts earlier. On a whim, he patted them down, checking for weapons or any other interesting gear that might give him an advantage in his escape.

As he patted around the front pocket of the first guy, Jon felt only a handheld and simple bill fold. He was about to move on to check his remaining pockets when he paused. Jon reached in the goon's pocket and withdrew the handheld and wallet. As he was about to start going through the guy's wallet to see if he could find anything useful, the obvious answer slapped him across the face.

Jon dropped the wallet onto the concrete and shifted his attention to the handheld. He tapped the button below the display and the screen prompted him to unlock with his thumbprint. He grabbed the unconscious goon's thumb and pressed it to the pad. The device immediately unlocked to let Jon inside.

Savvy with the basic operation of a 2050 Pinnacle handheld after the day's events, Jon navigated to the vehicle application, silently hoping this guy had a car nearby that Jon could 'borrow' for his escape. He tapped in the series of commands required to call the car to his location.

Jon almost jumped out of his skin as he was bathed in light. The headlights on the car directly in front of him in the small parking lot had just turned on, destroying Jon's night vision and momentarily disorienting him.

Whoever had just doused him in light now had the upper hand. Jon's fight or flight consideration leaned heavily toward flight at the moment. He moved to grab Claire by the arm and make a run for it until he could regain his bearings and dig in for a fight. Then the car owning the bright headlights rolled forward and stopped inches in front of Jon.

The bumper of the car stopped less than a foot from Jon's knees and gave him relief from the lights that had blinded him moments before. Jon squinted, forcing his eyes to re-adapt to the darker lighting as he looked into the cab of the car to face down his new adversary. What he found made him laugh out loud.

The car was empty. He looked down at the handheld in his left hand and laughed again. The car that had nearly sent him running was the one he'd called for using the security goon's handheld. And it had been parked less than ten yards from where he stood.

Jon quickly made his way back over to Claire, scooped her up behind the shoulders and under the knees, and carried her to the passenger side of the car. He quickly set her in the seat and shut the door, then made his way around the front of the car back toward the driver's side.

As he reached for the handle to open the door, a pair of lights on the other side of the car caught his eye. He caught a glimpse of a black van rounding the corner and turning toward him and the backside of Building 31. The silhouette of the van was replaced by two bright headlights advancing toward him from two hundred yards away.

Jon instinctively dropped down into a squat, taking cover below the driver side window. He could hear the whine of the van's electric motor as it approached. He saw the headlights brighten below the sedan around his feet. He crept toward the hood of the car in order to use the wheel to hide the silhouette of his feet. As he did, he poked his head up and tapped on the window to get Claire's attention. She looked at him and he gestured silently toward the approaching van. Thankfully, Claire understood Jon's warning and reclined her seat so her silhouette would no longer be visible through the tinted window.

With that done, Jon crouched in front of the front driver-side tire and withdrew the pistol from his waistband again. As the van drew closer Jon released the magazine of non-lethal rounds to double check the number that remained. Eight. He slammed the magazine back into the weapon and withdrew the full magazine of lethal rounds from the cargo pocket of his pants. He dropped it into his front left pocket to ensure it was quickly accessible if he ran through the rest of the non-lethal rounds before the fight was done.

The van rolled to a stop still facing directly at the passenger side of Jon and Claire's getaway sedan. He listened intently as two doors opened. He heard shuffling footsteps but didn't dare raise up to take a look and risk losing the element of surprise. Next he heard what was probably the side door of the van slide open.

"Get out," said a gruff voice.

"Ok, calm down. Where are you taking me?" asked a timid voice that Jon could barely make out. The same timid voice grew louder as it's owner emerged from the van into the parking lot. "I feel like I should be allowed to have a lawyer or a phone call or something."

Jon's pulse quickened as he registered the voice. It belonged to Tim Nguyen. Jon gripped the pistol a little tighter and listened closely to try and determine how many men were positioned around the van.

He heard multiple sets of footsteps approaching. He counted at least six. One of them was shuffling and dragging against the concrete as if being drug unwillingly toward the building. The sound drifted toward the back end of the car. The group was going to pass behind Jon's getaway vehicle en route to the back door of Building 31. Jon twisted his crouched body around so he could easily see in that direction and be prepared when the men emerged into his line of sight.

As he repositioned Jon was quickly reminded of the two Pinnacle guys he'd put down. They were both on the ground near the back end of the car and would be visible to the van crew any second.

"What the fu..."

Jon popped up firing. He'd honed in on the voice of the guy who'd seen his sleeping cohorts. He dropped him with one shot, buried in the man's shoulder. As his first shot was landing Jon adjusted his aim for the second man. A second later he was down too, a non-lethal round penetrating his left pectoral.

"Tim, get down!" Jon yelled as he trained the pistol on one of the men dragging Tim toward the door. Jon squeezed the trigger but the man he'd aimed at recognized danger and dropped to the ground just like Tim. The shot sailed over his head and Jon lost his line of sight behind the car.

Jon quickly swung the pistol slightly to the left and dropped the other man who'd been escorting Tim. This one responded too slowly and the dart struck his neck.

Jon counted three Pinnacle men remaining. Two were running back toward the cover of the van and the third was tucked behind the trunk of Jon's getaway car. Three men and five rounds left. Jon pulled in a deep breath and held it.

He trained the gun on the closer of the two fleeing Pinnacle goons. He heard the first shot clang against the metal grill of the van so he fired a second. The dart found flesh in the man's back and the fleeing man fell violently, face first, to the concrete of the parking lot.

Jon trained to the right, leveling the weapon on the second man fleeing for the cover of the black van. He squeezed the trigger a fraction of a second too late. Another round ricocheted off the van. But this time, his target had made it to cover on the driver's side of the van.

Two targets and two rounds left. Jon duck walked toward the rear of the car, hoping to creep up on the man he'd watched drop to the deck earlier. Before he could reach the back end of the vehicle his ears were assaulted by an explosion of glass as the rear windshield and rear driver's side window exploded into shards that rained into the car and onto Jon's head and shoulders. The remaining shooting gallery targets were starting to shoot back.

Unwilling to bet on two perfect shots with the non-lethal darts, Jon ejected the magazine and let it clatter to the concrete. He quickly pulled the other magazine from his pocket and slammed it into the bottom of the pistol before racking back the slide to put a very real, very lethal round in the chamber.

Then Jon dropped to his stomach and scooted his way under the car, still facing the rear, and hoping to get a shot on the guy hiding back there. Instead he found his line of sight obstructed by Tim. The Pinnacle thug had an arm draped over Tim's back and looked intent on using him as a shield.

Tim and Jon made eye contact. Jon still couldn't see the face of his target and any shot he took would put Tim right in the line of fire. Jon swiped his hand hard to the left, motioning for Tim to try and make a run for it. Tim's eyes told Jon he was terrified; frozen in place. Jon needed to make something happen fast. He had no idea what the other target that had made it to the van was doing. He couldn't afford to take so long that the remaining enemy got the drop on him, or worse, on Claire hiding in the car above him.

Jon crept forward on his stomach waiting for an opportunity. Tim watched him advance with wide eyes. Jon swiped his hand to the left again, silently imploring Tim to move. This time Tim complied, scrabbling up to his knees before the Pinnacle guy could gain a better hold on him. But Jon was out of position from his prone crawl and it took a fraction of a second for him to train the gun on his target. By the time he had, the man was already on his feet, trying to restrain Tim and stop his flight. It wasn't ideal, but it was the best shot he was going to get. Jon squeezed the trigger and blew the Pinnacle man's ankle apart.

The man screamed in agony as he fell to the ground.

"Run Tim!" Jon yelled from below the sedan. Tim broke to Jon's left and gave Jon a clear line of sight to the screaming, writhing man on the ground. Jon silenced him with a second round, this one to the back of his head.

One left. Jon scooted on his stomach to his right, trying to quickly climb out from under the car and re-locate the one escaped Pinnacle employee who had taken cover behind the van. Once he was out from under the car Jon climbed up on all fours.

"Don't move asshole," came a voice from above him. *Damn.*

Jon stayed still, praying the guy wouldn't pull the trigger and remaining deathly still so as not to spook him. He squeezed his eyes shut, trying to think of a way out. Then he heard a gunshot and waited for the pain of the end.

Instead, the man who'd been standing over him dropped to the concrete in a growing pool of blood. Jon stood to take in his surroundings. The right side of the man's head had a small hole and the left was blown to pieces by the exit wound. Jon looked to his left to find the shooter and saw Tim, doubled over ten feet away and vomiting the contents of his stomach onto the parking lot concrete. Tim was bent over next to one of the Pinnacle guys Jon had dropped earlier. One arm was propped against his thigh as he leaned over to vomit. The other was wrapped around the hand of the downed guard who's pistol Tim had used to bail Jon out of his most recent jam. Sometimes it's better to be lucky than good. Jon would never have pegged Tim for a hero.

Next, Jon opened the driver's side door of the sedan to check on Claire. She was shaking but unharmed. It was time to leave, and fast.

"Tim, come help me out," Jon called to the now dry-heaving Tim. Jon took position with his arms hooked through the arm pits of the Pinnacle man he'd stolen the handheld from.

"Open the back door then grab his feet. We're bringing him with us," said Jon.

Tim complied, moving on wobbly legs and opening the rear driver's side door, then stepping over to help hoist the large man into the back seat. Once they'd stuffed his large frame into the seat, Jon shut the door.

"Get in on the other side Tim. And if he starts to wake up, let me know."

Jon grabbed the non-lethal magazine from where he'd dropped it on the ground. He double checked that it still had two rounds left. He might need them if the guy in the backseat tried to regain consciousness.

Jon climbed into the driver's seat, squeezed Claire's hand in reassurance, then tapped the handheld, directing the car to take them out to the desert to Hendrick House. The quiet electric motor whirred to life and headed for the front gate of the Pinnacle complex.

The front gate was the only barrier left and Jon was ready to fight his way through it if required. But silently, Jon had experienced enough for the day. He had recovered Claire and he didn't want to see more death tonight. He took a deep breath as the car closed the distance to the exit.

He saw a security vehicle sitting near the guard shack but nothing indicating the gate was closed to outbound traffic. As his stolen car approached within fifty yards of the exit, Jon pretended to be busy on the handheld, forcing himself not to look at the guard shack, lest he draw the notice of the guards.

The vehicle crept slowly through the outbound lane, then made a right onto Barnett Avenue. Jon held his breath, expecting pursuers would burst through the gate at any moment. Then the car made another slight right and merged onto Pacific Highway, accelerating toward the interstate that would take Jon, Claire and Tim to the relative safety of the Casimir safehouse in the desert.

CHAPTER FORTY

Just under forty five minutes after leaving the Pinnacle campus, Jon's stolen sedan pulled into the circle drive in front of Hendrick House. The car had been relatively quiet during the trip. Claire had fallen back asleep ten minutes after they'd escaped, the sedatives she'd been injected with earlier still very much in her system. Tim had sat nervously staring at the large Pinnacle security man sprawled next to him in the back seat.

Once they were on Interstate 8 headed west, Jon had finally been able to relax. As the automated electric car screamed down the interstate Jon realized high speed car chases were probably a thing of the past. The Cloud moved cars and trucks along the interstate as though they were all part of the same organism. There were no accidents, no rubbernecking, no chain reactions of cars mashing the brakes forcing the traffic to act like a half mile long confused caterpillar. How do you chase someone when everyone moves at the same speed? Maybe the cops had an override.

In any event, using the Pinnacle employee's car to make the getaway appeared to have been the right answer. They weren't pursued at all and didn't draw so much as a glance as they'd left the campus earlier. The only exciting part of the drive occurred when Tim screamed because the Pinnacle guy had stirred in the backseat. To calm Tim down, Jon had spun around in the front seat and shot another tranquilizer dart into the guy's thigh. The darts were supposed to be non-lethal, and the guy weighed an easy two hundred and fifty pounds, so he'd probably be ok.

As the car came to a stop in front of Hendrick House, Tim and Jon climbed out. Jon rounded the car to the passenger side. He opened the door and lifted Claire from her seat. Cradling her, one arm behind her knees and another under her shoulders, he carried he to the front door. Meanwhile, Tim stood next to the car in a stupor, staring at the large unconscious man in the back seat.

"Tim," Jon called. "A little help please."

"Uh, yeah, sorry."

Tim walked quickly past Jon to the front door, swiped his handheld at the door, then held it open for Jon to carry Claire inside.

Once inside, Jon walked quickly to his left and laid Claire on the sofa in the large living room off the entry foyer. Once that was done he made his way back outside.

Climbing back into the car on the passenger side, Jon pulled the Pinnacle security guard's handheld from where he'd stashed it in the center console. He maneuvered his way between the two front seats, grabbed the man's heavy limp right hand and pressed his thumb to the sensor. Once the device was unlocked Jon maneuvered his way back out of the car through the passenger door. He tapped through the options on the handheld, directing the car to it's next destination. Once he'd confirmed the trip he dropped the handheld on the passenger seat, shut the door, and watched the car drive away. With any luck the passenger wouldn't awaken until the car was parked in it's original spot outside Building 31. There was nothing Jon could do to get rid of the Cloud record of where the vehicle had been, but he had no intention of hanging around 2050 long enough to allow the forensics of that process to track him down.

Once Jon was back inside he made his way to the living room where Claire was resting and flopped heavily into a plush lounge chair across from her. He ran his hands through his hair and sighed deeply before looking around the room. Tim stood awkwardly in the open space where the foyer met the large living room and stared off into space, stress smeared across his face.

Jon considered offering Tim a few encouraging words to comfort him and calm him down, but couldn't find the energy or the kindness to do it. In fact, looking at Tim, who was fully absorbed in feeling sorry for himself, made Jon angry. He didn't know exactly what had happened back at the Pinnacle campus, but Tim definitely hadn't executed the simple piece of the plan Jon had assigned him. Thankfully it looked like it was all going to work out - by dumb luck - but Tim's skittishness was a major liability. And who knows what role he'd played in allowing Claire to be taken in the first place.

Jon took a deep breath. What had started out as something

resembling sympathy for Tim had quickly turned to anger and resentment. Jon reminded himself that he didn't have all the details and his anger might be misplaced.

He sat back in the chair and watched Claire sleep. God knows what she'd been through in the last few hours. Worse, her sleep wasn't peaceful. She seemed tense and rigid, even in exhausted drug-induced sleep. Jon fought the urge to wake her and save her from whatever nightmare she might be in. She'd been through a strange form of hell today and needed to sleep off whatever drugs the quack doctor had fed her.

As Jon tried to relax, his thoughts drifted to Steven Pulling. Just picturing the man's face in his mind's eye brought Jon to a new resolution. When this was all over and Claire was safely back in 2023, he would demand answers or walk away. Pulling had been deceiving and misleading him with half truths and sketchy details since they'd met. Jon was used to being in control - of his circumstances and the outcome. Somehow Pulling had manipulated him time and again, to the point that Jon had traveled almost thirty years into the future and taken on a half-baked breaking and entering mission at significant risk to himself-all without even considering Pulling's motives until this moment.

Jon leaned forward in the chair again, pulling the hair above his forehead into his fist. Before he realized it he was pacing the large living room and his thoughts were headed down a Pulling-centered rabbit hole. Steven Pulling had dangled obvious bait early in their relationship - help for Dan Jones' family. Once the hook was set, Jon had set out to do Pulling's bidding by finding a way to break into the Casimir facility. But when Pulling didn't like the speed at which Jon was executing his mission, he obstructed his progress.

Then there was Claire. With everything that had happened, especially in the last twenty four hours (as Jon perceived them), there was no way him meeting Claire and their subsequent relationship was a product of coincidence.

Jon reached the end of the room farthest from the foyer and turned to pace back the opposite way. He started back across the living room when he registered a change in his surroundings via his peripheral vision. He looked up from the floor to find Claire sitting upright on the couch massaging the area around her temples with her fingers.

"Claire! How are you feeling?" Jon nearly tripped over his feet as he hurried over to kneel next to her.

"I feel like shit," said Claire, without looking up from the floor. "Where are we?"

"We're back at Hendrick House. It's three in the morning so we still have a few hours until the return trip, but this was the best place I could think of to lay low and wait out the rest of this miserable trip."

"How did you find me?" asked Claire, finally looking up at Jon with tears developing in her eyes. The anguish on her face made it hard for Jon to tell if she was on the verge of crying from pain, emotional stress, or happiness at having been rescued.

"It's a long story," said Jon as he got up from his knee and sat next to her on the couch. He pulled her head toward his chest and leaned back into the sofa. "It can wait."

Claire sniffled and Jon felt heavy tears fall onto his shirt. "How many people died today Jon?"

"Too many," Jon replied quietly as he ran his hand up and down Claire's back.

Then Jon decided to change the subject. He needed to move Claire's thoughts in a positive direction, and try to get her a few more hours sleep.

"Claire, why don't you let me make you something to eat."

"Ok," Claire replied meekly, her head still laying heavy against Jon's chest.

"Come on, let's go to the kitchen."

Claire sat up reluctantly allowing Jon to stand. He helped her to her feet and walked her back toward the foyer and the kitchen beyond it. They passed Tim, who was now seated on one of the lounge chairs near the foyer, staring off into space, without a word.

Jon guided Claire to her left, down the short corridor that connected the kitchen at the back of the house with the foyer in the front. He then helped her to one of the high stools that lined the island countertop in the center of the large kitchen. Once she was seated he made his way to the refrigerator.

Before he got there the heavy door to the study at the back end of the kitchen started to swing open. Jon froze, staring at the door as it came open. Before he realized it was happening, he was moving toward the door. His hands clenched into tight fists and he failed to notice his own fingernails biting into the flesh of his palms. His heart rate rose and he didn't register the rage-induced tightness in his chest. Then it all poured forth in one uncontrolled, almost unintelligible outburst.

"WHOTHAFUKAARRRRYOOUUU!?"

Steven Pulling squirmed slightly as Jon screamed into his face. Pulling turned his face a little to keep Jon's flying spittle off his glasses and to avoid their faces making contact as Jon yanked him closer by the front of his shirt.

"Please Jon. Take a deep breath. And allow me to rinse my mouth. The transport ride from below gets me every time."

Jon released his grip on Steven Pulling's shirt and took a step back. He hadn't previously noticed the sea-sick green color on Pulling's face or the chunky residue at the corners of his mouth. Stephen Pulling had vomited very recently, and Jon was immediately aware of it when he'd calmed enough to notice the smell of the man's breath.

Pulling motioned forward as if asking Jon's permission to continue into the kitchen. Jon stepped aside, allowing him to pass. Then, without another word, Pulling walked to the kitchen sink, turned on the water, and stuck his mouth under the spigot. After rinsing and swishing three times, he shut the water off then dabbed his mouth with a towel that was hanging nearby.

Jon hadn't moved. His feet were cemented to the floor near the study door. His eyes were glued to Pulling as his brain tried to comprehend what was happening.

Pulling casually walked around the large kitchen island and sat down on a stool two seats away from Claire. He looked down at the marble countertop and didn't make eye contact with either Jon or Claire.

"I know you both have a lot of questions. Let me explain."

Silence.

Jon's eyes darted over to Claire who had joined him in staring daggers at Steven Pulling.

Finally Pulling looked up at both of them and broke the silence.

Epilogue

Jon sat across from Claire at the table in her apartment. He slowly ran his thumbs across the back of her hands as he held them gently in his. Both of them were still shell shocked from the events surrounding their trip to 2050. Neither said a word.

They'd returned from the future a few hours earlier, each team returning from 2050 in the order they'd left. The return trip had been filled with much less excitement. As Team B and C arrived at Hendrick House, Jon, Claire and Tim had delivered the news about Denise's death. Except instead of telling the other travelers the true circumstances behind her death, the three in the know had delivered a contrived story of an unfortunate accident. As the story went (the story provided by Steven Pulling), Denise was drunk after an exciting night of exploring the future. Sometime after Jon had fallen asleep, she'd gone out on the balcony, probably for some fresh air, and somehow fallen to her death. By the time Jon awoke to find her missing she was already in the morgue and it wasn't safe to retrieve her remains for transport back to 2023.

The group had accepted the news with shock and a good deal of concern for how Jon was handling it. He'd feigned quiet trauma and a substantial amount of guilt at not having done a better job of looking out for her well being. Emotions he assumed they'd expect and emotions he actually felt on some level. As a result, the return trip was mostly somber and quiet, allowing Jon plenty of mental bandwidth to contemplate what to do next.

In addition to being in the dark about the real circumstances surrounding Denise's death, Team B and C also weren't aware of Pulling's visit to 2050 or what he'd shared in the kitchen of Hendrick House with Jon and Claire while Tim sat nearly catatonic in the adjacent living room.

Over the last few hours, Jon had replayed the conversation with Pulling no less than a half dozen times. After Jon had almost strangled Pulling when he emerged from the subterranean transport, Pulling had finally offered something that Jon was half-willing to believe was the truth.

***

"I know you both suspect that I somehow engineered your relationship. Well, you are correct that I targeted you both for Casimir Institute's time travel program. I've been forward to many variants of the future and in each of them you both played an influential role. And you both have skill sets that are uniquely well suited to help us solve the fundamental problem..."

"Which is?" Claire interrupted.

"We're not entirely sure," Pulling replied, pausing. "Something happens in 2065. We cannot travel beyond June of that year. And traveling to the preceding six months is extremely dangerous, offering no guarantee that a traveler leaving the safe house will be able to return."

"You know more," Jon said, furrowing his brow. "If you didn't there's no way you would be so convinced that Claire and I are 'influential' in the future."

Pulling raised his hands defensively. "Please Jon. The details are constantly changing. For example, what the two of you accomplished in the last twenty four hours has already changed things in ways that we don't know yet."

"What did we accomplish in the last twenty four hours?" Jon asked as he stepped somewhat aggressively toward Pulling. "You do realize whatever we did also cost Denise Steinfeld her life, right?"

"Yes Jon, and I don't take that lightly," said Pulling. "We didn't foresee Ms. Steinfeld's death. But at the same time, her sacrifice is part of a significant step forward in preventing disaster in the future."

"Oh my god!" Claire exclaimed in frustration. "Are you even capable of speaking clearly? Or does everything you say have to be filled with vagaries and foreshadowing?"

Jon placed a hand on Claire's shoulder, showing support while also encouraging her to remain calm.

"I'm sorry Miss Keen. I'm not trying to be evasive or confusing. It's just...these matters tend to be difficult to address directly and succinctly."

Jon cut in. "Let's see if you can be direct. Without your intervention, would Claire and I have found each other?"

Pulling clasped his hands together and rested them on the countertop. He rolled his thumbs around each other while staring down at them.

"Now's your chance Steven. If you really want us to trust you, give us a reason. Would we be together without your intervention in our lives?"

"I understand your frustration Jon. But your question is irrelevant. I have intervened. And you are together. Would you rather it hadn't happened this way?" Pulling stared back at Jon with an odd confidence.

Jon bit his lower lip at the rebuke and looked down at Claire. She was staring back at him, seemingly awaiting his answer.

"Okay, I see your point," Jon relented. "Let's get back to the real issue. How did our actions today help fix things in the future?"

"Great question Jon," Pulling replied with a smile. "I can't say for sure yet."

Jon's brow furrowed again as he and Claire both prepared to interrupt Pulling to show their irritation.

"Now before you get upset, hear me out," said Pulling. "As I alluded to you both earlier, 2050 represents a critical juncture. Pinnacle Implants have been developed but haven't yet been introduced to the public. NPU is still 'controlled' by Pinnacle Computing. Both these things will not remain true for long. By gaining access - and understanding - to the interface between NPU and the Cloud, you've given us a chance to continue the fight."

"What fight are you talking about?" Claire asked, her voice rising again.

"Ok, Ok," Pulling said as his hands gestured toward Claire in a gentle motion urging her not to get upset again. "The general sequence of events goes like this: Pinnacle Implants become available to the public. Then Pinnacle loses its control over the Cloud - more specifically, they are locked out of NPU. Then nations find reasons to fight each other again - with consequences as bad as the 1940s. Then pandemic. Then nothing. We can't travel past June 2065. Our assumption is that the Casimir sphere doesn't exist after that time." Pulling paused.

Jon and Claire stared at him with skepticism but waited for him to continue.

Pulling continued. "These events play out over the course of years, and we still don't understand all the details of how or why they happen. But we do know that the chain of events is set in motion after the Implants start getting installed in humans and connecting their brains directly to the Cloud." Pulling stopped again, looking at Jon and Claire to gauge if he'd softened their doubt.

"Then why not just prevent the Implants from being developed, or manufactured, or installed in people?" Jon asked, now interested but still holding on to his cautious skepticism.

"We'd love to," Pulling replied with a slight satisfied smile. It quickly faded. "But we have yet to figure out how to do that without making our presence overtly known. That's why we need both of you."

"Why should I…we, believe you?" Jon asked quickly. "How do we know that your tinkering with the future isn't the source of the problem?"

"You don't," Pulling replied matter-of-factly. "But think about what you've witnessed in the last twenty four hours. Think of what Pinnacle was going to do to Claire if you hadn't intervened. Do I seem like the villain in this contest?"

"Wait," Claire cut in. "For the sake of argument, let's say we decide to trust you and join your time traveling, world saving team." Her sarcasm was obvious. Jon was relieved it wasn't directed at him. "What does that look like?"

"You would make more trips like this one. The key difference is, now that we trust each other, the details of your future missions won't be kept hidden from you." Pulling looked down at his feet and shook his head slightly.

"You have to understand. It was never my desire to intentionally deceive you. But I have a duty to guard our capabilities above everything else. Until I knew I could trust you I couldn't reveal the full purpose behind bringing you to Casimir Institute." Pulling paused for Claire's response but she only crossed her arms across her chest and waited for him to continue.

"So if you join us you would travel more. Sometimes together, but usually apart and often to different times. We still have a lot to learn about the chain of events and even more to learn about how to disrupt it. You'll be busy." Pulling stopped again.

"What about Tim and the other two teams?" Jon asked.

"Don't worry about them. In many ways they were a tool to get you two here without you recognizing that I'd singled you out. But they will continue in the program and may serve an important purpose as we move forward. Time will tell."

The large kitchen fell silent. Jon had another question but was afraid to ask. Claire's demeanor had softened as she processed everything Pulling had said. And Pulling seemed content to basque in the awkward silence and wait for the next round of questions.

Jon cleared his throat as he wrung his hands together. "Can we travel back? Before 2023?"

Pulling looked up and made eye contact with Jon. At first he said nothing. Jon felt his hands growing moist as he rubbed them harder.

"I mean, do you ever send agents back…to adjust, um, events that have already happened?"

Pulling smiled again.

"We have an informal, unwritten policy that we don't influence the past. There are risks involved that we don't fully understand. It's often been a subject of intense debate."

"That doesn't seem like a firm no," Jon replied with a hint of hope in his voice.

"It isn't," said Pulling. "Despite all the debate, and some strong feelings, we've left the possibility open on the off chance we find it necessary to take such a risk in order to achieve our broader goals."

Jon felt like a fish that just realized he'd taken the hook.

He'd run out of things to say. He looked at Claire and she gave a slight shake of her head and remained quiet. Both were out of questions. Pulling took the queue.

"I hope I've convinced you that the Institute is worthy of your trust. And I sincerely hope you'll continue in our employ. We need you both." Pulling stood up from the barstool where he'd been seated.

"I'm going to allow you some time to consider everything we've discussed. Regardless of what you decide, the clause in your non-disclosure agreement that requires you to stay inside the facility has been waived. I hope you won't, but you're free to leave as soon as you're back in 2023. And please remember what I said earlier about my presence here and the importance of protecting the circumstances surrounding the events of today. Goodbye Jon and Claire. I look forward to hearing from you in the coming days."

With that, Steven Pulling walked back into the study that led to the subterranean transport. Jon and Claire just stared at the door as he shut it behind him.

***

Jon finally broke the silence at the small kitchen table. "What are you thinking Claire? Do you believe him?"

Claire didn't respond at first. She just stared at her hands that were still resting in Jon's. Jon didn't press.

He took a deep breath. "Against my better judgement, I think I believe him," said Jon quietly. "His story is too far-fetched to be a lie. We could go to the Casimir Sphere now and take a trip to the end of 2064 to validate what he said…but that seems unnecessary. I think I might actually trust Steven Pulling."

Claire looked up at Jon and finally broke her silence. "I agree with you. His story of the future is so absurd that I can't convince myself he's lying about it. Especially after everything that just happened. But I'm hung up on something else." Claire paused and took on a labored expression - like she was searching her brain for the right words to express what she was thinking.

Jon squeezed her hands gently, encouraging her to continue.

"I'm still stuck on his answer to your question about Casimir tinkering with the future. On some level it felt like he was acknowledging that Casimir's manipulation of future events might be part of the problem. I mean, he basically ducked your question by pointing out that Pinnacle was worse."

"For what it's worth Claire, they're human. Even when humans are at our best, there's still wickedness and evil baked into the cake. Even the most benevolent humans, at their core, are prone to greed, selfishness, and deceit. I've been in plenty of situations where I knew the motives of the people I was working for weren't pure. But the bad guys were worse. And Casimir might not be perfect, but from everything I've seen so far, Pinnacle is much worse." Jon stopped and squeezed Claire's hands harder.

"They were going to torture you from inside your head Claire. And regardless of whether or not they got what they wanted, they were going to do it until it killed you."

Claire winced causing Jon to realize he'd started squeezing her hands a little too hard at the thought of her being tortured by the fat guy in the lab coat in 2050.

"Sorry," said Jon meekly. "Listening to the miserable version of my future self talk about losing you…it propelled me at first. I would have done *anything* to keep it from happening. But now I have you back. You're safe. I don't feel an ounce of sorrow for the Pinnacle guys

I put down. And I feel something like obligation, or duty, to stop them from trying the same sort of thing on other people that cross them." Jon looked down at the table as he fell silent again.

"So what do we do now?" Claire asked.

Jon looked up at her and smiled. Still holding her hands in his, he slid out of his chair and went to a knee in front of her.

"First let's get out of here. Then let's get married. Then let's go lie on a beach somewhere for a couple weeks. Then we'll see what happens after that."

Claire didn't say anything at first. Jon started to get nervous as she stared at him in shock. The surge of confidence that had prompted his proposal receded quickly.

"Claire? I'm asking you to marry me."

Jon waited anxiously as he tried to decipher her expression. He saw the glimmer of tears welling up in her eyes.

"Claire?"

She nodded her head imperceptibly as a tear spilled out and rolled down her right cheek. Jon took a relaxing breath as his confidence and his smile returned.

"Was that a yes? You know you have to say it out loud right?"

"YES!" said Claire a little too loudly as more tears fell. "Of course, Yes."

I hope you enjoyed Casimir Beginnings. If you did, I'd love to hear from you!

You can email me directly - jwwalker@timespacepublishers.com

Or head to my website and subscribe to my email newsletter - www.timespacepublishers.com

If you've made it this far I'd also really appreciate if you'd leave a review at your favorite bookseller or Goodreads.

Thanks, and Keep Reading!

51079121R00222

Made in the USA
Middletown, DE
29 June 2019